IRONCLAD GOLD

IRONCLAD GOLD

AUSTIN HAYNES

To the men and officers of the Confederate States Navy.

Be sure to read the prequel to Ironclad Gold...

The Queen of Kings

1-SEPTEMBER 1864

Off the North Carolina coast

Captain James Munford focused northeast-by-east down the narrow length of his leather-on-brass spyglass—a gift from his grandfather. Made in Weil, Germany. Home of Johannes Kepler, the inventor of the telescope. Centered at the end of his scope, plying heavy seas ahead of gale force winds and against a tar-black sky, was the ass-knotting sight of wetted spars and swollen sails.

Where had they come from? They had never hunted this far north before. Not in four years.

So why now?

Munford, a pensioned Royal Navy officer chasing his fortune running supplies from the Crown's seaport of Nassau to the embattled southern Confederacy, swung his spyglass further north. And his breath abandoned him. The protective cannon of Fort Macon at Beaufort harbor were far behind him now and well out of sight.

His ship, *Hermione*, was plowing her way through the waves with all she had, and yet her pursuer was gaining on her as if she were tied to a pier. Munford's gut felt like razors. It could only be one vessel; the one Yankee ship with the panache to hunt this far up the coast.

It had to be the *Niphon*.

She was rigged with all sails billowing and her boilers stoked, primed for the great chase and eager to add *Hermione* to her litany of victories.

The devil tapped Munford's shoulder and reminded him: *Niphon doesn't work alone.*

No, she doesn't. What was the other one? Adger! The *James Adger*!

Munford ordered his helmsman, "Stay alive, Mr. Tregale. This one's got a playmate. She's approaching from the southeast, I wager."

"Aye sir!" Gorran Tregale, an English fisherman's son, had served under Munford in Queen Victoria's navy. Munford always bested his enemy. He trusted Munford with his life.

"And tell Pritchard cotton and kerosene. Cotton and kerosene, Mr. Tregale."

Gorran flipped back the rain cover on one of two brass voice tubes at their helm, one for the fire room where the boilers were and the other down to the engine room where Gorran's shipmate, engineman Ensley fawned over *Hermione*'s engines.

Gorran hollered over the wind into the fire room tube, "Pritchard. Captain's order: cotton and kerosene. Cotton and kerosene."

Below decks, in *Hermione*'s belly, Robert Pritchard grimaced at the voice tube in his grip. His sweat-soaked, Irish skin glistened in the fluttering firelight of Boiler No. 3, one of eight boilers he tended as jealously as a lioness tended her cubs.

"Aye, Mr. Tregale, you'll have your cotton and kerosene," he hollered back.

He thrust the tube from his grip as if it had bitten him. Cotton soaked in kerosene would fire *Hermione*'s boilers to a furious inferno that would wake Dante Alighieri himself from death and scare the bejeezus out of him. Cotton and kerosene was a dangerously explosive blend; but it was *Hermione*'s only hope for the speed she needed to slip by the inevitable Yankee blockade and into the safety of Wilmington, the starving Confederacy's last open seaport, and her only link to the outside world.

Pritchard passed a doting eye over his boilers. They made the steam that fed the engines that turned the sidewheels that clawed *Hermione* over the waves. "Master Howe, time for the cotton."

An enthralled fourteen-year-old Wilmington boy named Peter Howe gaped back at Pritchard through the withering heat as the towering man grappled a rope-and-tackle hoist to a monstrous bale of cotton.

Peter's head, shaved and fuzzy, barely passed Pritchard's beltline.

"Master Howe! Bear a hand here."

Peter seized a fistful of jute wrap protecting the cotton bale. He tugged and yanked at it with all the might his sapling arms would give, but the 500-pound beast just knocked his sixty-five pounds to the deck for his troubles, and the hot deck planks wasted no time searing Peter's bum.

He sprung to his feet, slapping the burn from the smoldering seat of his trousers.

So that's how it's going to be, is it?

A pair of heavy black shears hanging from a hook on a post waved to him in the flickering light. Perfect! He grabbed them and dropped them just as quickly. They were hot as a pot handle on Mother's stove. He flexed his fists and licked at his lips, building his courage. He lunged at them and grabbed them up again, grinding their burn in his tender palms with gritted teeth. He leaped at the cotton beast and with two hands and all the muscle he had, he split the metal bands that bound together its coarse jute wrapping.

Pritchard beside him ripped shards from the jute and wrapped them round the prongs of his pitchfork. He dipped it in kerosene and warned Peter, "Back away, boy."

Peter ducked for cover, slipped on *Hermione's* rocking deck and all over again plopped down hard as ever on his hip, worse than falling from a tree. Swallowing the cry that wanted out so badly, he forced himself up and hollered over the fiery din, "Captain is running her so hard. Something is amiss, surely."

"Never you mind that," Pritchard hollered back. "Now stand back." He shoved the soaked jute into the boiler's feed. The kerosene boomed, spitting flames from the boiler's mouth, melting the Kerry hairs from Pritchard's chest.

A second boom followed right behind it, from the hull where just on the other side the sea was waiting to break in and swallow them up.

Peter's teenage tummy knotted up. His frightened bowels urged him to dash for the head, but that was all the way forward. There was the cow pail in the corner for convenience, but there was no time for that: Pritchard needed him. Pritchard trusted him. None of the grownups back home had ever trusted him the way Mr. Pritchard trusted him. He would stay put so help him, even if he soiled himself.

He sunk his knuckles into the cotton bale, ripped a big wad of itchy softness from it and handed it to Pritchard. Pritchard was wearing a queer expression. "What, Mr. Pritchard?"

"That thunder from the hull just now: our bottom's kissing the shallows. Captain is running her close to shore. The closer we trace the shoreline, the better the breakers will muffle the sound of our paddle wheels. The thing is..."

Pritchard listened to the keel with his feet.

"What, Mr. Pritchard?"

"The waves. Sometimes...just sometimes...there's not enough water between us and the bottom. If we're not watchful, we'll break our own back."

The deck bumped again, toppling Peter into Mr. Pritchard. His little cheek smeared a streak in the sweat on the big man's belly. "We hit the bottom!" he cried.

Pritchard gave Peter's head a reassuring stroke and held him at arms' length. "Captain Munford's been a seaman a long time, Master Howe. He knows what he's doing. And this time we have the best pilot aboard."

"You mean Mister Burgess?"

Pritchard nodded. "They say no man knows this coast like he does."

"I don't like him."

Pritchard flashed an acquiescent smile. "Whatever that is we're carrying down there in our hold, Master Howe, Captain Munford thinks it warrants Mr. Burgess's fee. Three times the usual, I hear."

The sea floor punched *Hermione*'s bottom again, with so much force this time it sent Mr. Pritchard toppling headlong toward his raging boilers. He palmed his fall with both hands landing squarely against the boiler's scalding iron skin. The scorching burn ripped like lightning through Pritchard's nerves and knocked him silly back against an oaken post just behind him. Too stunned to feel, he gaped down at his angry palms in the quavering amber fire light.

The sea bottom belted *Hermione* thrice. The post behind Pritchard shoved him forward, shoulder first against the boilers a second time. This time, he emitted a howl in agony like nothing Peter had ever heard before, kicking up a queer knot in his bowel. He felt behind him and searched the seat of his pants and sighed, relieved that he hadn't done what he feared most.

Pritchard pulled away, hunched forward and whimpering.

The cotton wadding slipped from Peter's horrified fingers. A sheet of skin, big as his little hand, was missing from Pritchard's back. The tissue beneath it was pink and full of rage. He traced a peculiar stink to the boiler's metal side where Pritchard's missing flesh was stuck to it, cooking.

Peter's last meal splattered to the deck and onto his shoes.

Bowed over and clutching his gut, Pritchard rolled his eyes up to Peter. "There is no time for that, boy." Expelling his agony through heavy breaths, he reached down and gripped his pitchfork with swelling palms. A faint whimper slipped through his gritted teeth. He bobbed his head past the edge of tears to the wadding on the deck.

"Pick it up, Master Howe. Give me the cotton."

Peter picked it up and wetted the wadding with kerosene, and he skewered it, hard as he could, down the tongs of Pritchard's fork.

The volatile chemical blend dribbled down the fork's handle to Pritchard's grip and attacked his wounds with a vicious bite. Pritchard roared at his wounded grip as if commanding it to quit whining and hold fast. He spun round and rammed his fork into the boiler's feed.

Over and over he gorged the boilers with Peter's wetted wads till the heat in their cramped space below *Hermione*'s waterline was beyond livable. The steam pressure gauges were rattling like lunatics, and the needles on the temperature gauges had run out of numbers.

The tongs of Pritchard's fork finally fell to the deck.

Teetering between anguish and exhaustion on the edge of awareness, he ordered Peter, "Tell the captain we're at the maximum. Any more and we'll all be meeting again on Christ's doorstep. Now get up there, and be fleet about it."

Peter chased the ladder leading up from the fire room to the open afterdeck. As *Hermione* groped her way first down and then up over the cadence of rising swells, his feet were at one instant heavy as lead bricks and the next instant light as feathers.

At the hatchway, he gingerly poked through the tarred canvas blackout cover, careful not to leak too much firelight to the enemy on their stern horizon. A spray of chilly seawater graced his face for his trouble and sizzled to nothing on his toasted shirt.

Peter crabbed up and over the hatch's coaming on to the deck. As he searched for his footing, the nighttime jumped him and mugged him with instant blackness, and the sea for her part knocked his feet out from under him. His face met something hard with a brutal smack. Salt water with a faint stink of holystone oil and pitch fingered its way deep into his nose.

Peter whimpered through the pain of pulling himself to his hands and knees and back onto his feet. The bottoms of his bare feet chafed the insides of his rough leather brogans: ill-fitting shoes with a nasty knack for finding and rasping every blister and rise on a man's foot, socks or no socks.

He forgave himself a two-barreled cry and measured the shadows closing in around him. He tacked a wavering path side to side with the ship's heavy rolls, fumbling his way forward past vague shapes till his palm rested on something chilly and hard.

A handrail!

It was the ladder up to the midships deckhouse roof where the helm was with the big wheel that steered the ship.

Captain Munford is always near the helm.

Peter footed the first rung, slipped and mashed his knee. He spat out an adult profanity, one of the many he had picked up from the crew. His mother's image appeared where his phlegm had splattered onto the deck. He felt suddenly low. Despite all the deference and manners Mother had taught him as she struggled in her husband's absence to mold him into a man, it seemed the sea was a stronger woman: her moody temper roughing his edges and salting his tongue with every day he spent with her.

He sped through a prayer for penance and two-stepped up the ladder.

The deckhouse roof spanned the width of the ship between the sidewheel paddle boxes, the great shells safeguarding the paddlewheels that powered *Hermione* through the water.

Masts thicker than two stout men bordered each end of the deckhouse, one fore and one aft. Below the roof beneath Peter's feet were the officers' quarters and head, the galley and crew's mess, an accounting office, and the armory to which only Captain Munford had the key.

Up forward on the roof, just behind the foremast, two men manned the helm, suffering the open weather. A tall pilothouse to shelter them would only make *Hermione* easier to spot from a distance. Low and sneaky was what she needed.

Gorran Tregale had the wheel. The other man, the Cape Fear pilot named Burgess, was a Carolina man like Peter. Captain Munford had hired him at the neutral port called Nassau on the island of New Providence. He would guide *Hermione* over the stony shoals peppering the North Carolina seacoast and littering the approach to the Cape Fear River's mouth, and where the Yankee blockade under Rear Admiral Samuel Phillips Lee lie waiting for them.

All supplies to the Confederacy were now coming through neutral British Nassau. That way her suppliers in Europe could support her without sparking a war with Mr. Lincoln. Fast ships like *Hermione* plied the seas at high speed between Wilmington and Nassau and back, and men like Burgess were making a good living showing them the way.

Peter didn't trust Burgess. But he did like Gorran. Gorran had taught him everything about *Hermione.* Back home in Wilmington, Peter's friends envied him getting to crew her.

Burgess hollered over his shoulder, "That was Bogue Inlet we just passed, Captain. The shallows get treacherous ahead. Quick wits are critical now." As he did so, Burgess caught little Peter in his sights.

A voice over Peter's shoulder replied, "Mr. Tregale, prepare to relieve the helm to Mr. Burgess on my order."

"Aye, sir!"

Peter traced the voice up to a lanky figure standing atop the portside paddle box. With his spyglass to his eye and his back to Peter and the helm, he rocked easily with *Hermione's* every roll. The tails of his frock coat carried in the breeze as if he might lift and fly away at any moment. His was truly a magically powerful presence.

"Why are you on my deck, Master Howe?"

Nothing ever evaded Captain Munford's eye, even from behind.

"Beg to report, sir. Mister Pritchard has used the kerosene. The boilers are stoked to their fullest, sir."

Foreboding tensed Gorran Tregale's grip on the big wheel as he shared an uneasy glance with Mr. Burgess who whispered, "Feeding the boilers kerosene—many a weathered captain has blown his ship apart pulling such a stunt."

Gorran took a deep breath. "Not Captain Munford." *And certainly not Hermione!* He trusted the first without question, and had absolute faith in the second.

Hermione was the fastest of the new sidewheel steamers out of Scotland, built by William Simons & Company of Renfrew-on-Clyde. She pulled past twenty-one knots at her sea trials. The slender-waisted clippers of the day could skim the seas like dolphins, yet any one of them would need hang every rag of sail she had—and her skipper hang his hanky too—just to sip a taste from *Hermione*'s wake.

Munford stayed glued to his spyglass. "Very good, Master Howe. Now get below. This is no place for a boy."

Peter's chattering teeth rattled out, "Aye sir!" Hugging himself for warmth he traced his steps aft best as he could using the waves' white caps for light. He ignored the ladder's rail, preferring the heat of his arms against his ribs.

But the Sea—she gave *Hermione* another shove.

Peter bumped his way down the ladder in a most ungraceful manner and ass-skidded across the wet deck and into the port bulwarks. He tucked his banged-up body into a knot in the nook where the deck met the bulwarks, out of the bone-chilling wind, and hid his agony behind his eyelids humming a familiar reel to the rush of the passing waves. Between tiny breaths he counted the faces of the men they had left behind in Nassau.

Fifty-three men crewed *Hermione*. But for reasons known only to him, Captain Munford had insisted on just eight men this time. Things were strange this trip. Captain Munford was unusually muted. Nobody would talk about what was below decks. Not Pritchard. Not even the usually effusive Gorran Tregale would open his mouth about it.

Sopping wetness and bone-chilling cold forced Peter from his hideaway. *And Mr. Pritchard will be wondering where in the heavens you are.*

Gripping the gunwale that topped the bulwarks, he pulled himself to his feet. For just an instant he hesitated, squinting over the water into the distance. The faraway sky spat a crimson flash. Practically instantly, the air above him screeched like fingernails scratching his schoolboy blackboard.

"Missed!" he gloated.

A throat cleared behind him. Captain Munford was standing on the sponson, a built-in scaffold thing that skirted the base of the paddle box. The men used it when repairing the wheel and for boarding the ship.

"Are you injured, Master Howe?"

"No, Captain."

"Get below, then."

"Yes, Captain Munford."

"Mr. Tregale. Get me closer to that shoreline."

"Aye, Captain."

Gorran Tregale tossed Burgess a sly smirk. Running close to shore was their trump card to evade the Yankee with the surf's racket to stifle the drumming beat of their enormous paddlewheels and the ebony tree line behind them to mask their profile. And if that did no good and the Yankee dared come any closer, the shallows would rip out his bottom.

A muffled boom echoed in the distance. A second shot! It screeched between *Hermione*'s masts and smashed into the breakers.

From his perch on the paddle box, Captain Munford commented, "Your work is cut out for you tonight, Mr. Burgess. It seems the *Niphon* would have us for a prize."

"She's probing blind, Captain. That last one was their second miss in two shots."

"That's how it works, Mr. Burgess. The first shot short; the next shot long. Right now *Niphon*'s gunner is setting his range. His third shot will be true I fear."

Aghast, Burgess threw his attention forward down the strand to a notch in the shoreline. "Bear Inlet just ahead! It's time I take the wheel, Captain."

"Mr. Tregale. Relieve your helm."

Burgess accepted the wheel from a reluctant Gorran. Behind him, a rumble skipped off the bellies of low lying clouds. *Niphon*'s third shot was on its way.

Captain Munford hollered, "Keep your wits about you, men."

An enormous racket aft sent a shudder the length of *Hermione*'s spine. The force of it snatched the wheel from Burgess's grip. He tried to grab the fast spinning wheel, yelped in surprise and collared his broken wrist with his good hand.

On the open afterdeck, Peter hobbled back to the fire room hatch. He lifted the tarred canvas covering, doing his best to ignore the third rumble echoing off the clouds. His shoe just settled onto the first rung of the ladder down when *Hermione*'s stern exploded, nearly tossing him headlong down the hole. From up forward, he thought he heard Gorran's voice.

"Captain, we've lost our rudder!"

Seconds later, Robert Pritchard burst forth from the hatch. He barged past Peter and sailed up the deckhouse ladder. Peter dared not follow him.

Phobic tongues conjectured like fluttering geese.

"The wheel, Captain! She won't budge."

"It's the rudder. They hit our rudder."

"She's on a course away from the shoreline."

"Out to where that infernal Yankee is waiting for us!"

Captain Munford's confident baritone voice boomed. "Mind your bearing, men."

It came again: a double-thunder this time, rattling the darkness. Twin screeches zipped overhead. As Peter scurried for cover, something popped into his memory.

Thirteen!

This was *Hermione's* thirteenth run through the blockade: her thirteenth time making the wild ride for the protection of Fort Fisher's famed Mound Battery. Just beyond the battery, she would heave hard to starboard and slip into the sanctuary of New Inlet. From there it would be a safe cruise upriver to Wilmington.

But thirteen was bad luck.

A deeper and more familiar rumble of Mother Nature's thunder clawed through the faraway clouds. Peter's trepidation crept northeast, testing the horizon. Out where the clouds tangled with the waves, a wicked streak reached down and jabbed at the sea. And in the flash of blue-white light, for a split instant, shimmering black sails like wetted shark skin threw him a sinister wink.

Peter searched the empty deck around him, immediately aware of how alone he was among the cold and the shadows with only the thick aftermast for company, creaking under its heavy burden.

Beyond *Hermione's* shattered stern, the horizon belched crimson once again. Another screech ripped through the air and ended with a horrendous smack. Up forward sounded like all hell had broken loose.

Someone was screaming.

Peter weighed the orange warmth of the fire room down the ladder against the black and chilly night. *It's either up here and cold or down there in comfort—alone.*

He meditated none too long on the shapes in the shadows behind him from over his tiny bruised shoulder. The ladder back up to the deckhouse roof looked suddenly friendlier. Quick as a wink, he scrambled up it and slip-slid his way forward to the homey protection of Gorran and Pritchard. He fell against the voice tubes, all jittery and chest heaving.

That's when he saw it.

The foremast—it was gone!

A jagged stump poking up from the deck was all there was left of it. Their two boatswains were hacking madly with axes at a tangle of rigging sweeping over the starboard side. The broken half of the mast was jabbing the air from the water like a great finger. If it all weren't so deadly, Peter might have laughed at the comic sight.

Captain Munford sniffed at the heady air. "A storm is brewing. Check the wheel, Mr. Burgess."

Gorran helped the injured Burgess clock the wheel three spokes past twelve o'clock and hollered back, "She's got some movement, Captain, but she's not all freed up."

"Give me west-southwest as best you can."

But the helm wouldn't budge. "She's not responding, sir."

"Steer with the paddles, Mr. Tregale. Order Ensley: starboard wheel ahead one third; ahead one-half on the port wheel. Get us back on course, Mr. Tregale."

"Aye, sir." Gorran leaned into the engine room voice pipe to give the order when little Peter, hugging Pritchard for cover, interrupted with, "What's that whizzy noise?"

Gorran's expression sickened. "Grapeshot! On your bellies. Now!"

Instantly, holes the size of fat apples marched across every inch of the starboard paddle box behind them. Wood splinters puked from every standing structure, strangling the air like mad bats. The swollen air pressure stole Peter's balance. He tried for the wheel, missed and fell, knocking his noggin against the deck.

All sound around him thickened. Every movement slowed to a creep.

Gorran Tregale was mouthing something.

Burgess was jigging about with eyes big as eggs.

Captain Munford's commands were all cottony.

The second ship you saw in the lightning. Captain Munford needs to know.

Peter forced the words from between his echoing ears, "Captain. There's another ship—"

But the whizzing sound was back.

Captain Munford erupted with gaping holes. He flew from his perch on the paddle box and slapped to a stony halt on the deck. His lifeless visage staring right at Peter seemed to be saying: *Save yourself.*

Beyond Munford's boots, severed paddle halves knifed up through the port box like it was butter. With an ear-piercing squeal, the giant wheel jammed to a breathless halt.

Prone on the deck, Peter chanced a look down his legs. At his feet lay Burgess with his hand gripping Peter's ankle. Peter stuck his tongue through his teeth at the sickly mess of him and tugged his ankle free from the dead man's hold. Beyond Burgess, the starboard wheel was chewing into the sandy bottom. Suddenly, a horrible crushing seized his arm: a huge grip attached to Mr. Pritchard.

Pritchard pointed to the coast. "We must move fast if we want—"

The starboard wheel groaned to a stop. A wall of pressure slapped them both.

Pritchard staggered a moment, and then yanked hard on Peter.

The deck fell away from Peter's side.

Pritchard tucked Peter's tiny body under his arm.

The heat from Pritchard's heaving ribs reached through Peter's sopping shirt. His head bounced in chorus to Pritchard's steps. Everything was all wonky. Flashes of deck, bulwarks painted white, *Hermione*'s torn foremast, and the ladder to the foredeck. Was that another explosion? They were slipping down the rungs of the forward ladder, almost falling.

Pritchard set him down against the starboard bulwarks.

Peter felt the vibrations of "Where's Gorran?" crossing his tongue.

Pritchard shook his head. "He's not coming," he said, and grabbed something from the shadows behind Peter.

"I want Gorran."

"Raise your arms."

"What are you doing?"

"Put this on."

 Peter pulled away and hugged himself.

Pritchard shook a cork Ross Ward life jacket at him. "There's no time for this, boy!"

As Pritchard crammed the Ross Ward down over him, Peter's Adam's apple squeezed out, "Where's your jacket?"

"I'm staying here."

Pritchard tied the straps on the jacket, so big on the boy it swallowed him up.

"You come, too."

Pritchard took Peter's spindly arms in-hand. "I have to stay. You want Gorran to get to a hospital, don't you?" The boy refused to nod. "The Yankees will have doctors and a hospital." But his little mate wasn't having any of it. "Peter, do you remember my secret? Only you know my secret. I told you, remember?" The boy broke into tears. "I can't swim, Peter. I'll drown out there."

"I remember now." Peter wiped the snot from his nose. "Can't swim? That's stupid."

"So you see? If we want to help Gorran, I need to stay." He stroked the boy's hair. "Don't worry. We're British citizens. They'll just send us home."

Long voices with broad A's and dropped R's were hailing them from beyond the other side of the ship.

"They're boarding. Time to go, lad."

"No."

"Peter. You're going."

The deck fell down and away from Peter's shoes. "Stop it. Let me go. No!"

A strange accent from somewhere hailed, "You there!"

"I want to stay! No. Don't!" He elbowed and struggled and he hollered for help. "Mr. Gorran!" And then he weighed like nothing at all.

The stars, they swirled all round him and swarmed beneath his shoes. He panicked, reaching out for touch, for feel, for *anything*; but only the twinkling blackness answered.

He was flying. Like a bird. No. Like a rock.

With a slap his head hit something hard. A hollow rush filled his ears. Salty wetness flooded up his nose and scratched his insides. There was no air. Where was the air? He thrashed and he grabbed and he kicked through a lurching bubbliness. It was cold. Very cold and sounded like a million marbles. And quite suddenly the stars were back, above him where they should be.

Sound was crisp again. And the air—it tasted better than he ever imagined. He jerked around trying to find himself. His clumsy cork lifejacket kept pelting him in the chin. The stars and the crests of the waves blinked out. *Hermione*'s side loomed high over him, so dark he couldn't see her green paint. He tried to look up, but his jacket wouldn't let him. He flopped around in the waves trying to see. He thought just for a flash he saw a head looking down from over the side.

"Peter! Swim, boy. Swim for the shore, fast as you can!"

Peter contorted his neck and peered up into the shadows. Heads were multiplying around Mr. Pritchard and at once the big man was snatched away.

Peter's own voice bounced back at him from off *Hermione*'s hard side. "Mister Pritchard. Come back!" But Pritchard was gone.

And he was alone.

With the salt in his nose, and slap of the waves for company.

2-JULY 2005

Stephen Robert Laird's steel blue orbs could still the heart of a lion. His seasoned, six-four Anglo-Saxon frame eased the scales to an aged but still sinewy 245 pounds. At the moment, his stone hard mug was branding fear into a skinny twenty-something teetering over muddy water on the edge of Stephen's dive barge. The kid was supposed to be tending one of two divers down in the wreck just beneath them and stretching along the east bank of the James River.

"Get him up!" he demanded. "Get him up now!"

The young man wagged his diver's severed tagline back at him. "But I don't have him."

Stephen snatched it away and ground his fury into the lay of it in his hand, hewn hard by decades of tough work grappling his own share of lines. The other half of the tagline was attached to his best diver, the most experienced man in the water he had. And as the bitter end of the clearly knife-cut line reminded him, he was also his most troublesome. The line had a purpose, dammit! For communication. For safety. And so the diver could retrace his way back out of the rusting, mud-choked wreck.

Stephen turned his back on the diver's tender. He was at his wit's end. His rented compressors—big gas powered things—two of them— had both been seized by the rental company. They were needed elsewhere, the men who showed up said. No apologies. No mention of the money he had paid in advance. No mention of getting it back.

To get by, he resorted to stuffing his team's SCUBA bottles with air at a local dive shop. It was a pain in the ass and expensive as hell. The off-duty police divers he had hired to watch the place and be his standby divers had quit. Everything was going to crap and no matter what he did, he couldn't seem to stop it.

Stephen ran his worried hand through thinning-on-top, grey-over-blond hair with a pony tail that reached down to dead center between his shoulder blades. He spied the thick woods tracing the east riverbank. He knew who was behind this. *To hell with them all!* They'd have to show up with an eviction notice and force him off the property—which, by the way he had a dig permit for.

This is crazy. You know better. Goddamned SCUBA is too dangerous for this job.

He was ready to explode. His attention caught the girl in the corner of his eye: his lost diver's partner, standing there dripping on deck in her gear with her flippers in-hand. She was supposed to be down there with him, not up here!

He swung his anger her way. "What the hell happened?"

Her voice cracked between her thoughts. "I—I couldn't—I couldn't see him. Anywhere. He just—he wasn't there." She was a mess.

"That's what your buddy line is for!"

She raised a limp stub of sisal clipped to her SCUBA bottle harness. "But he cut it! I kept banging my light on my tank to get his attention. I swear it. But he didn't come back—or he wouldn't. The jerk!"

Wouldn't. That would be just like him to ignore her signal to come up. *Probably got it from that father of his.*

"So you left him."

She blanched at his accusation. "I stayed down till I was at 500 psi!"

Well, he couldn't ask her for more than that. He turned to their standby diver, outfitted in a single-80 with an extra pony bottle for emergencies. "Get down there and find him."

"You got it, Professor." The young man, built like a wrestler, grabbed his flippers. His tender shackled a tether to his bottle harness and helped him down the ladder on the side of the barge into the river.

From the air, Virginia's James River was a soiled green anaconda snaking a haphazard path from sultry Richmond to the runaway currents of the Chesapeake Bay and the open Atlantic, through sinuous twists and turns past parched woodlands, sunburned fields, and crusty flatlands blanched by the stark footprints of industry.

But on the ground, maybe one in a hundred thousand people knew of the James River's three secrets hidden beneath her warbling surface as she threw herself first hard left below Drewry's Bluff before yanking herself into a breakneck right just beyond the old Jimmy Dean estate.

Professor Stephen Laird's team of graduate archaeologists—with a sprinkling of doctoral candidates, including the idiot in the water—were after one of those secrets: the Confederate States ironclad gunship *CSS Fredericksburg.*

Stephen glared at the girl. "This is your fucking cock up!"

"You can't blame me for this," she protested. But his frozen expression said otherwise. "That's not fair."

"You want fair? Here's bloody fair: no more water time for you."

"What?" Her face flushed red over cashew-brown skin.

The standby diver's tender reported, "Standby diver in the water."

Stephen waved that he heard him. "You'll tend and wash gear till we're all done here."

She slapped her flippers to the deck. "But you can't do that!"

"Oh yes I can, and I am. And you watch your temper on my dig."

She wiped the snot from her upper lip. The whites of her eyes scalded to red. "You know I need water time to graduate. My masters—I've been working my ass off for it. It's all I've got."

"You can repeat your practicum this fall. There's another dig in November with doctor—hmm, what's his fucking name? Ah, I forget."

"But I don't have the money. I've used it all up."

Behind them the tenders hollered, "We have bubbles!"

"Not my problem," Stephen insisted. He rushed to the barge's edge with a stream of students.

She growled after him from under her breath. "Asshole!"

Someone at the barge's edge cried out, "There they are!"

Two heads were bobbing on the pollen-carpeted surface of the James.

The lost diver ripped his regulator from his mouth and pulled a squalling breath deep into his starving lungs. A varnish of green slime coated his mask. The standby diver guided him over to the barge's ladder.

"Up here, dude," someone said. "Take my hand."

"I got him."

"No, I got him."

A fluttering gaggle of frantic fingers seized hold of him and hauled him up the ladder onto the deck where he flopped without grace onto hard steel.

Someone commented, "Whoa!" and the lot of them stepped back away from his stench.

The errant diver sniffed at his arm. He reeked of muddy James River yuck. He rolled to his side and lay against his SCUBA bottle, appreciating the fresh air. He yanked his mask off and peered at his pressure gauge: 200 psi. It was the lowest he had gone yet, skip-breathing to steal bottom time. Any cautious diver would have called it quits at 500.

Screw caution!

He appreciated the ring of faces circling round him and answered their distressed expressions with a shit-eating grin. A bucketful of water slapped it away. His focus cleared and tripped over the fuming stare of his tender looming over him. In his hand he wagged the frayed end of the cut safety line.

"Want to explain this?"

"I gave you two pulls for slack."

"And I gave you four to come up."

Qeb blew him off with a dismissive sneer. "I wasn't done yet."

"Your air time was up."

"You kept yanking on me, so I cut it."

"And you cut your buddy line, too." His tender's expression flushed crimson. "You're a real fuckhead, Qeb Morgan, you know that?"

Qeb hollered after his tender as he crossed the wobbly plank connecting their barge to the tree-cluttered shoreline, "And you didn't charge my bottle with enough air, either."

The guy shot him the bird as he headed uphill for the porta-showers.

Exhaustion tinted the resentful looks clustered over Qeb. The summertime James was a simmering stew with visibility worse than zero. They'd burned a month of 12-hour days sucking mud and silt from the guts of the *Fredericksburg*'s hulking battery.

This was their practicum: the requisite life's blood necessary to escape the drudgery of their collegiate careers for the rewards of professional archaeology. From different universities, they had all converged on Stephen Laird's project for the required field time to receive their degrees.

And Qeb's recklessness was threatening it all.

Qeb weighed the look on his dive partner and girlfriend—his third in as many years. "What's up with you?"

"I thought I lost you." The dusk orange sunlight intensified the hurt in her gaze.

"I was fine. You know that. I'm always fine."

"How nice for you." She closed in and stood over him, fighting her tears. "Professor Laird's taking me out of the water. You know what that means?"

He said nothing.

"Do you?" she hollered. "I don't have the money to come back next year. My whole family's counting on me graduating in September. What do I tell them now, Qeb? What? Tell me." She dumped her things and hollered, "You can clean my gear for my trouble, jerkoff!"

Someone said, "Way to go, Morgan."

Another voice chimed in. "Yeah, fuckwad."

Qeb pulled his six foot self to his feet. At 185 pounds wet, his frame carried a slender runner's build. His clean-shaven complexion paled against his tattered black wetsuit stained green with algae. His leather black locks lay matted with mud over eyes the watery brown of Arbequina olives. He slipped out of his rig and as he set it down dirt-scuffed shoe tips toed up to his bare feet.

He straightened up to face their owner.

At the far side of sixty, Stephen Laird still presented an imposing persona. The tuft of grey chest hairs floating in the crook of his silk Hawaiian shirt rose and fell with the pulse of his breathing like terns riding a wave. His thinning mane tied back in a ponytail framed a scarred countenance of salt-parched skin that reached deep inside Qeb, snatched hold of his ego, and commenced to squeeze.

"I was—"

"I don't want to hear it!"

"But you might—"

Stephen flagged his flip-phone at Qeb. "I just had a talk with EMS. They were almost here. Then I had to tell them you were okay after all. Now I'm getting a bill I can't afford." He indicated to the other students. "Which of them do I tell won't be getting in the water because you just cost us air money?"

"But I was only—"

"Not anymore, you're not."

"But nothing happened." Qeb patted himself down. "See? No missing parts."

"This isn't about you: it's about teamwork. Something I've learned the hard way that you're no good at."

Qeb lobbed him one of his trademark half-smiles. "Teamwork's overrated. And I'm the best, most experienced diver you have. That's all that counts. You know that."

"Not anymore, it doesn't. You're not even so much as tending another diver until I decide what I'm going to do about you."

"You're going to take your best diver out of the water. That's a little counterproductive, don't you think?"

"You'll clean gear and wash down the deck."

"No way."

The blue in Laird's eyes rippled. "Excuse me?"

"I know what I'm doing down there better than any of these guys. Even you."

Laird teetered on his shoe heels. "Is that a fact?"

"You know my background."

"I know your father's background. I know your uncle's background. All I know about you is how you may have—possibly had—remotely even—saved a coffin that your father discovered, mind you—from being stolen. And probably all by accident."

Qeb thumbed his chest. "It was no accident! It was me who got her out of that sarcophagus in time, not them. They thought she was a goner. I got a medal. The Egyptian government paid all my college, too."

"You never let anyone doubt just how proud of yourself you are, do you?"

"Why should I?"

Laird began running some numbers in the back of his head. "You and that crazy Tim-Lee Polk—somehow you two think you know better than everyone else. And by the way, where the hell is he? He's your friend. He's been gone a week."

"How should I know? I'm not his keeper."

Laird suddenly solved his calculation. "I just had an Ah Hah moment! Manpower."

"Huh?"

Laird indicated to the team. "I just realized that I have enough manpower."

"I don't get it."

"Well, get this: I don't need you."

"The hell you don't."

"How is this for the hell I don't: you're finished here. I want you gone in thirty minutes."

"Very funny." Qeb grabbed his gear to go clean it.

"Put that down."

Qeb stalled.

"Put...that...down."

Qeb's gear slowly slipped down his leg to the deck.

"Get all your belongings and get off my dig."

"You're joking."

Laird's phone flipped open. "Get off my dig, or it's the cops."

His phone sang out a 9.

"What am I supposed to do? Where am I supposed to go?"

Laird's phone sang out a 1.

"Okay, okay. I'm going."

Qeb took a few steps, jerked to a stop and spun round. "I'll be waiting for your call, Professor, begging me to come back. In the meantime, good luck. You're gonna need it with these clowns."

3-JULY, 2005

Tim-Lee Polk fascinated at the fuzzy shape peeking up at him from the silt in the shadowy space buried beneath the reeds in the cove that gave the local kids the shivers, and a place for them to scare the vacationing summer kids from up north. With a slight shift to his right, it winked in the sunlight that spilled through the same tight square that was his only way in, and only way out.

Tim-Lee's reach eased closer to the shape through his almost-legally-blind focus. Six inches. Five. Four. It was curved, he could see that. His regulator exhaust bubbles warbled round his neck and kissed the too-sensitive edge of his ear. He slapped the tickle away with one hand. His other hand, anxious, snapped at the prize.

Silt bloomed off the hard surface beneath it, gobbling up his visibility.

Shit!

If only he hadn't been so damned cheap, and had had his glasses prescription fitted to his SCUBA mask.

He froze, afraid his own breathing would make it all worse. He prayed an Our Father as he reeled in his hand till it emerged from the cloud of silt and drifted up to his face. From the other side of his mask, his thumb and forefinger, white and bloodless, were gripping as tight as they could onto nothing at all.

Tim-Lee spent 100 psi of air and a piss in his surf suit till the silt settled enough to find the gleam again. Annoying flotsam pestered him as he passed his hand over the bottom washing it away.

Gently. Remember what Professor Laird always says. Stroke the bottom like a lover's leg.

Professor Laird.

Laird would be fuming by now. The vein over his left eye would be pulsing like a night crawler thrashing on hot afternoon asphalt. Once again he was shirking his duties to the team to chase a fantasy; sloughing his responsibilities onto his already overworked teammates at the controversial dig on the east bank of the James River just north of the big house once owned by Jimmy Dean the singer, actor, and sausage-and-eggs guy.

Laird had meanly debunked his mystery as nothing more than a Kindergarten nap time fable. So what. He knew better. It was real. No one could just conjure up such a story. Not even the dying old man in the article he had read at the State archives in Raleigh—a stunning surprise that had bitch-slapped the defeatist funk that almost convinced him to give up.

The woman at the archives service counter had only mentioned it in ambling conversation. "Nobody ever asks for it. Only reason I know about it is—oh, I can't remember."

She had had to show him how to coax a rather old and disagreeable seventies microfiche machine to read it and make copies of the article.

It was summer, 1961. So sweltering hot that the *Wilmington Morning Star* was prognosticating that alligators would be shedding their Eagle Island hideaways to ford the river and loot Wilmington's waterfront establishments of iced refreshment.

On a celebratory Fourth of July in that first year of the Civil War centennial, when southerners were aching for glorified tales of Dixie's fight for independence, the *Star* had rushed a reporter to the bedside of a dying old man.

A very old man. With a story to tell.

The night of the Fourth, as the first fireworks jetted into the sky, the *Star* presses were clattering out a special edition. The next morning—the Fifth—wagging tongues clucked over coffee and donuts at the headline splashed in fat ink across the front page.

Confederate Veteran Alive in Wilmington Tells All!

It was the story of the year.

And the clue that had rescued Tim-Lee's flagging resolve.

The light was fading from the old man's calculating gaze. But his mind had never dulled, despite his extreme 110 years. He'd been a boiler tender's mate aboard what he called *a wonderfully sleek and sneaky runner* built in Scotland.

"*Hermione*," he replied, when asked her name by the mayor, who had tailed the *Star* reporter with his curiosity ablaze.

The old man's physician was present too, as was the mid-fifties woman who owned the grand old house on Nun Street off Second, where the old man boarded.

"He's been here two weeks," she told the reporter before she showed him in. "All the way from California. He's been fine really, taking walks, visiting the downtown. It's surprising really, given his age. Says he was born and raised right here in Wilmington. Can you imagine, and at his age!"

Her voice dropped to a cupped whisper. "I think maybe he's come home to die."

But breathing had begun to come hard to the old man. His labored breaths interrupted his words as he described running the blockade into Cape Fear, and the night the Yankees sank *Hermione*.

"Spies must'a informed the Federals of our course. Word must'a got out about her secret cargo. The blockade ships—they usually roamed farther south of Masonboro Inlet, not so far north."

"Secret cargo?" asked the young reporter, who was wondering what he had done wrong to get this boring assignment

"S'what I said. They found us like they knew just where to look and chased us down—the *Niphon* and the *James Adger*. Like hounds after the fox."

The old man reflected for a moment.

"Now those two"—He emphasized his point with a bowed and boney digit—"they had a reputation. Together they wrecked more runners than any other blockader. And that night their intentions were clear. They meant to sink us."

"What was the secret cargo?"

"I never saw it. No one did. It was loaded aboard in Nassau in the night, and not by the crew. It was deep in her belly and covered. Any other trip, *Hermione* would'a been crammed full and her decks brimming with overflow. But not that trip. For that one her decks were cleared and forty-five men got left behind in Nassau. It was just eight of us. Captain Munford, Pritchard and me to stoke the boilers, Gorran Tregale and Mr. Burgess. Ensley ran the engines. And two boatswains to work the decks and rigging.

"Captain Munford"—He smiled wistfully—"I could never forget him even if I tried. There was no runner captain better than him. Well, he hugged the shoreline so close the sea floor was beating us all to heck. The Yankees—they shattered our foremast. I remember it like it was yesterday. The top half of the foremast went over the side and got all tangled up and it was dragging the bottom like an anchor, stealing our speed. The portside wheel was blown all to heck. And then the other one froze up in the sand.

"*Hermione* broke her back on the shoals. She split amidships. It was an awful racket. By then I was in the water. There's a black spot in my recollections, but somehow through it all, I was the only survivor. Captain Munford and Mr. Burgess—he was our pilot—they were killed by grapeshot. Mr. Burgess was from Smithville. You call it Southport now.

"But now that you got me talking about it, Mr. Pritchard and Gorran Tregale and our boatswains—they were all Englishmen, so God willing they were just detained for a while and sent back to England."

The old man glanced out the single window of his room. "God save their poor souls." He bowed his head and shook it remorsefully. "After Johnson's surrender in Durham...what with the Reconstruction and all...I couldn't bear staying around here any longer. Soon as I was sixteen I picked myself up and left for California in sixty-six. I signed on with a tea clipper in San Francisco. We ran the Hong Kong-London route. I never could come back here. I could never stomach those people coming down here after the war."

The *Star* reporter eyed him askance. "Then what is it that made you return now?"

Sound hesitated in the small but comfortable room adorned in aged Edwardian furnishings.

"I want my ashes placed in the surf. I want to rest with my shipmates among *Hermione*'s ruins."

His visitors shared bland expressions amongst themselves. The mayor shrugged: there weren't any laws against that. He asked him, "Where'd she sink? How far out?"

"Just off Bear Inlet. Swimming distance. I should know, I swum it."

The mayor, the doctor, and the *Star* reporter muttered amongst themselves. There were no wrecks off Bear Inlet. The young reporter suggested, "You must mean Bogue Inlet."

"Did I say Bogue Inlet?"

They smirked at his curmudgeonly retort. Could be his age. Could be time; time dulls the memory, you know.

"Quit speakin' s'though I weren't here. The dang shoal where she sank was in sight of the shore."

Faces flushed with graceful possibilities.

"There's never been any ship found there."

"Maybe she was salvaged after the war or cleared away for navigation safety."

"A hurricane might have torn her apart and spread her bits and pieces up and down the coast."

"The Marines!"

"Huh?"

"The Marine jets. That area round Bear Inlet is closed to navigation most times, so as they can practice their bombing. Could be she was bombed to smithereens by the Marines. Most of them's Yankees, you know."

When the old man's expression swept to livid, his doctor suggested, "That's enough for now. Let's everyone let him rest," and he began herding everyone out the door.

The old man hollered after them, "I'm not finished!" He indicated to the *Star* reporter, the first one at the door. "The kid stays here."

When the door latch clicked shut, he pointed to a chair. "Siddown." He let the kid's ass just touch the cushion before adding, "But first, fluff up these pillows behind my back for me, wouldja?"

The kid stepped over to the bed and punched some softness into the pillows, and then retreated back to his chair.

The old man studied him till the kid looked like he had to pee. "There's a bigger reason I came back."

The *Star* reporter's hands flashed something.

"No notes. You busy yourself writing things down and you won't listen like you should."

The kid rolled with exasperation and pocketed his note pad.

"I hear there's a little fib going round here passed off as the truth. Teaching it in schools, too, I heard. Children being lied to by their elders." He shook a shameful head. "That ain't right." He slipped a papal smirk at the reporter. "I bet even your parents told it to you."

"Told me what?"

"And you believed them, too. And why shouldn't you? They're your parents. And when they tell you something is so, who's to say otherwise?" He leaned over in his bed closer to the kid with a delinquent gleam. "Well, I'm here to say otherwise."

The kid pursed apprehensive lips. "What is it my parents were supposed to have told me?"

"Same thing I'm going to tell you. Except mine's the truth. I'm putting things straight before I croak in this here bed." He pointed a bent finger at the kid. "You make sure people know that when you print my story."

"Okay. But still, what's the fib?"

"The one about the secret ironclad built at the Beery Yard on Eagle Island."

The young man grimaced and moaned, "Oh Lord." He rose to gather his things.

The old man stiffened like a stove pipe. "Siddown, youngster!"

"I'm no youngster: I'm 24 years old, a graduate of the University of North Carolina, cum laude. And here you jerk me around about some old wives tale."

"Ain't no wives tale, neither."

"Then why is there no record of it? Know why? Because it's bullshit."

"They teach you to talk like that in the university, did they?"

"You're just trying to pull wool over people because nobody else from back then is alive to challenge whatever you say."

The old man's cheeks mumped up when a growl tried to break through his stiff white lips.

"Look here," the reporter said.

"No. You look here. You show a veteran some respect and plop your pugnacious Chapel Hill, cum laude self in that chair there."

The kid sagged. "What the hell. I got nothing better to do." He dropped his things and kerplunked back into his chair. "Okay. I'm listening."

"You're sure now? I mean I don't need to be wasting my time on you."

"I said I'm listening, didn't I?"

"Fine. What I'm about to tell you, it's God's truth." The old man thumbed his sunken chest. "I know because I was there."

The kid tossed back an incredulous look.

"She was much smaller than most gunboats, but she carried a few secrets. Newfangled engines, they said, that didn't smoke. Armor made of English steel, not iron, like every other ship. And strange, too."

"Oh? Strange in what way?"

"The armor plate—straight on the sides but the tops and bottoms came to points. All put together they looked like scales on some monster fish. A smarter man once explained to me that their shape is called a pylon. It's Greek."

"I think you mean a polygon."

"I mean what I said."

"You were what then, a boy? How'd you get to see this ship and these secret plates of steel? They wouldn't let some boy just wander into something so secret."

The old man patted the blankets over his legs.

"Weren't you listening before? I was a sailor, a boiler man's mate. I had skills. I could be trusted. I knew when to shut my mouth and avert my eyes when it was right. So Beery's Yard gave me work. So I didn't just hear about her or see her from across the river; I *worked* on her. I helped build her, dammit!"

"Alright, alright! I believe you. Don't go giving me that look. I do. But there's something important you haven't told me. Two things actually."

"What's that?"

"You haven't told me your name. And the ironclad—what was she called?"

A smooth smile softened the old man's thin, cracked lips.

"My name is Peter Howe, and she was called the *Recluse*."

When he read that, the name hit Tim-Lee like a bolt of lightning. Tingles ran all through him from head to toe. *Recluse*. She had a name. She was real, not some fable or a myth or some silly legend. He was right. He was right!

Let Laird laugh. Let them all laugh. We'll see who's laughing when I finally show them.

His visibility was cleared up now. He could see the spot again.

He coaxed the silt aside a tiny bit at a time, searching for the gleam, wishing with all his might for it to return. He had to find it. He just *had* to. If he didn't—Oh no! He couldn't even go there. It was too horrible to think of.

A disturbing voice tapped on him.

You're done for. You know you are. Everyone is so sick of your shit. Even your best friend, Qeb Morgan.

Qeb is a good friend. He'll understand in the end.

Maybe. But will Professor Laird?

Tim-Lee's insides pretzeled up. Even if Qeb did understand, it wouldn't change the fact that Laird was ready to destroy his career before it ever got started.

The voice decreed: *You'll lose your scholarship.*

Growing up in the Smokey Mountains had qualified Tim-Lee for most of the money he was living on, plus it paid all his tuition and books. Without it he was a goner. He would never finish his masters. What would become of him then?

The voice insisted: *You're throwing it all away for something people smarter than you say doesn't exist. There's nothing here.*

Well they're all wrong!

This was the moment. *His* moment. That unnerving and nauseous, exciting and salubrious instant brimming with trepidation and doubt that all great men experienced as they tottered over the edge of final discovery. Beneath him—He *knew* it!—lay the bones of a great warship, pleading to be found and begging for its story to be told.

There's no way I'm giving up now. Not this close.

Outside, beyond the reeds and the water's surface was everyone else, up there, moving about their day, clueless and unexpecting: the naysayers, the skeptics, and the ones who simply didn't care. They were all in for a big shock.

Tim-Lee's ego bloomed. He had even surprised himself, tracing down that *Star* reporter from 1961. Forty-four years ago the old man, Peter Howe, had befriended the man; had confided in him; and had entrusted him with a manuscript before his death. *He'd always hankered to get it published*, the reporter had told him. But he never had.

"Peter Howe passed soon after our interview back then. Actually we had three. By then I came to really liking the old guy."

And him?

"Oh, I followed my youthful oats and staked my career claim up in New York City. Made myself a nice egg, too. The kind of money a man could come home to and retire near family."

And the whole time, Peter Howe's manuscript had been collecting dust in a box.

The aged reporter had parted with it easily. "Take it. I did him wrong by forgetting."

Tim-Lee had gleaned through its dry and brittle yellowed pages, cover to cover, consuming its contents. Twice. It was that second reading when he picked them up, the little anomalies in Howe's storytelling. Bits and pieces of a bigger puzzle secreted here and there between the lines; trinkets for the stubborn soul tenacious enough to piece them together and make them work.

Anyone like himself.

Armed with Howe's puzzle, the nightmares auguring Tim-Lee's looming fall from his studies paled against the intoxicating imminence of his success. With each clue he uncovered, with each step closer, the very helix of his DNA twisted tighter in on itself. He couldn't sleep. His mind refused to shut up. His stomach tolerated no food beyond Pop-Tarts and coffee. Black. No sugar.

Three mind-numbing weeks it had taken him to build Howe's puzzle. He was sick with exhaustion. But now he was here, where Peter Howe's words had pushed him, beneath a soddy cove off a meandering tributary of the Shallotte River.

And there it was again, that little gleam.

Just when his fingertip kissed the round edge of it, the gleam suddenly plinked out. All light was washed aside by a swath of darkness. Slower this time, with the gleam safe between his fingers, Tim-Lee checked his back. Too late. The shadow had passed. Just the speechless reeds outside, waving with the current between streaks of muddy sunlight.

A gator maybe?

His eyes traced the square that was his only exit. Could it get in through that?

You idiot, you're scaring yourself.

The gleam in his grip smiled up at him. He pulled it close to his mask. His eyes hurt, trying to focus. There was an eagle on one side, something incoherent on the other. There were words round its periphery on both sides that he could trace, just not read.

He would need his stupid glasses to read it. *Damn it!* He'd have to go up and back to his car on the side of the public road tracing the pine woods, safely parked out of sight from whoever lived in the little white house by the cove.

He fisted the little gleam in his one hand and reached up for the square that was his way out with the other hand.

The sunlight slipping through the reeds vanished again.

The shadow was back.

It was big.

And it wasn't any gator.

4-A LOST FISH

All fifty-three Confederate blockade runners entombed in North Carolina's shell-strewn sea bottom had been meticulously charted and recorded. Add to them the sunken Yankee warships and that brought the number closer to seventy-five. Most of the wrecks lay blanketed beneath deepwater sand, but a few had broken up in the shallows, sometimes visible from the beaches. There was a time when, at low tide, determined swimmers could reach them to pilfer souvenirs.

The coastline stretching northeast as the crow flies from the mouth of the Cape Fear River was so littered with wrecks that the area had been unofficially labeled Civil War Shipwreck District.

Between summers the many inlets creasing the outer banks offered overworked, 21st Century Carolinians quick escape to the peace of the open sea. Then each June, pale-faced vacationers swarmed down from up north, transforming nautical civility into a cluttered mayhem of fishing charters, day cruisers, dive boats, and conspicuous yachts bedecked with half-naked snowbirds, captained by high-rise desk jockeys practicing rusty seamanship in a haze of alcohol.

Dr. Frank Morgan shook his head from the deck of his boat. It was a wonder no one got killed.

And the mess wasn't just on the surface. Thirty-five feet down, the seabed lay marred by plastic waste and vacation debris in a tangled lattice of fishing tackle lost in futile pursuits of the big catch and a no-shit sea story for the nighttime bar scene.

Hurricane Meredith had passed through just weeks before the summertime rush, stirring the shallows and exposing God knows what to snag anything kiting by, including Frank's new sonar towfish.

Standing at the transom of his boat, he rolled the towfish's severed feed cable in his fingers. "How much did you say it cost?" his brother, Charley asked. He had convinced Charley to come out on the water with him and run the new towfish for a few passes so he could know what he was doing before his autumn graduate students showed up.

"Twenty-eight thousand dollars."

"I guess you shouldn't have lost it then."

"I didn't lose it. It's just caught on something."

"You said you knew how to operate it."

"Hey, you're the one who does this every day. Where's all that expertise I hear about?"

"Well first, you're not supposed to use the thing in shallow water. Look. Says right here in the manual. See, Frank?"

"I see."

"You're not looking."

"I've read the manual."

Charley flagged the pages under Frank's nose. "But there's a picture here. Says don't operate shallower than 50 feet."

"I know what it says."

Charley peered over the side. "How deep is it here? I think I can see the bottom."

"You can't see the bottom, Charley."

"I don't know. Maybe you set the ballast too nose heavy."

"It wasn't nose heavy. I know what I'm doing."

"Towfish doesn't think so."

"The towfish doesn't think, Charley."

"I didn't hear you—" Suddenly the sky opened up with a mighty roar so loud Charley cowered behind himself for cover. "What the hell!" Two matte grey jet fighters ripped through the air overhead so close he could have hit them with his shoe. "They're kind of low, aren't they?"

Frank gave them an off-handed glance. "They're just showing off. They must be training. I guess we shouldn't be here, really."

Charley cupped his eyes from the sun. "Oh? And why is that, Frank?"

Frank moped at the water around them and the shoreline about a mile away. "These are restricted waters. It's legal for us to navigate through here. We just can't stay put." He indicated to the shoreline. "The Marine air station is just beyond Bear Inlet there." He swung his arm across the water all around them. "They drop bombs and stuff out here."

"Well that's just great, Frank. Glad you told me we'd be dragging that damn thing back and forth in the Marines' playground. Anything else you don't want to tell me?"

"There's unexploded ordnance down there. That's why there's no fishing allowed here."

"You mean fishing as in dragging a hook through the water hoping to catch a big fish?"

"Something like that."

Charley's gaze traced after the jets shrinking to specks in the sky out over deeper water. "And knowing this—that there are things down there that might not respond so well to us snagging onto them—you decided to make a third pass at that thing down there you saw on your screen, towing a twenty-five pound, three foot long lure behind us."

"As long as we're not sitting around out here."

"Seems to me we're sitting pretty still right now."

"Not for long." Frank looked over the transom into the water and came to a conclusion. "Um, can you to go down after the fish?"

"Yeah, well our friends are back." The jet fighter's wings splayed wide as they banked into a slow turn. "I don't think they like us here, Frank. And why can't you go down after it?"

Frank ground his hands into fists. "Because I don't dive."

Charley's tanned face screwed all up. "What kind of marine archaeologist doesn't dive?"

Frank thumbed his chest. "This kind. At least not anymore. Not after..."

Charley squinted into his memory. "Is this about that stupid dive you did going down inside Ptolemy's tomb? Geez, Frank. That was five years ago."

"You weren't there, damn it! I still get nightmares."

The fighters drifted past them again, slower this time. Helmets with beady black visors bugged at them through polished canopies.

"Frank. I think they want their playground back."

"We gotta get the fish, first."

"Why not come back for it?"

"Are you nuts?"

"I think maybe we want to leave here. Like now, Frank."

"I can't go back without it."

"Uh huh. I know that look on your face. You've been testing the rules again."

Frank glanced back from behind a guilty grimace. "The fish isn't just mine. There's a procedure for signing it out. All that bureaucracy for a dumb tool. It's stupid."

"Meaning?"

"If I don't come back with it in one piece, they're not going to be pleased."

"Like your boss?"

Frank faded to green.

"I really like the way I get a choice here, Frank."

"The planes won't do anything with us here."

"Well, what about them?"

Frank traced Charley's finger to a low white craft flopping over the waves, heading their way. A fat band, black-on-red, circled its beltline. "Shit, the Coasties. Quick, get rigged up and get in the water. I'll take care of this."

"Like I said, Frank. I appreciate having a choice."

The Coast Guard let Frank off with a slap on the wrist. They had backed off and were idling in the distance, waiting to see that Frank left the area once he got his tangled towfish aboard. The towfish had come free and was now safe and in one piece, dripping dry on the afterdeck.

Charley was sitting on the starboard gunwale out of sight of the Coasties, hidden by the boat's pilothouse. "That was uncomfortable," he said, pulling a line up from the bottom.

"We're fine. It could've been worse."

"What did you tell them?"

"That I was letting you work the towfish and you caught it on something and that you were down on the bottom fixing your screw up."

"Yeah? Well smartass, I got a pay day down there." Charley hauled up a net bag with something big inside it. "And I'm going back down."

"What? No! Are you nuts? The Coast Guard—they're right there watching us."

"Frank, I gotta. I saw something weird down there, near where I nabbed this." Charley set the net bag down on the deck with a heavy clump.

Frank eyeballed a crusty glob in the bag with the vague outline of a ship's bell. "Charley, it's against the law, bringing things up from these waters."

"Just shut up, will you, and give me a line. Not that one. Give me the heavier one."

Frank mechanically handed over the line. "What kind of weird?"

"There's something else down there. A lot of something else. They're big, and I'm getting us one. We'll just let it hang below the water by the boat and cruise real easy till those Coast Guard guys get bored and leave. Don't sweat it. I'll be careful. They won't see a thing."

Their boat—a chubby little diesel research vessel named *Badger*—chugged along contently as Charley steered them back to Beaufort. Frank, standing next to him, had his laptop open on the helm. Charley frowned at one of the images recorded by the towfish Frank had on his screen. Crisp and clear was the outline of a ship casting long shadows across an eerie orange bottom.

"She's broken into three pieces." Frank tapped different places on the screen. "This rumpled area here on the bottom separates the bow from the stern. And this jumble in the middle looks like machinery; possibly the engines or the boilers."

Charley chanced a longer look. A field of debris pitter-pattered aft across the bottom to the wreck's stern, which dipped beneath the sand. The jumble in the middle was bordered by two enormous wagon wheel looking things. "Is that a sidewheeler?"

"Looks like it. She could be a blockade runner."

"As in Civil War blockade runner?"

"Yeah. And she's not supposed to be here."

Charley peered over his shoulder at the strange polygon plate he'd brought up. At first he'd left it hanging in the water just as he said, secured with the heavy line to the bulwarks so the Coasties wouldn't see it. He and Frank waved to them and got underway. After they had some good distance between them, they banged themselves up muscling the thing up onto the deck.

It was heavy as shit. Tongue and groove edges traced the long sides of it.

"It doesn't look that old, but there were so many of them—dozens of them—and all of them with that same weird shape."

Frank eyed the dubious plate. "These are busy shores. A lot of junk probably lost or dumped here over the last hundred years. It could be just a coincidence. They were tossed overboard by someone—probably the military—and just by chance they landed all over that wreck down there."

"Nah! I'm not buying it, Frank. Not the way they were laid out. It was like they belonged there. Kind of like those Greek jugs in the wrecks you see in the magazine pictures."

"Amphorae."

"Yeah, those; the way they're always laid out on the bottom all neat and tidy. Well, that's the way these were. Neat and tidy. And ain't that the weirdest thing. Take a look and tell me what you don't see."

Frank scrutinized the plate. "Well...other than the shape and the tongue-and-groove edges, I don't see anything."

"Exactly! There's not a speck of rust on it anywhere."

Frank looked more closely. "You know, you're right." He straightened up and indicated to the plate with an open hand. "That's our answer then, isn't it? They can't be part of the wreck. They haven't even been down there long enough to rust. Now let me get back to these images."

"Fine, Frank. You do that."

Bogue Banks drifted slowly by on their left. Atlantic Beach was straight off their port. Up ahead were the sand dunes clawing up to squat Fort Macon. Any minute now, the fort would pop up off their bow, just to port.

Charley was the first to break silence. "You want to tell me what's bugging you?"

"Nothing's bugging me."

"You haven't said a word in a while."

Frank sighed heavily at the towfish.

"The fish is fine, Frank."

"It's not the fish."

"The plate then. We didn't get caught. We're fine."

"We're not fine. Not yet. Especially me."

"So what then?"

"Badger."

"This boat?"

"I kind of borrowed it."

"You said it was yours."

"It's hard getting my hands on the things I need. Everybody's always competing, so I just grab what I need and run with it."

"I'll bet that goes over well."

"Not usually."

Frank slapped the top down on his laptop and watched the visitors ambling over the grassy knolls surrounding Fort Macon.

"In fact, I'm pretty sure they're going to fire me."

5-REUNION

Frank's lab was a gleaming affair clinging to the farthest corner of the newest building at the Institute for Marine Sciences in Morehead City, a hectic summer haven for frazzled vacationers; but an otherwise peaceful burg straddling a slowly eroding peninsula on North Carolina's middle coast.

Evening sunlight shimmered off burnished steel counters and the nickel-plated fixtures of Frank's deep sink, where he sat meticulously picking away at an ulcerous crust of sea life cloaking Charley's ship's bell, trying to recover from the chewing out he'd just endured from his boss, Director of Marine Studies, Bob Moore.

Frank ignored Charley's trophy plate lying behind him, soaking in a high-pH bath to strangle decomposition, and consuming more floor space than his lab could afford. The dutiful hum of a battery charger wired between the stainless bath and Charley's plate in the water might fend off unseen corrosion with ease, but it was no match for the acidic thoughts plaguing Frank, cranking up his gastric reflux: a sort of civilian PTSD.

A feminine utterance behind him said, "Your boss didn't sound very happy."

The distantly familiar and almost forgotten voice pinched the nape of Frank's neck. "It seems I'm losing my only ally," he replied to the bell in the sink in front of him. Crusty flakes fell away from it revealing a bronze letter, a second letter, and then two more.

His fingers flinched when she said, "Your recklessness has been hard on him."

His set his brush on the countertop with all the patience he could muster.

"He's only trying to help you. You just keep getting in the way."

His stool whirled round on well-oiled bearings. At that instant a dormant memory of what she'd done to him five years ago in Egypt hollered *Hello!* and it dawned on him that he'd never decided whether he'd forgiven her or not.

He holed up behind crossed arms, wishing with all his might that she would just go away. "What would you know about it?" he said.

"Are you going to invite me in?" she answered, still hidden in the hallway shadows.

His arms rose and sank over a plumbean sigh. His wish wasn't working. "Come on in (if you really have to)."

Sultry air stepped aside as her curvy form, poorly hidden by weathered jeans and a roomy man's plaid shirt, emerged into the light. With measured steps Dr. Hillary Bascombe tacked into his lab. Her wispy smile locked onto him with a snap. Her eyes, with that damned magnetic green, snatched him up as easily as they had the first day they'd met five years ago.

Well, he'd met her. She wouldn't give him the time of day.

Hillary steered her gaze aside, appraising his digs, weaving toward him over scuffed linoleum floors cluttered with technology and tattered boxes boasting their contents in bold *Marks-A-Lot* script. She stopped in the middle of the room. To her right, spindly metal shelves grappled bare walls for dear life, straining under their burdens of dull mechanical artifacts.

The whole place had a weirdly aged stink about it.

Her attention drifted back to him. The solemn glow of a countertop lamp behind him cast his long shadow to her shoe tips. "You need some air in here."

"Right now it suits my mood."

She edged over to the plate in the bath. "Is this what you stole the *Badger* for?"

"I borrowed it. And no, that's Charley's work."

"Mm. Poor Bob Moore has both Morgans to deal with now. So, what is it?"

"I don't know yet."

"It doesn't look like much."

"We found a new wreck."

Something gleamed yellow at her from the sink behind him. "Can I see?"

He rolled the bell so she could read the letters cast into it.

She repeated the name aloud: "*Hermione.*"

"Charley brought it up with that plate."

She pulled up a lab stool for herself. "Anything in this hovel to drink?" she said, sliding herself onto it.

"Tap water," he retorted.

She fidgeted, clocking her stool seat this way, then that, nicking at his attitude till he made up his mind to be nice.

"There's beer in the refrigerator."

"Beer sounds nice."

"Fine." He fished through his refrigerator crammed with desiccant packs and small artifacts in containers of ionized water.

Hillary's curiosity toured his body from behind. He looked fit.

He wheeled round gripping a growler and pulled two coffee mugs from the overhead cabinets. As he poured, she commented, "Bob's voice carried all the way outside the building."

"I'm sure it did," he said, shuffling back up onto his stool. "He's sending some moron here to talk to me. More like fire me, probably. He just doesn't have the guts to do it himself."

"That's not why."

"How would you know?"

"Because I'm the moron."

"What? Shit! Sorry. Why you? Why at all?"

"Because you've been behaving like a child. His words, not mine."

"I know. He used those exact words just now."

"How about first you tell me about your wreck?" she said, past the disgusted look on his face.

"She's a paddle steamer, a big one. Charley and I—we were exercising our new towfish off Brown's Inlet. That crazy charter boat traffic pushed us off course and we snagged the fish on her. Bob really sent you? What are you supposed to do?"

"I guess the crazy traffic served a purpose then. Yes, he did, and right now I have no idea what I'm supposed to do."

Frank re-read the letters aloud on Charley's bell. "I won't claim to know every wreck on this coast, but this one's definitely uncharted. I'm positive."

"Nothing's positive in our world, darling. *Hermione's* just been forgotten. Try that little museum in Southport. Maybe they'll have something."

"The Maritime Museum? I called them. They had nothing."

They sipped their beers quietly, tensed by the electricity of each other's bubble.

His face pickled all up. "*Darling?* You don't use words like that." She had obviously picked up some local parlance. And was that a teeny twang he heard marbling her Oxford English? "Wait a minute. How long have you been here?"

"I was waiting outside till Bob was done with you, then it was my turn."

"Very funny. You know what I mean."

"Eighteen months."

"Eighteen months!"

"I'm Visiting Professor of Marine Excavations at the women's marine archaeology program at East Carolina. Did you hear me?" His preoccupied reply: *There's no one better for the job*, wasn't the response she was ready for.

"Bob wasn't in the decision process to bring me onboard, you know? I didn't know that then, but it was going to make my presence here very difficult. The UNC Board of Trustees was pressing for a marine archaeology program of their own. To compete with Eastern Carolina's program. Your program now...I suppose."

He hesitated, befuddled by a charmed glimmer of contentment whittling through the moldy fabric of his animosity. "So all this time, you've known I've been working here?"

"And I've heard all the horror stories, too."

He harrumphed at that and admitted, "I suppose I became available at just the right time for them. I had just finished working with Charley on a job in the Mediterranean for David Kittering. And things were still all abuzz over our recovery of Cleopatra."

He stole—No, he savored, really, a long peek at her red hair shimmering in the sinking sunlight, expecting a reaction that didn't come.

"The trustees arm-twisted Bob into letting me set up shop here. I was an alumnus, I had fame, and the trustees wanted me. So it was screw you, Bob. I can't blame his bitterness. After he bowed to them, the trustees twisted their knife in his wound by making me a Distinguished Professor. That put me senior to the other professors here. Most of them had been here for years. So, from day one I've been persona non grata."

He ran his fingertips over the bell's letters tracing the rises and dips in their cursive sweep.

"I've only made things more difficult for him by being the way I am. The IMS is a marine sciences facility—biologists, zoologists, chemists. It's not set-up for the rusty, crumbly messiness of archaeology. This lab is needed and I'm taking it up. I should have seen this coming."

"But?"

"I'm not really surprised by it all, I guess." Moments passed as he let the soft hum of the chemical bath massage his punch-drunk self-esteem.

She studied his profile, pinging on his ear, somehow delicate in its curves and arches. He was aging well. "You have questions," she said.

"Hm? Yeah, I guess I do. How did you and Bob meet?"

"That's not what you want to ask me."

The knob in Frank's throat bobbed.

"You want to ask me about Nathaniel." She recalled, "You're a Christian, aren't you."

"I was raised Methodist, but I haven't been to church in years."

"Nathaniel was an atheist." His eyelids fluttered. "You didn't know that."

She panned the walls, pulling her thoughts from the blemishes in the paint. "It's sad, really. He spent his life studying other people's gods, and yet he never believed in any of them. In the end, I think his doubts about God got to him. When he couldn't get up anymore, that bed terrified him. Till the very end he kept wanting out of it. When it was getting time, he struggled and fought. My God. The terror in his eyes. It still..."

She drowned her thoughts with the rest of her beer.

"Were the two of you happy?"

She expelled a mournful sigh. "It was good finally getting him out of that filthy Egypt." She caught his searching expression and admitted, "Yes. We were happy."

He reminded her of her near death on the Red Sea, with the African coastline just in site, and Nathaniel willing to let her succumb just to satiate his lust for a legacy. "You were lucky to get out alive."

"Nathaniel wasn't responsible, Frank. He was—"

"Insane?"

"You're still angry."

"He kidnapped a sixteen year old boy."

"I know he did."

"His hired thug shot at Charley and nearly killed his best friend, Theo Menkin."

"I know, Frank."

She too had pointed a gun at Charley to get her way with him. And after that worked, she rewarded Charley's cooperation by having him arrested on bogus charges of smuggling. She braced for the third blow when Frank would remind her of what they had done to him, too. When that blow didn't come, she escaped with, "So how is Charley?"

"Kittering keeps him busy; too busy if you ask me. It's destroying his marriage and the idiot doesn't seem to know it."

"Are we talking *the* David Kittering?"

"The same. After Cleopatra, we both worked for him on a German U-boat wreck off Tunisia."

"Sounds exciting."

"Twenty-three million dollars' worth of exciting." The fresh-scrubbed gleaming bars with swastika eagles stamped in them had weighed heavily in Frank's hand. "Charley stayed on with Kittering." He rolled his eyes round the room. "Me? Well, here I am."

Her faint touch made the hairs rise on his forearm. She set her empty mug on the counter. He followed her lead and did likewise. "But, you were telling me about you," he said.

"Nathaniel squandered his family's fortune chasing after her." She shook her head in retrospect. She'd been madly in love with a dying man; had followed him nearly to her own death chasing a dead woman he loved more than her. She still couldn't bring herself to repeat the name of the Egyptian queen.

"In the process, he defamed and extorted his closest friend."

"You mean Theo Menkin," he guessed.

"Yes. We lived in a self-imposed exile at Nathaniel's family estate. I wanted us in some cozy seaside cottage, but the quiet and security were good for him."

"I noticed the ring."

She splayed her fingers out in front of her exposing a slender band of gold with three small diamonds. "It would be five years next month. It was a private ceremony. The vicar came to the house, and some friends to witness. Theodore was wonderful about it all, really. And he visited us often."

Frank shook his amused head. "That's hard for me to visualize, those two in the same room together."

"At the funeral, Theodore's eulogy to Nathaniel was beautiful. I insisted that all Nathaniel's former colleagues make their appearances: all those bastards that had turned against him. Theo held Nathaniel's department chair then, so he made them all attend."

She glimpsed the insult edging into Frank's features and offered a penitent smile. "I wanted them to suffer, but not you. That's why I didn't invite you. I'm sorry if I hurt you. I was quite the bitch, you know. As I'm sure you can remember from working with me."

"At the time, I thought you were the sexiest bitch I'd ever met."

She stiffened just slightly. That was number two: two times he had slipped up and made a pass at her. Did he even know it? She dodged his compliment and parried with, "Whatever happened to that Egyptian boy?"

"You mean Qeb. He's my nephew now. Charley married his mother and adopted him. He's working on his PhD."

"You're kidding. Just yesterday he was a teenager." Her dismayed fingers rose to her cheek and tinkered at some faint lines in her complexion. "Oh my God. I suddenly feel so old."

"He's a big kid. His eyes come to here." Frank tapped the tip of his nose. "He finished his bachelors in three years with honors and got accepted right into doctoral studies. He's up in Virginia now, on the James River, working on an ironclad shipwreck."

"Ah. You must mean Stephen Laird's project."

"You know Laird?"

"I know *of* him." Hillary's curiosity coaxed her from her stool and back over to the plate in the bath. "So where is his wife now?"

"I don't think Laird's married."

"Charley's wife, you twit."

"Olufemi? They bought a place down in Wilmington after her parents passed. She's studying studio art at UNCW. It's amazing how it has awakened the latent artiste in her. She's really quite good."

"And lonely I imagine, with him gone all the time. She must be happy he's back."

"It's a surprise. Her birthday's in two days."

"So he's here near her and he hasn't gone and seen her yet? Tschah! He's still as dense now as he was then." She seated herself on the backs of her calves for a closer look at the plate. "Come over here. And bring a torch."

Frank drifted over and knelt beside her. "What is it?"

She took his flashlight. "There," she said, wiggling the beam. "Do you see it?"

"Not really." He retrieved a dental pick clipped to his shirt pocket.

"Here. Let me," she said, snatching it from him. She coaxed away a large flake of marine growth. An intricate design the size of a postage stamp punched deep into the metal blossomed in the yellow light.

"How'd you see that?" he said, totally befuddled.

"Skill. You'll have it someday."

"Just shine the light on it, smart ass."

He squinted into the bath, winced, and extracted glasses from his shirt pocket. They opened with a crisp snap. He caught her look and shrugged. "Computers have ruined my eyes."

His slipped them on and a watery image crisped into view. "Spero m-e-l—"

"*Spero meliora*," she said. "'I will aspire to better things.' It's a maker's mark—the foundry that made this plate." She ran her fingers across the dips and grooves of a knight's helmet topping a shield. "And this is likely the family crest."

Frank's attention drifted to letters adorning the lower extremity of the crest. "Am I really seeing that?"

Hillary shifted the light, hesitating before whispering the name stamped in capital letters: *Laird*. She scratched at some musty memories. "The Laird family owned a foundry and shipyard on the Mersey River, at Birkenhead." Her gaze grazed over the plate with growing interest. "Frank. I think this was made by the Laird Iron Works."

"I'm not familiar with them."

"They built ironclad warships for your Confederate Navy. The Confederacy didn't have the means."

"Sure we did. We built the *Neuse*, the *Alamance*. I shouldn't have to mention the *Virginia*. And what about the *Fredericksburg* that Laird's diving on?" Frank faltered. Laird. He looked at her, unsure. "You don't think there could be a family connection here: Stephen Laird and the Laird's that made this plate?"

Hillary settled her bum onto the floor and waxed thoughtful. "I've heard a story from round these parts."

"Oh? Tell me."

"One of my students here shared it with me. Her grandfather told it to her when she was little. He always insisted it was a true story. People whispered behind his back, she said, because other people didn't think so." She huffed, skeptical. "I tend to agree with them. It's far too implausible to believe really, thinking about it. It was supposed to have happened near the end of your Civil War."

"Do you remember it?"

"Oh yes. Implausible stories are the easiest to recall."

"You were right," he said when she finished. "That is hard to believe."

"I'm not so sure anymore," she said, her eyes fixed on the plate.

"You think this could be—that the bit about a special armor might be true?" She just shrugged. "Really? I mean, look at the condition of it. Not a speck of rust. This is no 140-year-old Civil War relic."

"After all the fascinating things Nathaniel showed us, how can you be so sure?"

He had to admit she had a point. He let his fingertips glaze over the family crest. "The Oxford PhD hanging in my office says I'm some kind of materials expert. I should live up to it and find out what this thing is really made of."

She studied him, half-cocked. "What do you say we work together on this one? It'll be just like old times."

Dormant visions of their foray together deep beneath old Quait Bay castle, down into the flooded bowels of Ptolemy's tomb forced him to shudder. "I hope not completely like old times," he said.

She chuckled from her midriff over a sentimental smile, handing him back his pick. For a split second their fingertips touched, passing a hot charge betwixt them. She snatched her hand away, breaking the current. Embarrassed, she cleared her throat. "I have to get back. Bob Moore gave me your mobile phone number. I'll call you."

As she headed for the door, Frank heard himself call after her, "You know. Despite all you've been through, the years have been very good to you."

She froze at the doorjamb. That was number three: three passes. She flashed him a fast smile and faded quick as she could into the hallway. Outside in the parking lot, she fobbed her truck door open, unaware of a tall dark young man watching her with hard eyes from across the lot.

Frank fiddled with the splitting ends of his beard wondering from over his empty breakfast plate about his nephew, Qeb, seated across the table. The boy was wolfing down the last of four scrambled eggs over toast like he hadn't eaten in days. It was still dark outside when he had come downstairs to wake up the coffee pot. Out of habit, he had flicked on the porch lamp outside his kitchen door. This time when he did, he practically swallowed his heart at the sight of Qeb mooning back at him from the pre-dawn darkness.

"You scared the bejeezus out of me," he said, holding the screen door open for Qeb. "How long have you been standing out there?"

"I slept outside on your hammock. It was warm. I'm fine," Qeb reassured him, toting a bulging military surplus flight bag.

"What's with the bag? Does Professor Laird have you on some kind of break?"

"Not exactly." Qeb plopped his trusty bag on the floor beside him. "Uncle Frank, can we talk? Something happened. To me. At the dig."

When Qeb finished explaining what went down on the dig, he was horrified by his uncle's best advice. "Tell my mother? Are you crazy? It would crush her if I told her. And then she'd kill me."

Frank tight-lipped a smile till his lips went white. Qeb had a point. His mother Olufemi came from humble beginnings in a blue-collar town on the Nile River. She was a widow and a struggling mother nursing aging parents and raising her teenage son when she had crossed paths with his brother Charley.

Or was it Charley crossed hers? The recollection tickled Frank.

Charley's diving and salvage business was deep in the red when he'd met Olufemi for the first time. Not watching where he was going, he'd run smack into her in a fresh produce market, so the story went.

He knocked her bags from her arms and spilled her purchases onto the store floor, listless veggies at her feet and citrus pin-balling down the aisles.

Charley sent her home with a promise of fresh groceries, paid for them, and delivered them in person to her house.

And she invited him to stay for dinner. It had been love ever since.

Qeb was Olufemi's pride and joy. She could never have dreamed of a college education for her son, no matter how many accolades his teachers lauded over him. And without Charley in her life, maybe still that might never have happened. But all that changed when they found Cleopatra. For Qeb's role in saving the queen and bringing her home, a grateful Egypt had awarded him a full scholarship to any university in the world.

Qeb had expressed his young admiration for his adopted uncle by choosing Frank's alma mater, the University of North Carolina. And here he was, graduated with honors, and a doctoral candidate to boot. It was a dream-come-true for Olufemi.

All Frank could think of saying was, "Are you hungry?" and he cooked the kid breakfast.

His own food had gone down like knots in his throat and was now just a glob in his gut. His eyes sought distraction in the tight little hallway and the stairwell behind Qeb, beyond the kitchen. Bad move. The stairs only reminded him that any minute now the fit was going to hit the shan.

"Did you remember your mother's birthday? It's tomorrow, you know."

Qeb froze in a half-chew.

"I guess not," Frank said. The table between the two of them seemed to be growing wider. "You've got to tell her, Qeb."

Qeb's fork clattered to his plate. "Not yet." He wiped his mouth and settled against his chair back. "Laird's just bluffing."

"You said it happened ten days ago. Ten days is a long bluff."

Qeb thumbed his chest. "I'm the best diver he's got, Uncle Frank. And the best tender, too. He needs me and he knows it. He'll call. You'll see."

"Don't be so sure."

Qeb's face flushed. "Yeah well, thanks for that."

Frank brushed some toast crumbs off the table into his cupped hand and dumped them onto his plate only to have them pitter-patter off the other side of the plate back onto the table. "Call him. Call him now and apologize."

Qeb straightened in his chair. "Apologize? For what?"

Frank's tone shifted to deep and steady. "This isn't just another thin-skinned professor getting all worked up about a botched assignment. This isn't going to go down well for you. He's not obliged to call you and he's not going to." He collected the miscreant crumbs in his napkin and wadded it up. "Ball's in your court," he said, and lobbed the napkin at the garbage can.

He missed by a mile.

Qeb leaned into his words. "That dig completes my PhD. He *has* to let me finish. Apologize? Fuck him!"

Frank wrinkled his face. With college in America, the kid's English had massaged into fluency, profanity included. "Maybe you should rethink your methods."

Qeb huffed and searched the surroundings for empathy.

"Look at you," Frank said. "Your pride's eating your insides out."

Qeb looked away. "It's not just *that* that's eating them right now."

Frank stroked the table's edge. He knew where this was going. It always did when Charley came up in conversation. "This is about you, Qeb; not about your father."

"*Adopted* father you mean."

Frank's stroking hand froze. "Charley couldn't love you more if you were his own flesh and blood."

"Strange way of showing it. He's always gone, always at work; there's always an excuse. And now look. I come to you in trouble and all you say is it's *my* fault. But him? No, he can ignore his family, cruising around the world chasing shipwrecks and gold for that Kittering guy." He leaned into the back of his chair and waved, "But hey, that's all okay."

Frank stole a fast peek at the hallway behind Qeb. There was a shadow in the stairwell.

"What about my mother? What about *her*? It's like he's totally forgotten us."

Qeb withdrew behind folded arms.

The feet on Frank's chair legs hollowed across bruised kitchen linoleum. He rose, stretched out his arm across the table and wiggled his fingers at Qeb for his plate, but the boy's folded arms only cinched tighter round his chest.

Frank slipped his fingers under both their plates, snatched their cups, and gathered their utensils. Outside the window over the sink, a new day was tip-toeing over the neighbors' rooftops. He turned the faucets on and closed his eyes, calming his temper in the soothing rattle of the water as the sink filled up. When the water sounded deep enough, he searched for the faucet handles from behind the solace of his closed eyes.

The faucets squeaked closed.

He opened his eyes and came back to the reality of dirty dishes mumbling amongst themselves in the water, and shot a stream of blue Dawn at them. He gripped a cup in hand and with a greenie pad stroked the coffee staining the hairline cracks lining the cup's insides. From behind him he could feel Qeb's simmering rage boring two holes into his back.

"If you need money," he said, "I can use some help at the lab."

Qeb had other things on his mind. "What was *she* doing at your lab yesterday?"

The soapy cup slipped from Frank's grip and kerplunked into the water, splashing suds across his beltline. The air against the nape of his neck frosted over. "She who?"

"Now who's not talking?"

A thankful summer breeze wafted in from outside through the screen door and slapped the chill away. "By the way, how is Stephanie?" he parried. "She's up on the dig with you, isn't she?"

"What? Oh. Stephanie. Yeah. Well, we split up."

Frank picked at some yolk hiding between the tines of a fork. "That's a shame. You two seemed good together. What happened?"

"I don't want to talk about it."

"Hm. You said the same thing when Heather left."

"What?"

Frank pulled the plug on the sink. "And Angela. When was she? Your junior year in college, wasn't it?" He snatched one of the knives before it could slip down with the water into the glopita machine.

"It was three years ago, if you got to know. What're you, keeping account of my girlfriends?"

"Like I said, maybe it's time you rethink your methods."

The sink drain yawned loudly, sucking down the last of the soap suds. The faucets chirped happily back on under Frank's grip, and he moved ahead with the tedious chore of streaming the soap suds off their plates, from their cups and their silverware. In abject silence he rinsed and racked everything in the dish strainer on the countertop. He was finished and was coddling the silverware in the drainer cups before Qeb finally spoke up again.

"I heard a rumor they cut your funding. Is that true?"

One of the forks jumped from the drainer back into the sink.

"Yes," Frank said, setting the delinquent fork back into the drainer cups. He snatched a plate from the rack and grabbed a towel. The plate squeaked appreciatively as he wiped it dry.

Qeb pushed a little harder. "So it's true, then."

The plate clattered into place in the cabinets that bordered half the kitchen that hugged the back corner of the little Beaufort house Frank had bought with his sign-on bonus to the IMS and some of his savings.

Qeb dug even deeper. "They're taking it away."

Their cups clinked happily while Frank, speechless, hung them on their cozy hooks under the cabinets. "Yes," he broke. His hand was shaking.

"Yes? That's it?"

"That's it." The silverware jingled as Frank nestled them in the drawer to his right.

"You're not going to talk about it?"

Frank slapped the drawer home. "Nope."

Qeb studied his uncle staring out the sink window. His uncle liked to jog. Still, he was gaining a little weight in the middle. His gaze slipped down to a brownish water stain on the floor at Uncle Frank's feet. "Why do you put up with this run down old house, anyway?"

"It's not so rundown that you haven't come here wanting to stay. Besides, it needs me. I fix things."

"You're not really a fix-it-up kind of guy, Uncle Frank. What was that?"

"What was what?" Frank said.

Qeb wheeled round in his chair and searched the hallway and stairwell. Slight footsteps whispered from the top of the stairs. "Is there someone here?"

Light warbling down from the upstairs hall spilled over jeaned pant legs and heavy boots. A hand gripping the stair rail edged into the light. Qeb pinged on a long scar on the hand's back. His father had a scar just like it from when Rufus MacLeod had sliced at him, trying to kill him.

Qeb crept up from his chair. "Dad?"

The figure hesitated in the shadow of the landing, and then edged into the kitchen light.

An incredulous Qeb gaped back at his uncle.

His father drifted into the kitchen. "Got a cup of coffee, Frank?"

Pressure slowly worked its grip round Qeb's throat.

A cup clinked from its hook, coffee sloshed, and Uncle Frank extended a cup. "Black. No sugar. The way you like it."

Charley sipped it twice, eyes locked on his son.

Qeb's heart was beating against his chest like it wanted out.

"Aren't you supposed to be on a dig in Virginia?" his father said.

Qeb's tummy felt like a wet towel rung from both ends. He eked out a feeble, "Aren't you supposed to be somewhere in the South Pacific?"

Charley measured Qeb's expression quickly going pallid. "I overheard you and Frank talking."

A strange sensation reached round Qeb from behind. He shivered from its grip. "Why didn't you...?"

Charley's coffee cup settled to the table with a *tock*. "Son, maybe you should sit down."

"You didn't call..."

Qeb's thoughts were dodging him. Everything was suddenly going all wonky. His father's face faded. From behind a ringing in his ears, he heard Charley say, "Is something wrong?" The walls clocked round him like a slow moving carnival ride. Every part of him was being consumed by a swarm of pins and needles. His thoughts frittered into disarray like so many leaves ripped from their branches by a greedy wind.

The words, "Qeb, are you okay?" echoed hollow from down a long tunnel.

He thought he heard his own voice say, "I don't feel right..."

And blackness fell over him.

A quivering thread of amber seeped through Qeb's parting eyelids washing aside the darkness that had tackled him down into unconsciousness. His folded arms were pillowing his head on a hard surface. He pushed down against it and straightened himself. He was in a chair. He didn't remember sitting down. All he knew was his ass was numb.

He rubbed at the goo in his eyes, searching for focus. Dad and Uncle Frank's concerned faces washed into view. A fumbling sound drew Qeb's attention to his father's right hand. Dad was twiddling that old brass nut again. It was from his old oil rig days before he met his mother. It once belonged to a close friend of his, was all he knew. Not much else.

Dad was upset. Dad always twiddled that nut when he was upset.

"How are you feeling?" his father said.

Qeb fingered the small rise of bone at the back of his head that had been there since he was little. "My head aches. What happened?"

"You blacked out. Looked like some kind of anxiety attack. That kind of worries me, son. A kid your age shouldn't be having anxiety attacks. No, no. Don't get up. Give it a few minutes. Want some water?"

"Juice. I need some sugar."

"Let me get it." Uncle Frank threw the door open to his refrigerator and dove right in, fishing around inside. Glass clinked. Plastic wrap rustled. And aluminum racks sang to the tune of sliding Tupperware. "Found it." A big plastic jug kerplunked onto the top rim of the door. "Cranberry juice okay?" he said without looking up.

Qeb managed a flaccid smile. Cranberry juice was all Uncle Frank would have anyway. Uncle Frank loved cranberry juice, especially mixed with cherry juice. Uncle Frank was weird that way.

"Yes, please," he said, and added, "With cherry juice."

Uncle Frank set a pint glass on the table, full up to the brim.

Qeb gulped it down, trying to pull himself together. Studying their guarded silence, he decided, "I think I'm okay now."

"Yeah. Sure." His father took a worried seat beside him and elbowed closer. "Maybe you better explain what's going on that makes a big healthy guy like you faint into my arms like a rag doll."

Qeb settled folded arms heavy as sand bags onto the table, and hunkered in on himself. He moped at a long thin scratch marring the table's top and said, "I don't know."

Charley studied the curves of his son's face and the firmness of his shoulders. He was maturing into a real babe-magnet. "I heard you arguing. You really let Frank here have it."

Qeb huffed an awkward sigh.

"You know, son, holding it all inside—I tried that. It doesn't work."

Qeb tinkered with the scratch in the table while his thoughts busted through the haze.

"It's my friend. His name is Tim-Lee Polk. There's something going on with him up here." He tapped his temple. "He doesn't seem to care about what's important anymore. He keeps disappearing from our dig. He keeps rattling on about some shipwreck that's supposed to be down here somewhere. Professor Laird—he's in charge of our dig. He's had it with Tim-Lee. He says he's kicking Tim-Lee off the dig. He'll lose everything. I just don't get it, why he's doing this."

"The toughest thing about friendships, Qeb, is we have to step back and let those we care about make their own mistakes."

"Yeah, well I did that alright. And now my best friend has disappeared. And I've lost my third girlfriend in three years." He flicked a humble eye at Uncle Frank and back. "And now I'm..."

"And now you're what?"

Qeb lifted longer eyes up to Uncle Frank across the table.

"I didn't tell him," Frank said.

Qeb withdrew back to the scratch. If only he could crawl down inside it, he could get away from all this shit and hibernate from life altogether. He gripped the table's edge tighter, whiting the blush from his knuckles.

His father reached over and cupped his hand over Qeb's hand. "Tell me what, Qeb?"

"Tim-Lee's not the only one. Professor Laird—Dad...he kicked me off the dig, too."

That took a bit for Charley to register and digest. "But why? What happened? Are you with this Tim-Lee guy going after this shipwreck?"

"No. No, it's not like that. No."

"What did you do?"

"Uncle Frank says it's my fault."

His father settled back in his chair, twiddling that nut again, only slower. Slower was not good.

Charley shoved the nut back into his pocket and clocked his coffee cup in little circles on the table top. "How about you maybe just walk me through it?"

The sun had reached 10 AM when Qeb was finished.

Charley searched Frank's face. Frank shrugged back. "You're his father."

Charley worked his coffee cup in little circles again. He picked it up for a closer look at the IMS logo emblazoned on it. He flipped it over and read the bottom: Made in China. *Figures!* He set it down in a trace puddle of cold coffee he forgot was in the cup still.

"Don't worry. I'll get it," Frank said, getting up.

Charley tied together the best thoughts he could over Frank's hand cleaning the spill.

"You know, I thought I taught you better than that. You know how dangerous the water can be, especially when we get an attitude. And I get a sense you have a big one going on right now. Maybe that's why your girlfriend dumped you." He glanced at Frank and back. "Still, it doesn't sound to me like what you did was bad enough to get kicked off your dig. Maybe I should talk to this Laird guy."

"No!" Qeb was horrified. "Dad, don't. Don't even *think* it."

"Okay. Fine." Charley searched the table's blond wood grain for other alternatives.

Qeb didn't like the look on his father's face. The last time he saw that look, his father had been in the mood to help and it had spelled big time embarrassment for him. Charley kept shifting in his chair like there were hob nails on the seat or something. "Dad, what's going on? You're thinking again."

His father pulled out that nut again and twiddled. Qeb struggled to count the rotations as it jogged through his father's fingers.

When a car outside passed by pleading for a new exhaust Charley straitened in his chair. He glanced at his Rolex and shoved the nut back into his pocket. He seemed to have reached some sort of decision.

Uh, oh, Qeb thought.

"Ok. Here's the deal. I won't tell your mother. Frank here won't tell her either, will you Frank?"

Frank flagged his palms at them. "Hey, this is strictly a father-son thing."

"Good. For now, son, we'll just keep this mess between the three of us."

Relief rushed through Qeb. "That sounds great."

"Till you figure out how you're gonna fix this."

"What?" Qeb blanched. "Me fix it? Fix it how?"

Charley flashed a look at Frank. "Someone once reminded me that the measure of a man is not in his years, but in his decisions. You've got a tough one in front of you, son. I'm sure you'll make the right one. Till then, I say nothing to your mother. Do we have a deal?"

Qeb collapsed behind a heavy sigh. "Like I have a choice!"

"Then we have a deal." Charley rose from his seat. Qeb followed his cue.

"About my coming home—"

"Dad, I didn't mean it to sound the way I said it."

"Yes you did." Charley cracked a smile only a son in deep shit and needing help out of a jam could savor. "It's okay. I get it. We'll talk later, okay?"

"Wait. Where are you going?"

Charley swallowed Qeb up in a warm bear hug. "I have a date," he said over his son's shoulder. "Today's your mother's birthday"—He pulled away, grinning—"and I'm her surprise present."

Qeb pulled away and wilted. "I know. I forgot all about it."

"She doesn't know you're here, does she; that you're not up on your dig?"

"Not yet," Qeb said with doom in his voice.

Charley ruffled his son's hair. "Worry not. I'll clear you with her." He fished into the pocket of his lime green-over-navy blue windbreaker with Kittering Enterprises in small white letters emblazoned over the heart and flagged his keys. "Meanwhile, I'm out of here."

The screen door slapped home behind his quick exit.

"I don't believe this."

"What?" Frank said.

Qeb jabbed an angry finger at the door. "Him. I don't get to see him in like forever, and just like that, he shows up. He was just here"—He tossed a hand at his father's vacant chair—"and now he's gone again."

Frank drifted over to the window over the sink. "Hey, he's here now. You could at least appreciate that."

"Are you kidding? He steps in and out of my life like I'm some kind of layover."

Frank watched as Charley pulled away in a strange pickup, probably a rental. "Yep. Unfortunately, that is my brother." Behind Charley, a sedan was just pulling up to the curb. Its paint was faded tan. One headlight had a ghostly white patina to it, just like every other car on the road.

"Um...about the rumors you've heard. They're letting me go next June. This is my last year."

The driver in the car outside was deliberating his house. Was she lost?

"And you were going to tell me when?" Qeb said.

"It's just that I hadn't figured out *how* to tell you."

"What are you going to do?"

"There's nothing I can do."

"What do you mean? There's got to be something you can do."

Frank folded the wet dish cloth he'd forgotten and draped it over the faucet. He skirted round the table past Qeb into the hallway.

Outside, a car door closed.

Frank reappeared with a light jacket and car keys in-hand. "I can't do this right now, okay?" The screen door's rusty springs yawned as he opened it to leave. "I'll be at my lab."

The door's wood frame slapped shut twice behind him.

Qeb yelled after him, "What for? They're firing you."

He dumped himself down into his chair and stewed in a reeking blend of self-pity over losing another girlfriend, over Tim-Lee's stupidity and Professor Laird's arrogance, his father's here-and-gone visits, and seething contempt for the people destroying his Uncle Frank.

And then behind it all, there was her. He'd seen her. There was no escaping it. She'd been to Uncle Frank's lab. What was she doing here? What the hell did she want?

A polite rapping on the screen door yanked Qeb from his funk. Without looking, he bellowed, "No one's home." The rapping persisted, etching into his paper-thin patience. "Go away!"

Silence. "Good!" he muttered.

The rapping, slightly intimidated, tried again.

"Ugh! Okay, okay!"

He shot to his feet and stormed the screen door. His shoe tip connected with its rickety frame, knocking the handle from his grip and sending the door smack into the face of his uninvited visitor.

She squealed and back stepped, goggling at him from behind hands cupping her nose.

"Shit!" he said.

Her steepled brow collapsed into offended furrows.

"I—I'm sorry. I mean—Are you okay?"

Her hands pulled away from gently freckled skin. She shuffled her face from behind a sniffle. "I suppose I'll live," she said in a hilly accent Qeb thought he knew, but couldn't define. Her hair tumbled in pitch black wavelets to breasts barely distinguishable beneath a churchy patterned dress that draped without curves to slender ankles over staid Mary Jane slip-ons.

He gestured her past him with open palm. "Want to come in?"

She measured the kitchen behind him with dubious reserve.

"It's okay," he assured her.

She muttered a modest "Thank you," and quick-stepped past him to the far side of the table for refuge, and gathered her courage from a coffee stain burnished into the table's blonde wood surface.

Her conscience warned her: *This is really foolish.*

"Something to drink?"

"Excuse me? Oh. Yes. Water would be fine." She fingered the back of the chair before her.

"Go ahead. Please. Sit down."

She sidled into the chair. The seat was warm. The freezer door behind her made a sucking sound. "No ice, thank you," she said.

He poured some bottled water into a glass. And there it was again, that shade to her tongue; somehow familiar with prolonged vowels, but squashed like she was trying to hide it.

She accepted the glass from him, aware of him as he rounded the table and settled into the chair opposite her. She sipped the cool refreshment.

He drummed embarrassed fingers on the table top.

She pulled the glass from her lips. "I'm fine, really."

His drumming stopped. "Huh?"

"The door. You didn't hurt me. I'm okay. My name is Emeline Polk." She pronounced *Polk* like *Powk,* her tone suggesting he should know it.

"I'm Qeb. That was my Uncle Frank leaving just now."

"People back home call me Gemma."

His expression was uncomprehending.

She smiled, doleful. "Tim-Lee never mentioned me, then."

He leaned into the table's edge. "You're Tim-Lee's sister?"

She looked at him like he'd just changed color. "You make it sound somehow implausible."

He shied away from her obvious pain. Where he had kicked the screen door was sticking out from its jamb, now one more thing for Uncle Frank to fix. Everything was going to shit for Uncle Frank fast, and he wasn't helping any.

"Sorry. I mean, I've known Tim-Lee for years, but I know diddly squat about his family."

"Diddly squat?"

"It means, like, nothing at all."

"Oh. The way Tim-Lee talked, you were his best friend."

"More like my only friend the way things are going. By the way, do you know where he is?"

The glass in her hand quaked. The muscles in her neck went stringy and the whites of her eyes leached quickly to pink.

"Gemma. What's wrong?"

"There's something you don't know; something about Tim-Lee."

Qeb lost himself in the dark spots where the paint was chipping from Uncle Frank's kitchen cabinets. *Tim-Lee dead. But how could that be?*

Gemma dabbed at her tears with a tissue. "I'm sorry. I thought I'd do better than this." She read the reticence in his eyes. He wanted details.

"They found him in some reeds—some boys in a boat. He had on one of those air tanks for going underwater. The police say there was a tear in the air hose and bad gashes to his head. They say maybe an alligator attacked him, or that he panicked from something and water might have got in his air hose. The Brunswick County coroner called it an accidental death by drowning."

"Brunswick County? That's almost South Carolina. What the hell—excuse me—what was he doing all the way down there? Where did they find him?"

"Someplace the old people call Turkey Trap swamp, in the Shalot—Shallotte—oh, Lord. However you say it, I certainly don't know. It's a river."

"I never heard of it." He hesitated for a long moment.

"What's that look for? What're you thinking?"

"Oh, nothing."

"Don't you dare push me away. You tell me."

"Well, it's just that Tim-Lee and Professor Laird—the last time I saw them both was at our dig. It's up on the James River."

"I know where Tim-Lee's dig is."

"The two of them—they were always arguing something awful. Tim-Lee's always blathering on about some ship he's going to find, and the last few months it's been all he talked about. It drives Professor Laird crazy. This little vein in his head throbs. That's how you know when he's really pissed off. Anyway, he'd holler at Tim-Lee to shut up about it. That would just get Tim-Lee on a roll, like he somehow enjoyed getting Professor Laird in a boil."

A vague giggle dangled in the back of Gemma's throat. "That's Tim-Lee, alright. Growing up, he'd pick up on people's weak spots and play them."

Qeb gripped the table's edge and pattered his fingertips on the top like a piano. "Well, the last time they argued was the last time Tim-Lee left camp. Everyone was just hanging around the fire, nobody saying much, when he says he knows for sure where it is. Well, Professor Laird—he goes and kicks the fire, burning embers flying at everybody and he's hollering at Tim-Lee something mean about letting it go or he would kick him off the dig. That's when things got ugly."

Gemma gawked back at him. "Ugly how?"

"Tim-Lee gets real quiet, like maybe Professor Laird finally got to his senses and he might finally give it all up. I was wrong. Instead he got mean. He mocked our dig and said what was the purpose anyway because it was just blocking progress, and that people didn't care any more about the *Fredericksburg* or any of that, and that they wanted riverfront housing and shopping malls and stuff like that, and that Laird should just let it all go and retire."

"Was he right?"

"Oh, yeah. You see, the Richmond politicians—they want Laird to pack up and leave, get off that land so it can be developed. But

Professor Laird, he's got an 'in' somehow that lets him stay put, so he just pushes back. And it worked for a while..."

"But?"

"Something happened. His funds, they just dried up. Like someone somewhere made a call to someone else and got to his backers."

"So he's going to do what Tim-Lee said about giving up the dig?"

Qeb chuckled. "You don't know Professor Laird. He just started paying for everything from his own pocket including air compressors for our tanks. And he even hired off-duty police officers for standby divers and to watch the place. That's expensive."

"Why's the *Fredericksburg* so important to him?"

"He says there's gold down there."

"Gold! Really?"

"Hey, don't ask me how he ever got that idea. He won't say. Not even how much. You ask me, he's the one who's nuts, not Tim-Lee. Nobody ever said there was gold in those wrecks before. Besides, the *Fredericksburg* and the *Virginia II* and the *Richmond*—they were fighting enemy gunboats trying to come up the river and attack the capital. Who puts gold on warships going into battle, especially seeing as how they're probably not coming back?

"He just keeps pushing us, and we have to do it because we need this to get our degrees. We've been clearing away past lots of good stuff down there, too. We found three cannon. Nice shape, too. All the weapons were supposed to be salvaged long ago, but there they were, stowed in a lower deck. You think he cared? He couldn't care less. He skipped right past them, had us dig deeper inside her. Then things got really bad."

"What kind of bad?"

"Our compressors got repossessed. The rental guys said they needed them somewhere else. And the cops—they suddenly quit." Qeb stalled. "You lost me. Where was I going with all this?"

"You said Mr. Laird thinks there's gold in the *Fredericksburg*, and that Tim-Lee said he was wrong. And that he said it right there in front of everyone else. And that Tim-Lee told Mr. Laird where there really was gold. I suppose he made Mr. Laird look pretty foolish."

"It was more the *way* he said it. 'Not after I find that gold,' Tim-Lee said. It was the first time Tim-Lee ever mentioned it. 'I know where it is,' he said. He spit when he said it, too. Told Laird he could shove his stupid dig. Then he stormed off."

Qeb's rubbing fingers stalled on the rise on the table top. "You could've heard a spider crawl, it got that quiet. And Laird's face, the way he watched Tim-Lee's back when he left, like he could twist a knife in it. That was the last time I saw him alive."

Gemma was catching every syllable, twisting the life from her tissue as she listened for more.

"I'm sorry," he said.

"The Brunswick County coroner took forever releasing his body. We only just buried him last Saturday, back home."

Qeb pieced together the Tim-Lee he knew. "He would never dive in that kind of water, for sure not alone. I don't believe any of it."

Her twisted up tissue hesitated beneath her nose. "Then you don't believe he drowned?"

"The police—they're wrong somehow. I don't know how, but there's got to be something more to it than that. There has to be. Like the thing about a tear in his air hose—that was his regulator hose. I used to fix regulators for my dad's salvage company. Those things are tough. They don't just tear like that."

Gemma blew her nose and bleated, "What else could it be?"

"I don't know, but somehow someone should find out." He deliberated as he looked at her. How quickly would the cops blow her off? She'd get depressed, give up and go home. Well, it wasn't his problem. He had his own hassles right now. "Anyway, thank you for not leaving me to hear about all this from the school."

She attempted a meager smile. "You may not want to thank me yet. I have another reason for coming. A favor, really."

"Oh?"

"I need your help. I need you to take a little drive with me."

Gemma's hand wavered at the keyhole to her brother's second-floor apartment. It was just a short ride from the UNC-Wilmington campus, but from Qeb's uncle Frank's place up the coast, it had taken her and Qeb just over two hours to get there.

Tim-Lee's one-bedroom place was the front apartment among eight: four apartments on the ground level and four more on a second floor. Access to Tim-Lee's place was by wooden steps painted in fading milk chocolate brown leading up to a covered breezeway. The building of eight apartments was one among four weathered seventies-era HUD-subsidized units hammered together during the Nixon administration for low-income families.

Today they housed mostly impoverished graduate students.

The door lock would not cooperate. "Stupid key—it just won't go in!" A chill whisked up the bottom of her dress and took a mean nip at the backs of her knees. The sudden bite tripped the key from her grasp and it fell onto the tattered mat gracing the door with the word WE–COME.

"Here, let me." Qeb retrieved the key and slipped it home.

Before he could open the door, Gemma set her hand on his. "Thank you for coming. I just couldn't do this by myself."

The door opened with a suck and sighed over gaudy half-shag carpet beneath it. Gemma crushed Qeb's hand in hers as they inched their way inside. A creepy quiet greeted them. Flecks of dust toddled in the rays of sunlight seeping past parted window curtains.

The air, musty and still, made Gemma sneeze. "What, no 'Bless you'?"

"Huh? Oh. Bless you."

She ran her other hand over the furniture, testing. A light sheen of dust clung to her investigating fingertips. Her other hand in his stiffened noticeably. "What an awful place. Who ever could call this home?"

"Well, at least with the dig up in Virginia, it's not like he ever had to spend much time here."

She tossed his hand from hers and approached a large table hemmed in by four walls that offered a poor excuse for a dining room. "Look at this mess." Her brother's passion was laid out before her: ranks and files of papers, maps, and a short stack of books in tattered, once-glossy jackets boasting their titles along their spines.

Qeb picked one up and opened the inside leaf. "That's strange. This is a Reference book from the Cape Fear Museum library."

"What's so strange about that?"

"You can't check out Reference books. Not usually. That doesn't seem like Tim-Lee, sneaking out Reference books."

"You're supposed to be his best friend. It never occurred to you that maybe they let him have it for a while?"

"Sorry. I didn't mean that the way it sounded."

Gemma steered away from him and wandered into the only bedroom. The door drifted half-closed behind her.

Qeb pecked through the stuff on the table. It was creepy the way it was all too orderly and still so messy. It was all somehow not right. "This is not good."

He thought he heard crying. Yes, he did hear crying. He coaxed the bedroom door ajar. "Gemma?" She was sitting on the end of the bed sniffling at a framed picture. The bed was made. Other than dust, things were tidy.

He sat down next to her and gently tilted the picture to see. It was Tim-Lee at maybe fifteen years old wearing a high school graduation cap and gown. Qeb remembered then. Tim-Lee's smarts had gotten him out of the hills and into college when other kids were focused on

JV sports and the Junior Prom. With her arms wrapped around him was a young girl clinging to his side and all smiles.

"Is that you?" It sort of looked like her, kind'a maybe.

Gemma just smiled as she stroked the glass over Tim-Lee's image. "The sad thing about losing those we love is we all get over it in time. Faces fade. We forget their smiles and the sound of their voices...and their dumb jokes." She did her best to humor herself, but it was a flop.

"It's okay to cry."

She set the photo down as if it were a hot pot, popped to her feet and ran out of the room.

"Gemma?" He started after her, but thought better of it and let up by the dining table.

She circled her own footsteps in the middle of the living room passing cursive pangs of gloom over the whole place. It bespoke of loneliness with a faint tinge of aged cooking oil lingering in the air. The walls were dreary beige. And the windows! Draped by curtains she could only label as puke fuchsia.

"I don't feel Tim-Lee here at all." She fingered a loose thread flagging from one of the curtains. "What did you mean just now, about something wasn't good?"

He indicated to the clutter. "All this stuff here on the table. I never realized how bad it got."

"Or maybe you just didn't want to." She wrenched the thread away from the curtain, rending a rip in its brittle dry weave and tossed the thread to the floor. She turned and faced him from over crossed arms and stiff feet. "I brought some boxes from the storage place. I guess I had better start collecting his things." She headed for the door.

"Let me help," he said.

She waved his offer aside without looking. "I'm fine, thank you. They're boxes. They're light." The front door clicked quietly behind her as she left for her car.

At the table, Qeb snuck a peek under a large nautical chart with a slight hump in the middle of it. Tim-Lee's laptop greeted him from beneath it.

That's weird. Why would he leave this behind?

Yellow squares flagged him from between the machine and the closed screen. He flipped the screen up and paused at a string of sticky notes tacked to the keyboard. Anxious words, hastily scrawled in Tim-Lee's familiar chicken scratch clamored for his attention: *Take this laptop to Qeb Morgan. The password is his father's middle name.*

The message was to Tim-Lee's family, or maybe the police. Whoever it was, it was disturbing. It meant Tim-Lee thought, or maybe knew for sure, that something might happen to him and that someone would be here to clean out his things and would find the notes.

Three file names were listed on the little stickies. Behind him, brown cardboard cradled in Gemma's slender arms nudged through the front door. "I found something," he said, waving one of the yellow stickies. He pecked *Rodger* into the password prompt.

"Where'd that come from?" she said.

He pointed to the large paper. "It was hidden under this chart."

The password *Rodger* worked.

The first file was a Notepad text file referencing an e-book. He opened it up.

"What is that?" Gemma asked.

"Looks like something Tim-Lee downloaded from online somewhere." He scrolled to the publisher's page. *1907. London.*

Gemma wafted past him back into the bedroom.

He scrolled past the chapters till he stumbled over one Tim-Lee had electronically highlighted. He read it aloud: "Jean Joseph Etienne-Lenoir."

"What?" she hollered from the bedroom.

Qeb squeezed a recollection from a vague sophomore class. "Jean Joseph Etienne-Lenoir. He designed a compression engine in the 1850's. If I remember right, it was pretty radical." His undergrad memories groaned awake from their slumber. "In the 1850s, steam engines ruled the day. But they worked at atmospheric pressure."

No response from her.

"That means at the same pressure as the air around us. Etienne-Lenoir designed a way to compress air for combustion, like your car's engine."

Gemma emerged with a carton stuffed with clothes. "I see. I'm going to the car." When she returned, Qeb's nose was to the screen. "Anything useful in that thing?" she said.

"Not sure, but Tim-Lee tabbed something here. Listen to this."

"Jean Joseph Etienne-Lenoir's timing could not be more opportune. America's war had been waging for two years. France was watching, sure that the South would win her independence. The South was a free-trade economy. France desperately needed a trading partner in America.

"Etienne-Lenoir had written the Confederate government wanting to export his new coal-gas engine invention to the South's farmers and factories. In reply, Richmond sent Matthew Fontaine Maury, an agent of the war department, to investigate.

"Maury saw an immediate use for the engines, but not for farms like Etienne-Lenoir wanted. Maury wanted them for powering ironclad gunboats, which bewildered Etienne-Lenoir. He insisted that his engines were for peaceful purposes and that to power heavy warships was way beyond their capacity."

Qeb sat back. "You know, I actually remember this." He rubbed away the dry burn in his eyes from the harsh screen light. "Maury was sent to Europe to convince England and France to build warships for the South. He went to Paris to see Etienne-Lenoir—"

Gemma sniped, "I really could use your help cleaning up."

"Please. Just listen for a second. Maury brought Alphonse Beau de Rochas along with him when he went to see Etienne-Lenoir. De Rochas had a theory for compressing fuel in an engine to fire it. Maury wanted to get these two guys together."

Gemma cried out, "I don't care!" and whisked back into the bedroom with another carton.

Qeb digested his own stomach acids as long minutes of quiet rustling beyond the bedroom door passed. Eventually, she reappeared on the fringe of his attention.

In one arm she had a full carton. "That's all of it from in there." She grabbed up an empty one and set it by his feet. "Can you empty the kitchen for me? Just the cabinets. Throw out whatever's in the refrigerator and..."

But he wasn't listening. He was all hunkered over Tim-Lee's laptop, scrolling through folders.

She set down next to him cradling her full carton in her lap. "I didn't mean to get cross. Go ahead. Tell me what you found."

"This queer note here: Get the old man's manuscript from the server."

"What's a server?"

"It's usually another computer, like a desktop." He took a quick peek around the room. "But this laptop's the only computer here from what I see. He mentions it in one of the three files on these." He wagged a digit at the string of sticky notes. "But I've searched everywhere. There is no manuscript."

Her porcelain features shifted to sly. "Maybe he's teasing you from the beyond."

"Gemma!"

"Tsk! So uppity." She tapped his thigh. "Back home they say humor helps with mourning."

"Not where I grew up." He got up and reached for the empty carton to go pack the kitchen like she asked.

She nudged it away with her foot. "Never mind, I'll do it myself."

He reset himself in his chair and between glances at the files on the computer screen watched her huff and puff and bang and slam things around in the kitchen. It took forever, three plastic garbage bags and two big boxes before she was finally done, the whole time daring him with her eyes to get up and help her.

Heading for her car with one of the boxes, she stopped and gazed at the screen as he tinkered. Emotionally exhausted, she set her box down and took a seat again.

"Tim-Lee used to call and we would talk. The last time he called, he was—excited wouldn't be the right word." She searched the walls for syllables. "More like fear. I could hear it in his voice." She kissed her index finger with the belly of her thumb. "We were always this close."

Qeb stroked the checkerboard feel of the fabric covering of one of the delinquent books on the table. "Tim-Lee was my best friend," he said. His fingers hesitated at the cover's edge. "I could've stopped him from going down there."

"No you couldn't. Not in a million years, you couldn't."

"I could have at least tried. Or gone with him." He forced himself to his feet, past the pain in his heart, and retreated to the nearest window. He shoved the curtains aside and smacked face-to-face into his guilty reflection in the glass.

"The last time we argued, I called him a stupid fool. Those were the last words between us before..."

Gemma walked in his footsteps to the window. Standing beside him, she dithered after something in the pocket between the folds of her dress. "A month ago, he sent me something."

Qeb turned from his reflection to her. His attention traced the swift slope of her sweeping forearm to a crumpled white cloth nested in her palm.

"This is why he went back." She extended the crumple to him.

A flat-and-round something teased his touch from beneath the cotton. He coaxed the folds aside. His breathing stumbled. The words *Republica Mexicana* circled an eagle fighting a snake minted into a tarnished but still obviously gold coin. He flipped it over and butchered the pronunciation of *La Libertad en la Lay* circling a book and hand.

His confusion was obvious.

"It's an escudo," she said. "I checked."

He studied her askance between pecks at the impressions on the coin. "It says 1854. This is what Tim-Lee was after all the time?"

She rattled off a rapid nod. "That's why that coin frightens me so much. He said he was sure there were more where that came from."

"Why would that frighten you?"

"Because I think he knew that someone else knew about them, too. I think he was right. And I think they maybe killed him for them."

"Say that again?"

Her hazel eyes hardened like gems. "I'm saying I think my brother was murdered."

"You don't know that."

"And those stupid police down there—they're too lazy or too corrupt to go to work and find his killers."

"Gemma! The police aren't like that. And what proof is there?"

The green in her irises swooned. "That's why I need you; to help me find the proof."

Qeb felt suddenly cold. "Gemma, I can't."

Her expression flattened. "You mean you won't."

"I mean I *can't*."

"Then you're not his best friend!"

"You know I am."

"I know nothing of the sort."

"Gemma, Professor Laird will be calling me back to Richmond any day now."

She fussed with her dress. "So that's it then? You're just going to go back to your life like nothing ever happened?"

"That's not fair. Tim-Lee—if he was here, he'd tell you how important this dig is."

"Liar! You said it yourself, he told that old professor his work was stupid. Tim-Lee hated it. And he knew people were laughing at him from behind his back. You said that, too. Don't! Don't you even dare try and deny it. All I know, maybe you were one of them. Were you? Were you one of them, calling Tim-Lee names, making fun of him?"

"We were best friends."

"Then prove it. Come with me down to Brunswick County. Help me find out what really happened to my brother."

"Brunswick—I can't."

"What I think you mean is that you don't care."

"I do care! You just won't listen. Professor Laird's dig is important for me, for my future."

She shot to her feet. "And Tim-Lee's murder isn't. Is that it?" She skipped the box of kitchen things, snatched up her car keys, and grabbed the coin from his hand. "Give me that!"

"Please, Gemma. It's my career!" he pleaded as she stormed for the front door. "Where are you going?"

She left the door ajar and clop-clopped high speed down the outside stairs.

He grabbed Tim-Lee's apartment key from the dining table and slammed the front door behind him, leaving the carton behind with all the other junk. He chased her down to her car. She was fighting the lock on the driver's side. He took the shotgun side and flipped the handle on the door. It was locked. Her door was open.

"What are you doing?" he asked her from across the car's roof.

"What do you care?" She slipped into the car, slammed her door and revved the engine.

"Gemma, wait. My door is locked."

She hollered from behind the closed window, "Get a taxi!"

Her tires chirped into reverse. She backed into a wide sweep and screeched into forward.

He dangled Tim-Lee's apartment key after her as she shot across the parking lot.

"But Gemma..."

At the curb, her weathered Ford *Taurus* squealed out onto the main drag and vanished amid a blaring herd of angry horns.

9-DECEMBER 1864

Commander Thaddeus Trask studied the Wilmington waterfront directly across the Cape Fear River from Benjamin Beery's bustling shipyard on Eagle Island. Panicked refugees from the outlying countryside had streamed into town just the day before, agitating alarm. Sherman's Union cavalry were blitzing across the South Carolina edge into Brunswick County. *Torching any building standing*, they said. *Homes. Schools. Hospitals. Even the churches for God's sake!*

Dread was flowing thicker than pine tar through Wilmington. Thaddeus had heard the mayhem erupt in the streets the night before. Looters were being shot on sight. The city fathers were pleading for decorum. Women were bawling for sanity.

A fire broke out at City Hall. Quickly extinguished, arson was suspected, grist for the rumor mill. Accusations ran high. The latest being that Union sympathizers were working to crumble the city's spirits as a prelude to Yankee invasion.

A hodgepodge of ships cluttered the city's waterfront. Lumber schooners, a few larger ships, and passenger steamers—idle and jobless—trapped in port by the Yankee blockade waiting for them at the mouth of the river.

Blockade-runners from Nassau and the West Indies awaiting new cargo lay anchored in the middle of the river, quarantined for fear of spreading malaria or yellow fever into the city. Those that had been cleared had packed up their lading and disappeared. One of them, a sleek side-wheeler, was cruising downriver, putting the town behind her. Rigs like her were the only ones swift enough to slip past the enemy's ships. She was trimmed low in the water, her holds packed with naval stores, lumber and cotton bales bound for the Virgin Islands. She would steal the night to slip past the Yankees on another mad dash for Nassau, or maybe Havana, where she would offload and stock up with precious provisions and return to Wilmington—if she got through.

Commander Trask admired her fast lines and envied her skipper, one more brave soul chancing death or starvation in a freezing Yankee prison to supply the South with elusive necessities from Europe. And of course, getting filthy rich in the process.

A traditional navy man, Thaddeus Trask had difficulty seeing himself in that role. His family boasted two centuries of naval heritage. He was their first graduate from the Union's fledgling naval academy at Fort Severn and top of the university's first graduating class, the Class of 1854.

Thaddeus indulged himself a smirk, preferring the squat hulking mass of his new command to the sexy cut of the runner. Secretary of the Navy, Stephen Mallory, had personally rewarded him command of her.

Her name was *Recluse*.

As he traced the sleek angles of her armored battery—the business end of her where her powerful cannon lay ready and waiting for targets—the hairs on his neck crimpled at a presence behind him. "Yes, Mr. Pond," he said, without looking at all.

"It really disturbs me, sir, the way you do that. Do I carry an odor?"

Thaddeus turned and smiled at his lieutenant. "No, Mr. Pond, you do not. It's in your step, I assure you."

"Yes, sir. Word across the river, sir, is that General Sherman's men have laid a path of waste a half mile wide from Savannah, Georgia up through South Carolina, and that they're heading our way as we speak." Pond's eyes welled up. "The puritan Yankee filth are plundering everywhere, spreading their smallpox and cholera amongst our women and children."

Thaddeus admired Pond. Pond was a passionate man of faith. After the war, he had said more times than Thaddeus could count that he would enter the seminary. "There's nothing we can do about that now, Lieutenant. That's for the army to worry about."

"Yes, sir." Pond's breath was visible in the chilly winter air. "Oh, and sir. General Johnston's press gangs are in town conscripting men from the mills and markets, filling their ranks. They raided Cassidey's yesterday. They seized a dozen good family men, I hear."

Trask drifted to the east end of Wilmington where J. L. Cassidey & Sons shipyard lay across the river.

Joseph Eggleston Johnston, commanding the Confederate army in North Carolina had ordered his policing soldiers not to waste bullets. Two hundred and forty miles north, Robert E. Lee's depleted and starving Army of Northern Virginia was fending off growing swarms of blue-jacketed attackers swelling around Petersburg like angry hornets. The gossip was the politicians in nearby Richmond could see the Lincolnite troops from their office windows.

Deserters were being hung without trial.

Thaddeus' crew was made up of some Confederate navy men, which was a kind term for it. But mostly the rest were civilian volunteers: ex-convicts, dockside workers and merchant seamen. All of them, to a man, were in fit health and perfect fodder for the trenches of Petersburg. He passed a wary eye around the Beery docks where *Recluse* was being outfitted for battle.

"General Johnston's press gangs may try that here, Mr. Pond. Post a guard. I want fixed bayonets and full cartridge boxes. No mussing around, Lieutenant. They come even close to here you will shoot on sight. Just tell the men, do their best to wound and not kill. There it is. You have your orders."

Pond beamed. "Yes, sir! I'll place three sentries at dock's end, sir, and some pickets at the yard's entry."

"That sounds fine, Lieutenant. Now, what's your progress with the cannon?"

Pond's finger danced across drawings of Trask's ship as he explained that her six rifled cannon were all in-place. "Powder and shot are aboard, dry stores, crew's effects. We are essentially ready for sea ahead of schedule."

"Outstanding, Lieutenant."

Pond wrinkled his nose.

"What is it, Pond?"

"That newfangled fuel smells awfully, sir. And those two Frenchie engines. Internal combustion! Who ever heard of such a thing?"

Thaddeus patted Pond on the back. "They'll work fine, Lieutenant. And think of it, no coalbunkers needed, and no boilers to blow us up. It makes us smaller, too. Even more so with the ballast system."

"Yes. And about that, sir. Who ever heard of flooding a boat on purpose? I should think the *Hunley* would have taught us it's better to stay above surface. And what maniac designed the exhaust to pass through a hole in our hull under her waterline?"

"With no stack, we'll be harder to see."

Pond snorted, "I only pray the heathen thing doesn't kill *us*!"

"We can trust Mr. McClintock, Lieutenant."

Confederate design genius John L. Porter had conceived *Recluse*. She was state-of-the-art. Her French engines were superior to the best steam contemporaries. Her British rifled cannon from Armstrong & Blakely were so new, not even the Royal Navy had them yet.

But it was Confederate naval engineer James McClintock who conceived her sneakiest weapon. McClintock had helped design the astonishing submersible *Hunley*. And like *Hunley*, by flooding small tanks in *Recluse's* hull, she could immerse her outside decks just below the waterline, reducing her to a turtle's back skimming the water; a near impossible target. With her rifled batteries, she'd deliver a deadly bite.

Trask's plan to destroy the blockade was simple. He would send a dozen ships to the bottom in the first night, disappear before dawn, and repeat his attacks nightly until Yankee admiral David Porter's fleet was decimated and demoralized. Lee and Johnston's starving armies of men in rags would get the food and supplies they needed so badly and the South would survive.

Pond fidgeted in the cold, eyeballing their armor. "This new English steel, sir. Is it really impenetrable?"

The South's steel mills were few, outdated, and poorly equipped. John L. Porter's earlier ironclads depended on heavy, two- and three-inch thick steel plate armor, cumbersome and dangerous to ship by rail. But these latest laminated steels from England were lighter and touted as much stronger.

"They say it can repel explosive shot, sir."

"I think we'll be seeing that with our own eyes pretty soon, Lieutenant."

Pond turned on his heels and moped at the half-finished ship behind them. "It's a shame about the *Dixon*, sir."

Thaddeus didn't bother looking. "Yes, Mr. Pond. That it is."

In the neighboring dry dock lay *Recluse*'s unfinished sister ship. Her critical English armor had been sunk by the *Niphon* and the *James Adger* just months ago. It was a costly loss. If he could only have his way, those two would be *Recluse*'s first victims.

"Nearby somebody hollered, "Peter! Let's bear a hand over here, lad."

Lieutenant Pond snapped his attention to a young boy maybe fourteen, maybe fifteen, scurrying over to a team of men working on some ropes and tackle. He nodded in the boy's direction. "Sir. Is it really wise; the boy I mean?"

"I don't follow you."

"Well, sir. I mean, security being prudent and with spies in the town over there..."

"You think he's a spy, Lieutenant?"

Lieutenant Pond blushed.

Trask considered the gangly youngster. He then nodded likewise over to the unfinished *Dixon*. "As you know, she's doomed because her armor plates were sunk."

"Yes sir."

"What you don't know, Mr. Pond, is that that boy is the only survivor of the ship that went down carrying the *Dixon*'s plates."

Lieutenant Pond was broadsided. He stared hard at the boy, measuring him.

"He was one of her crew. A boilerman's hand, if I'm not mistaken. The ship was run aground and severed in two beneath the boy's very feet. So you might want to give him a break. I think he's proven his worth as well as whose side he favors."

"Absolutely, Commander." Pond changed tack. "So tonight it is, sir?"

"Yes. Tonight." Thaddeus indicated to the monstrous tarps that had been thrown up to block the view of their construction from the town across the river. "These are coming down after dark. Meanwhile, place those guards, Mr. Pond, and then fetch after the yard superintendent. I want this dry dock flooded long before dusk."

"Yes, sir!" Pond called a uniformed fellow over to him and gave the order to place men at the pier's end and pickets outside the gate. The big boned man—thin in the middle from years of living off field rations and foraging stripped farms and wasted pastures for food—saluted sharply and double-timed it back to his men.

As Pond watched the man's back, his attention drifted to a little fellow behind a determined expression wending his way through the corps of Beery workers. His eyes were steady and fixed most definitely on him and Commander Trask.

"Oh, Commander, I do not like the look of that fellow. No, sir, not one bit."

Percival Laird pinched his nose. The pall of human musk was repugnant. Beefy, uncouth fellows scrutinized him too closely for his comfort. He slithered his slender frame between stacked crates to avoid confrontation. Clearing past the oafs, he picked up his pace. How he wound up on his back mystified him. Baffled, he gazed up dully at a tar-stained hand shadowed by a bearded grin.

"What happened?"

"Tar, mate," the stranger said. "Slippery. Got to watch your step round here." He pulled Percival to his feet. Percival traced the man's nod to a precipice behind him bordering a deep dark pit. In it lay the armored gunboat he'd been briefed about, setting on blocks.

"Thirty-five feet," said the stranger. "Your death be sure, you fell down there."

Percival brushed himself off. "Yes. Well..." He started to offer his hand in thanks and thought better of it. He left it to a curt nod. "Thank you."

Curious laborers circled round them snickered and none too quietly.

Humiliated Percival retreated, struggling to recover his self-respect. Twenty paces ahead of him, down toward the end of the dock stood the man he sought, clearly critiquing his every step. He was a fit fellow in a tailored tunic, and at the moment fury held his gaze.

"Commander Trask?"

"What the hell are you doing on my docks, mister? You could have been killed."

Percival drew in a deep breath. "You are Commander Trask?"

Thaddeus folded up the ship's drawings and thrust them against Pond's dutiful chest. "What is it you want, sir? I have a ship to launch." Thaddeus showed Percival his back and mounted the narrow gangplank leading from the dock to the insides of his new command.

Percival replied after him, "I would have a moment of your time, Commander."

Thaddeus kept walking. "Time's not something I can afford, mister."

Percival eked his way up onto the plank after Trask, wrestling temptation to look down as he crossed.

Halfway, Thaddeus turned on him. "What's this about?"

Startled off balance, Percival grabbed the rope railing for support. It swayed, uncooperative in his grip, pulling his attention to the pit beneath him, yawning up at him, deep and dingy.

"I have new orders for you." Percival swooned. "I think I'm going to be sick."

Settled across from Commander Trask, Percival shifted for comfort in a chair so tight the arms of it crimped his sides. He flashed his attention about, gauging the confines that passed as Trask's quarters, and wrinkled his nose. The air in the place was heavy with burning lamp oil and the musk of pitch. It was cramped and the ceiling too low, more suited to a boy. No windows. No fresh air, save for a single, sealed vent in the overhead, which was actually the foredeck above them, where right now men were hard at work. The tromping of their Neanderthal footsteps was already testing his patience.

He extended a folded document across Trask's desk. "You have new orders from Richmond."

"Where I come from, mister, a man makes himself known first."

Percival expelled an exasperated sigh. "Of course. Where are my manners? Percival Laird, personal aide to Treasury Secretary

Trenholm. I've come from Richmond with those orders for you. From your superiors."

Thaddeus hawk-eyed Laird from over the document. "Navy secretary Mallory sent this?"

Laird nodded once, his cool expression suggesting he already knew the letter's contents.

Thaddeus rolled in his chair, broke the red wax seal on the back and unfolded the parchment. A second smaller letter toppled out from inside and fell to the deck. As he felt for it by his chair and picked it up, his eyes flitted through the Navy secretary's words.

Your new assignment is of the outmost secrecy, Commander. Your country depends—Mallory had crossed out the words and replaced them with—*I depend on you to complete it with alacrity.*

An old family friend, Secretary of the Navy Mallory had doubtless anticipated that Thaddeus might have qualms about a change in plans.

You come from a fine and beloved family, Thaddeus. You are, in these extremely difficult weeks, counted amongst this government's most trusted officers. Mallory's script then shifted to heavier, angry sweeps. *A disappointingly thin cadre, I am sad to admit.*

Attached you will find your new orders from Treasury secretary Trenholm. Also, you will find included a separately sealed document. Mr. Laird is to retain this document until he deems fit to deliver it to you.

Thaddeus handed the small letter over to Laird. "He says this letter is for you."

"Yes, I know."

Thaddeus, I would not ask you to do what you are about to engage in doing were it not of the utmost and most critical importance to the survival of this government.

Thaddeus shifted in his chair. Secretary Mallory usually abstained from using Christian names in formal communiques. He pulled

Treasury secretary Trenholm's orders out from behind Mallory's letter. "I suppose you already know what these say, too?"

"That is why I am here, Commander."

Thaddeus didn't like the ugly bigger picture taking shape. Hesitant, he proofed Treasurer George Trenholm's orders. In a few sentences he slapped the orders onto his desk, staring hard after them. He searched Laird's eyes looking for—for what, he had no clue. Laird just sat there eyeballing his reactions from behind clasped hands against his chin.

"I think you are enjoying this."

"Not at all, I assure you, Commander."

Trask reached down to his side and retrieved a small flask from inside his desk. He took a strong swig of bourbon, thought about it, and took a second. Without offering it to Laird, he dumped the flask back in the drawer and slammed it home.

He pulled himself together and began reading through his new orders again. Their shocking contents swept down the paper in Secretary of the Treasury Trenholm's flamboyant script which he was witnessing for the first time. Thaddeus's innate defenses faltered. Trenholm was due the utmost respect, not alone for his position in the government, but because he had personally lost a fortune financing a twelve-ship flotilla for the defense of Charleston, South Carolina.

But still...

He set the orders down again. His hands were trembling. Trenholm's idea—it was preposterous. Maybe even reckless. And probably flat out hopeless.

There is no other vessel, Commander, upon which this government can depend.

Trenholm was pleading. Richmond was desperate.

The reclining mechanism of Thaddeus's chair curled loudly as he settled back. "*Recluse* is not designed for this, Mr. Laird. She's not an open-ocean vessel." His eyes swept to Laird. The man wasn't speaking.

He re-read Mallory's letter searching betwixt the lines, hoping his boss and friend might let slip some deeper explanation for such an insane request. But there was none. No hint, no clue. He struggled for composure, but wasn't finding it. It had been a bitch getting *Recluse* ready. He'd done everything Richmond had ordered him to do. He hadn't even heard of her till the day when Secretary Mallory had summoned him away from his previous ship without explanation.

When he'd gotten to Richmond, Mallory had relieved him of his command. "A new man has replaced you already," Mallory had announced.

"They were my crew for two years, Mr. Secretary. You might have at least allowed me to explain to them."

Mallory was unsympathetic. "This is war, Lieutenant. They'll get over it."

"Sir?"

"I'm promoting you to commander. You're to get down to Wilmington with all haste and oversee completion of two new ironclad warships. You'll put them to sea and you will destroy that blockade. And you will do it before the New Year."

Since the previous August, Thaddeus had done exactly as Mallory had ordered. *Recluse* was now armed and ready to do as she was designed. She was ready for war. But he'd lost the *Dixon*. Her English armor, so crucial to her completion, now lay rusting on the seabed.

Nauseous reality overwhelmed him none too gently. A greater moral burden now suddenly hung over him. All Wilmington had pulled together and had helped him to finish *Recluse*. The city's citizens had seen to it that his crew and the Beery men building *Recluse* were fed at least one good meal a day while they themselves went hungry.

Homeless and unemployed men and boys had helped outfit her asking nothing in return.

Fear seized Thaddeus with an icy cold grip. Only assured defeat would pressure Richmond into pulling a stunt like it was pulling now. He laid Mallory's letter over Trenholm's orders. They were too painful to look at.

"It would seem our confederacy is crumbling in on itself, Mr. Laird."

"They are merely ensuring that the cheese remains after the house collapses."

"*Recluse* is a shallow water vessel, Mr. Laird."

"Yes, you already made that point."

"She cannot make Nassau!"

"We don't get the privilege of choosing our orders, Commander."

Trask leaned across his tight little desk. "These people, Mr. Laird, have vested their own blood in this ship. They've put their backs and their hearts into her. They expect her to save them, to go down that river and punch a few big holes in that blockade out there and open up this port. *Recluse* is their ship, Mr. Laird. She and I have an obligation to them."

"This ship belongs to the Confederate government, Commander, not the people of Wilmington."

"Spoken like a true politician. Well, I'll remind you that this is not England, Mr. Laird. The government here serves at the pleasure of the people. That's what this war is about."

"Please don't lecture me, Commander."

Thaddeus leaned into his words, jabbing his desktop with his finger. "This ship belongs to the people."

Laird rapped on Trask's orders. "As tough as these orders may be, Commander, your close family friend, Mr. Mallory, orders you to do so."

Bile was welling up in the back of Thaddeus's throat. As he had snuck off from his last command, he would once again be sneaking away from the people who trusted him most, letting them down after taking from them. He would be abandoning Wilmington to eventual capture. If only the damned Yankees would attack now then things would change completely. *Recluse* would have to stay. They'd be compelled to defend the city.

Laird and Trenholm could go to hell. And Mallory, too.

"The Yankees have been bombarding Fort Fisher since the seventh of the month. One thing I've learned in this war is that things change fast. These orders—they're over two weeks old. I am telegraphing for confirmation."

Laird reclined back into his tiny chair. The arms dug into his ribs on the sides, forcing him back forward. "You're only putting off the inevitable." Out of sight he flexed his fists, stifling his anger.

"I'm exercising my authority as commander of this ship."

"Secretary Trenholm is subordinate to no one but President Davis."

"I report to Secretary Mallory, not to the Treasury."

"But you are the government's last hope."

"I am also Wilmington's the last hope."

Laird pounded the desk. "Wilmington can be damned!"

Slow down. Losing your temper only riles up his defenses.

"You disobey these orders, it's treason. You know that."

Trask's expression remained granite hard.

Percival took a deep breath. "Fine, Commander. Go sink the Yankees. Wilmington will be grateful. The people get to eat again. The army will get its weapons. General Johnston may even give you a medal." He leaned onto the desk and pointed an unruly finger at Trask. "But eventually it all comes back to following orders. You will be court-martialed. In wartime that's a death sentence, even for a man with Secretary Mallory for a friend."

Thaddeus sneered slightly. "And President Davis is a longtime friend of my father."

"I don't think President Davis will count for much in the near future."

"Now who's being treasonous?"

Percival rose from his chair. He thrust his hands into a pair of leather dress gloves. "I think we both know better where this country is headed, Commander."

Thaddeus produced a small necklace from inside his collar and fingered a tiny image at the end of it. To Laird's quizzical look he said, "Saint Nicholas, the Patron Saint of sailors." Laird's countenance shifted to reproachful. "You disapprove of men leaving their fate to faith?"

"Nothing of the sort, Commander."

But Laird's lie was as clear as print. "If you will excuse me, Mr. Laird, I've some business to attend to. I'll be with you momentarily about your wagons."

When Laird was gone, Thaddeus prayed quietly to himself. He had muzzled his own fears of defeat pretty well these past few months, but when the English prick proclaimed the fall of the South like it was a foregone conclusion he could feel his dispirited nerves beginning to snap.

Thaddeus measured Laird's dozen teamsters waiting at the far end of the pier. Two teamsters per wagon, six wagons in all. Each wagon was burdened with top-secret lading sealed in wood kegs. Ten kegs per wagon except one, fifty-nine kegs in all.

Percival couldn't help but notice Trask's attention glued to his draft horses: exquisitely powerful Belgian Shires, Clydesdales and Percherons. "Gifts to the South from Her Majesty Queen Victoria," he boasted. "And very well fed they are, too. Keeping them strong was critical for our journey down from Richmond."

Thaddeus's swelling contempt for Laird simmered his blood to the verge of boiling. "Across that river"—He pointed to the city—"are homeless refugees. Children. All of them starving."

Percival whittled his nose at the city. "Yes, well that is war, is it not, Commander?"

Thaddeus took a long step at him with his hand outstretched for his throat. "I should toss you down in that pit!" Instantly, the two secret service officers assigned to Laird's protection blocked his path. Their hardened eyes over mauled skin suggested going any further would be bad for his health.

"You will stay out of my way, Mr. Laird. Once we put to sea, I am the law. I'll have you in irons if you so much as stir up a tizzy with my crew." He gave Laird's protection a disgusted once-over. "And these two thugs of yours—I'll have them keel hauled." Then sneering at Laird, he hissed, "I understand you Brits are fond of keel hauling."

Thaddeus despised the British. They had feigned allegiance before to the Confederacy back in sixty-two. And then when the debacle of Sharpsburg gave Lincoln the victory he needed to pen the Emancipation Proclamation, the lime-sucking cowards withdrew their pretenses of military support behind the expeditious veneer of neutrality. And since then, Her Majesty's pensioned naval officers were making their fortunes running the blockades. British foundries were growing fat and happy overcharging the South for cannon and firearms.

And admittedly very good steel.

Thaddeus passed his eye over *Recluse*'s new armor. The South needed England and it chafed him painfully. That Laird was English and that he was so brazen about the South's assured collapse only amplified the insult to his self-respect that the tripe little creep had orders for him to abandon his duty to fight.

Percival wrinkled his nose at Wilmington across the river. What was Trask's passion for saving such a slum? When his wagons had rumbled into the congested port city his discriminating olfactory glands were assaulted by offal of curing smoke, dried goods, pickling brine and overripe fruit; leather, pitch, tannery chemicals, tobacco smoke, trash and yellow pine turpentine; manure and the heavy odor of draft animals, all of them commingling with the pungent stench of homo-sapiens.

The harsh mélange sharply reminded him of his Liverpool home.

Wilmington was a microcosm of the quickly shriveling confederacy. Her macadam avenues and cobblestone side streets crackled beneath a relentless din of boot heels, horse hooves and ox carts. Horses— bony, swaybacked and obedient—lined her markets, awaiting loads for their drays.

A steady flow of humanity: desperate, determined, confident, frightened, hungry, and yet smugly satisfied, cluttered the stone slab sidewalks lining Wilmington's thoroughfares. Dandies and businessmen, bankers, commission merchants and grocers, laborers and displaced farmers, merchant seamen, furloughed soldiers and amputees. Their tongues wagged in blithering dialects, a profane travesty of the English language.

Trask's eyes were on him.

Percival made a pursy little smile. *Look at him, the rogue. He's enjoying your discomfort. So, let him. The man has no idea what he is dealing with. He only sees things from the perception of a petty naval hack.*

Percival remembered Treasury secretary Trenholm's parting words: *Should these orders I've written prove insufficient for convincing*

Commander Trask of his new duties, you may avail yourself of more compelling measures to force his cooperation.

Percival miffed. Leave the bravery to other men. He preferred basking in the trust of the confederate treasurer, the most powerful man in Richmond. All bravery was getting anybody was killed. After the war, he would use Trenholm's letter of introduction to make his fortune. But first he had a duty to fulfill. And most distastefully, he needed Trask to complete it.

Percival's entourage of wagons slowly worked its way up the dry dock pier to a place beside *Recluse*.

Thaddeus's new orders hadn't described his cargo; only that he was to escort it and Laird with all haste to Nassau. "Seems to me, Mr. Laird," Thaddeus said, ensuring no one was within earshot, "that since I am handing my ship and crew over to you, you might tell me what we are carrying."

Percival sidled closer and muttered under his breath, "Oh you certainly will, Commander; but only as fair wage for getting us to Nassau in one piece."

10-AUGUST 2005

Qeb read the glowing text message on his candy bar cell phone for the dozenth time. Its curt instruction was trademark Stephen Laird: *Get up here. It's time to get back to work.* Who would even guess from it the heated argument between them had ever happened. It was exactly the message Qeb had been aching for.

So why wasn't he packed and gone already?

The screen timed out. He punched it back on and wondered at it. There was something else in Laird's message, or rather something absent from it: there was no mention of the missing Tim-Lee. Nada. Zip. Did Laird even know what had happened?

The screen blinked off, forcing his chronically depleted battery into power save mode.

He traced the single coffee stain tattooed into the wood grain of Uncle Frank's kitchen table. His finger circled round it over and over, massaging his thoughts from the present, tugging him back in time.

At twelve years old and devastated by the sudden death of his birth father, he had withdrawn into his school work at the expense of normal boyhood pursuits. After Charley Morgan entered his mother's life, his only social life circled round Charley's diving & salvage business in Qena, Qeb's childhood hometown back in Egypt.

At sixteen his role in Charley Morgan's miraculous discovery of Cleopatra's lost tomb had tossed him along with Charley and his older brother Frank before the public eye. In the aftermath of worldwide attention and the gratitude of a nation, the people of Egypt had awarded him a full scholarship to any school he chose, any university in the world.

It was then that Charley had married his mother and had adopted him as his own son.

Fired by the excitement and the overwhelming aura of success, he had chosen his Uncle Frank's alma mater, the University of North Carolina. The scholastic grindstone that had pushed him through primary school propelled him through college. Excelling under his uncle's tutelage, he crammed a four-year bachelor's degree into three.

His excelsior performance had earned him *egregia cum laude*.

A rapid knocking jolted Qeb back to the present: it was Laird calling. He grabbed his phone. "Hello? Hello, Professor?" He pulled the phone away and stared at it. The face was blank and cold.

The knocking repeated. It was the damned kitchen door. Someone was at the door.

"Coming!" he hollered, not too nicely. He jabbed his phone into his pants pocket and circled the table for the door. Fingers on the knob, he noticed the face through the glass and stalled.

"Qeb, open the door."

"I suppose you're here for Tim-Lee's apartment key?"

"No. Would you let me in, please?"

She drifted past him without waiting for permission. At the table she turned to him. "It's no good anyway. I needed the Super to let me in and empty the place. He changed the lock the other day when you—Oh, never mind that."

Draped over her shoulder was a fabric messenger bag ornamented in flamboyant swatches that reminded him of the ancient artistry he'd seen from South America. She took the far seat where he'd been sitting and let the bag slip from her shoulder.

"I'm thirsty."

"Water again?"

She made a face and asked, "Got something sweet?"

He peered into the refrigerator. "Got *Cheerwine*."

"I don't know it, but okay."

"How's a girl from Tennessee not know *Cheerwine*?" he said, popping open a can. A vibration in his pocket startled him, making him spill. "Damn!"

"I'm a mountain girl, remember? We don't come by such things often." She accepted the can, took a sip and swooned over the flavor. "Of course indoor plumbing we do have. And electricity, although that is new," she teased. "What's the matter?"

"This." He showed her his phone.

"Is that him—your professor?" She read the insistent command, all in caps, over washed out blue. "He's angry with you."

"He's always angry at somebody, usually me."

"Then you're going back?"

"I have no choice. I need the dig to graduate."

"Well, put that thing away and sit down. I want to talk."

"What about?"

"Just sit down and I'll show you." Laird buzzed him again. "And will you please turn that stupid thing off?"

Qeb jabbed his phone off and took a chair. "I'm sorry about the other day."

"Never you mind that. You remember reading on Tim-Lee's computer something about a manuscript?"

"Find the manuscript in the server."

"Yes." She placed her messenger bag on its side on the table. "When I was moving his things I found a desktop computer tucked under a shelf." She reached inside her bag. "And this was taped to the side of it." She handed him a soiled three-by-five card with the words SERVER in heavy black marker on it.

"It was one of those with the sides that open up. You know the two knobby things you turn and the side falls open? Well I did. And would you believe, it was empty."

"Empty. What do you mean empty?"

"I mean there was nothing inside it: nothing at all to make it work."

He admired her as she rifled through her bag again. He liked the way she cocked her head and the way her finger traced her eyebrow when she coaxed an errant lock of hair behind her ear.

She extracted something large and thick and plopped it onto the table. "That is, nothing except this." It was tattered and sad and looked like it had been stored in a damp basement for a long time.

"What is it?"

"Silly. What do you think it is?"

He re-read the SERVER card. Instantly, two and two smashed together. "The manuscript!"

Her eyes brightened.

"It's heavy," he said, sliding it over to his side of the table. It was maybe two inches thick, with a hard brown cover on the top and bottom and yellowed pages rough on the edges, bound with string. "Are these shoelaces holding it together?"

"I guess so. Careful!" she warned, when he opened it. "It's really old."

The pages were foxed and stiff. A dank smell nudged his nose as he turned them. Ink from the back sides had leeched through into the sentences scripted on the front sides. Automatically he began reading passages. Thirty minutes later he closed the cover.

"What do you think this is, Gemma?"

"I think it's what Tim-Lee wanted us to find. The way he hid it, I almost think he was afraid someone else knew he had it and maybe they were looking for it."

"Whoever gave it to him could have just as easily told someone else. Anyway, it's just some old journal."

She reached across the table and took his hand. Her touch zipped all through him. "Please. Do me favor and just read it through all the way?"

"Have you read it?"

"I'm not saying. I want you to read it for yourself. See if you find anything."

"Find anything?" He felt the cover, thinking twice about the contents. "What should I find?"

"Hints."

"What kind of hints?"

She smiled in a way that made his chest tight. "Hints that tell us where Tim-Lee's ship is."

"You don't seriously mean...?" But her eyes said otherwise. "You're going after it."

"You were my brother's best friend. Could you really let all his work just go to nothing: for his death to mean nothing at all?"

His hand recoiled from the book. "It's not about letting his death mean nothing or his work to go to nothing. It's about priorities."

She stiffened from head to toe. "You were everything to him, Qeb Morgan: the only one who would listen."

"I was a fool." He caught the pain in her face and re-thought his words. "You're not being fair. I can't just throw everything away."

"Haven't you already?" She yanked her gaze away from him. Across the floor, a speck of an ant was foraging for scraps along the quarter round trimming the bottoms of the cabinets. "Tim-Lee needs you."

"Gemma...he's gone."

She admitted to the ant, "I need you."

"You don't understand. My standing up for Tim-Lee got me kicked me off the dig."

She leered at him with knowing eyes. "It wasn't defending my brother that got you kicked off."

"Whether it was or wasn't doesn't matter. Laird wants me back now. I can't afford—wait. How do you know that?"

"Never you mind how."

"Tell me."

"It was just a stupid guess, that's all. Is it my fault if I was right?" A gaggle of pitch-black bangs swooped down over her furrowed forehead, twice as black against her porcelain skin.

His gaze slipped down the bangs and dangled smack in front of her magnetic stare. "I can't do this and neither should you. It's a fairy tale, Gemma. Give it up."

"Give it up? Cleopatra's grave was supposed to be a fairy tale, or did you forget that?"

"Finding her was a lucky accident. And besides, she was real. She was always real."

Gemma jabbed a hard finger onto the manuscript's tender cover. "This says Tim-Lee's ship is real."

"Just because it's old doesn't make it true."

She practically gasped, "And you call yourself an archaeologist!" She edged over into the chair next to his. "Qeb, look at me. Please? There. Is that bad?" Her touch inched out to his hand. "All I'm asking is for you to read what's in here and see what it says: anything about Tim-Lee's ship."

She took his hand between hers. The brush of her palms against his skin made him tingle and swell. "See if anything pops out at you."

He pulled away and retreated to the sink.

"I have no one else, Qeb. You're my only hope."

"I have responsibilities. I have a life."

Gemma's eyes tottered between rage and desperation. "And my brother lost his. He died for this stupid book, which makes him ten times the archaeologist you'll ever be."

The kitchen walls bowed under the power of her insult. The drip, drip, drip of Uncle Frank's leaking faucet drummed against overwhelming silence.

"I didn't mean that," she finally said.

"Yes you did."

"Maybe so, but Tim-Lee—I think he wants for you to find the ship."

Qeb whispered to the rooftops across the street, "He can't want anything, Gemma. He's dead."

"Now who's being cruel?" She stroked the table, swallowing her mounting tears. "You're the only one he trusts—trusted—to finish his work."

Qeb fingered the edge of the countertop. He gazed without seeing at the goings-on outside the kitchen window. "My doctorate—it's what I've been working for my whole life. At least it feels that way. Even when I was sixteen and all my friends were chasing the girls, my school work was everything. I never had any fun. I didn't ever have a girlfriend. Not till here. Not till college."

He wrung his fingers into the porcelain edge of the sink. "My father—my real father, I mean—he was killed when I was twelve."

The sound of her chair slipping across the floor nipped his earlobes. The anger in the air behind him softened with the approach of gentle footsteps. His nose told him she was close behind him. Her cinnamon-over-lemon scent had his nerves chattering. Her syllables brushed the back of his neck.

"Help me steal the senselessness from Tim-Lee's death."

From somewhere he found the courage to turn round and face her. "I'll read the book for you and—" She was closer than he expected, trapping him against the counter's edge.

"Before you leave for Richmond?" Her sweet breath fogged his defenses.

"Yes. Okay." A queer buttery feeling tremored all through him. "But I think you should go now."

The tips of her shoes touched his. "Don't worry, Qeb. You'll finish your doctorate. But why do it being Professor Laird's lackey?"

A throat cleared across the room. "Hello?"

"Uncle Frank."

His uncle was leaning against the archway between the kitchen and hallway. "I'm sorry. I hope I didn't interrupt."

"It's okay. We were just talking about this." Qeb pointed to the manuscript on the table and nodded to Gemma. "This is Gemma Polk, Tim-Lee's sister."

Frank stepped into the kitchen. "We didn't meet the last time you were here. I'm very sorry about your brother."

"Thank you, Dr. Morgan. Qeb speaks so highly of you."

Frank's attention drifted to the manuscript. His educated eye immediately recognized antiquity. "Do you mind?"

"Of course not," she said.

Frank gently sifted through the foxed pages.

Qeb volunteered, "It's the manuscript of a Confederate sailor."

"Really?"

"My brother was using it to locate a shipwreck," Gemma said.

Frank's eyes flashed. "What shipwreck?"

"An ironclad warship. I think my brother found hints hidden in there leading him to it when he...when he died."

"I'm sorry, Miss Polk. I didn't mean to pry."

"It's not you. I'm such a wreck lately. I should leave now."

Frank extended the manuscript to her.

"Oh no, that stays here. Qeb's researching it for me." She turned and smiled her softest smile for Qeb. "I'm hoping he'll help me trace Tim-Lee's path to the ship."

Frank's attention darted to his nephew. "Oh?"

Qeb shied away from the hard look his uncle was giving him. "How do I reach you?"

She took his phone and programmed her number into it. She snuck a quick peck on his cheek. "Keep it safe. Call me when you're done."

Frank settled against the kitchen counter, folding and refolding a tattered dish cloth long ready for the trash can. He watched his nephew from over his shoulder scanning his phone. "She's very passionate about what's in that book," he said.

Qeb ogled Professor Laird's last text. "She wants to finish her brother's work."

"I was able to figure that part out. You want to tell me what's going on?"

"Nothing's going on. She just needs a favor. It's the least I can do. Tim-Lee's death has been really hard on her."

"Sure it has. Just be careful, huh? She could get herself hurt, and get you hurt along with her."

Qeb thumbed his screen. Laird's text disappeared. He turned in his chair and said, "Why would someone hurt her, Uncle Frank?"

"Maybe I said that wrong. It just seems there are too many unanswered questions about that boy's death."

"Then what the police said about him drowning—you don't believe it either?"

"I don't know what I believe. I know bad things happen."

Qeb's phone glowed to life and vibrated.

"When are you going to answer him?"

"Who?"

"Don't, Qeb. He's been trying to get you for days now."

"How'd you—"

"All these years and you don't think I can read you by now?"

"I don't want to talk to him." Qeb's mood dipped into morose.

"Getting back to work might be the best thing for you."

"You mean so I can forget Tim-Lee's death faster?" Qeb set his phone down on the table. He coaxed it around in circles with one finger. "Is that why you rushed back to school after your parents died: to get over them?"

Qeb's words jabbed a wound in Frank that had never healed. "I don't remember," he said. He sniffed his dish cloth. It stunk of sour water. "You know, Charley lost a close friend. Maybe talking to him would—"

"I don't want to talk about it"—Qeb rose from his chair—"least of all to him," and drifted into the other room.

Frank tossed his stinking towel into the trash—he'd buy more—and traced Qeb's retreat to the front room. Qeb was standing at the window tinkering with something in his hand.

"Why did she have to show up and tell me? It would've been better not even knowing."

"You would have heard about it sooner or later."

"I know. It's just that—"

"—that your friend died and it's inconvenient?"

"Yes. No. I mean, yes…maybe." He studied the old key to Tim-Lee's apartment. "He always put up with my shit."

"That's what friends do."

"In my case, he was my only friend." A saltiness stung Qeb's eyes.

"You just met her, isn't that true?"

"Yes."

"You don't know her."

"Tim-Lee never said anything about having a sister."

"Is that a secret a best friend keeps to himself?"

"I don't know. I guess not."

"She's in mourning, Qeb. Emotions run high when you lose someone close to you. You said now she wants to do his work. Why? Why is it so important to finish her brother's work?"

"She said she wants me to help her take the senselessness out of his death."

"She could hurt you, Qeb. Tell her no."

"Could you tell a woman no who just lost her brother and came to you for help?"

A knock at the kitchen screen door saved Frank from answering. "Door's open," he hollered.

The screen door springs announced someone's entry.

Frank continued, "If it caused me as must pain as it's obviously causing you, I would, yes."

Footsteps were marking the kitchen floor.

"I don't believe you," Qeb said. "You're not that—"

The face attached to the footsteps appeared in the archway separating the hallway from the front room. The face's gaze swept from the back of Frank's head, across the room to Qeb and smiled.

"Hello, Qeb," Hillary said.

Qeb tottered on startled heels. His wetted eyes flashed to his uncle. "What is she doing here?"

"She's taking me to my lab. We're working on something."

Qeb back-stepped. "The two of you? Together?"

"She's helping me research that plate your father found."

Hillary said, "And I think I've found something out you'll be very interested—"

"Why are you here?" Qeb demanded.

Hillary's complexion washed to cool Carrara pink. Irritation edged into her voice. "I've my own lab here if you must know, near Beaufort."

Qeb gaped at Frank. "She's got her own lab? Here?"

Frank suggested to her, "Maybe you should wait in the truck."

Soon as the back screen door slapped home, Qeb attacked.

"So it *was* her I saw at your lab that day."

"You came by my lab?"

"I needed to see you. I was in the parking lot and all of a sudden— I couldn't believe it—there *she* was, coming out the door to your building. And with a smile on her face. I told myself, 'No way. That can't be her.' I was sure I was wrong. I had to be wrong. I needed to be wrong! She is supposed to be in England. Or better yet, burning in Hell."

"That kind of talk is unnecessary!"

"After what she did, she *should* be in Hell."

"Stop this, Qeb. Right now."

"I can't believe you. You preach at me, tell me to push Gemma away when she needs me, and all the while you let *her* back to our lives. How can you, after what she did?"

"She's not the same person she was back then."

"She's a crazy bitch. She held a fucking gun to your own brother. She used you and me as ransom."

"You need to calm down."

"Don't tell me to goddamn calm down!"

"I let you stay here, but I can easily forget that you are family."

"How can you even let her back into our lives?"

"We're done here. I'm going."

"How is it that she has a lab here?"

"She's Visiting Professor of Archaeology at ECU."

"Agh! I can't stand it!" Qeb threw up his hands. Tim-Lee's apartment key slipped from his grasp and ricocheted off the ceiling.

Frank dodged it just in time. "Enough! I want you out of here when I get back. It's time you stopped grousing like a child and got your butt up to Richmond and back to work. And while you're there, grow up."

Frank disappeared beyond the hallway into the kitchen.

Qeb hollered after him, "I'm through listening to you!"

The screen door squawked open.

"This crap you're pulling: you just helped me make up my mind."

The screen door slapped home behind his uncle's exit.

"Thanks, Uncle Frank. Thanks for making it so easy!"

11-A TRUCE

Frank's inquisitive touch ran along the edges of Charley's plate. In his specialty of archaeomaterials—the investigation of ancient building materials production and their uses—he knew of course that iron had been a primary shipbuilding material in the mid-19th Century. The majority of side wheelers littering the bottom of North Carolina's seacoast were pretty much all constructed of iron.

"How have you managed to evade discovery all these years," he asked the plate. "With all that goes on along this coast, how is it no one ever stumbled over you?"

"Stumble over what?" Charley said, standing in the lab doorway.

"God, I wish you wouldn't do that! You startled the wits out of me. Wait. What are you doing here? You're supposed to be at home with your wife."

Charley wormed into the lab. He drifted past Frank over to the refrigerator. "Any beer in this thing?"

A different voice, distinctly female and foreign replied this time. "Not anymore."

Charley sagged beneath a disbelieving sigh. He bowed his head to find his strength, puffed up his courage and turned round. Beyond Frank she stood in the doorway, back from the ladies room. Back from his past.

"It's been a long time, hasn't it, Charley Morgan?"

All he could say was, "I need a drink."

They all needed drinks. Charley ordered, "Jameson's all around," from the waitress at the watering hole across the street from the IMS. "And make mine a triple."

"Triples all around," Hillary said, handing the girl her credit card. "This will be on me," she said to Mrs. Morgan's boys. "How often does a girl get to splurge on two men on the same date?"

The three of them sat in their booth massaging their triples with Frank doing all the talking about how he had always known this place was just across the street and that it served a legendary Brunswick stew and yet still, he'd never stepped inside.

The hospital nearby had a newly expanded surgery. Maybe that was why the place was filled with drinkers so early in the day. Stressed families on standby were awaiting word from Carteret General that their loved ones had made it and were in Recovery.

"Lot of road work going on," he commented, changing the subject.

Hillary and Charley remained mum. Nervous, Frank prayed a fight wasn't brewing between them. "It's about time, too, all the taxes we pay here. Highway 70 is all potholes," he said of the highway running through Morehead City, also called Arendell Street.

"Bob's always griping how tourist traffic keeps getting worse and the DOT never fixes the roads. KFC down the street's going out of business. Have you noticed all the fast-food joints are closing down all over the place? Last month it was Cletus's Fish Fry & Steam Bar. Cletus's was here over fifty years, they say. Maybe it's a sign. People are finally eating healthier now."

He raised his empty glass and jiggled it. "Miss, can I have another?"

Charley took a deep breath. Thank God! Frank was finally out of gas. He eked a peek at Hillary across the table. She caught him red-handed and smirked from over her glass. He said, "So...how's His Lordship?" and washed his words down with a mouthful of whiskey.

"My husband is dead, thank you."

Charley coughed Jameson's onto himself and the table. "Husband?"

"Yes."

"And he died. When?"

"Three months ago."

A sudden movement startled their table. As if on cue, Hillary and Frank shuffled sidelong across their seats making quick room for some waitress—not theirs—who just popped out of nowhere: a sunny forty-something about Charley's age with a spare-no-expense complexion. And she was armed...with a fresh drink for Charley and a dry towel for his soiled lap.

She made no effort to hide from Frank or Hillary her watching him dab the dampness away from his crotch as she sopped up his spill with long slow strokes over the tabletop that couldn't help but show off her bronzed beach girl arms. When he was done, she exchanged a flirty smile for his wetted towel, flicked her hair over her shoulder with a flourish, and turned away with a swashbuckling swagger that clearly invited him to pursue her secret places.

Charley squirmed beneath Hillary's sidelong expression that was all over him. "That just seems to happen to me a lot," he said.

"You're married."

"Hey, I can't help it."

"Oh really?"

Frank interjected, "Why don't you tell Hillary what you've been up to?"

"Yes Charley. Please. Tell me how the man who discovered Cleopatra's tomb stays busy."

"Well, I haven't been held at gunpoint by anyone lately if that's what you mean," he snipped, alluding to when she forced him at gunpoint to steal for her Egypt's greatest treasure since Tutankhamun.

"And I haven't needed rescuing from the sea floor for years," she clucked, reminding him, how despite her bad behavior, he had nevertheless saved her life in the end.

He raised his glass to her. "Touché."

She raised hers back. "Truce?"

"Truce." He took a hit from his drink, set his glass on the table, and commenced to working it in little circles with his thumb and index finger. "So, maybe you can explain something."

"My being here, you mean."

He shrugged with his face.

"Well..." She shared the same history she had shared with Frank, the good and the bad, and that she was now teaching maritime archaeology at ECU. "To get myself back in the swing of things, you could say."

"And just by chance you wind up here?"

"Believe me. If I knew I'd run into you two, I'd have taken work elsewhere."

"Was that the Oxford snobbery I just heard, Frank?"

"Mm, I'd say it was that old Hempstead blue blood finally leaching out of her."

"Oh shut up, the both of you."

Mrs. Morgan's boys enjoyed a tandem chuckle.

Charley recalled a long-ago friend he'd missed for years. "Theo—do you see him much?"

"We're actually very close now, considering. I should say he's the reason I'm here. After Nathaniel died, returning to teaching at Oxford would have been too painful: too many memories, and too many ex-enemies. Theo called in a few favors behind my back and here I am. I'm very grateful to him, really. Now it's your turn. So, you're working for David Kittering, I hear."

"Since just after Egypt."

He recounted his marriage to Olufemi, adopting her son Qeb, and selling his salvage business to his partner; and how he got the German submarine job from Kittering, and how proud he was of Qeb. "Pretty soon they'll be calling him Doctor just like you and Frank." And then, too, his latest work in the South Pacific. He quieted there at that point and withdrew back into the softness of the booth.

He shot Frank a look.

"What?" Frank said.

"There's something else. I'm not the saint you think I might be, coming home for Femi's birthday. David ordered me off the ship."

Frank gripped the edge of his seat. "Charley!"

"I know. I'm ashamed to say it, but there it is."

Frank deflated back into the booth. "You didn't tell me that before."

"David says I need a long vacation. He just isn't saying how long."

"He's right. You've been away too much, Charley."

"Yeah, I know. Femi reminded me. Thing is, at sea you're safe from your guilty conscience. It's easy to forget. But back home—I don't know what I was thinking, showing up expecting she'd cry and throw her arms around me and..."

He drained his second triple of Jameson's. "I wasn't the birthday surprise I thought I'd be. She made me sleep on the couch. The night of her birthday! I couldn't sleep a wink. My guts were on fire. In the morning she asked me to leave."

"I'm sorry. But it's not like you've been there for her, Charley. Or for Qeb."

"You don't need to remind me. What am I gonna do, Frank?" He tossed down the last of his drink and snatched up an idea. "How about your place?"

"What? No. No! No way, little brother. You're not hiding from her at my house. You're going back down there to her and you're gonna get on your best knees and square things with her."

"I can't go back, Frank! She kicked me out. Besides...she's got me scared shitless."

Hillary butted in. "Do we finally hear fear in the fearless Charley Morgan?"

"Shut up, Bascombe. Or is it Your Ladyship?"

"It's *Doctor* Bascombe you prick. And she's testing you. You're just too thick to see it. If you don't go back to her, Charley Morgan, you *will* lose her."

"That's what worries me." He looked away. "More than anything else in the world."

"You're scared because you love her, you idiot." Hillary waved the waitress over and asked for their tab. "Frank and I are going back across the street. We've work to do on that thing you brought up. Illegally, I understand."

"It was—"

"I'm talking! You are going back down to Wilmington and you are going to beg Olufemi for forgiveness."

"You never met her, did you?"

"I'm not finished. Then you're going to call that filthy rich boss of yours and you're going to tell him you quit."

Charley and Frank replied in chorus. "What?"

"There's a name for him, you know, floating out there," she revealed. "He's called the marriage wrecker."

"Maybe that's true, but—"

Hillary accepted her tab from their girl and signed it. "In your case, it may be truer than ever."

"I can't just up and quit."

"It's time you made a choice, Charley." She thanked the girl with a $20 tip. "It's either Kittering or Olufemi. You should have realized by now, it won't work having both."

Back across Arendell Street, Frank swooned over the water mark on the plate beneath the bath in his lab. He sat on the floor massaging the hangover building up in his forehead. "I can hardly think."

Hillary squatted by his side at the pH bath. "You've become a lightweight."

"It's probably more because I don't drink much at all anymore."

"Tschah! Right. And the beers in your lab frig?"

"That belonged to my students. You were my guest. I was being polite."

"You just downed two triple whiskeys."

"I was being sociable."

She stroked his hair, tracing the grey. "You're a real mess, aren't you?"

He leaned back onto his palms on the floor. "Qeb and I—that was our first fight this morning. I mean our first fight ever. And I kicked him out. I lost my temper. I kicked him out."

Hillary settled onto the floor next to him, resting on her elbow. "He's got some things to get over. He's a grown man, Frank. He'll survive."

Frank lay back all the way and stared up at the checkerboard ceiling tiles. A brownish stain waved down at him. IMS's newest building and already it was leaking from somewhere. "I told him, 'Go back to your dig and get back to work.'"

A stray thread flagged at her from his shirt pocket. "Sounds like good advice," she said, picking the thread away.

"They had a big argument—him and Laird. Laird kicked him off the dig. He showed up at my house. Slept on my porch all night just to talk with me. Can you believe that? I need to be there for him."

She rested her palm upon his chest. "You have been, Frank."

"But I haven't. He lost a friend and I've been too busy being angry with him to see his pain."

"He'll be alright." She brushed back an unruly lock of his hair. "He'll go back to work on his PhD and forget all of this."

He cocked his head to her, guilt stamped all over him.

"That's what *he* said, that I was trying to make him forget his best friend." He retreated to the stain on the ceiling. "Then he asked me, if that was what I did when I returned to college after our parents died: got away so I could forget them and—"

Her lips on his were immediate, and warm in a way he'd long forgotten. The scent of her hair swooped over him caressing his pain and shoving his guilt aside.

He pulled back and wondered up at her looking down at him, her face full of trust. "They fired me, Hillary." His breathing stumbled. "They're taking my students away from me."

She searched deep into his pain. "It's okay Frank." She stroked his cheek. "It's all going to be okay."

And again her lips pressed his, drawing his pain away.

Hillary coughed up a half-shocked sniggle at Frank's off-color joke. "You're awful!" she said, slapping his shoulder. "I don't remember you having such a vicious sense of humor. Where did—" Her attention jerked to the lab door. Muffled voices were passing by on the other side. "Please tell me the door's locked."

He shrugged innocently. "It never really occurred to me to check."

"Bloody hell!" Horrified, she scrambled to her feet. Her shapely legs stretched down from the tail of her big shirt to her shoeless feet slapping out frantic footsteps to the solid double doors. Her fingers slipped round the euro-style handle, quietly so as not to spook unwanted ears on the other side.

She forced her weight into it. The handle wouldn't budge. "Thank God." She turned and rested her back against the doors and pouted at him, coyly stroking her calf with the sole of her foot. "I suppose we must get up and at least *appear* like we're working."

The site of her, playful and naked beneath her shirt stirred him anew. "I thought maybe we could, maybe one more time..."

"Yes, wouldn't you." She pushed away from the door and approached him as he forced himself to his feet.

"Leave it to you to wreck everything," he said, bunching their bedding together.

"Here. Let me help you," she said.

They retrieved the thick comforter they'd laid out on the warm tile and picked up their pillows. Frank kept them all with a cot for the long nights when he was too exhausted to drive home. As they folded the comforter together, he revealed, "I checked on what you said about the Laird Foundry."

She pressed her half of the folded comforter against him. "You checked on me?"

"You were right."

"Thank you, Dr. Morgan," she said, pressing her second fold into his.

"Laird built two ironclad warships for the South," he said. "Big oceangoing things with speed and revolving gun turrets. It surprised me, really. I thought those kinds of ships came years later." He set the bedding onto his cot over in a far corner. "The British government seized them before they could get over here."

"It does open up some possibilities."

Frank pondered the thing in the pH bath.

"All the experts say steel didn't take off till the eighteen-seventies, but I did some homework. In the late eighteen-fifties the British Admiralty was contracting foundries to come up with a new metal armor for their warships. I guess they weren't alone. In 1862, they showed off, conducting tests on the Thames River right out in public view, apparently to scare the French, the Germans, and the Russians who had their spies in everything. Your typical arms race: whoever designed the toughest armor plate first would be ruler of the seas."

"I suppose, with America at war with itself, your country was a convenient lab rat."

"You mean they tested their new ideas by supplying them to us?"

"Enfield did it. They sold muskets to both sides, North and South."

"Smuggling rifles is a lot easier than slipping past the blockade with steel and cannon. Wait. You're serious."

"Why not? If England had a newer stronger armor, she would be eager to test it. What better place than in a war? She wasn't at war then, so she did the next best thing. And if they had made some new metal, it might explain why there's no corrosion, yes?"

Frank considered the dozing slab with a different eye. "Maybe. Whatever material that is, it's hard. Whatever alloys are in it for that kind of strength could certainly add some serious defense against rust, even in seawater. Come here. I want to show you something. Take a look at this."

Across town in Frank's kitchen, arthritic pages crimpled in Qeb's ginger fingertips. He coaxed them along, dreading they might crumble at any time like autumn leaves. The author's fading recollections plodded along with a steady cadence, occasionally stumbling over halting technical gibberish, or like now, double timing into a spurt of excitement.

The author was one Peter Howe, and right now Peter's quilled ink script was racing along faster than ever portraying the armor plates delivered to Wilmington beginning in the fall of 1864.

Delivered to Beery's yard on Eagle Island, that nests in the Cape Fear River a short swim from the docks in Wilmington. They were in the shape of a honeycomb, with six sides. Not square, or flat and long like the armor of the old Virginia. Not made from rail road track mashed flat by great steam hammers and bolted onto wood. They were tall as me, as a young lad of fifteen and maybe five feet tall then. They came to a point on the top and on the bottom so a man could not lean them up, for they would topple over with a great crash. As a man many years later, I learned this shape was called a hexagon.

Many brave men and many ships had nearly sunk slipping through the blockades to bring these plates. From England, I was told. That's where they were made. A new metal rumored stronger than the armor of any ship built.

There were so many of them, stacked high and so very heavy. Very dangerous to move and set in their places on the ships' frames. Their edges were knife edge sharp. More than one man lost his finger to carelessness in this exercise.

Qeb strained his best imagination visualizing the hectic construction Peter Howe was describing. Lincoln's troops had attempted a landing at Fort Fisher down river. Time was running out. Peter's writing reeked of urgency and panic.

Ships' frames, Howe had written. Ships. Plural. More than one.

Frank Morgan coaxed Hillary's hand into the pH bath. "Feel that edge," he said, guiding her touch in the warm tingling water along the tongues and grooves tracing the edges of the oblong hexagon plate.

"Strange. They're much smoother than I'd imagine, having been immersed for so long."

"Those edges, they weren't cast into the plate. Those were machined."

"Is that significant?"

"Usually not, but in this case, with this thing so hard it doesn't rust—the tooling needed to cut those edges had to be even tougher."

"Frank, what's that look for?"

"Well, if our guesses are right and it does date from the Civil War, that means as early as the 1860's the Laird Foundry was manufacturing what might be the first corrosion resistant metal. And what's more, it means they had the technology—the harder tool steels needed to machine it—earlier than history gives them credit for."

"I'm not quite connecting the dots."

"It may not look like much to most people, but in archaeomaterial science, this could be a profound discovery."

"Surely there are records of it somewhere," she said.

"My doctorate is in antique materials. I've learned from the best professors in the world. And yet, I have never ever heard of anything even remotely like this."

Qeb eased back a page and double checked something he read that only just now registered. Had he read it right? Yes. He had. And there it was in clear script. *Special cannon*. With exploding shells!

The South, we had rifled cannon. Anybody with ears and a penchant for eavesdropping knew we had rifled cannon, but not like these. These were different. Armstrong rifled cannon, named for the Englishman who designed them. A Mr. Armstrong. A Knight, knighted by Queen Victoria.

Armstrong called his cannon breech-loaders, as they loaded from the back through a special door so the crew was not placed in danger of enemy fire as they would be if they were to reload from the front as was common.

They had a strange screw mechanism. I worked it myself. It allows a crew to aim and fire accurately twice in a minute. An English engineer came with the guns to oversee their assembly and train the crew. He said even three times a minute was possible with superior gunners.

There were no guns like them anywhere in the world, made especially for Recluse and her sister, and would fire the latest English exploding projectiles tested against the most robust armor. Six pound shot, carried in secret to us through the West Indies.

Qeb repeated aloud Peter Howe's words, "...made especially for *Recluse* and her sister." There it was again. There had been not just one, but *two*.

He massaged the book in his lap with germinating appreciation. It was here then that Tim-Lee had uncovered the name. He quivered all through himself. It was as if he could feel Tim-Lee's divine hand on his shoulder.

You see, Qeb. I told you so.

"Damn it, Tim-Lee," he said aloud. "I don't need this right now." He had his own responsibilities to worry over. He was so close to finishing years of crap and working harder than he'd ever worked, for teachers who were never happy. And for no pay either.

The devil in Qeb's conscience teased him: *Now you know Recluse was real.* This was one of those hidden hints Tim-Lee wrote about that Gemma had asked him to find. *And you told her yes. You promised. So what's it going to be? What are you going to do now?*

Frank indicated to Charley's bell, gleaming clean in the light. "You know. Charley and I—we broke the law when we took that. And we found a wreck that nobody's ever charted before; found it where we weren't supposed to be—on military property. I don't think you understand the implications of that. I don't think you understand the implications for me. This plate—it could really be something."

"Maybe the bell is your starting point? The *Hermione* had to be built somewhere."

The bell's scripted letters smirked at him from the faint light. He palmed his forehead with a slap. "You're right! Where the hell have I been? Of course! She would have been built overseas, probably Ireland or Scotland. Her records—they would have recorded her at the yard."

"If the yard that built her—whatever yard—is still in operation. Maybe her lines can offer you a lead?"

Frank snapped his fingers and wagged a digit. "The sonar scans."

He drummed the keyboard on his laptop. The thing crept awake and blinked dully at him. "Come on, come on you piece of junk," he grumbled. The scuffed and exhausted machine performed its usual stumbling song and dance boot up and grizzled slowly to life.

"Finally!" He drilled his way to the folder holding his scan files and pulled one up with a hefty rap on the ENTER key. "Here we are."

A muddy orange-over-brown image joggled into view, coaxing Hillary's attention to the fractured outline of a ship with three distinct areas of wreckage. Long dark shadows reached out from them across the rippled shallows.

"This raised area here—it separates the bow from the stern. Some kind of machinery: the engines or the boilers maybe."

Hillary squinted at a pile of jumbled mess in the middle. "Are those sidewheels?"

"Funny. That's just what Charley said. And yes, they are."

"Anything to tell you she might be a blockade runner?"

His fingertip slipped across the screen to a curvaceous hump stretching aft from the bow, covering part of the foredeck. "This here is called a turtle's back. It would have kept her from taking on water as she plowed through the waves. It tells us she was built for speed. It's a darned good indicator she was a runner."

Frank admired the images with welling excitement. "They came out really well. Qeb would love these. Shit. I need to call Qeb."

"Wait, Frank."

"No. I really screwed up, Hillary." He snatched up his phone from the countertop and pecked at the numbers.

"Let him go, Frank."

Frank pulled his phone to his ear. "I just need to talk to him before he goes, that's all. I need to tell him I'm sorry."

Qeb set the manuscript down. Reading any further was a waste of time. He had work again. Laird wanted him back on his dig. He'd go back up and put up with Laird's shit, get his doctorate and finally be free of all the years of academic misery that had been so much a part of his life for so long.

Uncle Frank said leave. So fine, he would. He would finally be on his own. It was all so easy now—so simple. He glanced down at the book in his lap.

Just give it back to Gemma and forget it.

But how could you, after what you had just read?

But how could it even be possible? It would mean everything everybody says about technology 150 years ago is way wrong. He fingered the profound words with the gentleness of snowflakes, as if they might fly off the page and be lost forever.

Among Recluse's technological fascinations, she had many exemplary surprises for the Yankees. But I must ask your patience with me, for my words will sound foolish as I am not sufficiently schooled to describe them in any other way.

First, that Recluse was a sinkable ship.

Mister John Brooks, CSN designed her with no stacks for coal exhaust. Mr. Brooks conceived and designed Recluse with the unique ability of taking on floodwater ballast to lower her profile on the horizon for battle and to raise her freeboard for swiftness.

In her hold were tanks of brazed tin with valves and piping with which to fill them with seawater, bringing her foredeck and afterdeck just awash so that her battery was all that protruded above the sea. Much like a turtle's back, but much more deadly with her rifled Armstrong cannon and her new armor. Her guns were fast and they were accurate and her armor would repel even exploding shot from the Yankee warships.

They would never see her coming. That is because of her second secret. The reader will recall my mention that Mr. Brooks designed her without exhaust stacks. Exhaust would only flag her approach to the enemy. You see, dear reader, Messrs. Brooks and Porter, and the Frenchman, Mr. Etienne-Lenoir connived a cunning system of steering the engines' smoke from the hull through holes in her sides just beneath the water.

Qeb closed the cover. His phone said almost five o'clock. Uncle Frank would be home soon. He had to go. He stroked the cover of the book. Not in a million years would he have believed he'd ever think of doing what he was thinking of doing now. Everything he was working for, for so many years. Could he really do it?

His father had died in an instant on the streets of Qena in a stupid accident. His father never saw much outside his hometown cabinet shop. Not even the stunning Thebes, which lay just down river. Qeb pulled and tugged at the faded images of his father buried deep in his fractured memories, but they refused to come out. Guilt welled up inside him.

His conscience counseled him: *You're not your father.*

They wouldn't understand.

Is that so important?

But Uncle Frank—what would he say? What would dad say? And Mother. It would be like stabbing her in the heart. He glanced sidelong at his surplus flight bag packed at the ready. *Richmond. The team hates me anyway, even my girlfriend. Correction. Ex-girlfriend. Ex-girlfriend number three.*

The team had to know Laird wanted him back. Laird could never keep a secret. They were no doubt praying he would never show up if Laird called.

He stroked the cover of Howe's manuscript. How could the *Fredericksburg's* bland wreckage possibly compare to the fantastical story filling its pages? He couldn't do it. A strange calm swept through him.

You're not going.

No. Not now. Not with this.

The manuscript seemed to heat up in his lap, stirring up images of the *Recluse* in action.

Rollers rumbled on crescent rails as cannon swung left and swept right, taking aim. Officers bellowed confident orders. Crewmen worked in orderly chaos. Cannon blazed with rifled accuracy executing mayhem upon the enemy who lay helpless to strike back, for *Recluse* lay too low in the water to sight her in their crosshairs and her armor laughed off their most deadly projectiles.

And the cuffs of the Yankee sailors' slops soaked wet at their ankles as the decks of their ships, one after another, settled into the waves, taking them to their graves.

Qeb's practiced work ethic panicked, demanding obedience. *You have to go back. Professor Laird is expecting you. You texted him you were coming.*

His conscience argued: *There are always other digs.*

His work ethic scoffed: *All your hard work tossed away for a girl.*

But Qeb's conscience delivered a trump card: *She needs you. You're her only hope.*

Qeb's phone vibrated in his palm. Caller ID glowed green. Uncle Frank.

He refused the call.

His conscience pushed him harder: *You know you want to.*

Yeah. I know.

His phone vibrated again. He stared at it till the glowing dimmed. Uncle Frank was leaving a message. He shoved his phone in his pocket and sandwiched Peter Howe's manuscript between soft clothes in his bag. He snapped it closed and heaved it up with a grunt and nudged his shoulder under the strap.

He wormed his grip round the kitchen door knob and squeezed it into a turn. His nerves stalled. *Is this even right?* He stole one last look around. *Yes, it is right. Right for me!* He turned the handle all the way till the latch slipped free and the door pulled off its jamb.

Fresh air swooped in all over him and hugged him hard. His heart fluttered, all queer inside. Finally! He was doing what *he* wanted to do and not what someone else was telling him to do.

For the first time in his whole life ever, he was being his own man.

13-UNDERWAY

Beery Shipyard, Eagle Island, North Carolina

Throngs of spectators massed on the Wilmington waterfront. All business had ground to a halt to celebrate the city's new savior. Handkerchiefs, flags, hats and hands waved, cheering *Recluse* as she headed out to sea to redeem them from their Yankee scourge. The greenish patina to her armor would blend her well with the waves. Only ten inches of freeboard separated her deck from the water. Street talk was she could skim the sea so that low and quiet that she could lurk up to her unsuspecting prey like an alligator.

Thaddeus preferred the open air of *Recluse*'s spar deck to the stuffiness of her interior and even more so, the uninvited company of the annoying Mr. Laird. In front of him rising no higher than his waist was the roof of her pilothouse, a small rectangular affair with viewing slits all around to see when steering the ship in battle. Inside, with *Recluse*'s steersman, Lieutenant Pond awaited his orders, anxious to show off his new ship.

Thaddeus leaned into one of the slits. "Back her out, Mr. Pond."

"Aye, sir. Engine room. Astern one quarter."

Coffee-and-cream water boiled from her stern as *Recluse*'s twin propellers backed her out and free from her flooded Beery dry dock. Forty-five feet in beam, she was slightly narrower than her predecessors.

Somber men and weeping men alike lined the pier and watched her slip out into the river. She was a wonderful sight, potent and deadly. She would thrash the blockade! Richmond would sue for peace and finally, Southern independence would reign.

Recluse's bow cleared the dock. She was fully afloat and on her own. Her crew's cheers spilled from her open gun ports, ten in all: three each fore and aft, with another two each, port and starboard.

Whoops and yelps rose from *Recluse*'s proud Beery builders.

Thaddeus ordered to Pond, "Let's give them what they came to see, Mr. Pond. Port engine all stop; starboard engine ahead one quarter. Steer hard to port."

Pond's neck tingled with excitement. "Aye sir. Port engine all stop; ahead one quarter, starboard engine."

Recluse centered herself down the river, presenting her broadsides to the people lining the shores. They wondered at her sleek lines. Stories had reached the barstools and the Market that she boasted a host of modern secrets and experimental weapons. Her armor, they said, would stop anything the Yankees lobbed at her.

Yet as he acknowledged their good wishes with a hearty wave, Thaddeus's heart sank. He was abandoning these generous people, leaving them to fate and it sickened him.

Wither this war ends, how will you ever live with yourself?

He knew all too well what news would horrify his men when *Recluse* pulled into Nassau. The Yankee hordes would have finally subjugated Fort Fisher and would be occupying Wilmington. The last seaport in the South would vanish. The South would fall, her hopes of independence dashed, with *Recluse* never lobbing a shot!

"Okay, Mr. Pond. Both engines ahead one quarter. Watch your markers for the shoals."

"All ahead one quarter, Commander. Watch my markers, aye!"

Lieutenant Pond peered through the slots at the bright world outside. They were just passing Cassidey's yard clinging to the south edge of town. Workmen were lining the docks, silent and resolute. Some doffed their hats and bowed their heads.

As he studied the Cassidey men's faces, Thaddeus sensed a presence behind him. He needn't bother to look. "You see that, Mr. Laird; the looks on their faces? It's so clear even from this distance.

They are depending on us. And thanks to you, we are a nothing now but a big lie. I hope you can live with yourself."

Percival pouted with disdain at the motley and exhausted workers. "You'd best get over this pious guilt, Commander. You'll need your wits about you. Try and remember *Recluse* is doing as the government deems best for the people."

Thaddeus flashed a fiery look at Laird and peeked around beyond him.

"If it's my guard you're seeking, I sent them away. We're completely alone."

"You sure you want to gamble your life up here with me?"

Percival pulled his watch from his vest. "You're an officer first, Commander. Not a murderer."

He flipped his watch open and noted the time. The float down to the mouth of the Cape Fear would be dull. They would be leaving by way of Smithville, passing the protection of forts Johnson and Caswell before beginning their mad dash for Nassau. He studied the pathetic crowds, thinning down as they left the city behind. The sight of them was droll.

"I'm going below, Commander. I have work to do." As he strode aft along the spar deck to the companionway at the center that led down into the gun deck, all the way he could feel Trask's furious gaze scalding his back.

Thaddeus's stony expression followed Laird's descent down the companionway, wondering what the man was up to. Refusing any assist, Laird's teamsters had removed three score powder kegs from his magazine only to replace them with fifty-nine small kegs marked Gun Powder. And now tucked among *Recluse*'s ballast stones, almost four score lead ingots now lay.

Mallory's telegram the previous day had been curt: Do as Mr. Laird instructs. You will make course through the Yankee fleet. You are not to fight. Make all haste for Nassau. There you will offload the government's property. Mr. Laird will dismiss you and your crew when he is satisfied you have met the government's requirements.

Thaddeus wondered: *And then what?*

It was a bitter pill he was swallowing, and that bastard Laird had enjoyed watching him choke it down. Queerly, it dawned on him that to rid himself of the man, reaching Nassau could not come soon enough.

He gave Pond one last order before going below. "Maintain one quarter, Mr. Pond and make for Smithville."

"Smithville it is, sir."

Thaddeus pulled the collar of his heavy wool greatcoat against him, fending off the chilly December sea breezes. Tinkling yellow candlelight reached out to him across the darkness from Smithville on the westerly shore. A familiar growling filled his stomach. Families would be coming together to share whatever they managed to cobble together for dinner. Even in these hard times, southerners were resolute to celebrate traditions.

It made his homesickness all the more painful.

Behind him to port and out of sight, Thaddeus knew bodies were watching him like cats in the night; men manning the tiny island battery eyeballing *Recluse* slipping by their deadly cannon without so much as a whisper; and no doubt just as he was, wishing they too were home instead.

Directly ahead a welcome light flickered from the Lower Lighthouse: the extreme eastern end of Oak Island. From here the Cape Fear River traced a fast S-curve, first left, skirting around the Island Battery, then right, around Oak Island and past Fort Caswell.

"Give me standard rudder to port, Mr. Pond."

"Standard rudder she is, sir, at fifteen degrees to port."

Fort Caswell was drifting by to starboard. A heavy fog was building over the treacherous Middle Ground Shoal below the fort. *Recluse* would steer a careful heading directly south for the light at Bald Head. From there, she would follow the Bald Head Channel away from the blockade using the shoreline for cover.

Fort Caswell's shadowy outline receded in *Recluse*'s wake. Bald Head lighthouse and the mouth of Bald Head Channel closed on *Recluse*'s bow. The friendly light was fading fast in the thickening fog.

"Come to starboard, Mr. Pond. Full rudder."

"Full rudder. Thirty degrees to starboard she is, sir."

"Ahead one third, Mr. Pond."

"Ahead, sir. Increase speed to one third."

"And Mr. Pond, I want you to—"

A deep thunder rumbled from the direction of Fort Fisher beyond Smith's Island, the huge mass of land astern of *Recluse* and separating Fort Caswell from Fort Fisher. Thaddeus listened intently. Echoes scampered over the bottoms of low-lying clouds and withered to silence. Though rumors of an assault on Fisher had been running for weeks, the air remained queerly still. The Yankee ships were not firing a shot. It was no attack then. Maybe a blockade-runner had exploded?

Thaddeus squinted at the face of his pocket watch. His night vision wasn't so good. "Mr. Pond. The time please."

"1:48 AM, sir."

"What in God's name was that boom?"

"You should be below, Mr. Laird," Thaddeus said, watching the northern horizon, anticipating another volley indicating the Yankee fleet had commenced bombarding Fort Fisher. But only minutes of eerie silence hung over them. Not even his English pain in the ass eked a syllable.

The Smith's Island shoreline faded into the growing fog. Thaddeus felt his face. His skin was damp. His intuition was hollering at him. "Mr. Pond. Ready the guns."

The blackness beyond the slits on the pilothouse remained quiet for a moment, and then Mr. Pond replied, "But sir, our orders..."

Thaddeus's tone was reassuring. "Ready the guns, Mr. Pond."

"Yes, sir."

"And Mr. Pond. Extinguish all lamps on the gun deck before opening those shudders."

"Sir?"

"This fog may break. Lamplight is visible for miles. We don't want to call unnecessary attention to ourselves."

Laird insisted over Thaddeus's shoulder, "Do not engage the enemy."

"With God's good graces we will not, Mr. Laird. Reports are the Yankees have shifted their ships to attack Fisher. We should encounter no resistance this side of the island. Still, I would be imprudent pretending such circumstances were assured."

A heavy metal-on-metal grating rose up from just below them. The gun port shudders were opening. Menacing black snouts emerged from their darkened gun ports, stark contrast against the milky fog.

"If you engage the enemy, Commander—"

"I will do my best not to, Mr. Laird, but it may become unavoidable."

With unsure steps, Laird's vague image disappeared in the mist. Somewhere in the milky white, he banged his knee on something and cussed loudly.

Thaddeus had a good laugh.

Pond's voice crept from out of the pilothouse. "May I come out there, sir, onto the spar deck? This is my first time at sea. I've never been in a sea fog before."

"Yes Lieutenant. Mind your step up the companionway. And the deck is wet and slippery."

Beneath Thaddeus, *Recluse* slid effortlessly across still water. The throb of her strange combustion engines was not even discernable from where he stood. A muffled expletive drifted forward from the companionway. Thaddeus turned his back from the bow and watched aft for Pond.

Pond broke through the mist rubbing his head. "Sorry, sir. That ventilation duct back there—I plowed headlong right into it. You know, I don't—" Pond's expression went wild. "Dear God!"

Thaddeus spun round. A dark wall wide as ever and tall as a house rolled out of the fog. In an instant, it closed on their bow impaling itself on *Recluse*'s solid cast iron ram, tossing Thaddeus and Pond forward like rag dolls. Pond's face slammed against the pilothouse.

From out of the fog and somewhere up high, cries of surprise echoed against masts and hard deck. A bell clanged in alarm. Drums somewhere were beating to quarters. Commands—clearly New English—spilled down through the mist and melted on *Recluse*'s armor plates.

Thaddeus pulled himself from his knees. "We've rammed a Yankee." He gripped the edges of the pilothouse slits and hollered inside to the pilot, "All astern. Full speed. Now!"

He turned to Pond and halted. Pond's jawbone was just visible in the gash on his chin. Blood dribbled down onto his uniform. "Get below Lieutenant. See to the battery first, and then have the surgeon look at that."

"Look at what, sir?" Pond felt around, unaware of his wound. He pulled his crimson fingers from his jaw and paled. Woozy, he wobbled and fingered his way aft to the companionway.

Thaddeus spilled a rapid succession of orders for the pilot to relay to the battery. *Recluse*'s forward cannon boomed. Her explosive charge blasted a gaping hole at the New Englander's waterline.

The throaty cough of linear musket fire rattled down from the Yankee's main deck. The shots were wild. The Yankee's weren't yet sure what had hit them or where.

Recluse withdrew her ram from the Yankee's side. Immediately, seawater spilled into the gaping wound she had inflicted. Over Thaddeus's head, panic was spreading through the enemy's ranks. They were sinking, and fast.

A dull pop, a flash of white phosphorous, and a distress flare rocketed skyward through the fog and disappeared. A lifeboat splashed into the water. The crew was abandoning ship.

Beyond the mayhem and under clearer skies, a low black huntress churned her way northwest along Frying Pan Shoal. Against the lens of her watchman's spyglass a far off streak of light arced across the horizon. A distress flare! And for just an instant, gray moonlight trickled past a momentary break in the heavy clouds, illuminating the squat outline of a large cheese box on a low flat deck.

14-TWO LITTLE SCAPEGOATS

"Pull over."

"But we're almost there."

"Pull over. Please!"

Qeb forced Gemma's late-Nineties Ford *Taurus* off the road onto the shoulder. Gravel crunched beneath them as they slid to an urgent stop. Gemma shoved her door open and tore from the car, stumbled and tripped and collapsed onto her hands and knees.

Qeb watched the road from behind the wheel trying not to listen to her heaves. This was obviously getting to be too much for her nerves.

But she had insisted. "I want to meet those two young boys. I have to know what they know about Tim-Lee's murder."

"So, it's murder now," he had said over coffees after he had called her from Panera and she came to get him. "You're so sure?"

"I don't know. All I do know is it wasn't any accident. I will not accept that."

"How are we supposed to find out where they live?"

"We have to go to the police. They'll have their names and addresses."

"Gemma, the police aren't going to give you that."

"Maybe they won't, but somebody there will."

"You know someone there?"

"No, but somebody always talks. People can't resist the chance to gossip."

"And you learned this where?"

"Hush up and drive, will you please?"

But wary hesitation had greeted them at the Shallotte City police department. Gemma had pressed and pushed for answers on her brother's death. It would have been easier pulling teeth from a tiger.

A frazzled detective burdened with the case replied to her as cordially as he could muster, "Miss Polk, there is no evidence suggesting any wrongdoing. Please accept that. Your brother's death was an unfortunate and very tragic accident."

Gemma flew into a tizzy, hand-tying the detective into breaking the hard news to her.

"We've closed the case, Miss Polk. Accidental death. I know it's difficult. But please understand that these things—it's unfortunate, but they happen sometimes. You're a Christian woman, we can see that. Perhaps it's time to spend quiet contemplation with God and move on."

At the twin glass doors exiting the brand new Town of Shallotte police station, Gemma froze with her hand on the cross bar. She hissed reprobation through clenched teeth, "Say a prayer. Fuck him, that pious pig!" and broke into sobs.

Qeb flashed embarrassed eyes back at the busy station. No one seemed to have overheard her seething accusation.

"They get upset like that sometimes."

The voice's eyes were kind and empathetic. "It's not you, dear. People round here—they get uppity when strangers come round and stir things up."

Gemma turned and rumpled her nose. The foyer reeked of virgin carpet and the chemical stink of new construction. From behind her counter, the station receptionist met her puffy tears with an apologetic smile.

Gemma preached from between sniffles. "My not being from here has nothing to do with anything. They're the police. They're supposed to help people. All they did is go and shove my brother away in some folder somewhere. Tim-Lee's death means nothing to them."

She crossed the space between them with deferential steps. "If it were your brother, would you let them get away with it; just slide him away in some file?" She broke into heavier tears, pulling an, "Aw, honey," from the receptionist, who stood up and handed her a box of Kleenex.

"What about you?" Gemma asked from behind a tissue. "Do you think his death was just an accident?"

"Me? Oh! I'm nobody, dear; certainly no detective."

But Gemma's expression said she wasn't gonna get off that easy.

The receptionist gave her a long look, turned round and announced to no one in particular, "It's my smoke break." She grabbed a stylish little purse and came round. She waited and let Qeb open the twin glass doors for her.

Once outside and under the shade of a single tree, she said, "It's about time somebody figured out for good if it's all true or not."

"If what's true?" Qeb said.

The woman pulled a pack of cigarettes from her purse and lighted one up.

"No thanks," he said when she offered him one.

She looked him over with just a trickle of interest slipping through her indifferent, front-desk cover. "It's been over 150 years," she said. "And still people are getting hurt over that stupid boat."

Qeb and Gemma shared cautious glances.

She plucked her cigarette from her lips. "You haven't heard, then," she decided. "People say there's gold on it. All my life people been saying that. Since when my granddaddy was around. Maybe that's what keeps people going out there."

"What kind of gold?" Qeb asked.

"Sweetie, how many kinds of gold are there?"

"What did you mean by people still getting hurt?" Gemma said.

The receptionist spoke to the faint stream of white smoke drifting skyward from her cigarette. "Those two boys who found your poor brother, God rest his soul. They weren't the first to be snooping around out there. That cove's always been a magnet for trouble. Since I was little, people been sneaking round out there. Us kids mostly, but lately, there been strangers."

"You mean like my brother?"

She indicated to a picnic table. "Sit down over here with me." Settled in, she continued, "The old woman that lives out there—that property's been in her family since just after the war, so they say. I don't know."

"Which war?" Qeb asked.

"Oh honey. The Civil War of course." She sighed in mock exasperation. "Anyway, there been all kinds of Power Company and utility people out there lately. Working where I do, you hear things. Seems rich developers from out of state want her land to put up condominiums or some such nonsense. Rumor is they want to dredge the estuary too. I guess so people can bring their big boats, like we ain't got enough of that round here anyways.

"Last week some young people from the college were out there protesting, blocking the county inspector. Something about the eco-something-or-other. Anyway, she ain't selling. Everybody knows that."

"So, what's the problem?" Qeb said.

"Problem is those developers won't quit. Money does things to people's right thinking, you know? Seems they been talking to the State about eminent...eminent..."

"Eminent domain?" Gemma said. "But that's only if the public benefits. You can't take someone's land so someone else can profit from it."

The woman shook her head pitifully from behind a smirk. The end of her cigarette glowed as she savored a long hit. "This is North Carolina, darling. You'd be surprised what counts as for the public benefit around here."

"So they're just going to take her land from her?"

"Oh, they have to pay her, of course. Fair market value. But if the value drops, then the State doesn't have to pay her as much. I see you're confused. Let me put it this way. Forgive me, sweetie, if I'm unkind, but your brother's death? Well, that's the best thing ever happened for these developer people. After all these years with people messing round out there at that cove, somebody finally got hurt."

Her touch to the back of Gemma's hand was soft with compassion.

"People won't look on that place the same way they used to. Nobody's gonna want to go near there now. So that means her property becomes kind of unsavory to the public eye. Now her property taxes can be dropped and the State gets away with offering her peanuts. If she refuses, they'll just take her to court and convince some good old boy judge to force her to accept.

"Those developers will move in and do what they want, and the politicians will hike up the taxes again when all those expensive condominiums are done. They win on both ends of the deal. And then the first Sunday after, you'll see their disgusting smiles at church. It's all so disgusting."

She wetted the dryness from her lips and took a chance. "You been out there yet?"

Qeb and Gemma shook their heads.

"Well you be careful. She's a frightened old girl. Got no family I've ever heard of. She doesn't have the money to hire a lawyer, so she's fighting it the only way she knows how."

"How's that?"

"We're a Castle Doctrine state, honey. Thank God for that, but if she's afraid that somebody snooping round out there might be coming to hurt her—well, she's done it before."

"Done what before?"

"Shoot at trespassers."

"She's *shot* at people?"

"Mm hm. Even hit somebody once."

"Why don't you arrest her?"

"Oh honey, she don't mean no harm. It was just rock salt anyway. Whoever it was, they probably just hurt in the seat of their pants for a week or two while driving to work."

"Sounds like she should be locked up or put in a home."

"Trespassing's a crime, darlin'. Besides"—She tapped off the ashes from her cigarette—"people been used to hearing gunfire out there. My officers in there—they're tired of the calls. Usually wind up being nothing. Everybody round here knows how she is, except maybe the summer people. We give them enough warning. If one of them's dumb enough to trespass on her land, then they deserve what they get."

She indicated to her cigarette, almost burned to the filter, "This is my timer. I gotta get back."

"Um..." Qeb started.

She looked at him almost expectantly. "Yes darlin'?"

He glanced at Gemma, who'd gotten up and was standing by her lonesome with her back to them. "She's really hoping we might go see the boys who found her brother, maybe talk to them."

"I was wondering when you'd get the courage to ask me. That is why you're down here, isn't it? Don't blush, honey. I do work with the police, after all."

Qeb grinned a little. "I thought you said you weren't a detective?"

Her smile back was winsome. He was a hottie and beginning to rile her nerves in a way they hadn't been riled in some time. Oh well. She shelved her impossible dream for a later fantasy and pondered Gemma with empathy.

"Her brother's in God's hands now, but the questions in her heart need answers, and not the kind God can give. Let her be with her thoughts." She tapped the top of his hand. "You come inside with me a minute."

Qeb fiddled with the note the receptionist had slipped him with the names and addresses of the two boys' families. "Tell you what," she had whispered to him with a twinkle. "I'll call them, tell them you're coming."

The first family was sheepish, but polite. They knew from the call that the sister of the dead man found by their boy and his friend wanted to come meet them. She was only searching for answers that might ease her pain in mourning, and certainly meant no harm.

"There was flooding from the hurricane," the father explained. "The Shallotte River and the estuaries were higher than normal—very inviting to two disobedient boys with a boat."

The mother had insisted, "We're sure they used the flooding as an excuse for adventure."

"You mean the wreck?" Qeb asked her.

That's when the father got suddenly defensive. "We don't know about any wreck. Only thing we've ever heard about is there's some old truck down there. Old folks round here say gangster's stowed liquor down there during the Prohibition. Maybe so. Sounds far-fetched, you ask me, hiding liquor underwater. But we don't know about any wreck."

Curious, their son Robby had peered round the corner in the house. Gemma had seen him and waved with a big smile. When he turned and dashed away, his mother had surrendered a sheepish smile. "You'll have to forgive him. He's not usually like this, so rude and all. I just can't understand what's got into him."

The second family was easy to find. When they pulled in the drive, Gemma suggested, "You go ahead. I need a moment."

"That's exactly right," the second boy's mother said, when Qeb repeated the first family's story about the hurricane and flooding. She shot her son a punitive look. "They've been told to stay away from there. I just never expected they would do something so stupid as to take that boat out there. They know better than to go near that cove. Everyone avoids it."

"Why?"

"The old woman who lives there—"

"She's an ex-convict," the boy boasted. "Mean, too. She'll shoot you, you don't watch out."

"You hush!" his mother said. "She's just alone, poor thing. She just wants her privacy."

"She shot at a boat last year," the boy blurted.

"I said hush! Just tourist snoops wanting to see the cove. Nobody really knows who did what."

"What's got people so curious about the cove?" Qeb said.

"That's where the wreck is." The boy spread his arms wide. "It's a big one. I seen it."

"Saw it. And no you didn't." His mother offered up an embarrassed smile. "Everybody round here has heard the stories about the lost ship."

"But the other family—the father—he said it was just some old truck down there."

She smiled only slightly. "That would be Robert. Robert's made up his own mind about the whole thing. My daddy—he told me the ship story at bedtime. And his daddy told it to him." She licked her chapped summertime lips. "Some people you talk to will go on about there being gold."

"Yes. We heard that."

"Don't get all excited. It's just to keep people interested in the story. You know. The summer people? They all come down here for history and legends. Don't you believe any of it: it's just some old truck down there. Kids been sneaking swims there since before my parents were in school."

Behind Qeb, the car door shut.

The mother looked past him. "Is that her: the sister?"

"Her name's Gemma. Gemma Polk."

The boy's mother frowned a moment and recalled, "People from church say there been people on the property lately, people not from round here. Gossip is someone wants to buy the land."

"They're gangsters!" her son said.

She knuckled a Christmas noogie into his scalp.

"Ow!" He retreated from her grasp and pouted sidelong up at her.

Gemma stepped into view from behind Qeb. "Gangsters?" she said, grinning with big eyes at the boy.

The boy gaped at her and seized his mother's protection.

"We mind our own business, but there's something going on there," his mother said.

A door in the back of the house opened and shut again.

Gemma wiggled her fingers at the boy, leaching color from the boy's complexion.

Booted footsteps approached, just out of sight.

"What makes you say that?" Qeb asked the mother.

There was a clatter in the kitchen.

The boy gripped his mother's hand.

"Ow, honey. You're crushing mommy's hand."

He clung even closer to her side, his terror fixated on Gemma.

A faceless voice boomed from the kitchen, "Why don't you people mind your own business?"

Gemma lost her smile and glared at the boy in a way that said, "Don't you dare say anything!"

A large man strode into view. The boy tossed his mother's hand aside and charged him. "Daddy, that lady—she scares me."

"Maybe we should go," Gemma suggested.

The mother volunteered, "I'll walk you to your car."

Outside, at the bottom of the porch steps, she picked up a small something. When they got to the car, she handed it over to Qeb. "He's a good boy. But he's at that age, you know?"

It was a diver's ditty bag: a mesh net bag used for stowing goodies found on the bottom. Inside it were three small gray bricks, maybe four or five inches long.

"What are they?" Qeb said.

"I have no idea. He got them from whatever that is down there in that cove. He knows he's not supposed to go diving without his father, but that's what they did and that was his prize. I won't have them around here, and he won't be in the water again for a very long time if I have anything to say about it. I swear he'll be the death of me." She turned to Gemma. "Miss Polk, I'm very sorry for your loss. Your brother—what was his name?"

"Tim-Lee Polk."

"Well, Tim-Lee will be in my prayers tonight. I'll ask our pastor to mention him next Sunday."

Gemma brushed the hair from her sight and blessed her with her softest mountain girl smile.

"Thank you. You're very kind."

Fluttering movement pulled Qeb back to the Now. Gemma was beside the car brushing orange clay from her hands. He reached round to the back seat and grabbed a roll of paper towels and handed it to her with a bottled water to clean up.

"Oh, look at this!" she whined after rinsing her mouth and hands. Two large orange-brown blotches marred the front of her flower patterned dress. "It's all just shabby now."

She sidled into her seat and slammed the passenger door after her.

"You okay doing this?" he said.

She stared ahead, glaring at something in the distance. Just in site, down the road was the white house where the old woman lived.

"Gemma?"

"I'm fine! You think I came all this far just to turn around?"

Then her hand slipped over his on the seat.

"I'm sorry. I don't know what I'd do without you." She picked at the damage to her dress. "I have a bag in the back with jeans and a top for just this kind of thing."

"There was a Kangaroo mini-mart back there. You can change there."

"There's no time for that. I'll just change here in the car. Give me the keys for the trunk."

15-CHRISTMAS EVE 1864

Off Smith's Island, North Carolina

The groaning figure sprawled out and coughing on *Recluse*'s gun deck was soaking wet and barely with it. His dirty blond hair crowning his hungry face was matted with blood over a melon of a bump just over his left eye. A smattering of moist spots marked blood stains on his dark blue uniform. He wore a crackerjack jumper over generous blue trousers. A blue neckerchief dangled from round his neck.

Recluse's boatswain, Timothy Myers, handed Thaddeus the man's hat. "That was on the deck, sir."

Thaddeus rolled the hat round in nimble fingers. A blue ribbon circled round the bottom of it bore the name in tired gold print: *USS Sassacus*.

"He must have fallen from that ship, sir," Myers said.

Recluse lay still in the water. Her shipwrights had scurried topside to check for damages after the collision and had found the man lying on the foredeck unconscious. "His shoulder is dislocated, but otherwise he's in one piece."

Thaddeus nodded. He stole a peek outside through one of the open gun ports. Night had faded fast to dawn. A strip of yellow was rapidly parting the sea from the sky. Soon the sun would burn away the fog, and *Recluse*'s cover. A thin strip of sand and trees in the distance marked the coastline.

He handed the man's hat back to Mr. Myers. "Take him below. See the surgeon looks at him."

"Aye, sir." Myers flagged two of his men to help the sailor below decks.

"Just a moment." Percival stepped between Myers and Trask. He indicated to the Union man. "Are you mad? We can't afford a prisoner."

"You are suggesting we toss him overboard?"

Percival's hard expression anchored onto Thaddeus. "If that's what it takes."

The *Sassacus* man pleaded with a cottony tongue, "I can't swim."

Thaddeus insisted through gritted teeth, "His wounds will be tended to and he will be confined and fed, and released when we arrive in Nassau."

Laird's expression swelled at Thaddeus's mention of their secret destination. He remembered a pair of launches served as *Recluse's* lifeboats. "Then put him in a launch. Give him a canteen and compass, and set him adrift."

"He remains aboard, Mr. Laird, and that's the end of it." He nodded at Laird's two bodyguards close by. "Any more from you and I'll toss you and your twins there in the launch instead."

Thaddeus overheard the Yankee moaning. He was gripping his arm and grimacing. And he appeared more lucid. "Earlier this morning," he asked the boy, "just before two o'clock, there was a great thunder and the whole sky lighted up. What do you know about that?"

The Yankee's misgivings skittered over the stern expressions of Thaddeus's crew circled around him. They would not like what he had to say. "It was a powder ship, sir. The *Louisiana*. She was floated onto the shallows before Fort Fisher so as to blast a great hole out of that damned dirt mound—Your pardon, sir—out of that mound so as General Butler's soldiers could storm through and take her. Sir."

A distant rumbling drifted in with the wind through the open gun ports.

"That would be the bombardment, sir. It's started. Admiral Porter will be readying the fort for the invasion. After the bombardment, launch boats full of soldiers will put ashore and storm Fort Fisher."

"When?"

"Why, tomorrow, sir."

Percival leaped at the reality. "You see, Commander. The invasion! It's our perfect time to sneak through the blockade. All attention will be on the attack. We can't just sit here idling away in petty argument. Let us get underway, now." He clocked his cold condemnation onto the *Sassacus* sailor. "And now he knows our destination. We can't let him go. But we can't afford a prisoner compromising this mission."

"What can he possibly do, Mr. Laird?" Thaddeus measured the sailor's build beneath a uniform that looked three sizes too big for him. "I'm guessing you're happy enough just to be alive. How old are you, son?"

"Sixteen this March, sir. And yes, thank you for saving me. The best Christmas gift ever, sir."

"Christmas?"

Boatswain Myers reminded him, "It's Christmas Eve morning, sir. Tomorrow's Christmas Day."

"I'd completely forgotten." Thaddeus shook a melancholy head. "And the invasion's tomorrow, you say; on Christmas Day?"

"It's General Butler, sir," the boy replied. "They say he doesn't care a wit about holidays."

Myers chuckled with a friendly pat on his friend and commander's back. "Merry Christmas, Commander." The surrounding gunners joined in with some good humored aplomb.

Thaddeus smiled. "We've been so busy I completely forgot."

The *Sassacus* man flinched at the sting that greeted his fingers fiddling after his head wound. He moped at the blood on his fingertips and groused about his predicament. "It figures, sir. We weren't even supposed to be this far south."

"What do you mean?"

"This place, sir—these waters south of the big island."

"You mean Smith's Island."

"I'm not familiar with the island, sir, but this area—it's not our normal post."

Percival interrupted, "Enough of this chatter, Commander Trask. What are you—"

Trask palmed him for silence. "You were saying, son?"

"Our post is north of here, sir. Cape Lookout, it's called."

Trask replied with a fuddled look. "That's halfway up the coast, on the outer banks east of Beaufort. What are you doing way down here?"

"Well, sir, it was us who towed the *Louisiana*—the powder ship, sir—down from Hampton Roads. In Virginia that is, sir."

"Yes, I know where it is."

"We came down mid-month—December eighteenth I think it was—to deliver the *Louisiana* to those that was to tow her onto the beachhead near the fort. That would be the twenty-third, sir. When she blew, that was the signal for the barrage to begin."

"But that noise now—it doesn't sound like much of a barrage to me, just a few cannon."

The boy stared at the sky outside one of open gun ports, showing some confusion. The Confederate was right. It seemed that only a feeble firing was going on. "Don't know about that, sir. Maybe they're just warming things up. Maybe something went wrong." He looked away and said to the deck, "Like went wrong with us."

"What do you mean?"

"We were the fourth ship in the front line of the reserve facing that great Mound Battery. We were to be part of the barrage. All the crew—we were all excited to be part of it." He noted the faces round him, glaring down at him. "Sorry sir. I mean..."

"Don't you mind them, son. Go on."

"Well, sir, there was a fire broke out, a grease fire. We couldn't seem to put it out. As if it were some living beast and fighting us back.

It started to sweep the lower deck and the order was given to withdraw from the line. You see, sir, it was getting too near our powder magazine. If we blew, we would take half the line and the one behind us to the Lord's gate. So the skipper—Captain Calhoun, his name is—he withdrew us from the line and we steamed south. We beat the fire, but two men, sir—they were burned badly. Captain Calhoun—he steers us round that big island and then inland for these shallows. Right worried the men were, sir. We didn't hear a pigeon's twiddle what it was all about. And then Captain Calhoun musters us and reports we had new orders from Admiral Porter himself to anchor south of that island and give hell to that battery at the light house if they gave any protest."

Percival interrupted, "Commander Trask, I'll have a word with you in private, please."

"In a moment, Mr. Laird. Go on boy."

"Well, sir, it's just that these shallows"—He hugged his injured shoulder—"*Sassacus* is a fast girl, sir, but she likes a deeper keel, not these shallows."

Percival growled at Thaddeus from under his breath, "Commander. Your orders! We must proceed."

Laird's tone of voice was not lost on the Yankee. He hovered in confusion at the way the foreign civilian was addressing the Confederate commander. No man speaks in such a tone to a ship's captain like that.

Thaddeus let his attentions slide over his gunners, one by one. He had eighteen of them: three for each of their six newfangled breechloader rifled cannon. The bunch of them were shifting on their feet and passing rustled whispers amongst themselves. Laird's insubordination was not going over well with them.

"Lieutenant Pond."

Idling by one of the gun ports, Pond popped to life. "Yes sir?"

"Order the men, stoke up the Frenchies," he said using the crew's not-so-loving nickname for their coal gas engines. At present, their bow was pointing southeast to the open Atlantic. "Bring her east by south, two thirds, Mr. Pond."

Pond shared a confused look with the mass of gunners. "Sir?"

Thaddeus addressed the lot of them. "This attack needs to be stopped. We will circle round Frying Pan Shoals and come up from the seaward side. We're going to show those fat blockade ships just what *Recluse* is capable of."

His men shared hazy looks at first and then cried a collective "Hurrah!"

Lieutenant Pond boasted a toothy, "Yes, sir!"

Laird protested loudly.

Thaddeus argued, equally loud.

The Yankee prisoner watched them with great alarm. The Confederates were fighting among themselves!

"Your cargo will have to wait, Mr. Laird. Another duty calls: the duty that comes with this uniform."

But when Thaddeus showed his back to Laird, a voice called out, "Sir, watch out!"

Thaddeus spun on his heels and came face to face with the barrel of a revolver in Laird's grip. "Your duty is what it is, Commander Trask. We head for Nassau."

Thaddeus closed on Laird. "Now you listen here!"

Percival thumbed the hammer of his pocket revolver. Its cylinder rotated, lining up a .31-caliber round with its compact four-inch barrel. One of Trask's gunners took a long step at him. "Back!" he ordered. The man froze on his toes, measuring Percival's resolve. "I won't hesitate to shoot," he said. But he could see it in their faces, they didn't believe him. Two more gunners were inching closer to him, testing his bluff. He swung his revolver round before any of them could catch his movement. The revolver's cough slapped thick against the heavy wood interior of the gun deck.

A young voice yelped. Older heads turned.

The *Sassacus* sailor's hand lay clasping his breast, from which blood seeped through his jumper and fingers from the wound in his heart. His questioning pleading eyes hopped from one face to another. His gaze slowed at the end of them and settled on a rotund deck hand. He said nothing. He just looked at the round Confederate with horror on his face. Then without a whimper, he toppled back onto the deck.

Percival swung his aim back at the crew and thumbed another round to the barrel.

A gunner volunteered, "You'll never get out of here, Mister. And every moment you stand here playing at murder gives those Yankees out there more time to find us."

"Order your men to step back, Commander Trask."

Trask stalled.

"Please, Commander." The P-word tasted filthy on Percival's tongue.

"Step back, you men. Give him air."

Mr. Myers was kneeling over the sailor's body. "The boy's dead." He stood up and glared at Laird. His chest seemed to swell twice its size. "Was that necessary?"

Laird's fury flashed to the crumbled blue uniform on the deck and back at Trask's gunners. "We have orders. They must be carried out," he growled, attempting his meanest look on the men. But it wasn't working. It was time to pull his trump card; time to establish his authority or fail in his mission. He retrieved from his breast pocket and extended to Thaddeus the small sealed letter that had accompanied *Recluse*'s new orders.

Thaddeus threw him a confused look. "I thought this was meant for you?"

Laird's look was dark and sinister. "I already know what it says."

"I see." Thaddeus flipped the letter over to open it and halted at the sight of Jefferson Davis's presidential seal frozen in maroon wax on the letter's seam.

"Go ahead, Commander. Open it. I want your men to hear it."

Thaddeus passed a faithful eye over his crew as he broke the seal. Maroon wax crumbles tinkled onto the deck at his feet. When his eyebrows arched not unnoticeably, a crewman said, "What is it, sir?"

He said to Laird, "I'm not sure this is appropriate for the men."

At that, his men stated to grumble.

"Alright, alright, keep it down." He met each of their faces as he read aloud Secretary Trenholm's script reiterating the importance of *Recluse*'s new mission and the critical value of the mysterious cargo she now carried. The crew shuffled uncomfortably at the mention of defeat and exile in the secretary's words.

Thaddeus stumbled as he began the next to final paragraph. "I think this part is for you, Mr. Laird."

"Let them hear it from you, Commander."

Trask swallowed the dryness in his throat. "You are hereby authorized to arrest"—He glanced at his men—"to arrest and...and to confine Commander Trask if he refuses to comply with his orders."

Percival absorbed the men's reactions to the powerful words. New found humility and respect would change their attitudes. He was after all the government's personal representative. But as their collective gazes turned on him, their countenances grew hard and ugly.

Thaddeus choked on the closing sentence. "If you deem necessary, you may apply capital force to assume command of *Recluse*. Successful completion of your mission is paramount."

Percival leaned into the men. "You men hear that. This mission is paramount. You will do as Commander Trask orders you and get us to Nassau." But any ideas he harbored of taking charge were cowering beneath a heightening wall of fear cresting over him, for a wave of murderous intent was etching into the men's features.

Thaddeus wrestled a rising urge to quell Laird's big mouth for good. The opportunity would present itself again, he knew. But right now it looked like he had an edge that Laird wasn't aware of. It may well be that Mr. Laird was aware of the letter's content, but he obviously had not read it as he implied that he did, for below the final paragraph was a single and very potent command.

If safe exit from Cape Fear is impossible, Commander Trask is ordered to...

The words were too astounding to finish.

"What's wrong, sir? Why the fearful look, sir?"

Thaddeus masked his shock beneath a smile. "It's nothing, men." But it wasn't nothing; not that at all. Truth was he wanted to vomit.

How could Secretary Trenholm—a man of such character, a man who had foundered his own fortune for the success of their Great Cause—how could he order such a thing? But he was. And to prove it, his gnarled initials soiled the bottom of the letter. And beneath them, President Davis had approved Trenholm's mandate with a sweeping, angry pen. But the most devastating blow was the familiar flow of ink beneath the president's signature: the signature of his own lifelong friend and confidant, Secretary of the Navy Mallory.

Thaddeus had known Stephen Russell Mallory as 'uncle' since he was a boy. Nineteen thin years separated their births. Uncle Russie, as Thaddeus grew up calling him, could be his older brother. In fact, as Thaddeus had no siblings, Uncle Russie had taken great pleasure filling that gap in Thaddeus's life.

Russie had been the one to introduce him to the sights and sounds and scents of the sea when he was little. And in return, as an adult and just before the war, Thaddeus had taken Uncle Russie's own son, Stephen Russell junior north to New England to ogle over the great whaling ships, even finagled the boy a ride on a whaler making from Nantucket into the Boston yards for repairs.

Fending off the burn of the acids stressing his nauseous ulcer, Thaddeus counted the movements of his fingers folding the letter with its three powerful signatures, and stuffed it in the breast pocket of his tunic over his heart. He dulled his own suffering by measuring the pain on the faces of his crew. Uncle Russie had once said of the hard toiling whaling men: *A captain serves his men before all others. He is the heart and soul of his ship and his crew.*

"I've made up my mind." He closed on Laird and pressed himself against the end of Laird's pistol.

A head taller than Percival, Thaddeus was intimidating. His suddenly icy countenance sent shivers down Percival's back.

Thaddeus could feel the gun's hard barrel quavering against his tunic. "You have a decision to make, Mr. Laird. Shoot me now or put that thing away."

All around them the shoe soles of *Recluse*'s crew searched the deck, feeling for a jump off point. There was no way the foreigner was going to shoot their commander. But if he did; if he were that intent on dying, then they'd oblige him quickly, cutting him down in a messy flash and tossing him out by bits and pieces to feed the sharks.

Only the creaking deck and the gentle clop of dangling wood tackle separated their unspoken words from the silence ringing in their ears. Then something strange just nicked the air outside. Experienced attentions steered past the open portside gun ports and the sloping bulkheads boxing them in from the sea outside. Discomforting looks fluttered amongst them. No. They weren't mistaken. They had all heard it, and beards darkened over blanching faces. Men flinched. And despite all that was promised from their newfangled armor, their practiced instincts won out and they dove fast for immediate cover.

It came fast and it came hard.

The stony silence was thrust aside by the swelling growl of an approaching shell. Something godawful heavy whammed against *Recluse*'s battery. A horrendous boom resounded through her innards.

In all his twenty-eight years, Percival had never heard such an indescribably frightening thunder. It jarred his bones and rattled his teeth, stealing his train of thought.

In the distraction, Thaddeus grabbed Laird's pistol and cried out, "Lieutenant Pond to the pilothouse! Master Stevens below to the engines, please. Lieutenant Meade, your men to their guns. Boatswain Myers, deploy your men. Assist the gunners. Watch for fires."

A chorus of yes, sirs filled the battery.

"Sir!" A crewman was indicating through one of the port gun ports to something outside. "It's a monitor, sir."

Thaddeus hurried over to take a look. Curious, Laird followed behind him.

Percival was too fascinated to be scared. Slithering out from the receding mist beyond the wounded Yankee side-wheeler, *Sassacus*, a monitor to the rescue was clipping a path directly for *Recluse*. Her wrought steel Ericsson's turret, taller than a man by a few feet and disdainfully snubbed as a cheese box on a raft clanked through its heavy cast metal gears. As the turret crept round with calculated intent, tiny bits of near-dawn light pulsed over her damp curved armor, eight inches thick and peppered together by orderly ranks of hammered rivets.

Two malevolent up-and-down slots as soulless as a cottonmouth's stare swung into view. They winked at Thaddeus as if to say: *We have a secret.*

He peered back at them and shuddered. He knew that secret. They weren't yet visible to the eye, but he'd read enough about them—the two Dahlgren shell guns that snuggled inside the turret. One of them, the one on the left, was an enormous fifteen-incher so big around it couldn't even poke its business end out through its own gun port. But the snout of it was there well enough, peering back at him from just inside its port like a prisoner in his cell making dirty faces at passers-by from behind the bars that held him back.

The other one was a different matter, a smaller eleven-incher on the right that had no such problem poking its snout into the open, and was just now sticking its nose out again for another shot at them. Instantly, the black hollow of its barrel belched fire, spitting a shot sent whistling across *Recluse*'s stern.

Thaddeus deduced, "They're bracketing us in their sights."

"Bracketing. What does that mean?" Percival said.

Thaddeus extricated himself from the gun port. "It means, Mr. Laird, that the next shot will pound our broadside." He hollered to his men, "It's about to get noisy in here. Lieutenant Meade, are your gun crews ready?"

"Aye, sir!"

Laird practically screamed, "Your orders are to not engage the enemy under any circumstances!"

"I don't think the enemy knows that, Mr. Laird. Now, if you will, I suggest you stand clear of my gunners. Lieutenant Meade, are you ready to test out these wonder guns of ours?"

"Aye, sir. That we are!"

"On my order then, Mr. Meade, I want you—"

There could never have been in history—nor would there likely ever be one again—as lucky a shot as the third shot that struck *Recluse*. Sixteen pounds of cast iron ball clipped the inside edge of her port forward gun port and whizzed clean through it, exploding the Armstrong rifle behind it and blasting its crew to pieces.

The ball ploughed through two other crews and stained with their blood, it crashed against the sloping oak of the starboard bulkhead. Outside, *Recluse*'s English armor bulged outward from the force. Inside, the deadly shot bounced off the starboard bulkhead, ricocheted off the deck and flew across the battery through five more men, knocking hell out of a second Armstrong gun before slamming against the port bulkhead and spending itself by smashing a hole through the deck.

Men below cried out in horror. A voice called up, "The hull is hit. We're taking water!"

Thaddeus panned his surroundings through a ringing fog, searching for his senses. Men and parts of men lay strewn about the deck. Other men were scurrying about. Equipment and two of their Armstrong guns were shattered from their carriages and were now nothing more than so much trash.

Boom!

The battery thundered again with another impact.

One of the Armstrong guns got off a shot.

Boatswain Myers had his hands to his knees and was looking down a gaping hole in the deck. He looked Thaddeus's way and waved him over. His mouth was moving, but Thaddeus couldn't hear him. Everything was all thick and garbled.

He picked at his ears, searching for the cotton, but nothing was there.

Myers was standing in front of him now. He had a tight grip on him by the arm and was shaking the bejeezus out of him. His words were just scratching through. "...flooding below...Can you hear me, sir?"

Thaddeus shook off his concussion and tried to speak, but his syllables only rumbled incoherent behind his ears.

Myers was frowning at him and shaking his head. "What, sir? You're not making sense, sir. You men," he yelled around him, "keep down the chatter. Someone get the surgeon."

From somewhere in the mess the surgeon's voice reported, "I'm already here, Mr. Myers."

A second Armstrong gun reported. Its gunner's jaw dropped at the result. "Jesus, do you see that? Did we do that?" The enemy cheese box was sporting a third hole clean through her thick turret plate, black smoke billowing from it. "Fire again! We'll kill her sure this time."

"There's another one!"

Boatswain Myers's words were starting to clear. "Commander, the monitor—there's a second one. She's coming fast and we're taking on water below. Can you hear me, sir?"

"I think we've killed one of them, Boatswain Myers," the gunner hollered.

Thaddeus winced behind a nod. "I can hear you now, Mr. Myers. Where is Mr. Pond?"

"Just here, sir." Pond was covered in blood. He knew he was wounded, but from Myers's stare he guessed he was in worse shape than he assumed.

Boom! Boom!

Mr. Meade's Armstrong rifles were returning a steady fire now. The cheers from the men suggested to Thaddeus that Mr. Armstrong's invention was exacting good work upon the enemy.

He hollered over his fading deafness to Mr. Pond, "Jesus, Lieutenant, can you make it?" A flap of Mr. Pond's scalp was folded back on his head, revealing a small bit of white beneath torn membranes.

"Yes, sir," Pond said, gingerly feeling about his wound. "Oh yes, sir, I've had much worse than this."

"Very well then, Lieutenant. Bring us about, west-southwest fast as you can."

"Yes sir!" Pond turned and bounded forward for the pilothouse.

Thaddeus called after him, "I want full speed ahead, Mr. Pond."

Pond hesitated on the three steps leading into the pilothouse. "Our heading, sir?"

"Make for Shallotte Inlet and be quick about it!" But already he could feel *Recluse* heeling away from the turn as she proceeded into her own wake.

"Mr. Meade, close the port gun ports. Prepare your starboard guns; we're coming about. And I want that stern gun at work too."

"Aye, sir. Starboard ports are just open, sir." Meade turned into his gun crews. The place was a disaster area. "Clear those guns. And you! Get that rubbish out of the way."

Thaddeus felt something thick in his palm and realized he still had Laird's pistol. He read the small print stamped into the barrel. It was a nice piece, a Hartford Pocket Model, 1849 Samuel Colt's Manufacture. He peered at the ass-end of the cylinder, notably devoid of any nipples, though the original round ball rammer mechanism was still intact.

"You've had this modified to take premade cartridges. That's an expensive endeavor, Mr. Laird. Secretary Trenholm must be paying you well."

"I do okay," Percival said, extending his hand for his gun back.

"What should I do about the murder, Mr. Laird?"

Percival studied the dead sailor, now covered over with a blanket, detached from any remorse. "He was the enemy."

"He was a boy."

"Boys have been killing each other in this war for four years, Commander."

"He was cooperating! You shot him in cold blood. The law will see that as murder."

"If you must, Commander, go ahead and press the issue when we arrive in Nassau. But I think you will see the tide turn quickly against you. I have influential contacts in Richmond and Nassau. My report to Secretary Trenholm will address how you compromised our mission. It will say that in my best judgement we could neither house a prisoner onboard, nor could we release him; therefore I had to take things into my own hands, painful as it was, because you were unwilling to fulfill your duty as commander of this vessel. Think about it, Commander. Which of us do you think will endeavor at your court-martial? They will see it my way. I assure you."

"The way this war is proceeding, Mr. Laird, you may find that all your high-powered contacts are more fearful for their lives and on the run, and are little concerned for your grievances. Boatswain Myers!"

"Yes sir?"

Thaddeus handed Myers a key on a small ring. "Issue side arms to all the officers and one for yourself. Then I want you personally to keep an eye on Mr. Laird here."

Myers shot Laird a satisfied look. "Yes sir!" Quickly, he ran below decks to retrieve side arms for five men.

Thaddeus opened Laird's revolver and emptied the unspent cartridges from the cylinder into his palm and pocketed them. He seized Laird's arm none too gently and slapped the empty pistol in his hand. He pulled the man close and snarled beneath his breath into his ear, "I don't want to see this thing in your grip again on my ship. If I do, I'll have you shot on the spot. Understood? Now, see the surgeon and make yourself useful with the wounded."

16-CHRISTMAS DAY 1864

The Shallotte River, North Carolina

"This is a hell of a way to spend Christmas Day, sir."

"A hell of a way it is, Boatswain Myers," Thaddeus said from behind his pair of *Chevalier Optics* field glasses.

The monitor in his sights was just passing the mouth of the tributary that fed Turkey Trap Swamp and was creeping northward up the Shallotte River proper just over a mile away. She lay so low in the water that her cheese box turret appeared to glide unsupported in the haze blanketing the river's sheen. Scoffing any need for stealth, the black soot of cheap bituminous coal plumed blatantly from the tall stack marring the sleek flatness of her stern deck. As if sensing him watching her, she slewed her turret slowly round and stopped it dead-on with her guns trained straight up into the swamp, directly at Thaddeus. The wound *Recluse* had inflicted upon her marred her beauty like a mole on a dance hall doxy.

Miles away to the east, behind him and Mr. Myers, the skies rumbled with cannon fire. The invasion the young *Sassacus* sailor had presaged was in full swing. From his vantage point on shore, standing among the skinny yellow pines lining the swamp, Thaddeus could only imagine how many enemy ships itching for a fight were gathering outside Shallotte Inlet at that very moment with their coal boilers stoked and their engine stacks pluming, daring *Recluse* to come back out and show herself.

The swamp water lapping at Thaddeus's boots was black with silt and stunk awfully. He shivered in the bone chilling cold. Behind him *Recluse* lay hidden in a deep cove, invisible to the Yankee's spyglass. He prayed the monitor's skipper had dismissed the reed-choked tributary *Recluse* had traced back into hiding. Deceptive as the thick marsh grass appeared, the tributary might still be just deep enough for the monitor's hull to clear without grounding.

He hoped not. And he hoped the monitor's skipper lacked the intestinal fortitude to try.

The second monitor was nowhere to be seen. It was clear now that the pair of them had been posted on the south side of Smith's Island to contest the lighthouse battery and Fort Caswell at the mouth of the Cape Fear River, when they had sighted *Sassacus*'s distress flare. Spotting *Recluse*, they had pursued her with difficulty, quickly left in her wake by her powerful French engines. With no exhaust from her on which to measure their aim, their shots fell short and wide.

But congratulations for quick wit were premature: he had eight dead and a dozen walking wounded.

Despite listing to starboard from rising water seeping through the cracks in her hull where the monitor's lucky shot had punched her below her waterline, *Recluse* had kept her speed up well as she gassed her way through the Shallotte Inlet.

The waters leading to the inlet were charted four fathoms deep. If the Yankees attempted to give chase, the bottom would rise up fast and grind their keels to a halt in the breakers. Once inside, the Shallotte River snaked wildly through grassy marsh. If the Yankees did get through, they would not dare venture far up river for fear of fouling their screws or running aground.

But Thaddeus's hopes of easy escape had been quickly dashed. The first monitor had sliced her way through the inlet without even slowing. Her heavier sister was not so lucky. Stuck in the sand, she would need the high tide to free her off the bottom.

Recluse traced her escape up the easterly Little Shallotte tributary, a dead end leading deep into Turkey Trap Swamp. Unsure of his next plan, Thaddeus had spied the cove only when *Recluse* was immediately upon it, so well was it hidden.

With God's graces, the Yankee would tire of the ruse and withdraw. For now, he seemed to be idling at the mouth of the tributary. Had he figured them out? Her stack suddenly puked up a thick plume. She was putting her engines up to speed.

Thaddeus watched as she reversed, slowed to a stop, and then swung into a long curve presenting her bow to the tributary. His gut knotted up like a fist.

The monitor was underway slicing her way straight down the path *Recluse* had followed.

The boy's name was Steven Kirby. He was twelve, he said. He lived between the Hewitt farms. His breath plumed in the cold air. His throat hurt awful, he said. He had run as fast as he could through the trees searching for the Confederate ship, he said. The Hewitt's and Kirby's had witnessed *Recluse* slipping into the swamp. When the Yankee ship turned into the tributary to follow, that's when the shore batteries showed themselves and opened up.

"It protects the town further up river," the boy said.

Thaddeus listened to the boy with growing alarm. The second monitor had freed herself up and had chugged through the inlet. The two of them were now playing havoc with the meager shore batteries armed with puny field pieces manned by pensioned reserves.

"But that's not the worst of it, sir," Kirby admitted between breaths, hands on his knees. He felt like puking. "Blue bellies. Horse soldiers. Hundreds of them. Coming up from Charleston."

Thaddeus, Boatswain Myers, and Lieutenant Pond who had brought the boy to them shared troubled glances.

"Everyone knows you're here, sir," Kirby said. "They're expecting you'll whup the Yankee boats and scare off the cavalry."

But Thaddeus knew different. No ironclad on earth was going to fend off any attack stuck in a cove. "Mr. Pond. Break out the weapons, arm the men. I want the wounded off the ship," he ordered. He indicated to the woods. "Get them in there to a safe place,"

"Sir?"

"You heard me." He waved his hand across the pine thickets. "Give me a perimeter of men 500 paces out there. Set up pickets beyond that—say another 200 paces. I want to know about anything that moves out there."

But Pond was no field officer. What was a picket? "Yes sir," he said, without asking.

Thaddeus read Pond's confusion. "The men will know what to do, Mr. Pond."

"Yes sir."

"Mr. Myers?"

"Sir?"

"I need you here with me and Mr. Laird."

"Sir?"

"When the men are deployed, Mr. Myers."

Myers stared after his men with their two-banded Enfields, shorter versions of their three-banded cousins preferred by the army, but better suited for the tighter confines of sea duty. He had been with some of the men most of the war. As they disappeared into the woods with Lieutenant Pond, a bad feeling crept up inside him.

Thaddeus scribbled a note on paper and handed it to the Kirby boy. With it he gave the boy a twenty-dollar gold piece. The boy's eyes grew threefold. "When you get home, you give that to your mother, you hear?" Kirby's little head nodded rapidly. "But first, I want you to take that note to the tall officer you saw leaving just now. You tell him I said he must follow those orders."

"Yes, Captain!" Steven Kirby emulated his best salute and ran like a deer into the trees, and like a deer he vanished instantly.

"Sir?"

Thaddeus offered Myers a pondering look. "A change of orders, Mr. Myers. I've ordered Pond to get the men out of here; to do their best to evade capture and escape back to Wilmington."

Percival Laird couldn't believe his ears. "What the bloody hell?" Standing nearby in the fresh air, he had not uttered a syllable since escaping the stink of blood and guts aboard the ship.

"This war is soon to be over, Mr. Laird."

"Are you out of your mind?"

"I'll not order my men to their deaths."

Percival flushed crimson. "Boatswain Myers, get Lieutenant Pond and have him bring the men back here."

Myers remained stock still, wondering if the Englishman could swim.

Percival practically lathered at the mouth. "Tell him, Commander!"

Thaddeus expelled a loud sigh from between puffed cheeks. "Mr. Laird, your constant harangues are really getting the better of my patience." He reproduced the small letter Laird had had him read to his men and slapped it against Laird's breast, taking especial effort to shove him off balance.

"You said you knew what was in that. Maybe you don't."

Percival moped down at the letter held against his breast. He took it in hand and opened it, and started to read.

"Just go right to the very last sentence. The one just below where it says you can kill me if you have to. It will interest you, I imagine."

Percival's horror fluttered across the final words. "But...but they can't mean this. They can't do this to me."

"It would seem they have, Mr. Laird. Perhaps you want to read it aloud for Mr. Myers? Then you can explain our cargo to him."

Percival studied Myers, all beefy and big. "I don't think that will be necessary."

"Go ahead. Tell him what we've been toting around in our bilges."

Percival fingered the letter, evading Trask's burning gaze. "You've no right to judge me. I may not be a soldier like you, but my life is on the line, just like yours."

"Except you don't face a Yankee prison camp; they'll ship you back to England or set you loose on the streets up north. That letter may say you can shoot me for not trying to make Nassau, but that last line orders me to destroy your cargo if we have no hope of getting there at all."

Boatswain Myers reached for the letter in Laird's hands. "I can read it myself."

Percival snatched the letter away.

"So how much is in those kegs?" Thaddeus said.

"What?"

"And don't tell me those are fifty-nine kegs of powder."

Percival caved under the weight of Trask's indictment. "Three hundred and six—three hundred and sixty-thousand dollars."

Myers's jaw dropped.

"And about $55,000 for the ingots."

"Christ, Commander," Myers said. "That's over four-hundred thousand dollars."

Thaddeus drilled into Laird. "How much are they paying you? Don't give me that look. You're not in this for free."

Percival threw his guilt to the horizon. "Ten percent: thirty-six thousand dollars, in gold." He could feel immediately the heat building in the air between them.

"My men, Mr. Laird, earn $27 Confederate per month...when they get paid...if they get paid."

Trenholm's Treasury hadn't paid his men's wages in two months. Indifferent detachment was not one of Thaddeus's strengths. So he paid them all from his own quickly deflating savings. And of course, none of them knew it. "How far does $27 last, do you think, with bread at five dollars a loaf? No, that's what I thought. You have no idea what—"

The edge of the woods exploded with a furious snapping of brambles. One of Lieutenant Pond's men came bursting through the brambles. "Sir! Enemy cavalry are engaging our pickets." The man had run hard through the trees. Thrashing branches had mapped his countenance with bleeding scratches.

Hadn't Pond read his orders?

"Report!"

"Yankee cavalry, sir." His breath plumed in the chilly air. "They made Old Stores, sir, up at the end of the river."

"The Kirby boy. I sent him to you with new orders for Mr. Pond."

The crewman waxed ashen and shook his head. "They killed that boy, sir."

His words were weak. "The men, sir—he was running through the trees, sir, waving something in his hand at us. The men—they hollered at him to get down; to stay low. He must not have heard, sir. He just kept on hollering for Mr. Pond when the Yankees opened fire. They shot the boy, sir." The man shook his head. "You can't tell me a man can't tell a sprout from a grown man."

Steven Kirby's freckled cheeks popped into Thaddeus's memory, a memory the war had already flooded with the faces of dead men, young and old, that he'd known and commanded.

"Damn them, sir. He was just a boy."

Thaddeus placed an empathetic hand on the man's shoulder.

Steven Kirby never reached Lieutenant Pond, meaning the lieutenant had never gotten Thaddeus's change in plan. Instead of at sea commanding *Recluse*'s rifled cannon, the green navy lieutenant was out there on dry land fighting veteran cavalry with repeaters against his own crew's dated single-fire muskets.

"Those cavalry, sir: I wager they're Sherman's men making their way to the river into Wilmington. There's no one defending that road, sir. And by now both Admiral Porter and General Sherman know we're here. That boy was right, sir. Everything's coming apart. The men are in a mean mood, sir. They think the farmers gave us up to the enemy."

Thaddeus could hardly blame the starving people giving them away. They were tired, hungry, sick with disease, wishing for the end to come and forget the whole mess and just recover what shambles were left of their lives.

Thaddeus barely heard his own realization slip through his lips. "(It's over.)"

The men weren't sure they heard right. "Sir?"

"How many? The Yankee cavalry: how many are there?"

"A company at least of skirmishers. Maybe a hundred men. Damned carbines they got, too, sir. And in the cover of those trees, we got nil chance, sir."

Thaddeus snatched the letter back from Laird. "You'll report back to Lieutenant Pond. Order him to withdraw pickets."

"Yes sir!"

The man's chest puffed. He was no foot soldier, but from behind his cannon back aboard ship, they'd make a mess of the Yankee horse soldiers and blast that confounded cheese box waiting for them at the mouth of the river.

He stamped his feet for warmth, tracing the path of Thaddeus's pencil across the back of the letter. New orders! He could practically read them without seeing. They'd scrap their way back out to sea, past the monitors, and return to the Cape and fight the decisive battle. It was etched all over his commander's face. He could see it, thank God!

Thaddeus folded the letter and handed it to the man. "This is for Mr. Pond's eyes only."

"Report back to *Recluse*, sir? Ready her for battle, sir?"

Thaddeus slipped him a vague smile. "Take that to Mr. Pond, fast as you can."

17-MUCK, ROCK SALT & KISSES

The pebbly clay beside Gemma's exhausted Ford spilled away from the road's edge and disappeared beneath a scraggly carpet of sunbaked grass monopolizing on the only bit of ground that separated a starving yellow pine woods from the crackled asphalt road that passed by the old woman's property.

The ground's hardness greeted Gemma's first steps with jabs at the soft soles of her worn-but-comfy Mary Janes. She was the first to reach the dry grass. She lifted her ankle up and slapped at some itching that started soon as she stopped moving. Qeb was messing with the back of her car.

"What ever are you doing? Come on."

The car's trunk closed with a hollow *whomp!*

"Alright already," he said.

She watched him with fading patience as he strapped a long black tube no fatter than a broom handle to his forearm. At the bottom end of the tube, hanging down to his ankles, there was a circular ring that looked to her like a big Mercedes Benz hood ornament. A little square boxy thing was attached to the rod up near Qeb's hand. He was walking her way when he stopped in his tracks and commenced to twiddling with the little box.

"Will you quit?"

"I'm just making a setting," he said.

"Why can't you just leave it? You're going to trip on that thing."

"I want to bring it. Maybe we'll find something."

The two of them wormed their way into the woods separating the road from the estuary. The yellow pines closer to the road and more accustomed to freshwater soil, quickly abdicated ground to a mob of red cedars that were perfectly happy with whatever water God would give them, saltwater or fresh.

The ground beneath them descended from a firm milk chocolate to a mushy espresso-black. With progressive steps, their soaked shoes sank deeper into a gushy roux of rotted fauna and dead things.

"Oh! My feet are soaked!" Gemma tugged at her foot, sunk up to her ankle. The gush finally gave, but kept her shoe. "Ugh!"

"Are we whining?" Qeb teased.

"You hush up!"

"It stinks out here," he noticed, as she fished with her hand into the muck. "And these stupid brambles: I keep snagging on them."

Gemma beat the muck and won back her shoe. "And now who's whining?" she said. She took off her other shoe and slapped the both of them against his chest—"Here. Hold these."—and forged ahead barefoot, on her own.

Holding her shoes in his free hand, Qeb waved his detector after her with his other hand. "But I'm already carrying this." But she only faded further into the thickets. "Hey. Wait up." He hung her shoes on a bush and chased after her with his detector tangling on every branch he tried to miss.

Somewhere up ahead of him, Gemma called out, "It's the cove. We're here!"

The squishiness between her toes was cool. The air was slight. The brambles had withered away to salt marsh hay and dense needle rushes. When Qeb drifted into the corner of her eye, she noticed, "You're scratched and bleeding."

"And I'm itching like crazy." He palmed his neck and grimaced at the thin wash of red stain on his fingers. The soil beneath his heels collapsed and gushiness crept over the necks of his sneakers. "I think I'm sinking." He teetered on unsure legs and tumbled backwards off balance.

"Whoa!"

Gemma snatched his free arm. "Shh! You're gonna get us caught."

"As opposed to you charging through the brush like a bull?" he said, straightening himself up.

"I did no such thing."

"Did too. And you just hollered back at me loud enough for the whole world to hear."

She turned away from his jibes and took in the view, standing ankle-deep in wetness. Indifferent cordgrass all round her poked up through a thin veil of lime algae over snoozing water. From beyond the grass, the deeper cove glowered in dirty-brown and gunmetal blue. A dense line of cordgrass and rushes bordered the far side of the cove. And beyond them, a severe lawn—maybe an acre—was home to three very large trees. At the far end of the lawn was a thick wood. The lawn ended on the right with thick brush bordering the estuary.

Qeb sloshed into the water beside her, not caring about his waterlogged sneakers.

She took his arm in her hand and squeezed. "This is Tim-Lee's cove. It has to be." She indicated out to where the water was bluer and snaked through thick patches of man-high reed grass. With condolence in her voice she guessed, "I suppose that's where they found him. Out there."

She dropped his arm and stepped out up to her knees in the cove.

"Gemma," he said.

She wasn't there.

"Gemma!"

"What?"

"We can't stay long."

"I know. But this is it, I'm positive." She skimmed the water's surface with her finger tips. "This is where the manuscript finally brought my brother."

Qeb could swear the water washed to pitch black when she said that.

She heard a sloshing behind her and felt his touch on her arm. She looked back at him and smiled. "I'm okay."

"Are you sure?"

"Mm hm."

"Okay. Look, I'm going to give this thing a try, okay?"

"Okay."

Her gaze reached out to the small white clapboard house across the cove. It had one big ground floor with a small upstairs; screened porches, front and back. The front porch had a screen door on the side with three short steps down to the yard. Just to the right of it, a single window, the old type that let all the heat out in the wintertime, was lighted from the inside. A second window farther down and another in the upstairs were both dark.

Whoop! Whoop!

Gemma jerked round. Qeb was waving the end of his contraption back and forth over the ground. "What ever are you doing with that thing; and what is it?"

He was twiddling with the knobs on the box again. "This *thing* is a metal detector. I'm just adjusting the sensitivity."

"Well why ever does it have to be so loud?"

He turned something till it clicked. "All done." He spied after the house for movement. There was no sign of life. "Maybe she's not home. I'm gonna look around some more, see how this thing does." He had just begun to sweep the detector over the grass when distant springs squawked and a door slapped against its jamb.

Gemma whispered loud as she could, "It's her!"

A faded flowered house dress draped easily over the thick figure of a woman in her later years. A small bag dangled from her hand in one arm.

Breathless, they watched her amble from the house across the lawn to an opening in the brush by the estuary's edge at the back of her yard. A gaggle of geese met her expectantly, honking and gathering round her. She was talking to them, her words only slight from so far away. She began tossing something to them from the bag. Jealous seagulls swooped in for their share and a cackling frenzy ensued. The woman laughed gleefully and ordered them all to behave themselves and share.

Qeb's knees felt like concrete by the time the bag in her hand was empty.

The woman said something to the flock and waved goodbye. Slowly her thick ankles picked up her sandaled feet and carried her back toward the house. Halfway there she stopped and stood in the yard as if she had heard something.

Her head turned their direction.

"Shit. She sees us," Qeb whispered.

"Just shush."

"She's looking right at us!"

"Just stay still."

The old woman's attention drifted back to the estuary that fed the cove. The geese were loitering, hopeful for the possibility of seconds. The gulls had moved on for better pickings elsewhere. An endless stretch of minutes passed before she turned back to the house and headed inside. The side door of the front porch screen door slapped closed behind her.

"Whew!" Qeb said. "That was way too close."

The sloshing out in the cove was almost instant. Gemma was navel deep in the water, past the cordgrass wide out in the open for anyone to see. Her tank top was off. She was topless with nothing but her jeans on.

He freaked out. "What are you doing?"

She pointed to the deeper water. "That's where Tim-Lee found whatever it was he saw. I'm going in there to take a look."

"Are you nuts?"

Consternation filled her face. "What is wrong with you?"

"With me, nothing; with you, maybe a few things. Shit, it's her again. She's back."

Gemma turned to see, but from where she was, only the top of the house was visible beyond the cordgrass on the other side. "What's she doing?" she said, working herself breast deep into the water.

"I don't know."

"Just make sure she doesn't come over here."

"How am I supposed to do that?"

But she was gone. She'd slipped under the water.

He squatted in the grass on the edge of the cove, sucking air through his teeth when the chilly water seeped up through his pants and clutched his nuts.

The old woman turned on the water spigot below the kitchen window. A faint metallic yawn warbled from her watering jug as it filled up. She shut off the spigot and ambled somewhat arthritically round the back of the house and busied herself watering a strip of autumn flowers tracing the porch.

Gemma popped up for air, taking in a loud gasp. The splash of the water sounded like thunder. Before Qeb could warn her, she disappeared again beneath the surface.

Crazy girl!

The old woman rounded the far end of the back porch and disappeared. Cautious, but getting bored, Qeb crouched low and chanced sweeping the cove's edge with his detector. He passed it over the thinner grass and shallow water. A small tick registered on the detector's control. He swept the coil back over the spot.

Tick-tick-tick!

He slipped the end of the detector under the water.

Tick-tick-tick-tick-tick!

He sank the coil deeper, just into the rotted leaves carpeting the bottom.

"Qeb!" Gemma was back up.

Startled, he jerked round and hissed, "Don't do that!"

Treading water, she said, "There's something down here."

The he noticed. The old woman was back. She must have heard: she was practically looking right at him. Not paying attention, he let the detector's coil sink deeper into the muck on the bottom. The reader went haywire, barraging the air with rapid fire ticking. His panicking fingers fumbled with the controls.

"Stupid audio volume!" His horrified eyes flashed to the house.

The old woman shuffled a few steps toward the cove and squinted. Her fading vision passed over the grass and the water, first left, then right.

He jabbed a finger at the house and told Gemma, "Get under."

Instead she said, "Are you listening?" not bothering to whisper. "There's something down here."

The old woman dropped her watering can and double-time shuffled her edematous calves back up into the house through the back porch, trailed by the echoes of her clomping orthotic shoes.

"She went inside. Get out of there. We got to go. Now!"

The clomping shoes were back.

"Oh shit! She's got her shotgun."

"I need another look."

"Are you nuts? Get out of there."

A gravelly voice hollered, "Who's out there?"

Qeb toed behind him, feeling his way back to drier ground. His anxiety stayed glued to the woman's dress pattern drifting closer behind the brush just across the cove. Something hard that wouldn't give snagged his sneaker. He struggled, wiggled his shoe free, but tripped and slapped his detector's coil against a stone.

The thing howled like a goose in protest.

The woman bellowed, "There you are! What are you up to, you skinny prick?"

Gemma thrashed her way out of the water and through the cordgrass with her jeans clinging to her skin.

"Who is she? What are you two doing skinny dipping in my cove?"

Gemma grabbed her tank top and wrestled it down over her chest.

Qeb snatched her wrist, "Come on!"

Pock!

The brush just ahead of them shagged to the rhythm of raining pebbles.

Qeb yelped. "She's shooting at us. What's so funny?"

"You just go," Gemma said, pushing him on. Her bare feet stumbled in gush and danced over prickly twigs as they went.

A passing bush grabbed at Qeb's detector. He flagged his arm fighting to free it from the bush's grip. "Stupid thing!"

"Just leave it," she said, strangely jovial.

"This dumb strap on the arm cuff—it won't let go."

Pock!

Pebbles rained through the cedars, barely over their heads.

The cuff's Velcro strap finally gave. Gemma grabbed him and pulled him through the cedars.

He tripped all over himself trying to keep pace. "Please tell me," he called after her between gasps for air, "what's so funny when we're being shot at?"

When they reached the friendly protection of the yellow pines bordering the road, she stumbled to a stop and fell with her back against a tree. Her belly jiggled in the throes of humor.

"My shoes. You lost my shoes."

He looked around them. "I hung them on a branch. They're around here somewhere."

She rested her head against the tree and rolled mischievous invitation his way.

"You're crazy, you know that?" he said, checking the cut on his wrist where the Velcro took a bite. It was okay, just a scratch. His attention drifted beyond his wound to her navel and slid up her body. Her nipples were hard beneath her thin, soaked tee.

"I dare you, Qeb Morgan. Tell me that didn't excite you."

"It scared the shit out of me!"

"Not even a little bit?"

"She was shooting at us. And you were laughing the whole time. There's something not right up here with you, is there? You're not really insane or something, are you? I mean maybe that's why Tim-Lee never told me about you."

"You jerk," she said, slapping him playfully on his shoulder. "I just can't help it. I've always been like that, since forever. I mean, one time when I was little, a bunch of us threw snow balls at a Catholic school bus. The driver, he stopped and he let all the kids out after us. I remember I ran as fast as I could. But I couldn't stop laughing."

She rolled her head sidelong at him with a winsome smile. "Ever try running when you're laughing? Your belly hurts so bad, and you can't hardly breathe." She rolled her head back and looked up into the high branches. "They almost caught me." She took a deep breath that pronounced the topside curve of her size-A breasts.

He tried not to stare. He wasn't doing so well. He shifted on his feet, hoping she wasn't seeing the rise in his pants. "You're really weird, Gemma Polk. Look, now you got me laughing." He almost peed his pants.

She took another breath. "You see. There's hope for you after all." Her head leaned forward away from the tree. Her expression grew serious. "I saw it, Qeb; what Tim-Lee found down there. And it's not some sunken truck like those people said, neither."

"Why hasn't anybody else seen it then," he said, checking the feel of the cuts in his neck.

Her breathing was calming down. "Maybe the hurricane. Maybe the flooding washed all the junk off of it. How should I know?" Her eyes fixed hard on him. "There's a way inside."

"You went inside it? You could have drowned."

"Oh! Anyways, there's a square hole in the side—will you stop picking at those cuts?"

"They sting." He searched beyond the threes. Her car was just barely visible. "I think there's a kit in the trunk for—"

She took his wrist and pulled him to her. She passed her tongue over the red scratch on his wrist and then licked the ones on his neck. A rush zipped all through him. He hid behind his eyelids and groaned with relief.

She whispered into his ear, "Is that better?" and peered past him at the path back to the cove. They were okay. The old lady wasn't coming.

She cupped his head in her one hand and nibbled his ear lobe. She stepped back and lifted her tank tee up over her head and let it fall to the ground. A gentle swath of soft freckles trickled down the slopes of her breasts into her slight cleavage.

"My clothes are soaked. I'll catch my death."

"Wait here. I'll go get you some dry—"

She pulled him back to her. "Shut up," and slipped her tongue between his startled lips.

His heart raced like a frightened thoroughbred. His loins weighed heavy with the rush of blood. The scent of her slipped inside him and tickled his tummy. He tried to pull away, confused what to do. Her grip on his wrists was gentle, but firm.

He moaned, "We could have died back there."

"It was only rock salt, silly." She took both his hands in hers. "Can't you feel it—the rush—the excitement? It's like—" Her expression hesitated. "Oh, and you're going to love this."

She drilled two fingers in the small coin pocket of her wet jeans, skin-tight against her figure. "Close your eyes. Now hold out your hand. You can open them now."

Qeb's pulse tumbled at the sight of the gold coin in his palm, about the size of a quarter. "You found this back there...down there?"

"Mm hm."

"But how did you see with all the weeds and mud and junk?"

"There was a clear spot. There's something down there on its side. And this was just there, lying in the sunlight on the side of whatever that is down there." She shrugged, girlish. "Just lucky, I guess. Or, maybe it's a sign?"

He felt a warm tingle down where he hung freely. Just beyond the coin's gleam in his fingertips, her petite breasts were calling out, begging for his touch.

"It's just like the coin Tim-Lee sent you. That must mean..."

"It means my brother found the ship. It means it's down there, Qeb, in that cove."

He twiddled the coin between his fingers. It was almost like new. "It's amazing," he said. His focus drifted past the coin to her. "You're amazing."

Her eyes glimmered like jewels in candlelight. Her breathing was paced and sensuous.

"I really have to make love to you."

She coaxed him closer to her and said back, "Well, it's about time."

18-DEMISE

Percival Laird's head swirled, awhirl in confusion. His was such a stupidly simple assignment; so simple in fact that his ego and self-worth had been offended at first by his apparent demotion from the gilded halls of high government to the chilly outdoors and the mud and muck of a common teamster.

Get the kegs from Richmond down through the Yankee lines and to Wilmington and load them aboard the best ship available. Slip past the blockade and slink across the sea to Nassau. Four days. Could it be that tough? Then arrive and deliver the kegs to Secretary Trenholm's waiting man and he'd be done with it, paid richly for his services. No more worries for the rest of his life.

And yet here he stood watching his dream of affluence degenerate into an appalling calamity and going all to shit in the matter of one stupid day. He stewed in his own rage alone on the shore, ordered by Trask off the ship for his own safety. And alone he was, for his bodyguards had hit the woods running to save their skins.

It was just as well: the thing he needed most at the moment was distance between himself and the self-important commander.

Percival paced the brink of dry ground bordering *Recluse*'s hideaway cove. The crisp reports of federal cavalry carbine fire echoed through the thick and dormant yellow pines, answered by the throaty musket reports fired from Trask's sailors receding into the woodlands surrounding Turkey Trap Swamp.

He struggled to measure the erratic gunfire. The reports of the muskets were fading. The Yankees were pushing hard on Trask's seamen, herding them farther away. That might be good at first, maybe. Steer the bastards clear of the ship so they don't discover it. But there was a problem, something the insubordinate Trask had overlooked.

They'll never make it back here. You're never getting out of here.

Percival swung his gaze over *Recluse*. This cove—no one of any intelligence would have tried to escape those enemy monitors by backing themselves into a corner like this cove. But Trask—he knew. He had been keeping tabs on the reports from Wilmington of the federal advances across the North Carolina border. He'd have to have known they'd be this far by now. Trask also had to know his seamen were no match for battle-hardened cavalry.

Percival cupped his ears, fending off what his conscience was screaming at him.

Trask had armed and ordered his men ashore to save their lives. They'd either evade the federals and run, or be captured. But no such army fast on the heels of victory could afford the time to feed and tend to disheveled prisoners. Trask's men would be paroled instead of jailed because the war was as good as over already. And Trask knew it.

He deliberately sabotaged your mission. The damned man is a traitor.

And who was to say his plan had worked? Infantry skirmishers—the front line feelers of the main army—would be trailing the cavalry, foraging and snooping for trouble. Any time now, blue sack coats might be popping through the thickets.

Percival shifted on his feet. Thirty-six thousand dollars: ten years' income. It was the pay that was waiting for him in Nassau. Such money he could parley into a life's fortune. At least he had his gold.

His eyes egged onto *Recluse*.

My gold!

All $3,000 of a small fortune he had saved in Richmond was locked in a trunk he had had his teamsters bring along with them. It was all he had that he could claim was his. And right now it was thirty feet from his reach on that damn scow.

It's your own stupid fault.

He should have run. He should have fled the capital with all the rest of the rats and the cowards when he had had the chance. No one would have held it against him. The senators, the congressman, even the general staff were all looting the coffers and clattering off for the hills.

Who would blame you?

But no, not him. He had to stand his post at Secretary Trenholm's side.

A tingling attack of panic swarmed over him, trampling his confidence and taking prisoner his calm and his cool. Instantly, it looked like four years of head-strong struggle and strife would stand for naught. Four years within the halls of the highest levels of the Confederate government kowtowing to scoundrels, pandering to people whom he detested, and socializing with hillbillies in silken attire in his strivings for a position of influence in the future and independent Confederacy. And now, for all his patience and commitment, it looked like he would have not a single paltry farthing to show for it.

A queer ringing blossomed in his ears, giving pause to his runaway fears. It was eerily quiet. His gaze poked upward at the pines overhead. Grey and leafless branches, scraggly and cold and creaking against one another in the gloomy winter wind, returned his questioning glances with "So what?" expressions.

The gunfire—it was gone.

Recluse, all angles and menacing, tugged his attention back on her.

She didn't like him. Percival could feel it, the way she was chilling his blood. She watched him there, as if she could read what was chinking away over the worn gears of his overstressed and underappreciated mind. Truth was she frightened the hell out of him.

He slipped a sidelong glance at the far side of the swamp. Out in the water, reed grass thick as a rug and all brown and bowed over in death, teased him with the idea of running across them to the far side and escaping the doom of his impending poverty.

Go ahead. If the icy water doesn't kill you, she'll slither out after you and drown your ass.

But the half frozen muck beneath him sucked in protest each time he lifted his feet.

He was fucked. There'd be no future for him in the rubble of post-war America. He had conspired in the American disunion for his own monetary gain and political position. After the war, it would be worse. His former Richmond connections, seeking new office with their Yankee overseers, would receive him with disdain. Southern Society would abhor him as a loathsome opportunist. And were he to seek his future in the North, his British heritage would make him a target of suspicion amongst the hypocritical descendants of colonial traitors to King George.

Percival's anguish evoked memories of sooty, sprawling Liverpool. He sneered, disgusted by thoughts of failure; of being cajoled by his formerly envious lickspittle peers back in Britain. His only alternative it would seem was a gloomy exile in Canada, Her majesty, Queen Victoria's desolate tundra.

Palming a tree, he voided his stomach.

You're pathetic.

He straightened himself.

That's your answer then: Canada?

He primped himself with a clean hanky.

You killed that sailor...

Percival stiffened. He'd completely forgotten. Where was his remorse? Had it been that easy? He'd taken a life, flippantly, without forethought and wasn't feeling anything for it. He searched his formative years—all the blather berating murder as venal sin. It was all tripe.

He paused. Somewhere down in the ship's bowels, Trask and his boatswain were doing what navy men did to scuttle their own ship. Whatever they were doing, it was working. Water was edging over her stern. She would take his gold and his secret cargo down with her to the muddy bottom.

Maybe that's not a bad thing. Look around you.

The woods surrounding *Recluse* in the cove had quieted. The Yankees had never shown.

They're not coming. They have no idea you're here.

That was true. As far as the world was concerned, no one knew anyone or anything was here. It was a stinking swamp, so why would they? And Trask's crew: if they were captured, they were army conscripts and civilian volunteers. They weren't wearing navy uniforms that might stir suspicion.

Percival edged up to the water. The Yankee monitor down at the mouth had given up the chase and had withdrawn. They were truly alone.

No witnesses.

A swarm of indefinite possibilities hummed fresh in Percival's imagination. As a fascinated boy in Liverpool, he'd witnessed sunken boats and lost equipment retrieved from the bottom of the Mersey River, and once with his father on the English coast. Times were changing. Men were finding ways to work underwater. Former impossibilities were becoming possible now.

Percival shed his malaise behind a smirk.

There you are, then: a solution to your problem.

His creative juices were flowing again. Catastrophe fluttered away like ash in a breeze. Percival studied the woods. They were secluded. Thick pines lined the opposite bank. No homes. No sign of life. He had his answer. He would purchase the land, own the cove and with it *Recluse's* wreck and her secret.

A sudden motion startled him. The surface at *Recluse*'s freeboard effervesced. The water buoying her simmered violently. Brown swamp water swept over her stern deck.

Of course, he would have to remain mum for a time after the war.

But Secretary Trenholm knows. He would hardly forget.

In the postwar recovery, Trenholm's minions would most certainly come looking for him.

Maybe. Maybe not.

The war had ruined many fine fortunes. The recovery would ruin even more as the Yankees restructured the South. If they caught up to him, Secretary Trenholm would be imprisoned along with the rest of President Davis's administration. They'd all be too preoccupied with recovering their freedoms to care about him.

They may forget, but Trask could remind them, or he might come back here himself.

Trask was the last impediment to Percival's plan. No. There was the boatswain, too. He had two impediments.

Recluse's fore and aft decks were gone. Her armored battery rolled slowly to starboard as she settled into the swamp. Acrid water spilled into her open gun ports, the growing weight of it tugging at her, pulling her down, away from the surface. Her port bulwarks rolled upward from the water, reaching out to Percival, clinging to life, hoping. Her innards rumbled with muffled commotion. The shattered cannon were tumbling against her sinking bulkheads.

Percival rippled with excitement. He had never before witnessed such a thing as a ship dying. It was...magnificent! And only suddenly so because—because why? Because his future was not lost after all: he had a plan, a plan that could work. One that meant things falling from his reach right now, here in this stinking swamp, would be reachable once again.

With a little help from the right class of people hardship need not to be his fate after all. Poverty might sully his doorstep for a short time after this ridiculous war, but it would never cross his threshold. Oh, quite the contrary. For before him now, sinking into safe keeping was his own windfall of riches: the exiled treasury of a fallen nation.

Recluse shoved her starboard bulk deep into Turkey Trap Swamp's sodden, mushy bottom, built up over tens of decades from soft leafy decay. The last vestige of her sloped port battery settled nearly flat with the water's surface. *Recluse* protested, hanging there for a half-dozen seconds with the water lapping over her armor, nudging her down to her final rest. With a collapsed sigh of the last air within her, she gave in and receded out of sight.

Percival remained glued to the black water, tracing every swirling eddy. Watching. Waiting.

Maybe God has saved you the trouble.

Still, he listened closely for movement. But dammit to hell, his heart was rendering such a ridiculous racket hammering his chest.

There! There, in the water. Burbling bubbles.

Percival snuck his hand down into his trousers pocket.

Nobody knows you're here. Keep your senses and this will be quick and easy.

He stroked the soothing smooth grip of his revolver, a five-year-old Colt's Revolving Pocket Pistol that had never failed him in a pinch, and extricated it from his specially sewn deep pockets, stitched with just the right girth and depth for the purpose of concealment and easy retrieval.

With a boiling rush, Boatswain Myers broke the surface first, gasping for air. Unaware of Percival's presence, he jerked first left, then right, searching for signs of Trask.

Percival raised his pistol and aimed for the back of the boatswain's big head. His aim fluttered. Myers wasn't looking. This would be easy.

Can you really shoot him in the back? Percival affirmed his aim. *Of course I can.*

He squeezed the trigger. The Colt spat a deadly report. Blood exploded from behind Myers's left ear. Myers rolled round. His eyes, enormous in their shock, settled on Percival, their glimmer already gone, and he sank beneath the water.

Thaddeus Trask broke the surface with mouth agape, squalling for his breath. Fresh air flooded his hungry lungs. His thigh seared with pain. He felt around himself. His trousers were torn. His fingers fumbled over a gash in his leg. He remembered now. He had gotten tangled in some rope and cannon and had had to wrestle himself free. The cut was deep, and from the feel of it, it wasn't going to be pretty when he saw it.

"Myers!" he called out. "Boatswain Myers!"

But Myers was nowhere to be seen.

Three times, Thaddeus forced himself beneath the water into the darkness, probing, feeling, searching, until his body gave out and his hope surrendered to the reality he'd lost his friend. He must have gotten tangled. They hadn't counted on the cannon shifting and sliding down the sloping gun deck all around them. But he was sure he saw Myers making for the surface.

Something wasn't right.

Thaddeus's hands reached up and opened the water's surface above him. He poled out into the open air and tread water. He foddered around with his feet wondering if he might feel *Recluse* down there beneath him. How deep could it be here, so far into the swamp?

But no, she wasn't there. She was just too far down. Nausea crept up and took hold of him. How would he explain his actions to his family? What would he tell Mallory? How could he face his own men— Lieutenant Pond? His beautiful gunship: his country's last hope for shattering the blockade and the hope of a renewed chance at independence. Without so much as a single shot at the enemy, he had scuttled those hopes.

But you had to do it. Whether it was here or out at sea, you know you had to sink her.

Yes, he did. Ever since that foreigner, Laird, had shown up things had begun to feel not right. And where was Laird, by the way? The intensity of his orders with their tone of sheer panic: it was all too much of a rush job. And when they had passed Smithville and none but the watch was awake, he had sent Myers below to do some snooping. When Myers had returned to him in the dead of night with the gold coin in his palm, everything blew up in Thaddeus's face.

He and his ship of volunteers—all of them hungry and all of them still aching for a fight—they had all been whored along with his country's hopes of victory, sold out to the highest bidders for the self-interests of the soon-to-be exiled Confederate government.

He had had to do it. And the sheer chance of smacking into that ship and being run into this swamp had come with God's good graces. To sink her at sea meant possibly drowning some of his crew. After all, their two gigs were too small to hold everyone. At least now, his crew had their lives and their futures.

And you have yours.

Yes he did. He had done what was right in his heart and his gut, and he would go home now and rebuild his life in the wake of this godawful war.

A noise in the trees snatched his attention out of his daydream. Pond. His men. He had to find them. If they had followed his orders to the letter he'd catch up with them at Fort Johnson. They'd get their orders there, if there were anyone there to give them.

But he couldn't do it. What if Myers were down there, still alive, just trapped in a pocket of sour air? He would be telling himself right now that any minute his commander would find him and get him out.

Thaddeus cursed himself and forced himself once again beneath the water. He fingered his way through a gun port into the sooty darkness. Stilling himself, he tried to listen in the water for anything telling him Myers was trapped in a bubble of air somewhere. His throat's apple started tightening. As he kicked himself further inside, he drove his noggin so hard against something he coughed up half the air in his lungs.

The sting was horrendous.

He forced himself deeper, grinding his molars against the urge to gasp.

But there wasn't any air pocket. There wasn't any sign of Myers. He had killed his friend. He could have scuttled the ship himself, but he insisted on Myers's help, and now Myers was dead for it.

Hopelessness and his own desperate need for life forced Thaddeus back to the surface. His starving chest was threading up his throat reaching for the spot of air hiding in his mouth. He searched the sloping side of the gun battery now directly overhead with his fingertips and his wits for the gun port that was his way out, found it and pulled his way up through it the way his lungs were pulling his insides up after them.

Again he broke the surface, this time teasing the delirious edge of blacking out.

As his blood cells gobbled oxygen with a vengeance, he meditated on his own good fortune. *You will survive this war.* He would forget failure and go west, maybe San Francisco. *Yes, San Francisco!* And there he would captain a merchantman to the Far East. He smiled at the thought of it. He would find himself an exotic Asian woman, the ones he had heard about from clipper sailors. He would marry her, buy a tall house on one of those steep hills he had seen once when traveling. They would raise a gaggle of kids. *Daughters, all of them.*

Five of them! He would pamper and spoil them, and make them difficult for their future husbands. God help them.

A muffled cough startled Thaddeus from his fantasies.

The ridiculous smile sagged from his face. He wasn't exactly sure why, but the hackles on his neck were beating like drum sticks. He was suddenly and very uncomfortably aware of his vulnerable situation. Slowly, he shifted round in the water and squinted at confusing globs of color. He wiped the silt from his sight enough to make out that there was a sole figure standing on the shoreline. He rubbed the goo from his sight again, harder this time, and focused.

Slowly, the shadowy image washed into disturbing clarity.

After so many years of war, the end of a six-shooter pointed his way was nothing new or especially unsettling to Thaddeus. But what sent the last chill of his life through his body was the stony expression of loathing and determined murder in the eyes of Percival Laird behind the cold, cocked hammer of a gun.

"But you've got to believe us. Look at that coin, Uncle Frank. Will you just look at it? Gemma found it down in the cove." Qeb gave her a second-thought glance. "And...and there was something else. She saw something."

"You were foolish to pull a stunt like that," Frank chastised. "You could have gotten yourself killed, just like your brother."

"Uncle Frank!"

"And you. Why aren't you back at your dig? Why are you still down here?"

"I'm—I'm helping Gemma finish Tim-Lee's work."

Frank threw his hands in the air. "I can't talk any sense to him. Maybe you can."

Hillary palmed her chest. "Me? He's your nephew."

Qeb threw her a face crumbling with penitence. "Dr. Bascombe. I—I shouldn't have lost my temper like that, the way I did."

"Never mind that. Miss Polk, I don't expect you to understand. But you, Qeb—achieving for your doctorate brings with it a heavy burden of responsibility. You should know better. In our science it takes more than just coincidental evidence like that coin to validate a hypothesis."

"But this is more than just some hypothesis."

Hillary chucked him an unconvinced chin.

"I don't believe this. You sound like Uncle Frank: like...like you've just given up."

"Is that what you think of me, Qeb; that I've given up?" Frank said.

"Seems like it. I mean, where's your passion? Aren't you even curious why there's a Mexican coin on the bottom of a cove in North Carolina?"

"There could be a hundred reasons how it got down there."

Gemma interrupted, "Dr. Bascombe. You're right. Maybe I wouldn't understand. But I do know you're one of the most respected marine archaeologists today. I can't believe you got there by doubting your way through evidence. I read about you and Dr. Hempstead. You stood by him when other people were laughing at him."

Gemma gambled a couple steps closer. "But—and please, forgive me—it seems to me that you and Dr. Morgan are the ones doing the laughing this time."

Hillary shot Frank a look.

"Maybe we should tell them?"

"Tell us what, Uncle Frank?"

"About the plate your father brought up."

"What's that thing got to do with any of this?"

"I don't know where to start, so I'll just get to the point. That plate is one of dozens lying on the bottom. They're all over that wreck we found. Hillary and I have been doing some research. Well, her mostly—with some people in England who've been very helpful. Anyway, it seems it's no coincidence those plates are strewn all over what we now know is the wreck of the *Hermione*."

Gemma gripped Qeb's arm. "Did you hear that, Qeb? It's her."

Hillary said, "Then you've heard of her?"

"Peter Howe's manuscript," Qeb said. "Before he worked in the Beery Shipyard on the *Recluse*, he was a stoker in *Hermione*'s fire room."

"Oh my!"

"Yeah, and he writes about her running aground, too; and that there weren't any survivors. And get this. In the 1960's he returned to Wilmington to die. He wanted his ashes put to sea where she wrecked."

"So, he knew where she went down?"

"I guess so, since he was on her when she wrecked."

"Can we see this manuscript?" Hillary said

"I already showed it to Uncle Frank." Qeb tossed Frank a dirty look. "He wasn't interested."

"I'm sorry, Qeb. I had a lot on my mind. I shouldn't have been like that."

"Yeah. Okay, I guess."

"Wait," Frank said. "What was the name you said just now, the one before *Hermione*?"

"The *Recluse*. They built her at the old Beery Shipyard. And she wasn't the only one. There were two. Peter Howe only worked the *Recluse*, but he mentions the other one."

"It's them, Frank. It must be," Hillary said. "Qeb, does the manuscript describe the plates?"

"Pointed at the top and bottom, and grooved on the edges."

"Like tongue-and-grooves on wood floors, maybe?"

"How'd you know that?"

"You two should see this." Frank flagged them both over to Charley's plate

Standing with her toes to the bath, Gemma gaped at the thing in the solution. "Qeb, look!"

"Yeah, I see it."

She squeezed his hand in hers. "It's just like Peter Howe says."

Frank knelt down and wagged a light into the solution onto the makers mark. "Take a peek."

The letters beneath its crest tittered back at Qeb. "Am I really seeing that?"

"Yes," Hillary said. "It's the Laird family crest."

"But how can that be?"

She expelled a loud sigh and admitted, "It's time I tell you a story, about a great shipbuilding family. In England."

When Hillary finished, all the loose pieces Qeb had put together to make some sense out of what he knew toppled like a house of cards. *Tim-Lee, wherever you are I hope you can see this.* His disbelief slipped out with a skeptical accusation. "This is too unreal. So how come no one knows about any of this?"

"We don't know. We can only guess. Maybe because the British government could not afford for it to leak out that they were supplying advanced armor to the Confederate navy. When the war ended, prudence might have dictated that the whole thing was better buried. Maybe events in Europe after the Civil War clouded the story into obscurity, and it was all forgotten.

"Out of ridiculous luck, a friend of mine in Scotland traced where *Hermione* was built. He was allowed to peruse the archives. Her last manifest was there." She produced an envelope with a platoon of postage and stamped *Par Avion*. She smirked, a bit proud. "Snail mail is more secure these days. You never know who's snooping into our computers. But nobody pays attention anymore to the Post."

Qeb and Gemma struggled through scanned copies of cursive penmanship to a line describing a vessel named *Hermione* bound for Nassau in autumn, 1864. The contents of her cargo manifest was nothing more than columns of ditto marks and a comment at the top and bottom reading Captain's Eyes Only.

Qeb waved the scanned manifest at his uncle. "This proves the *Recluse* was real."

"No, Qeb. It only proves that, when she sank, *Hermione* was carrying a cargo no one wanted to mention."

"Dammit! Just once, can't you stop putting up obstacles and stick your neck out for something?"

"If you two can sheath your swords, I think I have an idea," Hillary said.

"Fine!"

"Okay, what?"

"Your father might be able to help."

"No! No way."

"Stop being such an ass," Frank snapped.

"I'm not being an ass."

"Oh, ho, ho, yes you are. You're being just like him. When are you finally going to get some sense in that thick head of yours and put away all that shit you think you have against your father?"

"What do you know about it?"

"Oh, shut up, the both of you!" Hillary shouted. "Look, Qeb. Here's what I know. You're father works for the wealthiest and most connected and well networked marine archaeologist in the world. David Kittering can get whatever he needs wherever he needs it, whenever he wants it. And that includes your father, who David holds in the highest regard. So if you can put away all that rubbish in your head and maybe act more like the man I know your father is, then maybe he will help you and Gemma, and actually see what that is down there you think it is.

"He's the only one, Qeb," she added. "If you're sincere about helping Gemma—if your friend Tim-Lee's legacy really means anything to you, then you have to stop this war with your father and forgive him. No matter how much it hurts. If you really want to see what's down there, you need his help. You have no other choice."

Qeb chewed on his cheek, wedged between a rock and a hard place. "I'll think about it."

"You don't have a lot of time," Uncle Frank said.

"What do you mean?"

"Your parents are leaving in two days on a long vacation, courtesy of David Kittering. They'll be gone for a couple months."

"This is it, kiddo," Hillary added. "Decision time: it's now or never."

20-A MOTHER'S LOVE

The shock of the slap to his cheek sent sparks all through Qeb, knocking his sight into a flash of blackness. His nerves cringed from the back of his head to the tips of his toes.

"Mother!" He palmed the sting to his face. Never before had she struck him. Not ever.

His mother wailed from the depths of her heart, "What have you done?" Tears streamed down the gentle curves of her face, each drop dangling from the soft edges of her jaw before falling to its demise in the fine weave of her favorite house dress.

Fingering the ringing in his ear Qeb begged her, "Mother, it's not worth crying about."

Olufemi raised her hand for another strike.

Her palm, angry red with throbbing pain, pleaded, *No!*

Her hand drifted helpless to her side. She looked up at him as if she were meeting a complete stranger for the very first time, and plopped into the soft chair behind her. "How could you do this to us; to *me*? What have I done to make you do this thing? You are smart. You have always been so smart. And now you are throwing your future away for—" She glanced dismissively at Gemma in the living room of the small bungalow she and Charley bought when they relocated from Egypt.

"Why are you doing this to my son?"

"Mother, Gemma's not doing anything to me, or to you. Tim-Lee was my best friend. I'm only helping her find out how he...how he..."

"How my brother drowned," Gemma said.

Drowned. Olufemi fluttered her eyes at the harsh sound of the word.

"Mother, I'm doing this because it's important; more important than anything I've ever done."

Olufemi shot to her feet and readied another slap, but her strength was too withered to deliver. "How dare you say such a thing?" She collapsed back into her chair and bawled loudly, filling the room with her anguish. "And when you find out how he died, or why he died," she demanded, "what will you do then?"

Qeb wrestled himself from the humiliation that was circling thick arms around him. He straightened himself and stole a breath. "That's why I came to you, Mother. I..." He glanced at Gemma, who nudged him on with a supportive nod. "That is, we...we need your help."

"My help?" Confused, she pulled a clean hanky from her dress pocket. "How could I possibly help my son ruin his career?" she said between sniffles. She rolled the hurt from her shoulders and set her hands and hanky in her lap. "Why would I want to?"

Qeb knelt before her and rested his hands on hers in her lap, feeling right away their desire to escape his touch. "I'm helping Gemma and her family because they need to know that Tim-Lee's death wasn't meaningless. They have a right to know what really happened. They need to know that he will get the recognition he deserves for his discovery."

Her gaze strolled over the patterns in the arm of her chair, evading him. "How can I possibly be of any use to you with that?"

Qeb swallowed hard, choking on a sudden reality: his mother's absolute trust in him that was always there in the past wasn't there now. "Uncle...Uncle Frank says...he says you're leaving, on a vacation."

A teeny glimmer of a smile brushed the corner of her lips. "With your father."

"And you leave the day after tomorrow?"

Her hands fluttered beneath his as she spoke to the far wall. "Mr. Kittering has given us plane tickets to Egypt. I will see home again. Your father and I will have time together, like before Cleopatra."

His throat squeezed. "Mother, what if…" She still wouldn't look at him. "Could you…" He glanced back to Gemma again, who could only wince back hopeless, but with understanding. "Mother, wouldn't you like to go back when the weather is cooler?"

Olufemi jerked her head round to him. Her features were speechless. When he tried wrapping his fingers round her hands she snatched them away.

He crumbled before her on supplicant calves. "You know how you like the October air better." His voice was suddenly small and alone.

"You are asking me…" She couldn't say it.

"I—we…we need dad's help too. We can't do this without him. He knows stuff, and…and he has equipment."

His mother's tiny body began to tremble. "So it's not me you need; it's your father you want."

"That's not true, Mother. Without your help, dad can't stay and help us do this. Mother…Mother, please."

Olufemi considered her son without batting an eye. She straightened in her chair, wiped her nose and jabbed her attentions at Gemma. "How do you know my son?"

Gemma stole a timid step forward. "I didn't know him before. I needed help, from someone, from anyone, and I took a chance. I came to Qeb for help. The police took forever returning my brother's body to us. They insisted Tim-Lee's death was an accident. I can't believe them. I won't believe them. I know his death—"

She hesitated. That word *death*. It was too horrible.

"The people at Qeb's college were so understanding. They knew he knew my brother and where he was. I drove up to see him on his dig, but he wasn't there. Professor Laird had…well, Qeb was already gone."

Olufemi's hurt blazed at her son. "Yes, I know about Qeb and Professor Laird. And I know Qeb tried to keep it a secret from me."

"Mrs. Morgan, Qeb got the police to give us the addresses of the boys who found my brother's body so I could talk to them. And he has helped me research the manuscript that tells us so much about what my brother discovered. It's an amazing story, greater than anything going on up there in Virginia that Qeb could be working on."

"You are being arrogant," Olufemi scolded.

"I don't mean to be. But without Qeb's help, I cannot hope to do this on my own."

Gemma produced some of her own tears. "Without your help, Tim-Lee will be just a name on a gravestone in the hills back home, and his discovery will be lost and forgotten."

Olufemi considered her son at her feet. "What is this discovery?"

"It's a shipwreck, Mother; one that doesn't exist if you ask people like Professor Laird. But it does exist, and Tim-Lee found it." He shoved his hand into his pocket for something and held it up for her to see. "Then Gemma showed me this." His mother's eyes gripped the golden flash in his fingers. "It's there, Mother. Tim-Lee's lost ship—it's really there."

Strong fingers snatched the coin from his grasp.

"Dad!"

Charley looked over his son to Gemma. "You found this where?"

"It was lying on the outside of whatever that is down there. It was in the daylight; otherwise I would have missed it."

Charley studied the coin more closely and frowned. "Is this Spanish?"

"It's Mexican."

"Well, who knows? It could have been dropped down there last week."

Gemma drifted over to him. She took the coin from him and flipped its date round to him.

He read the numbers. "Or maybe not. Still, this doesn't prove a wreck—"

"It's there, Dad."

"Qeb, you're just wishing it's there."

"But we have proof. You saw it yourself at Uncle Frank's that morning."

Charley's eyes glazed over: Femi wasn't supposed to know that he was home sooner than he admitted. He planted his fear onto the coin hoping she didn't catch Qeb's slip-up. "Okay. So, say it is there. Now what? Your girlfriend goes home and you do what, sweep floors somewhere till you figure out how to make a living with an incomplete education?"

Qeb recovered from his bended knees. "She's not my girlfriend, Dad."

Gemma slipped her arm under his and smiled coyly.

"Yeah, I can see that," Charley said.

"What did you mean by sweeping floors?"

"It was nothing." Unimpressed, Charley handed the coin back to Gemma. "I was listening in the hall." He took Femi's hand in his. "I think you were asking your mother for a favor: something about giving something up?"

Qeb batted his eyes at the both of them. For the first time he could remember, he was afraid of them. "No, not give up. Not that. I only meant that maybe in the fall—"

"There's nothing you can do, Qeb. You might know where it is; you might *think* you know where it is, but you two don't have the equipment to finish the job." Charley studied the panic seeping from his son's features. "And that's it, isn't it? That's really why you're here: not to explain yourself to your mother; not to apologize for breaking her heart. You're here because you want something."

"Charley?"

"You hid at your Uncle Frank's, not a word to her, leaving her to learn from complete strangers that you were dismissed from your dig."

"Charley?"

"What are you going to do when the school boots you from your program?"

"Charley!" Femi's hand squeezed his. "I will do it."

"Femi?"

Her eyes pleaded. "He is my son."

"Femi, please. I've made a mess of us."

"Yes, you have. But now you are here, and we can do this together for our son; for our family." She could see he wasn't quite connecting the dots. She tinkered with the hairs on the back of his hand. "I am asking you to help them."

"But Femi."

"You have the equipment."

There it was. The dots connected.

Charley swept astonished eyes over the three of them: Femi begging, Qeb breathless, and the girl Gemma standing next to him all poker-faced.

"Femi, you know my situation."

"I am sure Mr. Kittering will have you back if he knows what you are doing."

"What does she mean, Dad, have you back?"

"Your father was fired."

"What!"

"Mr. Kittering was not pleased with your father that he refused two vacations."

Qeb measured up his dad. "Refused? What, we're not good enough for you to come home?"

"It's hard to explain."

"Mr. Kittering fired him so he had no excuse for not taking a vacation. Then Mr. Kittering bought the plane tickets and the hotels for us."

"Hotels. As in more than one?"

"First we go home to Egypt and then we fly up to Paris. I've never been there. And then to Ireland. That was my choice. What a strange little country. I want to see it."

Qeb felt suddenly very dirty.

Gemma stepped in. "You go on your trip, Mrs. Morgan. This is all my fault: I pushed Qeb to ask you. It was wrong of me."

Qeb shot her a queer look. "You what?"

"We can go see his uncle. I'm sure he would help"

Charley guffawed. "Frank?"

"Uncle Frank is cool, Dad. And there's Dr. Bascombe."

Charley's brow reached for the sky. "I seem to recall you blew up at him for allowing her back into his life, and now you want her help? Oh, that'll work. I can see it now. So tell me, what's the first thing you're going to do; what's your plan?" They didn't say much. "Just what I thought: you don't have a plan. Okay. This wreck—where is it, and who owns the property? You can't just stroll in and start tearing things up without permission."

Gemma and Qeb avoided his eyes.

"Ah. So it *is* on private property."

"We were going to ask the old woman if...maybe..."

"Is this the same woman who shoots at trespassers?"

Qeb shuffled a bit. "How'd you hear that?"

"Never mind. So, are you listening to your son now, Femi?"

"But Charley, Miss Polk's brother—somebody must be able to do something? Mr. Kittering—he is a rich man, with powerful friends. Maybe you can talk to him."

"Femi! I can't just go up to David and ask him to...ask him to—I don't even know what I'm supposed to be asking him."

But her touch was gentle and its tender squeeze was subtle. "Femi..." He surrendered with a heavy sigh. "Crap."

Gemma studied the thoughts crossing Charley's expression. "Then you'll do it?"

He nodded at her with his eyes.

"You *will* do it?" She turned to Qeb and landed a smacker on his lips. "Oh! Thank you, Qeb. And Mrs. Morgan, how will I ever be able to repay you?"

"There is no repaying. You go and find your brother's ship."

Gemma bear hugged Charley. "Thank you!"

"Hey, I haven't done anything yet. David could say no, or maybe he won't have an answer. The woman doesn't have to let us on her land either, and—" A sudden idea bitch-slapped him. He palmed his forehead. "Damn. There is something!" He snapped suddenly exuberant fingers.

"What, Dad?"

"Something we can do to find out exactly what's down there."

"We can't go back there. If we try to dive that cove..."

"You're not even close, Qeb. We'll need a small plane, but yeah, it could work"

"A plane? Dad, what are you thinking?"

"I'm not even sure yet. But for now you'll just have to trust me."

Charley and Qeb quick-stepped it from the air conditioned comfort of the Odell Williamson Municipal Airport out over scorching concrete tarmac to the Kittering Enterprises Cessna *Turbo Skylane* waiting for them in the smothering heat blanketing lower left Brunswick County.

"Damn air's so thick you can spoon your way through it," Charley groused. Beneath his steps, the beach-side airport's recent tarmac extension blazed white-hot in the sun. "And this glare—I'm going blind."

Qeb waggled his Persols at Charley. "You need a pair of these."

Quick as a wasp, Charley snatched the pitch black sunglasses from his son's smart-ass fingers. "Thanks."

"Hey!"

The flood of abrupt whiteness sent Qeb's sight running for cover. He grabbed Charley's near arm and searched his father's face. "Get your own," he said, snatching his Persols back.

He slid them back down over his tearing eyes.

The Cessna's two-man crew just ahead of them floated into view in a soothing bath of Polaroid protection. What a strange pair they made: a broomstick and beach ball. One guy was short and rail thin. The other was as husky as he was tall. Qeb had watched when Charley greeted them after they had landed. The big man was obviously familiar to him from the bear hug he laid on him, but the formal handshake Charley offered the other guy hinted that he was a complete stranger.

The big guy was a jovial man named Rand. He sported a grey-on-white beard that more than made up for the hair he was lacking upstairs. At the plane, Rand indicated to the two seats in the back. "You take the one here, my man," he said to Qeb, pointing out the rear seat on the plane's right side. "I'm gonna need you on my side when we do this thing."

Charley shoe-horned himself into the plane's cramped rear on the left side, just behind the seat of their pilot, a chain smoking needle of a man named Gulp.

Gulp hopped up into his seat, clipped his seat belt on and donned his headset. He flipped a switch and spattered something to the tower. He checked on Charley seated directly behind him and shut the door on his side.

That's when Qeb noticed.

"Hey, where's our door?" he asked Rand.

"We took it off." Rand jabbed a fat thumb to the storage compartment between them and the tail. "It's in the back. I don't need it in my way when I'm working."

Qeb's fingers searched after his seatbelt while his eyes traced the outline of where the door should be. His left ear was half-listening to Gulp up front yammering to the tower something about a low altitude clearance.

"Don't worry kid," Rand said. "We're only gonna be at 500 feet. Not too far of a fall if you slip. Hey, I'm kidding. It'll be fine, I promise."

Gulp cupped his headset and frowned at Rand. He shook his head and grumbled something into his Mic.

"What's up?" Rand asked him.

Gulp slurred something about "northern Southerners" and released the plane's brakes with a snap. He punched the controls and the Cessna's prop roared to life.

Rand grasped a handhold over his head and hollered over the din, "Hold on to your hats, guys." The Cessna *Turbo Skylane* screamed down the runway heading southwest-by-west like a straight-track dragster.

Qeb white-knuckled his seat and ogled the asphalt runway whizzing past the gaping hole beside him and Rand. Mostly Rand. The runway suddenly dropped away fast in a steep climb that mashed his guts against his back and took his breath away.

Gulp quickly banked a hard left, curling the Cessna round east in a dramatic sickening roll that filled the door hole on Qeb's right side with blue sky. Gravity tugged hard left at his fear of heights. He gaped to his left, straight down through Charley's window at broken swamp land, a washboard neighborhood of dockside houses, and a flotilla of boats of all sizes tracing over dirty water like snow white comets.

A creaking sound from Rand's seat in front of him panicked him. Would Rand's seatbelt hold, or would it snap under his weight and send him tumbling onto Gulp?

Gulp would lose control. They would be doomed.

He swooned as the Cessna snapped back to level.

Rand grinned back at his obvious nausea. "Fun, huh?"

"Yeah, fun." Qeb swallowed the trace of puke in the back of his throat.

Charley rapped on his arm. "Better tell him where we're going."

Qeb reached forward and pointed to a green-grey causeway separating the mainland from a thin strip of sand blistering with overdevelopment. "That's the Intracoastal Waterway up ahead. Then there's the Shallotte River mouth. Just keep heading this way."

Gulp replied, "Eyupe."

Gulp wasn't much for words, even less for ones Qeb could understand. Rand was different. Rand liked to talk. The way he yammered on with Charley, you'd think the two of them hadn't seen each other in years, though from the conversation, they'd worked a lot together.

"Hey Gulp," Qeb asked.

"Eyupe."

"Where'd you get a name like Gulp?"

Rand interrupted, "From the way he drinks his beer."

Gulp snapped back, "Id'n not!" in an accent Qeb couldn't hope to place. "Iffo' Gulpeign." It sounded to Qeb like gull pain.

"Yeah, sure," Rand said. "Next he'll tell you it's Cajun."

Gulp shook a fist at Rand. "Acadian. Quebecoise!"

"Yeah, yeah. Don't fret so much." Rand winked a delinquent grin to Qeb as they crossed the mouth of the Shallotte River. "And pay attention to where you're going. You got maybe some hairy ground flying coming up here soon. I need you concentrating so Gloria doesn't have to work more than she needs to."

"Effe-you!" Gulp said.

When Qeb asked, "Who's Gloria?" Gulp raised his eyes to the heavens. "Oh Lordy, God."

Rand leaned forward for a second and sat back up again. His right hand fiddled with the down low side of his seat till something clicked. He turned his seat completely round to face Qeb, which was easy to do now with the door completely gone.

In his lap was a buff metal box. As he opened it, a shit-eating grin divided his chin from his nose. Inside, nestled in grey cushioning, lay what looked to Qeb like the telephoto lens of a big ass camera, but way fatter.

Rand lifted it out like a newborn father and leaned closer past the whistling wind that made it so hard to hear. "This is Gloria."

Gloria sported a buff black finish. On her one flat end there was a dull yellow circle. Her other end was all boxy and angular. On her top she had a little screen tucked kind of deep down in a rectangular recess straddling her back.

Rand cradled her in his arms. "She's a pain in my ass mostly, but I love her."

Gulp hollered, "Ey won' let 'nother man touch her, neither."

Rand exclaimed, "You got that right."

Rand and Gulp had flown up from Kittering's Charleston staging facility, where Kittering Enterprises kept two crewed research boats, a warehouse of equipment, and a team of specialists. Kittering operated a dozen such staging areas, worldwide.

"It makes things easier when your resources are closer to their projects," Charley had explained when Qeb asked, while they were waiting for the plane at the airport.

"She looks heavy," Qeb said.

"Nah, she's only about three pounds."

"So what's so special about her?"

Rand stroked her back. "You could say she's a sweet mix of ground penetrating radar on steroids, armed with a sweet blend of echo sounder and high-resolution acoustic imaging sonar, all mashed into one."

"I thought sonar only worked in water."

Rand placed a finger over his lips. "Yeah, and until Gloria's patent is firm, Mr. Kittering prefers that people go on believing that."

"How does she work?"

There were four touch pads lined along the edge of Gloria's little screen. Rand pointed to the one at the end. "With this nifty little function, Gloria takes repeatable signatures to make vertical cross-sections of the sub-sea bed. She paints three-dimensional images of what's hidden maybe twenty, thirty meters beneath the sea floor. What's more, she can resolve to just tenths of a meter. That's piddly, dude. We're talking resolutions to just four inches. Did I lose you?"

"Kind of."

"Look at it this way, things down there buried in the muck come out so sharp you can practically reach out and touch them."

"I see."

"You're not impressed. Okay. Well try this: Gloria can do all that from 500 feet in the air, through the damn trees and rain if she has to."

"Whoa!"

"Yeah, whoa. And there's nobody else in this industry but us who can do that." Rand patted Gloria's behind. "Whaddaya say to that?"

"I say that's pretty cool. Can't wait to see her work."

Rand sucked on his cheek. "Don't get too excited. She's not really much to watch." Then his brows arched with price. "But what comes out of her brain is pure joy. You just wait and see."

"River splittin' up ahead, kid," Gulp hollered.

"My name's Qeb."

"Eyupe. Whi' way?"

"That way." Qeb pointed past Gulp to the east branch of the river where the Shallotte whittled down fast into a varicose tributary snaking through thick salt grass that faded into a breaking late morning haze blanketing the distant town of Secession. "That mobile home park coming up on the left, just up ahead. We pass that and we'll be almost there."

Rand snapped into action. He had donned a crazy looking harness at the airport, not a word why. The why was clear now as he clipped Gloria to it with two small spinnaker shackles. He twiddled again with his seat and clicked into a turn that put him looking straight out the hole where the door should be. His chubby fingers danced across Gloria's touch pads.

"Okay Gulp," he hollered. "Waiting on you, buddy."

"Eyupe."

An orderly mobile home community was easing by on their left. Just past it the narrowing tributary took a wild left and then reversed her decision heading south before easing herself into a meandering easterly creep. Beyond a slight knee in the creep, the trees on the north bank thinned out and a huge cove poking north at eleven o'clock steered into view.

"That's it!" Qeb shouted.

Rand measured it in split seconds, four times as long as she was wide. "Gulp. Let's make a first pass right up her alley."

"Eyupe."

Gulp banked the Cessna slightly southeast-by-south over some houses and a shut-down causeway on the south side, dipped into a steep bank the other way, and set a flight path along the cove's backbone heading north for eleven o'clock on the dial.

Rand hollered over the wind to Qeb. "We'll take three, maybe four passes and then get the hell out of here. Don't want to spook that old bird living down there, do we?"

"No we don't. She's got a shotgun."

"Wha' shotgun?" Gulp said.

"She shot at me and Gemma. Cops say she shoots at people all the time."

"You might'a said'n sob'm 'bout that a'fore," Gulp said.

"Ah, just keep your eyes ahead and you won't see anything," Rand huffed.

"Mebbe I hear sob'm though."

"You can be such a girl, sometimes, you know that?"

"Prettiest gurl you ebber be goin' whi', da' fo' sho.'"

"Yeah, yeah." Rand set his feet up on the lip of the door sill with Gloria hanging from her harness between his thighs and contorted himself over the little screen on her back.

Qeb glanced to Charley sitting next to him in the cramped back of the four-passenger *Turbo Skylane*. Charley's thoughts were out the window. He hadn't said more than six words in the past fifteen minutes.

"Thanks, Dad, for the plane and these guys. For everything."

Charley smiled out the window. "It's nothing."

Rand commanded Gulp to do a run from the other direction. "This time come over the house with the cove on my side."

"Dad, what's bothering you?" Qeb asked his father. "I can see it in your face."

Charley said to the ground out his window, "You ever think of so many things at once you didn't know for sure what you're really thinking about?"

"That's been me pretty much since before you and Mother got married. I've been working so hard for teachers and grades for so long I don't think I know who I am anymore, or what I want."

Charley's empathetic smile reflecting in the window slipped past Qeb unnoticed.

"Christ, Charley!" Rand exclaimed, reading the teeny images on Gloria's micro-screen. "Your boy may have found something here. There's a big bastard lying down there." He hollered over the racket outside to Gulp, "We're definitely doing four passes."

Gulp said, "Was a woman in d'yard watchin' us, fust pass. Mebbe betta feather'n the prop so's not t' rile her up."

The Cessna drifted round northwest-by-north for their third pass and slipped into a lazy coast just above the approaching tree tops bordering the cove.

"Dere she id," Gulp said. Her light dress was apparent against the grass. "She got som'in in her han'," he said as they cruised over the cove.

Rand was tweaking Gloria. "That last run over the house was kind'a crummy. We need to get way lower this time, buddy."

Qeb freaked. "Are you crazy?" The roof of the house was coming up on their right. They'd skim the tree tops between it and the cove.

"No sweat," Rand insisted. "We'll be gone before she figures where we are."

"But she shot at me and Gemma. Gulp, don't do it."

"S'okay kid," Gulp said. "We'll kill d' engine an' coast."

The Cessna feathered into a glide path between the house and the cove with the quiet of a hawk, the whole time Rand with his eyes glued to Gloria's screen. Near cove's end, Rand sat up and boasted, "Beautiful!"

Bam!

The Cessna heeled right from a punch, knocking Gloria from Rand's grasp. She slipped between his knees and glanced of the door sill on her way out of the plane.

"Fuckinay!" Rand exclaimed. Gloria's tagline to his harness twanged to rod straight. She clocked this way and that like a pendulum in mid-air over algae colored water.

Gulp read his gauges and said in flat syllables, "Oop! She done sob'm', look like."

Qeb indicated to the belly of the left side wing over Gulp's head. "Is that bad?"

Rand ogled a series of tiny holes peppered into the wing's underside. "Better skip the fourth run, Gulp. Get us out of here."

Gulp peered at the damage. "We okay, I'm thinkin'," he said, and steered west for home.

"Okay? But there's holes in the wing."

Rand reassured Qeb, "It's nothing, really. Take my word; we've been in worse shape."

Qeb eyed Gloria back in the safety of Rand's lap. "Is she okay?"

Rand stroked Gloria's curved back. "She took a couple dings, but she's alright." Then he squeezed Qeb's shoulder and said, "Just you wait till you see what she's got in here for you, kid. You're gonna bust a gut."

Qeb reached for Gloria. "Can I see now?"

"Hey!" Rand snatched her away and cuddled her into the snug safety of his generous lap.

"Patience, boy. Patience."

22-REVEALING RECLUSE

There was nowhere to turn, nowhere to steer his haggard attentions without slamming headlong into another ugly reminder that this was no longer his place; just another cruel reminder that once again he had tried to find home, and once again he had failed.

In the short days after the ax severed Frank from his future, a gooey pall of unrealized achievement had oozed in through every pore and crack in the walls and ceiling, smothering his lab's signature frenetic energy of hope and discovery beneath a hardened lacquer of gloom. Even opening the windows was useless, few as they were, for the depression inside was far too thick for the refreshing outside air to push its way in.

The usual and weirdly comfortable clutter of minor artifacts collected and catalogued by Frank's former students was now glaringly absent: wrapped, packed and stacked in crates out in the hallway awaiting pickup, addressed to the research labs back at Chapel Hill. Their only traces were the scuffs they left on the floor and an acidic whiff of rusty iron in the air.

By year's end he'd be history. His lab's new tenants would stride in through the door, victorious and self-absorbed. The once excited chatter of Frank's students was now withered and fallen to a fine dust over the floor and would be swept away with all traces gone beneath a shiny new veneer of wax.

But it was worse than that.

The Board of Trustees weren't done twisting their fingers in his wound. They needed him to hang around and oversee the transfer. If he did so, they'd make the necessary calls to see he got a proper place elsewhere. To ice the cake, they had waved money at him.

And he took it. Like a whore.

Thank God Mama isn't alive to hear of it.

And now he was paying for it simmering in a percolating funk; a deteriorating fixture without meaning. If only he could throw the money back at them and flip them off.

To hell with them!

But he couldn't. It was too late. He had already blown a hefty chunk of it on bills.

And then there was that thing about him, that when he thought of it, he wanted to crumble to the floor and scream out to God to come and take him away and relief him of his shame. That thing about him being—that even if he could escape this place to freedom—he would have no idea whatsoever what to do with all the free time.

Good God, what the hell's happened to you?

He was pathetic.

Frank evaded the cold walls closing in around him, his jobless tools on the counter, and the flutter of the far fluorescent lamp that—Dammit to hell!—just wouldn't give up the ghost and burn out for good.

His urge to break out and cry suddenly withered and toppled with her touch. He turned slightly, just letting Hillary standing next to him on his left see the redness in his eyes.

She squeezed his hand and kissed his tear away. "I'm here."

His heart fluttered. At least today he had her.

Hillary caught Charley's eye on them and lobbed him an attempted smile of friendship. From Frank's right, Charley tossed back an equally uncomfortable nod.

Frank took solace in the shoulder-to-shoulder presence of Hillary and Charley beside him. The three of them were standing behind Qeb who was seated at the not-so-gleaming anymore work counter, with his laptop open.

All eyes were on the laptop's screen. Its keys clattered like skittering cockroaches as Qeb searched the image files Rand had downloaded from Gloria. "Found them," he said. "You guys ready for this?"

Hillary hugged Frank's arm.

Charley wavered from one foot to the other.

"Here we go." Qeb banged a singular peck to his keyboard.

The image was stark in its simplicity. Shades of blue from chilly to freezing, darkest at the deepest points to almost black at the sharpest edges of the unmistakable shape of a ship against the surrounding soil. Her shape at one end was pointed. Her foredeck was modest, flat, and uncluttered. Her back end was hard to make out, covered over in fourteen decades of dirt and debris. Fades of green traced a sloping superstructure reaching up to the cove's bottom. Oranges and yellows flagged where it poked through the muck into the open water above it.

Hillary hugged tighter on Frank's arm.

Frank cupped his hand over hers. "Charley, are you seeing this?"

"I'm right here, and yes I am."

Qeb opened another image. "Rand said this was the best one." He sat back in his stool and crossed his arms. "All these years that thing was down there, and nobody even knew it."

"Maybe they did. They just didn't want to say anything."

"Or maybe they just didn't want to believe it."

"I think dad's right, Uncle Frank. It was just easier not believing it."

"Why do you think that?"

"Just the way people acted, even the police. You could see it in their faces. They didn't like us asking questions. It didn't matter Gemma was just looking for answers to Tim-Lee's death. And the two boys—the ones who found him—their parents weren't much better. The father of one of them—he got so mad at us his wife had to walk us to the car."

"Speaking of Gemma, where is she?" Frank said. "She should see this."

Qeb squirmed in his seat, just slightly. He moved his cursor with a heavy finger and pulled up another image.

Charley added, "That's right. She was with us at the airport when we were waiting for the plane. Where'd she go?"

Qeb struck ENTER with noticeable irritation. "She went home."

"Is something wrong?"

"Nothing's wrong!" Qeb fingered little circles on his computer's mouse pad

Frank suggested, "Well in any case, you've helped her a lot. I'm sure she's grateful. She'll be back."

Circles, faster now, dashed Qeb's cursor over the command bar to Gloria's image software.

"Why not just call her?" Charley said.

A pulldown menu flashed open and the image collapsed.

"Shit! Really, Dad? Now look what you made me do. Anyway, I did call her. Here it is. Good. Besides, all I ever get is her voicemail."

"And she hasn't called back?"

"No."

Hillary butted in, "Well that's rather rude."

Qeb tossed her an unappreciative pout. "It's the way she is, okay? So no, she hasn't called back. Anyway, I left her a message, so she knows we found Tim-Lee's ship."

"Well, this discovery the two of you made," Hillary said, attempting détente, "you can both be proud."

"Tim-Lee's the one who found it, not us."

"Of course." Qeb's tone was clear. He still hadn't forgiven her.

"So, what now?" Frank wondered.

"David has seen these images by now," Charley said. "I'm sure they have his attention. And I told him what Qeb and Gemma said about developers wanting the land, so if we're gonna do anything, we better do it fast."

"You think he'll go for it?" Frank said. "What can we do if he doesn't? I mean we know it's there, but it's on private land. And the State—the red tape alone could take months."

"Frank?"

"And by then that woman in the house could have sold."

"Frank."

"And by the way, that's a watershed. The ecologists could tie us up for years. They might even sue to stop us and—"

"Frank!"

"What?"

"Kittering Enterprises can raise her. And if it comes down to cutting red tape, I'm sure David's got it covered."

"But Charley, look at this thing." The curiosity gears in Frank's head started to whir. "I mean that's no small thing there." He pecked the keyboard through Gloria's images from over Qeb's shoulder, awing at the distinct traces of an ironclad gunboat. He'd seem enough photos of them to know. "She's got to be maybe, who knows how long." Maybe it was possible. "And her beam—I don't know. And look where she is. How do you reach her way back there in that tiny river, let alone get her out of there once you do?"

"Frank, I'm not saying it'll be easy, but it's do-able."

Frank backed away from the keyboard, kneading his beard in thought. The gears in his brain downshifted, chewing through his doubts. "Maybe. But Charley, if we're going after it—"

"Going after what, Frank?"

"Bob! I didn't hear you come in."

Bob Moore wandered up to the counter, leaned past them and peered at the glorious swath of colors on Qeb's laptop. "Looks interesting. What's going on?"

"Um..." Frank's gaze flashed to the pH-bath on the floor still undisturbed by all the packing out. "I should show you something." He led Bob over to the bath. "You haven't seen this yet, I don't think. Charley found it."

"Oh, yes." Bob acknowledged Charley with a nod. "You discovered this and an uncharted wreck. In restricted waters as I recall. Don't look so worried, Frank. I won't tell."

Frank shared a surprised glance with Charley and said, "Er, Bob. Thank you."

"So speak up. Tell me about this plate here in the bath taking up all this space."

"Dr. Bascombe and I—we've been doing some research."

"Ah. Dr. Bascombe." Bob smiled formally at Hillary. "You're not spying on our little operation here for our friends over at ECU, are you?"

She looped her arm through Frank's arm. "I promise. I'm just here helping a friend."

Frank filled Bob in on the plate. "We think it's somehow tied to that shipwreck there on Qeb's screen." He indicated down to the family crest stamped into the plate. "This maker's mark here, it's English. It dates back to the Civil War. But that's not the interesting part. The interesting part is the material itself. Old as it is, and clearly some kind of industrial purpose to it, you'd expect it to be iron or maybe cheap steel. Thing is, it's not. It's an alloy, and a very good one. I had it tested."

Frank indicated to a notch of missing material. "I sent a sample to the research labs back in Chapel Hill." He fished into his pants pocket and pulled out his house and car keys. A nickel-sized hockey puck with the swirling red, black and white logo of the Carolina *Hurricanes* dangled from the key ring.

"Watch this."

He plucked the puck from the ring, set the puck on the plate and flicked it with his finger. It shot away easily and settled. He did it again, and then handed the puck to Bob.

Bob looked it over. "It's a magnet." He handed it back, unimpressed. "You a hockey fan?"

"Exactly. It's a magnet. And yeah, when I can actually get to a game."

"Okay. So what?"

"It didn't stick to the plate because the plate's not magnetic." Frank watched Bob expectantly, waiting for enlightenment to pop on.

"Frank, I'm a marine biologist, remember? This is all Greek to me."

Frank puffed his cheeks and expelled exasperation.

"From the test, this plate is chromium-nickel steel, six percent carbon. In metallurgy that's called an alloy. We use them today for just about anything we want to last or to be strong. But alloy steel wasn't even around in America till after the Civil War when it was first smelted in Brooklyn. But that was a commercial failure. And I'll emphasize again that was after the war was over. This plate, Bob—this is an alloy steel with at least ten or twenty years of development behind it, discovered on a ship that sank in 1864."

Bob still wasn't following him.

"Okay. Let me put it in perspective. Producing steel like this in the mid-19th Century was expensive and labor intensive, and the quality was hardly worth the effort. This stuff is far superior to any of that." He waved away any contest and pointed a digit at Bob. "And that's the rub."

"Why's that?"

"Because metallurgical history says this wasn't around until almost 1900."

Bob simply shrugged. "So maybe the plates are more recent than the wreck. It could be just a bizarre coincidence. Maybe they fell down there in the same place as the shipwreck."

But Frank was ahead of him and shaking his head. "We've already been down that path. The maker's mark dates the plates to the same period as the wreck."

Hillary added, "Dr. Moore—Bob—in 1864, the British navy was pursuing new armor for its warships. We believe they developed this alloy. We know now they had been testing the plates, firing at idle targets. But that wasn't enough. They needed real-world results. There was just a little problem: England was not at war in 1864. But America was. We think the British government provided this armor to the Confederate navy for their ironclads."

Bob searched their faces. "You're serious!"

"The South needed armor for its gunboats. The British Admiralty needed battle tested data."

Bob's eyes fell back onto the plate. "Tell me more about the shipwreck."

"She's the *Hermione*." Frank indicated to *Hermione*'s bell sitting in a special place on his big counter. "She was built in Scotland and was apparently a very successful venture for her owners and her crew. We couldn't get any absolutes on her cargo when she went down, but we do know on her last voyage she pulled into Nassau and took a pilot aboard to guide her into Wilmington. That's not unusual. What's unusual is she took on no additional lading when she stopped over in Nassau. That's not normal. It had to be an expensive opportunity wasted."

Hillary added, "The more lading a blockade runner delivered, the more profitable the trip was for her crew and owners. And remember, they're putting their lives at stake with every trip. But this time,

Hermione's captain resisted loading her down. He was keeping her light for speed."

Frank indicated to the plate. "He was delivering this plate and dozens like it. Armor plates meant for an ironclad gunboat. One they were building right here near the end of the war."

Bob nodded to the image on Qeb's laptop screen. "And you think that's it."

"Yes."

Bob's expression flustered. "Frank, Wilmington building an ironclad; that story—it's an old wives tale. It's just a legend."

Frank pointed to the laptop. "There's your legend, right there."

Bob stiffened. "You don't know that. By the way, where is she, exactly?"

"In a cove off the Shallotte River."

"Off the Shallotte River, in a cove. And that makes sense to you? I know the Shallotte River. A lot of swamp down there. It doesn't exactly sound to me like somewhere some ironclad would fight it out."

Frank rested his supportive palm against the warm center of Hillary's back. "We think maybe the crew was hiding her. Maybe even scuttled her."

"Oh, now it's even getting better. You're suggesting they took the trouble to build a new warship with some advanced armor—smuggled mind you through a blockade—only to turn around and sink it themselves without firing a shot? That's ridiculous!"

"Okay, then you tell us, Bob. What the hell is that warship doing down there in that cove?"

Hillary snuggled Frank's hand in hers to calm him down and sidled up between them.

"It was built too late. The war was already lost. The government in Richmond might have feared that, had Washington discovered England was providing armor to the Confederacy, it may have seen it as an overt act of war against the Union. The Civil War was as good as done. There was no hope of the South winning. Wise minds must have prevailed. Why escalate a war that was clearly over into an international conflict that might drag on for another decade?"

She hesitated, measuring her next words.

"I think Washington did know. It would explain the silence, why Washington recorded nothing of it, and why Southern propriety hushed wagging tongues. Those who did know the truth packaged reality as a myth to prevent more bloodshed. It wouldn't be the first time a nation lied to itself to evade a war."

"That all sounds just dandy, Dr. Bascombe; all clean and perfect. Well I'm not buying it. I grew up here, Doctor. A kid can't grow up here without knowing something about that war. Now I'll tell you something. Three out of ten blockade runners ran aground so close to shore you could swim out to them with a mask and snorkel. At low tide you could almost wade out to them. I know this because I did it when I was a kid.

"So you say people knew there was some kind of nasty truth to hide. Well, for that to have happened, Union salvage crews would have had to have discovered the plates in the first place before anybody else could report them to Washington. How are you going to keep a bunch of sailors from blabbing about it?"

Hillary shrugged. "Who can say? Sailors follow orders. Maybe they were paid to be quiet. I don't know. The war was ending, people were exhausted. All anybody wanted was to go home. Maybe the fall of Fort Fisher and Wilmington overshadowed any further interests in her wreckage. After a war, priorities change. Things get forgotten."

"But let's just say someone in Washington did know about it, and let's say they covered it up still. This alloy as you call it, it would have been valuable to someone. Our own navy perhaps? What's that look on your face, Frank?"

"We have no idea how many plates were on the *Hermione*. Maybe someone did take a couple for testing. But if they took the whole load, someone would have noticed. I think Hillary's right. The myth was created to hide the truth that a criminal act of war took place between England and the North. It was created because we couldn't tolerate more war."

The tension in the air sagged a bit.

Bob massaged the pain welling up in his throbbing temple. "I don't know. That's some hell of a theory, Frank. People round here might think you're touched a bit upstairs," he said, tapping his forehead. He laid somber eyes on the plate. It was exquisite in its pathetic condition, lying in the bath looking up at him. "You know, it's sad really. This is exactly what the trustees hired you for."

"What do you mean?"

"I mean you should go for it. Go find out what that really is down there."

"Am I hearing the same Bob Moore I work for?"

"You were meant for this, Frank. Let's just agree the Board gave up on you too soon."

Bob's angst flamed out with a frustrated sigh. He cleared an obstruction in his nose and said, "I've made a decision." His haggard eyes met Frank and Hillary studying him side-by-side. He only just then noticed how natural they looked together.

"The IMS, Frank—it's at your disposal. All of it. The whole shebang. Anything you need that we have, it's yours."

"But the Board—as far as they're concerned, I'm gone. You do this and you'll get yourself in a heap of trouble."

Bob's rueful gaze drifted to *Hermione*'s polished bronze bell warming under soft light. It hung there for three moments before drifting back to Frank.

"Then I guess it won't hurt the Board if they didn't know, will it?"

The steady rattle of rain against stiff autumn leaves massaged Charley's troubled mind into a settled calm. It was a big step he was taking: a step he'd so far evaded by rushing for cover in the urgencies of his everyday job, safe and sound at sea, ever procrastinating with a stream of excuses that—though they made sense at sea—here on firm land revealed themselves for their harsh foolishness.

"Charley."

It was all so glaringly obvious now. It always was. He just refused to accept it.

You've just been too scared to look.

"Charley?"

Thing was, he hadn't told Femi or Qeb yet.

Why not?

"Charley! Are you there?"

Because you're still scared shitless that it's too late.

He closed his eyes and raised his face to the rain, savoring the metallic taste of the drops on his lips. The warm pitter-patter against his skin shushed the fabric of his fears into gentle folds, one over the other, over again, folding, shrinking ever smaller till they were nothing more than a tumbling spec in the darkness.

See how easy that was?

"Goddammit, Charley! Where are you?"

Charley's eyelids fluttered open. He stumbled out of his fog, teetering on loose feet, and fumbled with something fat in his hand. He pulled it to his face and squeezed the TALK button on the side.

"I'm here. What's up?"

"Chrissakes, Charley! Where you been? We're all waiting on you, bro." The California voice spilling from Charley's two-way radio chirruped with beach boy exuberance. "The water pumps are gassed up and ready when you give the word. Divers are on the bottom ready to come up. They're all done down there."

Charley shoved himself into reality with his hot hand across the back of his neck. "Roger that, Conley. Go ahead, bring the divers up. When they're out of the water, start taking in on the straps."

"You got it, bro."

A thoughtful voice pulled up just on the edge of Charley's sight and said from beneath the generous hood of a Columbia rain slicker, "So, how's it going?"

"Oh hi, David. Divers are just coming up. We're pretty much ready to bring her up."

David bobbed his head. His eyes skittered over the mostly submerged rust-on-white welded steel framework filling most of the cove in front of him, glistening in a sheen of rainwater.

"I never get tired of this, you know," he said with fatherly pride in his voice. "This is my umpteenth wreck and still I get excited."

Charley stayed mum, his attention moored to a splatter of rust on one of the columns of the frame in the water.

David flashed a disappointed smile and turned away. He reached out over the water, stretched a bit further, and pressed the hard sole of his cane against the frame, shut his eyes and connected with the machine, absorbing its subtle vibrations through the teakwood curve of his cane's handle. He lowered it back down to his right side, beside the knee he'd injured a year before, smacked hard against an unyielding ship's ladder in stormy seas. "You got her sunk down there pretty far, don't you think?"

"Her" was a floating self-propelled semi-submersible gantry nicknamed *Mini* for her narrow beam that made her perfect for tight jobs like this one.

"I guess," Charley said. "It took a lot to fit her in here." He pointed to the opposite side of the cove where Conley's team was just pulling the first diver out of the water. The lawn behind them was all scarred up with excavator tracks. "We dredged out 150 years of accumulated Mother Nature on top of her so *Mini* could straddle her. We kept clearing away and she kept growing. She's a big one."

David panned up past the raindrops splattering his face. Most of the trees overhead had been cleared away to make room for when *Mini* rose back up with the wreck. On the surface, including her machinery up top, she poked near thirty-five feet into the air.

"Got any numbers for me?" he said.

Charley retrieved his PDA from the pocket of his baggy army surplus trousers. "A hundred-fifty feet, stem to stern. Beam's forty-five feet. Her draft is fifteen feet."

Charley toggled his head. "That one has me confused. I mean, we had to dredge out the tributary. How'd they even get her all the way in here in the first place without grounding her in the mud?"

David considered the wind swept seagrass of the tributary. "Things were different then. It might have been deeper. How'd you figure the draft?"

"There are faded Roman numerals painted on her hull at the stern. Oh, and she's got two screws with a single rudder in the center. That's interesting, too."

"Why's that?"

"Qeb did some research. You remember the *Virginia*—the Confederate ironclad everyone calls the *Merrimack*? Well, she also had two screws. But they were big puppies: seventeen feet in diameter. These screws on this gal aren't even half that: about seven and a half feet each. Either she was very slow, or she's got some hellacious engines in her."

"Interesting."

Charley gave the tributary a once over, tracing it out to the Shallotte River. "You gotta wonder, you know, what they were doing way down here? There's no way out."

"Maybe they didn't plan on coming back out." David studied the slate gray skies. "This rain's gonna get worse. There's a squall down in Savannah. Weather's threatening a hurricane warning."

"Yeah, we heard. Figures! All month we get sunshine. Now when we need it most, we get a storm."

"Got anything else for me?"

"She's plated with the same plates that are out on that wreck we found. You can see it in the silt in the creases between the plates. Same stuff, I'm positive. Frank's right. That wreck we found off Bear Inlet and this ship are connected."

"Well, if they are, we'll figure it all out pretty soon. You've done well. You're ahead of schedule. What do you have under her hull for support?"

"Full hull splints both sides of her keel so she doesn't break her back when she leaves the bottom."

"That's good thinking."

"It was a bitch, I'll tell you. It took us thirty-four round-the-clock shifts opening up this cove so we could squeeze *Mini* in here, including dredging that tributary just so we could get her up here and get her back down to the river again. I just hope we dredged deep enough so once she's hanging onto that thing, she doesn't go and ground herself in the muck somewhere."

David hadn't been on-site for it, but it was an exercise that he was well tuned to. It had cost him a ghastly sum of money to stimulate approval from the politicians in Raleigh and Brunswick County.

He studied his star employee. "So, are you excited?"

"I'll be excited when Femi and I get that vacation together."

"Pretty soon. You're almost finished."

Charley snorted. "We've been at this so long and hard, I forgot all about any kind of finish."

A sudden clap of electric current snapped David's attention to a team of motors bolted to the platform crowning the top of *Mini*'s gantry frame.

Mini fascinated him. She was Charley's design: backyard simple and had paid for herself many times over in the three years since Kittering Enterprises had constructed her for shallow-water operations just like this one. She wasn't made to submerge under water completely, so all her pumps and motors and plumbing and controls, winches and other mechanical clutter David didn't need to understand were all gathered up there, up top.

Mini's electric motor controls whispered in satisfied standby. When Charley gave Conley the order to bring her up, they would kick the motors alive. Their spinning shafts would spool up powerful hydraulic pumps. The pumps would growl into action, zipping heavy oil down through pipes big around as beer cans to *Mini*'s submerged pontoons where nestled inside, hydraulic motors at the other end turned her ballast compressors.

The hungry compressors would gobble damp, stormy air from the outside through filters big as milk crates mounted up top on her platform. They'd suck that air down through long tubes, squash it to high pressure, and stuff it into *Mini*'s flooded ballast tanks, shoving the water out.

And *Mini*, with her monstrous load, would begin her rise back to the surface.

David snuck a grave look at Charley and wrung his hand into the silky smooth finish of his cane. "I had a talk with your brother Frank."

"Oh?"

David hoisted his nose and tested the iron in the damp air. "It seems his employers are having second thoughts about letting him go. Perhaps his boss talked some sense into them."

Charley shook the rain from his radio. "I think it's more them having second thoughts about what's going on right here."

"Do you?"

"Once you got the politicians on your side, it couldn't have been more than ten minutes before the phone calls started. A lot of tax dollars I bet trickle down to that university."

He indicated to the clutter in front of them. "This is gonna be the find of the decade. It's exactly what the university wanted from Frank all along. That Board jumped the gun and now they're sweating bullets about it." He turned to David with eyes hard as stone. "And they didn't dismiss Frank, either: they fired him. And they did it dirty too, bribing him to hang around."

The rain was ratcheting down to a fine, misty drizzle.

"Well, there's been a change. They asked him to stay."

"What!"

"I don't think he's answered them yet."

"Crap!" Charley's jaw tensed behind bronzed skin beneath his sodden blond beard, just starting to gray. "I hope he tells them to go to hell."

David tamped the ground with his cane. "That IMS facility—it's the perfect location."

"Perfect location for what? What are you getting at?"

David counted the receding drops hitting the water's surface. "I asked Frank to accept."

The rain stopped.

Charley rammed his hand deep into his trousers pocket, yanked something from it and began deftly fumbling it between his fingers.

The air between them thickened with the odor of wet wool.

David was all too familiar with the meaning of the thing in Charley's hand: Charley was stressing. Charley stressed a lot. And over the years, the dull antique nut from an old-school diving helmet had picked up a distinctly brassy gleam.

The last two divers popped their heads above the water.

Conley's voice chortled over Charley's radio, "Divers up!"

Charley's fingers fumbled faster.

"Charley, you there?"

"Don't you think you better answer him?" David said.

Charley snapped his radio to his face and barked, "Yeah, divers up. Roger that."

One of the divers pulled his regulator from his mouth and beamed a gleaming smile at Charley from across the cove. Charley didn't notice. His eyes were on fire.

David waved to Qeb for him and snatched the opportunity to shift gears. "Conley's been all about your son's work. He thinks Qeb's exceptional."

Charley's eyes flashed across the cove to his adopted son.

"He wants me to make Qeb an offer and bring him onboard."

The plastic seams of Charley's radio groaned under his shrinking grip.

"It could be good for him, considering—"

The movement was lightning fast.

David flinched from Charley's finger in his face.

Charley stapled hard eyes onto him. "Don't you dare! Don't even think it."

David steered Charley's hand aside. "You could let him decide?"

"My absence alone has been hard enough on his mother. You do that, especially now, and it'll kill her. Qeb's going back to school. You're going to promise me you won't even hint to him anything of the sort, you got that?"

The heady air between them ceased to move.

"Alright, Charley."

"No. You promise me."

"I promise, Charley. Jesus, what's with you?"

David shifted his attention fast across the cove beyond an armada of portable tool compressors and generators and light carts and other industrious clutter, to the small white clapboard house beyond it huddled in the center of autumn vegetation. Everything this time had been going so well, but in the end his world would fall apart. For the first time in his life, he was actually considering retirement.

"I guess we see now if this was all worth it."

Charley's twiddling fingers slowed up. He studied the lighted windows of the house. His gut just below his ribs was so knotted up with anger that he had to force the words out. "She's a tough old girl." He ceased twiddling altogether, expunging his temper into the nut with his thumb.

"It took you what, five weeks?"

"Six with the closing," David corrected. But he had done it: he had won her to his side, at least temporarily, saved by a peculiar law unearthed by his platoon of overpriced attorneys.

In the wake of the one hundredth anniversary of the War of Northern Aggression, North Carolina politicians had passed a bill in the Sixties granting private citizens wider latitude when engaging in archaeological activities on their own land.

Before then, the State usually scrutinized retrievals of historical artifacts of significance on private property. But with the centennial celebrations rekindling public passions for ancestral history, fueled by a bulging surplus of cheap World War II mine detectors hawked in the backs of hobby magazines and comic books, relic searching swelled and—well, there you had it.

The law had two catches.

Catch One was any work had to be paid-for—not voluntary. If educated volunteer specialists performed any work—say university professors or college students—all bets were off and the State could roll on in and take over the whole shebang. And it had to be funded by the owner's own pocketbook; no big-moneyed enterprises allowed.

Catch Two was what saved David in the end. He just twisted it a little. Catch Two said an owner having performed digs on their own property could not sell that property prior to twelve months accruing after official closure of the archaeological operation.

What paper-shuffling bureaucrat came up with that one?

But Catch Two was the trick David had needed. He would buy the place, raise the wreck, and then re-sell the place back to her one year after the project was done. So for a cool three million the place was his to get the work done. In the meantime, the old woman was on a lease for peanuts and would get it all back for a paltry $250,000.

He didn't mind the loss. Giving made him feel good, which was probably why he was still just a multi-millionaire and not yet a billionaire.

Damn! His knee was killing him.

For diversion, he studied the tiny flotilla of small boats lining the opposite bank of the tributary two hundred yards away. Environmentalist protestors and curious history buffs, or what was left of them. They were once a cluttered mayhem so bad the Coast Guard had deployed a patrol. But with time and boredom, they had dwindled down to just a few hangers-on.

Charley commented, "Those are the diehards."

"Got to give them credit for their commitment," David said.

Charley's radio chirped, "Ready, Charley."

"Okay, Conley. Fire them up."

A squad of twelve band winches standing duty at intervals atop the long sides of *Min*'s upper frame lighted into action humming and clicking, searching for just the right strain on their six lifting straps looped under *Recluse*'s hull.

David observed, "I see you chose the new composite straps. Is this really the right project to gamble with something new?"

"They'll be fine, David."

Sensing the right strain, a mesh of tiny tension gauges stitched into the fibers of the straps fed signals back to Conley's computer. Conley rapped a command on his keyboard and to the winches' computer controls, commanding them to stop. "Straps are set. Time for *Mini* to do her thing."

"Roger that. Bring her up. I'll tell you when to light off the water pumps."

"You got it, bro."

Charley checked his watch. "We're doing good time today."

"You're a natural at this, Charley. It's what you're meant to do."

"My decision still stands." Charley side-stepped, putting some distance between them.

David's cane hand worked into the wood. "Fine, have it your way." He shifted his weight and tugged his cane from the waterlogged muck. "I think I'll wander over and see Conley."

Charley's eyes clung to David's back as the hobbling man traced their makeshift path carved round the cove. His thoughts receded to a faraway place, and for a measureless moment he was nowhere at all.

"Your decision still stands. What decision is that?"

The new voice nearly tripped him into the water.

From across the cove, Qeb hollered "Gemma!" waving wildly in Charley's direction from where David was just walking up to him and the other divers, out of their rigs and standing around.

As she waved back to Qeb, Gemma stepped up beside Charley.

Charley extricated his foot from the gush in the water. "I suppose you've made his day now that you're back." He straightened himself up and said, "So are you? Back, I mean."

Her smile tumbled a bit. "I'd love to be, but I can't promise anything. Tim-Lee's death—it's been hard on Momma, you see. I don't mean to be mean and hurt Qeb. But you understand, don't you? Being a brother and a father I mean. Giving up things for family must come easy to you."

Her eyes lay long on his with a knowing look in them.

"But I explained to her, 'Momma I just got to be there.' All this, it's all too important to Qeb. I wouldn't miss it for the world."

"Just for Qeb? Not for Tim-Lee?"

Her expression chilled just slightly. "Of course for Tim-Lee."

It was then that he noticed the change. Her dowdy dress and staid loafers were gone. Beneath a zipped-open deep grey hoodie, she wore a black tank top revealing enough to abolish any impressions her flat-chested dresses had left behind. Curvaceous black jeans wended their way down to red, white and green socks puffing from the tops of sturdy black hiking boots bejeweled with chrome tongues for the laces.

"He's not going to be used to you in pants."

"What, this?" she said, studying herself. "I put the dresses away for a while. With Momma in mourning, they just weren't right."

"Well, I'm sure he'll like the change. He's been trying to reach you. He's been worried about you." He stifled his urge to ask her how it was she knew that today was the day they were raising *Recluse*. "He hasn't been able to get you off his mind. His concentration—he's had to work hard keeping his attention where it needs to be."

Her brows arched slightly, eyes on Qeb, waving to him again.

Before Charley could stop himself, he blurted out, "I would almost bet that he's in love with you."

She stiffened, just instantly, but enough for him to see.

Her arm fell to her side. "Tsk. That's silly. His kind doesn't fall in love with my type."

"You're exactly the type his kind falls in love with." He thought he heard exasperation in her sigh. "You could have returned his calls."

"You're angry with me."

"I don't want him hurt, that's all."

"He'll come through all this just fine." There was a faint tone of finality to her words.

"What do you mean by that?"

She indicated to *Mini* in the water. "All this. It's all gonna change his life forever. I suppose now every university is gonna be tempting him with offers, maybe even Mr. Kittering. There's the media with all the public exposure. And after what you guys did with finding Cleopatra, there won't be a moment's peace for him for a long time."

It occurred to him that the girly look in her expression had quickly matured ten years. He put a little distance between them. "You're not here to stay. You're here to let him down."

"He doesn't need me in the way. And I think someone's trying to call you on your radio."

"Maybe you should ask him?"

"My life's not mine yet, Mr. Morgan. I have other responsibilities."

He spat into the water. "Yeah. Your family. Your mother. You said that already." He turned to her and said, "I need to ask you something."

But she was already gone, tracing the path round the cove, dismissing him with a wave. "You might want to answer your radio. I'm just gonna wander round and see Qeb."

Charley couldn't pull his eyes off her. What was it about her that had his alarm bells tinkling? Not their full-blown clanging, like when something was in-his-face obvious; just that little better-watch-out kind of tinkling. He couldn't put his finger on it, but there was definitely something about her that was rubbing him the wrong way.

Conley's interruption jolted him. "Charley!"

Charley snapped into his radio, "What?"

"Where's your head, man? I've been calling you and calling you. Are you ready?"

Charley scrunched his radio in his fist. "Shit, Conley! Do you need me to come round there and flip the damn GO switch for you? Grow up! Do your damn job and let's get this fucking show on the road."

"Jesus, Charley. Whatever! (Christ, what's with him today?)"

Mini's dozen winches hummed back into action, juggling their straps under the splint beneath *Recluse*, gently nudging up their tension. One motor's overpressure safety valve squealed open. Charley and Conley, standing across the cove, shared hopeful glances.

A second motor's safety screamed open too, then another followed. Like dominoes, the other valves began lifting and bypassing their motors.

The motors were starving for oil. Their straps were slipping.

Conley's falsetto voice spilled from Charley's two-way radio, "The load's too much."

"Increase the settings on the safety valves," Charley ordered.

David, standing next to Conley, radioed his protest.

"I know what I'm doing David." He skipped the radio chatter and hollered across the water, "Do it now, Conley!"

Using a new technology called wireless, little green electronic cards in each of the valves soaked up signals from Conley's computer to increase their settings to allow higher, more powerful pressures.

One by one the squealing valves hushed back to closed. The starving winches hummed stronger and their straps creaked with renewed tension, tugging at *Recluse* stuck in her muddy bed.

Conley reported, "We're in the yellow, Charley." The straps' tension gauges were reporting back to his computer their pull in the tens of thousands of pounds. The gauge readings were drifting from cautious yellow to deadly red. "Charley, we gotta stop. Let me settle her back down. We can send the divers in and—"

"We're fine! Keep going."

Suddenly, a muffled thunder drifted through the water and *Mini*'s huge frame shuddered. Conley's falsetto voice pitched up two octaves. "Charley, something's wrong down there."

"She just broke free off the bottom, that's all. But we're not home free yet."

"You want the compressors now?"

"I want them just pissing air, just enough to keep her coming without her popping loose too fast and breaking her back."

Mini's compressors engaged, coaxing the flooded water out of her ballast tanks.

"Slowly, Conley. Easy."

"I'm on it, okay?"

This part of the job was not as easy as it might come over in a barstool conversation. With too little air seeping into the ballast tanks, the mud's suck might not let *Recluse* go. But jab too much air to them, too fast, she could bust free with a pop. They'd lose control and *Mini* would rocket to the surface, dragging *Recluse* after her, maybe in pieces.

Or rising too fast, *Recluse* would break the surface. Her water-logged weight would shock the straps, parting them in frayed halves. Or a strap winch might slip and drop its load. And once one went, the others would follow like tumbling dominoes. *Recluse* would crash back down and break in two.

It would be a disaster.

A faint boom from deep within *Mini*'s bowels brushed Charley's ears. Instantly, the ground beneath him punched the soles of his boots.

"That was it! She must be out of the mud now," Conley reported. "Wait. She's not coming. Charley, I think we better release more ballast."

"Just give her a moment to pull herself together," Charley said, with his eye pegged to the splatter of rust on *Mini*'s column.

"Just a little jab, Charley, that's all."

"Patience, Conley." The pumps overhead driving the compressors spun with a hum that said everything was working fine. Two enormous blobs of air busted the cove's surface. "There we are. Tanks are empty."

Mini began rattling all through herself with a mechanical *tock, tock, tock, tock, tock, tock, tock.* A nut and washer toppled from the platform into the water. A paint bucket full of rags followed after them.

Shhhtutt, tutt, tutt, tutt, tutt, tutt, tutt.

The rusty splatter edged up, maybe an inch. Hard to tell. Charley's TALK finger hovered over the button on his radio. Two inches; make it three. His finger squashed the button. "She's coming up."

The splatter edged higher, picking up pace, passing eye level.

From across the cove, Qeb hollered between hands cupping his mouth, "Dad. The water. Look," and pointed at the brownish churned water whitening with the approach of *Mini*'s pontoons.

Between them, a swelling shadow shoved up against the surface. The cove's water rose in protest with nowhere to go. Spreading long, the rising shadow reached out fore and aft beyond *Mini*'s ends.

The bulging cove strained as the big pontoons, round like two whales' backs, broke surface and eased into the open air. With a burst of energy that could only be likened to the sound of a busting dam, the cove's surface ripped open from over *Recluse*'s flat top and gushed over the sloping sides of her dull, sodden steel battery.

"Hold that," Charley ordered. "Set the strap winches to auto-adjust. Get her back down a bit. Keep her top just level with the surface."

Conley practically squealed with excitement. "We're already on it, bro."

Silty water washed down *Mini*'s towering frame like a South Pacific downpour. Her controls clattered and slapped, easing her strap winches in or out to keep *Recluse* from breaking the surface.

Conley let out a *whoop!* "She's trim," he said, reporting that *Mini* was level and stable in the water.

"Roger that."

The water from *Mini*'s frame subsided to a hushed trickle.

And Charley's radio finally shut up.

The winches' hum-click-clicking seemed to double in the growing silence. Speechless eyes just stared. Tongues gripped by wonder could not shape their words.

A damp stink stained the air.

And in the distance a lone seabird cawed.

After the divers got out of their wetsuits and everyone had had a chance to piss and eat a quick lunch cabbed in from town, David joined Charley on the cove's far side again.

"Okay Conley. You know what's next."

"Yes, sir, we're on it." Conley's tone was strangely subdued.

Charley frowned at his radio

"We had a talk," David said. "We both know how Conley gets excited sometimes."

"Well it's good timing, because now comes the hairy part, and it's been years since we've done this on something so fragile."

David nodded, uneasy. "Yes. Let's hope we're not too rusty." He wheeled his attention over his shoulder to the far mouth of the tributary where a rolling haze was blanketing the Shallotte River, gobbling up all details, save one.

Reflecting through the haze were the nail polish red hull and gleaming white upper decks of Kittering Enterprise's heavy lift ship, *K-Four*. Her bow stood tall as an eight-story building. Marking her stern stood two equally tall, box-like stacks: her machinery spaces. From where he stood, they looked like two completely separate things floating in the water. But hidden in the haze, *K-Four*'s well deck stretched between them: a low, flat surface with absolutely no character whatsoever.

But what lacked character had purpose. Big purpose.

K-Four was a semi-submersible wonder: a float-on, float-off ship— Flo/Flo for short—designed to intentionally submerge herself till her well deck lay beneath the water's surface whereby extremely heavy loads like oil rigs, floating dry docks, even navy ships, could drift over the deck such that when *K-Four* rose up again, she'd bring them up out of the water high and dry, sometimes nestled in a cradle or set on blocks.

A dark horizontal slit marked *K-Four*'s bridge. From somewhere inside that slit, curious eyes behind powerful binoculars were no doubt watching the progress at the cove. Silly thing, but he waved to them, over half a mile away.

A sudden revving of engines nudged David back to the task at hand. Husky little outboards warbled from the sterns of three skiffs, eager for the next and most precarious phase of their project. It was time to slide *Recluse* out of the cove and take her down the estuary to the Shallotte River, where *K-Four* would accept her.

"Okay Conley," Charley said. "David and I are boarding Skiff Three. We'll meet you in the middle of the tributary. Is Qeb with you?"

"Roger that. Give us, say, ten minutes to button things up here and board Skiff One."

Conley glanced at Qeb standing in dry clothes beside his girlfriend from Tennessee. She was drop-dead hot and fawning all over him.

"And yeah, Qeb's here with me. I'm going to give him the helm once we get clear of the salt grass. Maybe get him some real experience and put her over the well deck. What do you think?"

"Well, he did find her. He should share in the glory." He crossed his fingers out of David's sight. "I'll leave it to you. It's your call,"

Trailing *Mini* from behind, Conley and Qeb, in Skiff One with a remote control, would drive *Mini*'s pontoon propulsion to ease her out of the cove and steer her into a westerly heading, and then creep her down the tributary at one knot.

Charley and David in Skiff Three, and the rest of Conley's crew in Skiff Two would lead *Mini*, advising Conley of their course and warning of obstacles in the water.

The rest of the crew, machinists and equipment operators mostly, would stay behind and begin the drudgery of cleaning up.

David was first in the boat. As Charley stepped aboard, David blocked him, staring past him at something.

Charley turned round, following David's gaze.

She hadn't shown the slightest interest since the project had invaded her privacy in a swarm of foreign machinery and incomprehensible accents. Her fading lawn was brown with thirst and trodden flat in the sweeping tracks of machinery traffic. Her pet plants circling the house were drooped over and folded with neglect.

She had paid them no heed, these strangers in her midst, with their industrious racket well into suppertime, and their working on the Sabbath. Never once had she succumbed to any inkling of curiosity.

Yet there she stood now on the steps of her back porch, in a dated house dress of proper autumn colors.

David smiled big at her and waved for her to come down and take a look before they left.

Unaffected, she made no attempt. Just stood there, arms folded, hawking their every move from behind her salt air complexion.

24-THE HOMECOMING QUEEN

The Cape Fear River, October 2005

The steel railing bordering the deck just below *K-Four*'s pilothouse reeked of cool in Charley's hands. The deck beneath his 10-1/2-wide, Justin Original work boots—*made in America, thank you very much*—shone with a fresh coat of spit-shine, four leaf clover green. The overhang above him and the bulkhead behind him were lavished in crisp white paint, meticulously applied. Not a nook or cranny had been missed. With *K-Four* heading into public view, David Kittering was sparing nothing to make sure Kittering Enterprises shone proud.

This was day two since they had raised *Recluse* from her muddy bed. *K-Four* had idled, half-submerged as she was wont to do, in the Shallotte River and waited patiently as *Mini* drifted over her well deck with her precious load. Once in place, the "All Go!" command had been given, and slowly *K-Four* had broken the surface with *Recluse* and *Mini* riding her back.

It was an all-hands evolution that had lasted well into the night beneath the smile of the biggest moon the Farmer's Almanac had registered in a century. With their work finally complete, the crew had whispered in wonder at the edgy behemoth looming over them, bathing in blue-white moonlight.

K-Four had paid her mystic burden no mind, sleeping deeply that night anchored in the Shallotte River, creaking in her dreams to the chime of buoy bells in the distant darkness.

After the morning meal of strong coffee, buttermilk biscuits, and the cook's pride—scrambled eggs with andouille sausage, chopped bell peppers, and pearl onions dusted with a healthy dose of *Tony Chachere's*—they departed through the Shallotte Inlet and traced the coast east, rounding Fort Caswell on their port side and edging past

Southport on their left, where superstitious eyes lined every edge of the quaint town's sparse waterfront.

Standing at the rail, Charley shuffled his joints and bobbled his head. *K-Four*'s doddering pace was driving him nuts: like two steps forward, one step back. That and Qeb refusing to talk to him. The kid hadn't so much as traded eye contact at breakfast.

He needed off this damned ship. Just step right off when they docked and adios! He'd go home and see Femi and forget everything.

Yeah. Sure you will.

After they docked, work would keep him busy long after dark, which wasn't all that far off, low in the sky as the sun was now. Winter. He despised her. The islands and the Pacific had rescued him from winter for so long he'd forgotten her hijinks. Now here he was, back, with winter gripping him in her clutches and laughing at him, too loud for him to hear. Like an old girlfriend who never left home, she had never changed. The same old same old: dark in the morning when he went to work, dark when he got home, and icy sunshine in between.

He wondered, would they notice if he jumped ship right here, right now, into the river? It was shallow here, for sure. He gazed over the rail. Not so far down, either. He might get sore, but no broken bones.

Ah! A damn gator or something would probably nip him in the leg and give him rabies.

K-Four glided gently forward making barely a ripple in the water. Campbell Island was just passing by on Charley's right as he looked aft down the river. Campbell Island. It was their marker. The rest of the way, a hodge-podge of sandy islets peppered the river, making a general nuisance of themselves to ships' traffic. From here on, their hired river pilot up on the bridge with the captain would be much concerned.

"There won't be any other ships in your way. The police have the river shut down. Not even a bass boat or kayak is allowed on the water till you guys are tied up." Or so Frank said.

He had called the night before. "This place is nuts, Charley! People are coming from everywhere to see what you're bringing in. The mayor's got a big ceremony set up for Saturday. There's bunting all over the place. And Confederate flags. Little ones on sticks for kids are ten bucks. What a rip-off. And bigger ones flying from just about anything you can call a flagpole.

"Anyway, Hillary and I got lucky and found a room in a restored mansion, a Bed-and-Breakfast. Someone cancelled or something like that. It's expensive as hell. Anyway, can you believe she actually suggested we ask Femi if we could stay with her? Hillary, I mean. I don't think she realizes that situation. Femi's never going to forgive her."

Sure she will, Frank. Just give her time.

Frank and Hillary.

Together.

When this was over—after the city welcomed the ship home, after she was settled in her new place, and after David Kittering started doing whatever it was he had planned for restoring the thing—he was definitely going to need some quiet time just to adjust to the shock of all the changes.

"Anyway, the hotels are booked solid. And the traffic! What a mess. Snarled to a dead stop just about everywhere. If we didn't find our room, we would have had to sleep in the truck. But then, thing is, there's no place to park anyway because the police won't allow parking on the streets."

"Probably safety reasons," Charley had guessed. "They don't want a repeat of what happened up north. That bomb in the train station. A couple of years ago, remember?"

No, Frank didn't remember.

Charley stroked the rail in his hands over the chips and gouges missing from the layers of paint beneath the latest coating of gleaming white marine enamel. How do you forget something like that, so many people hurt? Maybe no one was killed, but still. He twisted his palms round the rail, searching its uneven edges and slight craters. The tiniest inkling of a smile teased the roots of his beard, blonde-going-gray. The feel of simple imperfections against his skin like the feel of his favorite fat pen in his hand: a simple pleasantry that softened the hardness of workaday life; so inconsequential, but somehow so meaningful.

Like the birthmark on Femi's neck.

He snatched his grip from the rail.

That tiny birthmark he loved so much, just beneath the nape of her pitch black hair. A simple nothing, so small; but without that little blemish Femi wouldn't be Femi. And just like the uneven feel of the paint on the rail, he'd gotten so used to it that he'd stopped seeing it altogether.

He'd taken it for granted.

He'd taken *her* for granted.

A lumpy blend of dread gripping a double-barreled load of fear faced off with him: dread that the decision he'd finally gotten the guts to make, he'd made much too late; with one barrel-load of fear being she would leave him anyway, and the other barrel-load being his fear about his new future packed hard with all its unknowns.

Unknowns. There were so many unknowns ahead of him: stability, consistency, order, structure. All of them had been the backbone of his working life since the navy. The oil rigs too. Okay, maybe not so much when he'd gone into business for himself in Egypt, but even then there had been the same two constants: the feel of a steel deck beneath his feet and the pungent aroma of overworked water.

And there'd been Olufemi.

In the worst days of his independence, Femi had kept him steady. When the specter of inadequacy visited him in his sleep, greeted him when he woke, or jumped his back during the day to prophesy his financial demise, Femi would bitch-slap him back to his senses. She would comfort him when he felt most alone as a friendless American expat, and she would mend his heart when life made him feel small.

Femi.

The sometimes clean, sometimes not water.

And a steel deck beneath him—all of them, they were home.

Somebody rapped on the glass of a porthole behind him. Did he want some coffee?

His waved, "No thanks," and distanced himself from his unwelcome observers into the privacy of the autumn sunlight.

He had worked so hard—so damned hard!—all his adult life to find that home, to make that home, to make something good of himself, give purpose to his life, and fill it with friends and people he loved.

And still somehow, he had fucked it all up in the end.

He took in the chilly air hanging over the Cape Fear River. Maybe things aren't as fucked up as you think. Maybe you made the right decision in time to save it all.

It was the right decision, wasn't it?

Isn't it?

Thing was, he was only half the decision. Olufemi was the other half. And to his horror, she wasn't committing herself. She was actually *thinking* about it. And it was that hesitation in her that had slammed everything home for him, and everything came crashing down.

For the first time since God knew when, he was scared out of his wits. Because even if Femi did say yes, there was that little string that was attached with it: a very long and knotted string that would ask him to do the unthinkable.

Give up the ships.

Ships like *K-Four* were in his blood, in his deepest sense of self-worth. They had sown the very fiber of his adult life. The ships in the navy. The rigs on the oil patch.

He enjoyed a sentimental smile. Yes, even his salvage barge *Opportunity* in Egypt.

His smile sagged. With them all in his past, what would take their place?

The hackles on his neck stirred.

An unwelcome voice stepped out from a dark corner in his head. *There is always me.*

He wasn't fooled. He knew right where it came from.

His courage crept over the railing to the thing down in the well deck. He studied her with distrust from the safety of his vantage point three decks above her. All through the project at the cove, she'd never amounted to much more to him than vague Technicolor images on Qeb's computer screen. Even bringing her out to the river to *K-Four*, she'd slipped along just beneath the waves, never showing herself.

Not a hint. Not even a teasing sliver.

But when *K-Four*'s well deck broke the surface and the river's water washed over her sides, nothing in all his experience had prepared him for what rose from the saline. When the "All Clear!" was finally passed, he had traced the ladders down to the deck, eyes fixed on her settled on hefty wood keel blocks, towering over him, dripping cold memories and filth.

Aft of her on the well deck, between *K-Four*'s machinery spaces that looked like two giant cigarette packs guarding the corners of her stern, men were tending to *Mini*, cleaning her up and refitting her. Another team was spraying a film of oils over the *Recluse*'s armor, a concoction invented and patented by David Kittering that would, till better means could be applied, fend off the inevitable attack of corrosion from the open air that would kick in at a rate of destruction that would make your head spin.

He had approached her with halting steps and had loitered under her bow, his mind drawing a blank. His hand had reached up and his fingertips had kissed her wood hull. She was slimy, hard, and cold. Cold like nothing he'd imagined. He had tried to pull his touch away, but couldn't. Something in him was refusing.

He remembered the involuntary words *What is it?* slipping past his lips.

She then emitted a sudden stink that had engulfed him and squeezed the breath from him, chilling him to his deepest insides. Vague images had entered his thoughts. Harsh words, a loud holler, and then a muffled bang. Like a gunshot. And then it was over, gone just as suddenly as it came. His hand had fallen away from her and hung before his face.

He remembered searching the prints in his fingertips. That's when it came. Or was it they?

It's happening again, isn't it, Charley?

That time in Egypt when *she* came in his sleep. He would never forget it. And she wouldn't let him. And again, in that thing buried under the river bottom. Why the hell did he have to be the one to find it? She had showed herself and he had done what he could to steer his fear aside, but then she touched him, scaring his soul right out of him and sending it scurrying up to Heaven to wait for him there, not daring to come back.

It was since then that he realized, not all things that spoke were alive.

He looked up at her with fierce eyes.

No. It's not happening. Not again. I won't let it. Not ever.

Still, the entire trip from Shallotte, he had avoided her like the plague, hiding in the crew's lounge, hovering over coffee, black, no sugar, cupped between his trembling hands.

When word was passed over *K-Four*'s intercom that they were just rounding Fort Caswell, he had worked up the courage to visit her again, this time from a safe distance on the cramped machinery deck just below the pilothouse, and three decks above the well deck. And when he chanced a peek down at her, he had stiffened, waiting for the images to return, and the angry words. And the gun shot.

But only the chill in the air lay between them.

Whatever it was or was supposed to be, it was gone now. It was only her down there now, alone and quiet, like a ship asleep at pierside.

Ships have a human way about them, especially at night. Things in their shadows clink and clatter. Their bowels rumble and their bones groan as they search in their sleep for a comfortable trim or heel. They off-gas steam like farts and dispense bilge pump waste over the side like piss. But not her. There was nothing human about her. She had lain submerged in that cove back there, down in the dark, drowned and lifeless.

And still, his all-too-busy sixth sense wasn't convinced one bit that she was dead.

A century and a half of biological detritus had seeped into the cracks between her armor plates, giving her a particularly reptilian appearance. A mossy hue emanated from all over her. She was an ugly thing, squat and angular, menacing in her filthy condition in the mid-afternoon sunlight, like a waiting alligator ready to snap up its next meal.

And she was beginning to stink like one.

A ridiculous sadness trickled through him. She was so big in her presence and yet so vulnerable and defenseless. He tried to humor himself with Chunky bars: a candy treat from his childhood, a foil-wrapped square with sloping sides. That's what she looked like, a big Chunky bar on a flat boat.

Maybe she wasn't so ugly after all.

Her curved hull reached forward from her mid-ships in a slow sweep to a point at her bow. A single bollard was the only object disturbing the perfect flatness of her steel foredeck that reached out to her hull freeboard, also made of steel and unmarred by the obtrusive presence of bulwarks or gunwales.

Her gun battery had been fashioned and joined to her deck with exquisite skill suggesting an almost seamless transition from flat deck to sloping sides. A single hatch in the center of the front part of her battery faced his way. He'd snooped inside there when the machinists had tethered some pumps to draw out the muck inside her. Cold dankness and a numbing blackness had greeted him, and the queer sensation of a presence not really there.

Like the one that had visited him in his dreams in Egypt.

The squawk of a door opening behind him brushed aside the images cluttering his thoughts. Unsure footsteps approached him from behind and passed him by. He glanced sidelong at the shape as it assumed a spot at the rail beside him. Qeb.

Beyond Qeb, where the Brunswick River slipped into intercourse with the Cape Fear, the bottom tip of Eagle Island was just sliding into view. Charley worked his jaw, toying with a bump on his back tooth.

Time's running out. Now's as good a time as any.

"So, when do you think you'll be going back to school?" He searched for brush strokes in the green deck paint. A hundred silent seconds seemed to pass. "S'okay. I didn't mean to pry. I know you got a lot on your mind and—"

"I'm not sure I am going back."

Charley squashed out an imaginary cigarette on the deck. "That's a shame. All your busting ass. All your hard work. Quitting now, it's almost like giving up the fight three days before victory, don't you think?"

"I'm not a quitter."

"What else would you call it?"

Qeb's gaze retreated to the passing riverbank. "You don't understand."

"Try me."

Qeb leaned into the rail and clocked his attention down onto *Recluse*. "These past few weeks with Gemma—they remind me of the excitement we had before, you and me." His attention was snatched by the call of a passing gull. "You remember that, you and me? We were so close then."

The gull settled onto *Recluse*'s battery. Its dirty white feathers against *Recluse*'s motley dark made it seem twice as bright. "I want that all back, the excitement and the feeling of doing. Not watching. Not just studying. And Gemma's given me that, showing me a whole different way of looking at things. Until her, it was like I was walking through life just doing the motions without really seeing."

He and Charley evaded each other, the both of them retreating to the isolation of *Recluse*'s armor, all moody and grey with red-brown stains streaking down it like a bad roof.

"I'm sure mom has told you by now, but I'm not very successful with girls."

Charley watched Qeb's hands wringing the color from the rail.

"My last girlfriend, she dumped me up there on the dig, the same time Professor Laird dumped me and kicked me off the site. Did you know he threatened to call the police when I wouldn't leave? Right there in front of everybody. And all the others watching. I swear they were loving it. I felt this big."

A sliver of daylight slipped between his thumb and forefinger.

"But Gemma—she sees things in me Professor Laird can't, or won't. Uncle Frank, too. But her, she's not like them. She treats me decent." He stepped back from the rail and indicated to *Recluse*. "If it wasn't for her, I might never have looked any further than Tim-Lee did. I would have gone back up on Professor Laird's dig. But now, that's not going to happen."

"You don't know that. Did you even try?"

Qeb glanced at Charley's feet. "Gemma convinced me not to go back."

Charley's grip on the rail whitened his knuckles. "So, it was her all along."

"Don't sound like that. I couldn't make up my mind between the feeling guilty and the just wanting to get away. She helped me choose and she was right. Dumping school and finishing Tim-Lee's work. It was the right thing. This is real life. Now I know I can do this work, not just pretend."

"Qeb."

"No, Dad. No more school..." He shook his head at the muddy trees tracing the river's edge. "I can't do it anymore. I can't. I won't."

Charley closed the gap a little between them. "What you did for your friend, it's a great thing. Down there is the proof. You've done well by him. No one can ever deny that." He leaned into the railing. Its familiarity pleased the soft underbellies of his forearms. "Do you remember when I tried to get you to quit school for a year and help me on that project down in New Zealand?"

Qeb turned his back to the rail. His mind scampered across the gadgetry on the bulkheads and deck, trying to recall. "The oil barge thing, yeah. But no, I don't remember you asking me that."

"I said then that I wasn't convinced they were teaching you anything useful in those classrooms. I was positive what you needed was real field experience. More than anything any of those professors could teach you."

He half-turned and squinted south into the sunlight behind his son. "You remember what you said?" Even in the sun's glare he could see the muscles in Qeb's jaw flexing just so slightly. "You said, 'It doesn't matter what I can do in the field. Without my doctorate, I'm nothing.'"

Qeb's eyelids fluttered.

"You don't remember that, do you?"

Qeb's grip wrung deeper into the rigid comfort of the railing.

Charley took a single step closer. "One last crummy dig. What is that, a year maybe? Then it's over."

Qeb's Adam's apple bobbed. "A year. I'm sure to you that's, like nothing."

"Gemma will wait. She'll be here for you when you're done."

Qeb pushed the rail away. "You just don't get it, do you? I want to live my life with her, Dad. I want to do things together with her, now. Not in another year or two or three or whatever." His gaze dove overboard to the gushy safety of the passing river bank.

Charley's throat kicked hard, deep down behind his heart. "Have you asked her?"

"Asked her what?"

"What *she* wants."

Qeb squinted back at him as if he'd spoken some incoherent language.

"What would she say to you tossing in the towel now?"

The wrinkles of Qeb's frown aged him two decades in a single second.

"She'd say it makes no sense, that's what she'd say."

Qeb's frown flattened instantly. "You don't even know her. And I'm not going back."

Charley searched the tiny details of Qeb's ear and down the unblemished skin that swept round his cheek and jaw, for the real truth behind his hardnosed resistance. He sought it in the olive brown of Qeb's eyes and found nothing. Frustrated, he traced the fine sweep of Qeb's twenty-something leather-black hair. Maybe the answer would seep out from between the follicles.

Qeb couldn't stand it any longer. He was no match for the slow steady chipping of Charley's chisel against his defenses. "I love her, Dad."

There. You said it.

Something electric zipped through Charley. His throat kicked again, harder this time. Was this what a heart attack felt like?

"Did you hear me, Dad? I said I love her."

"You can't love her. You hardly know her."

"I know her enough to know my feelings for her." Qeb gave his father a sidelong once-over and straightened himself. "There's something else."

Oh, great. Here it comes.

He turned and faced his father. "I'm going to ask Mr. Kittering for work. I'm going to do the work, not just study it. You said ask her. Well I'll ask her that, and we'll see what she says."

Charley seized his son's arm. "Qeb, you need to think about this."

"Ow! You're hurting me." Qeb yanked himself free. "Forget the dig, will you?" he said, massaging the pain from his bicep. "Professor Laird won't let me back."

"Sure he will."

"I told you what happened. Why won't you listen?"

"Just go see him and apologize, for chrissakes."

"It won't do any good."

"Sure it will. Just tell him—"

"Dammit, Dad! Don't you get it? I lost my fellowship."

Somewhere up forward, a hatch slammed hard.

25-SHIFTING SANDS

The Cape Fear River's green blue over brown water hissed by along *K-Four*'s hull through the silence that widened even more the gap that was growing between Qeb and his father. Qeb barely heard Charley say, "I see."

The hatch behind them squawked open. Qeb did a half-turn and shook his head at somebody behind them. Voices muttered, shoes shuffled, and the hatch squawked closed again.

"Gemma's all I've got now. She's all I think about." He indicated to *Recluse*. "You know me. You'd think I'd be all over that ship right now. But I'm not, am I? No. I'm up here thinking about her. She's all I think of anymore."

"And you love her."

"I do love her." Qeb stamped his words with a committed nod. "I do."

"And that's dangerous."

"Love dangerous? You want to explain that?"

"It's dangerous because when a man falls in love, he loses all reason."

Qeb smirked. "I'll remember to tell Mother that."

"What I mean is we guys—we don't manage love as well as women do. We get stupid. We forget what's important and we lose our sense of priorities."

"Listen to you, talking about love and priorities like they're incompatible."

"They are now, and you need to get a grip on that. What's so funny?"

"You, lecturing me on priorities when you leave your own wife home alone for months and months."

Qeb waited for the reply that never came. "You know," he said from behind moist eyes, "I can't talk with you about this." He noticed David Kittering down below snooping around *Recluse*, at something on her hull. "I'm going down there to talk to David."

"About a job?" Charley snapped.

As he descended the ladder to the well deck, the tears Qeb had been holding back finally busted the dam. He stopped halfway down and cried alone in the shadows of the ladder well.

David Kittering deliberated *Recluse*'s hull as if unseen words had been scribed into her fibers. "Amazing, isn't she?" he said, when Qeb strolled up. His head shook slowly, almost imperceptibly. "She's in incredibly good shape." He waved to a place in her hull where the planks were punched out like something inside had kicked them. "If it weren't for that damage there, I'd almost bet she would be seaworthy."

Kittering half-turned to Qeb, smack into the bloated redness of the boy's eyes.

Qeb flinched under the pressure of Kittering's questioning look and tossed his attention onto a sprig of growth comfortably settled between the planks of *Recluse*'s hull.

"What's bothering you, kid?"

Qeb reached out and plucked the sprig. "It's just my dad." He rolled the crumbling sprig between his fingertips. How many years or decades had it been living there, he wondered. He let it all fall to his feet. With a sigh, he swept the dirt from his hands. "It's nothing, really."

Kittering doubted that. "Father-son stuff is rarely ever just nothing."

Qeb wiped the back of his wrist across the bottom of his nose. "You asked me once before, was there anything you could do. Well...there is something."

Kittering handed him a handkerchief from his jacket pocket. He said nothing. Just waited.

Qeb's eyes, glistening like glass, met Kittering head-on. "Fire my dad so my mother can have him back."

Kittering tottered on startled legs for a long moment before admitting, "I almost wish I could." A vague smirk came and went across his face. "But I can't."

"Why not?"

"I just can't."

Qeb blanched. "What you mean is you think you need him more than his family needs him."

"Not at all."

"Then why the hell not?"

Kittering ignored the mean edge to Qeb's words. "I can't fire your father because he already fired himself."

Qeb's fury crumpled. "I—I don't understand."

Kittering pulled a tri-folded letter from inside his windbreaker. "Your father resigned." He extended it to Qeb. "Go ahead. Read it."

Qeb glanced up at his father. He wasn't looking. He was watching the city of Wilmington approaching. Still, he hunkered back beneath *Recluse*'s shadow so Charley wouldn't see. He read the letter, read it again, and brain-farted into a blank space.

Gentle fingers reached out and coaxed the letter back from his grasp.

"What're you going to do?"

"Refuse it, of course. And I'm still sending him and your mother on that vacation you asked them to postpone."

Qeb flinched from Kittering's penalizing tone. "And when they're back?"

Kittering's expression softened from stern to reminiscent.

"Your father once told me—and this is strictly in confidence. I never told you this. But he's been dreaming of working with you after you graduated. He has this...this idea of the three of you working together somehow. You, him, and that drifty brother of his."

Qeb glanced up at his father again. Charley was looking to port now and half-waving to the crowd lining the waterfront at the tug yard on Battleship Road.

K-Four's horn wailed out two blasts: one long, one short. The drawbridge was approaching. Almost over Charley's head, the Ocean Highway was jammed with onlookers. Traffic had stopped completely. The drawbridge was up to let *K-Four* pass underneath.

"He hasn't shut up about your doctorate for months. He was driving my crew nuts; part of the reason I kicked him off my ship."

"You kicked him off?"

"That I did." Kittering said, as they passed underneath the bridge.

People were looking down onto them from over the bridge's railing. Flashing blue police lights were at each end of the bridge. Traffic was frozen stock still. Uniforms were pleading with the crowd for their own safety.

"Do not climb onto the railing. Stay off the railing."

Some kids waved down to them. But for the most part, the countless faces were muted, awing down at the thing on *K-Four*'s back: the thing they'd always been told was a lie; the thing their parents, and parents' parents had dismissed as one of History's reprobate hoaxes.

"Charley is one of the strongest men I know," Kittering said, waving up to the kids. "But you know something? I wouldn't be at all surprised that—if for some reason you couldn't finish your studies—I think it would just about crush his heart." He didn't look at Qeb. He just waved.

Kittering's words jabbed hard at Qeb's gut, in that tender place just above the navel. "Why are you going to refuse his resignation?"

The Wilmington waterfront was closing on their starboard side. There was a voice on a loudspeaker, somewhere up ahead.

"I'm going to help your father get his dream, Qeb. Kittering Enterprises is setting up operations up in Beaufort. Kittering Explorations, we're calling it. Kind of a spin-off operation. My lawyers are doing up the paperwork." He cocked a twinkling eye Qeb's way. "He doesn't know it yet. It's my secret." He turned and faced the boy. "And you, too. You'll have a fleet of three boats, a couple crews and a warehouse."

"But—"

"There will be equipment and a lab for your uncle."

"Uncle Frank?"

"I've already discussed it with him."

"Mr. Kittering—"

"Call me David."

"Mr. Kittering, about my doctorate—"

"I know. You're not done yet."

"No, you don't understand. I'm not graduating."

"Very funny."

"I'm not joking."

David faltered. His expression went this way and that.

"You don't know me, Mr. Kittering."

"That's a laugh. Your father never shuts up about you. I probably know more about you than you'd ever want me to know, believe me."

"He only remembers me the way I was. That was years ago. I've changed. I'm not that easy to get along with. I can't keep a girlfriend. I don't even have friends really, except for Tim-Lee."

"Excuse me, but what's all this got to do with you not graduating?"

"I rock the boat a lot. I caused some trouble with Professor Laird, enough that he kicked me off his dig. I brought it on myself, I suppose."

"I'm sure we can convince the university—"

"No!" Qeb snapped, then cooled down. "I mean, Professor Laird gave me the chance to come back and I refused. And for that, I lost my fellowship. Okay?"

David's expression collapsed. He looked like he took a punch.

The rustle of activity on the waterfront round the other side of *Recluse* wormed its way through the gaps between her keel blocks and traced the sweep of her hull. The racket seemed to spark something in him. He scratched his chin, thinking. "This Professor Laird—do you mean Dr. Stephan Laird?"

"You know him?"

"Never mind that. So the college—they've already dismissed you, not just threatened it?"

"I got the news the day before you arrived to help raise the ship."

David mulled it over for a minute. "Well, I'll tell you something from experience. There's nothing yet I've found that can't be fixed by applying large sums of ready cash to the right palms."

"You mean bribes?"

David plopped his hand on Qeb's shoulder. "I prefer calling them incentives. Let me make a call. And then we'll see if we can't do something about Mr. Laird."

Qeb pulled away. "No."

"Excuse me?"

"I deserved it, Mr. Kittering."

"No, you didn't."

"You weren't even listening to what I said just now."

"Listen here, kiddo. You need to dump the self-pity thing and think of your father." David steered his attention back up to Charley eyeballing the waterfront. It seemed a brass band on shore had struck up Dixie. "You *do* realize what you've done, don't you?"

Qeb traced David's gaze up to his father. "I've ruined his dream, that's what."

"No you haven't. And I wasn't talking about that." David stroked *Recluse*'s cool wood hull with the love of a sculptor caressing his finally-finished work of a lifetime. "I was talking about this lady. What you've discovered here—she's going to upset a lot of people."

"Tim-Lee Polk discovered her, not me."

"Well then, Mr. Polk's discovery is going to upset a lot of people."

"Why is that?"

"History, Qeb. History will have to be rewritten and engineering textbooks revised. And those hacks in academia will have a lot of explaining to do." But the boy wasn't with him. "You really haven't been inside her, have you?"

"I've had things on my mind. Once we got her onboard, I just..."

"Then you haven't seen."

"I thought I would wait till we were tied up. There will be time."

"Come with me." David waved for him to come aft. They stopped at a spot just abaft *Recluse*'s midships. David placed his hand on a dark, metal hole in her hull.

"Any idea what this is?"

Qeb studied the end of a metal pipe leading into the ship's insides, all black with age. It was about a foot in diameter. The end of it was curvaceous and smooth, blended into the wood all round it by a long dead craftsman who clearly had practiced his trade with a passion.

A recollection flashed through Qeb's grey matter, shrinking his brow into deep furrows. "In the old man's manuscript, he said something about the engine exhaust coming out under the water. It was so there would be no smoke to give them away."

"That's what you're looking at, kid. There's another one on the other side."

Qeb traced the sweep of the hull up to the freeboard. "Why will that change history and school books?"

David snickered and shook his head. "You see? You can't quit school now; you still have too much left to learn. Anyway, way back in 1876 an obnoxious German named Nikolas Otto was credited for the first functioning compression engine. Since then, every kid who goes to engineering school is taught about the great Nikolas Otto. In basic Thermodynamics it's the Otto Cycle. And what respectable work on engine history would exclude him? But this old girl is going to change all that, because of what she's got in her belly."

David admired *Recluse*'s hull, reading every ripple and rise in her planks. "She's full of surprises, this one." He studied Qeb a little deeper. "You said back there you didn't look inside because you had things on your mind. What kind of things?"

"Just things?"

"Come on, kid. Out with it."

Qeb cleared his throat. "Well, when we were getting ready to pull out of the cove—Gemma promised to come along out to *K-Four* with us and take the ride upriver with us. Then, just like that, she said no. She wasn't coming along, she said. She said she would rather drive."

"And that's why you've been walking around here with that hang-dog face?" But the boy's expression was clear. He was in deep hurt. "Her family is in Tennessee, yes?"

"Uh huh. Tim-Lee once said they had hundreds of acres in the mountains just over the state line. You'd never guess it, as broke as he always was. And Gemma—she was so hot yesterday. I couldn't take my eyes off her."

"You really have it for her deep, don't you?" The boy's expression suggested he wanted to share something. "Go ahead, you can tell me.

It'll stay just between you and me." David made sure Charley up on the rails wasn't watching.

"It doesn't matter," Qeb said. "I already told him."

"That you love her?" He snatched Qeb by the arm when the kid lost his balance. "Whoa! Hold on there."

"It's that obvious?"

"You're kidding, right?" He squished paternally at Qeb's shock. "I guess not. Look at me, Qeb. You don't get to be my age without magically learning somewhere along the line how to read people. It's okay. Don't be upset. I was in love myself a couple times. Or maybe it was three. It was a while back, but not so long ago that I can't remember what it's like when someone steals your heart. I'd say it's pretty obvious she's got yours cupped in her hands."

"Can we please not talk about this? This Dr. Otto; what's he got to do with this ship?"

David expelled a disappointed sigh. "Okay. We'll do it your way. So anyway, this Dr. Otto character has been occupying a pedestal of honor for years. Now, thanks to you and your friend, we have proof he plagiarized his design."

"Stole his design? That's crazy." But it was clear the old man wasn't joking.

"From a French fellow by the name of Alphonse Beau de Rochas."

Qeb faded a bit till recollection struck home. "In Peter Howe's manuscript he talks about some kind of new engines. I researched it. De Rochas—he had a theory for compressing fuel for combustion."

"Good for you. I'm impressed. Well it just so happens that Monsieur de Rochas patented his four-stroke engine theory before the Civil War and a full fifteen years before Herr Otto's first successful engine farted to life. And Otto used de Rochas' theory to do it."

"But that's not really stealing, is it? Putting another man's theory to work?"

"Maybe not; but you at least share credit where credit is due. In the end, Otto did no such thing. The way history has it, you'd think he worked out the kinks all by himself." David patted *Recluse*'s hull with a strange smirk on his face.

Qeb's confusion tip-toed past David's palm on *Recluse*'s hull and into her pitch dark belly, slowly fitting the pieces together. "You're saying the de Rochas engines are in there, aren't you?"

"Your friend, Tim-Lee would have liked that, don't you think, shaking up the academic world reconciling a historical fallacy?"

Maybe, but Qeb's heart only sagged further. "I think the way it all turned out really sucks." He bowed his head and nudged a pebble on the deck with his shoe tip. "He was my best friend. The last time I saw him, we had this fight. I said things. And now I can't take them back." He traced a crease in *Recluse*'s hull, searching for penance. "Professor Laird was so hard on him. I sometimes wonder if he just hated that Tim-Lee might actually find her. Tim-Lee took all the crap from all of us and still he never gave up. Not until he..."

"I don't think Professor Laird hated your friend. Not so much as he might have hated that Mr. Polk had found what he had lost: the passion and commitment for his work. You have it too."

Qeb raised a skeptical cheek. "I don't have the strength he had, to put up with people's crap and keep going."

"Of course you do. *Recluse* is proof of that. Your friend showed you the way. Yes, he died. But in finishing his search, you've put meaning in his death." He placed a fatherly hand on Qeb's shoulder. "That's the kind of strength only the best of friends can give."

K-Four's horn on the pilot house roof tooted twice.

Qeb cleared his throat. "We must be there." He wiped something from his eye. "We're coasting to starboard."

"Yes. We'll be closing on the city side of the river first. Then we'll back down and slip across the river stern-first into our spot on Eagle Island."

They strolled round to *Recluse*'s bow to watch the Wilmington waterfront drifting closer as *K-Four* nosed round.

Up forward, *K-Four*'s bow shadowed over enthralled onlookers clustered on the manicured Riverwalk Park that traced the river. She was a big rig. With her bow barely kissing the shoreline, the full length of her stretched out to the middle of the river. Astounded faces hung quiet and mouths dangled agape at the enormous mottled grey thing squatting on *K-Four*'s flat back. At the far end if it, twisted propeller blades hung idle from braces bordering a single rudder.

K-Four's horn gave three short blasts. Her well deck shuddered as she slipped into reverse engines and pulled away from the faces on the waterfront, and shoved her stern aft across the river to Eagle Island. There, as she edged into a slip cut into the island especially for her, an enormous shadow swept over her, drawing all eyes aboard skyward. To port, looming over them was the imposing presence of the USS *North Carolina*.

The order was given, "Secure lines fore and aft."

Starboard hawser lines were heaved to waiting hands on the new pier just completed in the nick of time a week before. There was an enormous wood grandstand, maybe fifty feet long and a dozen rows high, with a podium at its center. Bunting was draped from anything that might hold it. A few vehicles were parked on the pier. A moment later, the word was passed, "All lines secured."

Instantly, *K-Four*'s horn blasted a celebratory series of long and short blasts.

The great warship beside her, USS *North Carolina*, blew honors in reply.

From across the river and almost on cue, hand-held, aerosol horns—a bargain at $10 each, two for $15—small boat whistles, car horns and tolling church bells loosed a rolling tsunami of racket across the Cape Fear River that side-slammed the cliff-like bulkheads of *North Carolina* and spilled over *K-Four*.

Confederate States Ship, CSS *Recluse* had come home.

David rested a friendly arm over Qeb's shoulder. "Yes indeed, you've sure made one hell of an achievement."

He squeezed Qeb close and looked at him as a father might.

"And as for you fellowship, let's see if we can't do something about that."

Evening: the chilly suppertime of an autumn day when it's still early as the clocks chime five, but much later to the eye. The Sun, cheated by the human calamity of daylight savings time, pouts from just over the brim of the Earth. Her lighted fingers slip through the spindly leafless trees of Eagle Island and reach across the gentle ripples of the Cape Fear River for one last begrudging grip on Wilmington.

But force of habit persists. She lets go, and sinks beneath the horizon with her receding rays flattening all color in a swath of drowsy orange.

A gentle rumble cracks gunmetal clouds rolling in from the east and drizzles the city in a soft misty rain.

On the Riverwalk, fascinated and yet somehow frightened eyes wonder at the dark and distant beast across the water blanketed now in the garish spill of halogen work lights that brand its sometimes curvy, mostly edgy shadow into the hard flat sides of neighboring USS *North Carolina*. It lay sleeping now on the long flat back of that strange ship that slithered in that day with her mountainous bow and two boxy whatever-the-heck-they-were towering from the back end of her.

Strolling lovers linger, the unattached loiter, and nighttime tongues whisper.

"That big red ship—I read about ships like—it's actually made to sink."

"Be quiet!"

"It is."

"You're just making that up."

"Really. Just enough so other stuff can float over its back and then it can lift them out of the water when it comes back up."

"A ship that's supposed to sink? That's crazy."

"Baby, how do you think they got that thing on its back?"

"I don't know, Herbie. And I don't care how far it sinks; you're not getting me on that thing."

"Well I guess you don't have to worry then, because I don't hear them asking you."

"I'm bored. And it's raining. I thought you were taking me to dinner."

"I am. And it's almost time for our reservation, so come on."

Downtown Wilmington buzzed with partied excitement, a preamble to the next day's official homecoming ceremonies for the thing in the shadows across the river. The rain was picking up. On the sidewalks, umbrellas were out and shoulders hunkered in against the October dampness. Cars shushed over asphalt glazed with a pre-Halloween drizzle. Raindrops pattered against nightspot windows, twisting the neon colors and amber table lights within. Everywhere it was standing room only, crammed tight in the immovable mugginess of shoulder-to-shoulder humanity and uproarious chatter. The beer taps were tipping as generously as their jovial revelers. Liquors were flowing and wine glasses were toasting over excited debate.

"You can't really believe that! I do. You think that's really it, over there? I do. Forgive him. He's a romantic. I think it's hideous, you ask me. Sinister's the word you're looking for, darlin'. Well, I think it's beautiful, and you all should have more respect. Respect for what; some old wreck? They should'a just left it where they found it. Fool! I'm talkin' 'bout the brave men who died in it, fighting for The Cause. Oh pooh on The Cause! That's so long ago, who cares 'bout that anymore. Bartender! Over here, another round!

"You ask me, I think it's the one. Well who's asking you? He's right. It's that one they made at the end of the war that was gonna sink those Yankees, damn them all. (Sorry John. I know you're from New Jersey). S'okay. I got a thick skin growing up in Newark. You have to forgive my husband, John. He's confusing reality with legend. Am not! That's a myth, sweetie: a child's bedtime story. We all heard it growing up. I don't care. I say that thing over there is proof the fairy tale is a lie. It always has been. How could you say such a thing? Why would our parents and their parents lie to their own children and grandchildren? If granny ever heard you say such things. Maybe it is better that she can't, God rest her soul.

"Me, I say that's it. There's no other ship it could be. Oh? And who says? Well, what else could it be? Maybe she's the *Richmond*, or the *Virginia II*, or the *Fredericksburg*? Ever think of that? That's dumb. Any ten-year-old knows all three of them are lying in the mud beneath the James River, a half-day's drive from here. And in another state I'll remind you. That's right. We could be wrong about that. Yeah, and maybe you need another drink.

"What about that old man gramps told us about when we were little: the one that came visiting in the Sixties? The old people say he said it was true. Yeah, but that was the Centennial. People were all riled up remembering the war. They would'a believed anything then. Oh, who's gonna believe the ramblings of some old thing more'an 100 years old anyway? I heard a hundred-eleven actually. I remember from sixth grade. Oh Lord, can you imagine being that old? How awful! Yeah, all messed in the mind and crappin' your drawers. Hey! Mother's 105 and she's sharp as a tack. So ask her then. I will. Tomorrow."

Across the street in a raucous waterfront watering hole called The Bollard, but known as Mace's, Frank was enjoying an alcohol-fired debate with his soon-to-be-former boss, Bob Moore when Hillary interrupted them.

"Frank, isn't that Charley's wife over there?"

Frank craned his head over the crowd.

"There, near the door."

"You're right. It is her." He waved wildly and shouted over the din, "Femi! Over here."

The top of Olufemi's head barely broke the gaps between the crowded shoulders. Her face popped in and out as she jumped up and down trying to see.

Hillary knuckled Frank. "Well go get her, Frank."

Femi's arm shot up and waved crazily.

"She's okay." He watched the little knob of black hair wending a path toward them through a sea of shoulders and laughter. Bodies parted marking her progress through the crowd. She busted past the last barrier, pressing a beefy gentleman twice her size out of her way.

Barely higher than Frank's heart, she hollered up to him over the din, "Where is Qeb?"

Frank indicated across the river. "Over there still. I called and tried to get them to quit for the night, but..." He shrugged his shoulders.

Olufemi caught a movement next to Frank. A strange woman standing with him said, "You're Charley's wife."

Olufemi struggled with the woman's features in the multicolored light. "I don't know you. How do you know me?"

Hillary extended her hand to her. "I'm Hillary. Hillary Bascombe."

The name didn't register. Femi ignored the gesture and wheeled stressed eyes back to Frank. "Something is not right. I am afraid for Qeb and for Charley."

"Afraid? Why? What's wrong?"

The kitchen door next to the bar opened and a long light settled across Hillary's countenance. Olufemi recognized her immediately and gasped. Even in the thin light, her instant hostility was obvious.

"Femi, it's okay," Frank said. "She's a friend."

"I remember exactly who she is. Why is she with you?"

He placed a gentle hand against her upper arm. "Never mind that. Tell us why you're afraid for Qeb and Charley."

Olufemi fished into the deep pocket of her rain slicker, the whole time seething at Hillary, the woman who had threatened her husband with a gun, who had lied to the police and had him arrested. It mattered not that that was half a decade ago. She still hated her. Finding what she wanted, she yanked her eyes from Hillary and slapped an envelope against Frank's chest. "This letter came today for Qeb. I opened it. I read it. Two times, but I still do not understand it."

She accepted Frank's drink from his other hand so he could read it. She wrestled her swelling urge to drench Hillary's face with it.

The envelope bore the seal of Brunswick County. Its weathered appearance was a testament to the weeks it had suffered in the mail system chasing Qeb down, crumpled, scuffed and streaked with the signs of automated postal equipment. He opened the tri-folded letter inside. His brow over uneasy eyes crumpling deeper with each sentence he read. When he finished, he pursed silent lips for a long minute.

"What is it, Frank?" Bob Moore said.

"The Brunswick County Coroner." He rapped on the letter. "Femi's right. It doesn't make sense."

"What's it say?"

"They want to know what to do with Tim-Lee Polk's body. It says they will have to bury him locally if the family doesn't come and claim his body."

"You mean a John Doe's grave?"

Frank shrugged. "I don't know. But this cancel mark is a month ago. The deadline in the letter is already passed."

Hillary said, "Frank, what's wrong?"

"Qeb's girlfriend, Gemma: Tim-Lee was her brother."

Bob suggested, "And?"

"He's the body. Gemma said her family buried him in Tennessee."

Bob toasted an idea. "So maybe the letter just got lost in the mail. It wouldn't be the first time."

Olufemi said, "Frank, what is that look on your face? You scare me."

"I'm sorry, Femi. I don't mean to." He stuffed the letter back in its tattered envelope and slipped it into her soft hand. "But I think we really do need to get over there, and right now."

He snatched up his keys from the bar.

"Frank. Wait. No. We can't drive over." Bob pointed to the silent TV over the bar. "The highway is out. There's a wreck on the bridge."

Behind an overworked reporter with bad hair and too much makeup over scrolling white-on-black subtitles was a scene of tangled automotive chaos on Business 17 West connecting town to the other side of the river and Eagle Island. Red, white, blue and yellow lights flashed harsh against the tired bottom of a toppled delivery truck and the crumpled remains of two tiny cars.

"My boat's docked down on the waterfront."

Frank gaped at Bob. "You brought that dinky thing all the way down the coast from Beaufort? Are you crazy?"

Bob shot him a cockeyed grin. "That's right. You haven't seen my new baby yet, have you?" He patted Frank on the back. "You're in for a big surprise, buddy. I got her shipped up from Louisiana last week. But to answer your question insinuating my nautical abilities? No. I tied up halfway here and spent the night at a friend's place in Topsail Beach. And while you were looking for a place to bed down in this crowded nut hole, I was kicking back on the porch with Gentleman Jack and lemonade and the sounds of the surf."

Chagrinned, Frank suggested, "I suppose that means you're too broke now to pay the tab. Never mind. I got it." He slapped four twenties on the bar and nodded to the girl behind the bar. "Let's go. Hillary, how about you wait here with Femi?"

"How about we're coming along with you, instead?"

"Just stay here. It's faster that way."

He turned to leave with Bob. Short Femi met him toe-to-toe. "They are my son and my husband. I am coming with you."

"Guess that's settled," Hillary said. "And don't give me that look, Frank."

On their way up Water Street paralleling the river, Hillary spoke between rushed strides. "Frank, there's something...about that gunboat. Something I learned...I haven't told you...told you yet. Will you slow down?"

That was when she noticed the battleship was directly opposite them, across the river. They'd been walking quite a bit. Her bloody damned feet were hot as Dante's inferno.

"Where is this bloody boat, Bob?"

Bob indicated to the town's largest hotel all the way at the north end of the waterfront. "I'm moored near the Hilton. It's just at the other end of the Riverwalk."

Hillary spied the glowing red Hilton logo. "All the way down there, in these shoes?" She was torturing herself in some pumps she'd bought on a whim to impress Frank. She never wore pumps. She hated pumps. Shoes designed by men who never had to wear them. She had a special spot reserved just for them after tonight. In her garbage.

"Hey, we're lucky I was able to even get a slip this close. So just take the damn shoes off, why don't you? Walk in your stockings."

Hillary ripped the shoes from her feet. She grimaced at the feel of her expensive silk stockings—another whimsical purchase—chafing on the cold stone walk as they huffed and puffed the rest of their way north along the waterfront to a manicured copse of trees where Bob said, "Down here. Follow me."

They made a hard left and clomped down onto a grey wood boardwalk. Over their right shoulders and from a hundred feet up, the Hilton H wrapped in a glowing red swirl paid them no mind.

A small squadron of private boats of all shapes and sizes were tied up to a skinny floating pier paralleling the boardwalk. The thing was barely wide enough to walk side-by-side, two-by-two without toppling over the edge and into the water. At the end, Bob leaped onto the last boat in line.

"I can't believe how out of shape I am," Hillary complained, breathless from their double-timed hustle almost the full length of downtown. She placed a hand on Frank's shoulder for support. "Frank. About what I was saying—"

Frank stroked her hair. "How about you tell me on the way over? Holy shit, Bob."

"She's a real beauty, right?" Bob boasted from the deck of his latest purchase: a pristine, pre-owned 2003 Regulator Marine center-console, open-ocean fishing boat. He extended a helping hand up to Olufemi first, guiding her petite and hesitant steps aboard. "Careful. Watch your step."

He couldn't help but enjoy Frank's priceless expression, frozen in place on the pier. He outstretched his arms to fore and aft. "She's thirty-two feet long. Twin Evinrude E-Tec 300's. She'll do thirty-four knots in the right water." His smirk spread to a sly grin. "If you can stomach it, that is."

"Jesus Bob," was all Frank could say.

"Yeah, well how about you two lovers up there make yourself useful and undo those lines."

As Frank stepped aft to undo the stern line, Hillary traipsed barefoot after him. "Frank, we really need to talk—"

He tossed the stern line aboard. "Get the forward line, will you?" he said to her, nearly bowling her over when he jumped aboard. He crossed the deck to the boat's port side and studied the shapes in the lights across the river. Not a sign of life. Aboard *K-Four*, the bridge lights were out.

That's not right, is it?

"I don't see the guards. Where are the guards? *Ow!*"

He caressed the sting where Hillary applied a horse bite to the back of his arm. "What was that for?"

"Just walk away from me when I'm trying to talk to you."

He rubbed at the sting. "Hey, I'm just worried, that's all."

The twin outboards behind them woke up with a tandem growl. "You all best sit down for this," Bob said. He shoved the throttles forward and let the engines fly.

Hillary and Frank grabbed each other as they toppled sidelong into their seats. Safe in their places, he let go, but she kept her grip on him.

"Now that I have your attention, you can listen for a change. I got a call. From Richmond," she said, forcing her words between the river's punches against the boat's bottom. "A student of mine. From years ago. When I was a green professor at Oxford. The little shit. He was always testing my boundaries." She smirked slightly at a thin memory.

"It seems he's a naval historian now. He works someplace all hush-hush up on the Potomac in Maryland. Anyway..." She measured him in the faint light. "I told him about that ship."

"You *what?*"

"I know! I promised. But..." The wrinkles in her brow seemed to be competing for pity with the grimace in her smile. "I'm sorry."

"God, Hillary. No," he said, in an almost-whine. He flopped back into his seat aghast. "I can't believe you did that. I told you about those people up there. They're government, Hillary. You can't trust them. You can never trust their motives."

He looked here and there across the water back at the Riverwalk like he was considering jumping and swimming back just to get away from her. "Why would you do that?"

"I had to, Frank. We had to know *something*." Her eyes clocked forward and across the water to the squat ugly menace on *K-Four*'s back. "So I asked him to look into something for us."

"Hey, not 'for us.' Don't try and include me in this blunder." When he said it, he noticed and turned to face her. "If you're so sure you can trust this guy, why do you look so worried?"

"That part's complicated." Her long hair waved crazily in the breeze.

"Complicated. So what did he tell you?"

She hollered over the racket of the engines and the water slapping the hull. "He says that there is a record that proves that that thing over there did float out of here near the end of the war, just like the legend says. But it's the motive the legend got all wrong. It wasn't leaving to save the city in some great battle. That wasn't her mission. The mission had changed. No one knew about it. Maybe not even the crew."

Her eyes swung back to his.

"Not till the last minute anyway. The people here believed she would save the city. Maybe delay a Union victory. At least until England joined the war."

"England was never going to join the war, Hillary."

"Shut up, Frank. The point is a crime took place here, and that ship over there was the tool."

He looked at her funny. "Are you getting emotional over this?"

"History, Frank. It's what we do, isn't it? Or have you forgotten, drowning in self-pity over being sacked? Ugh! I'm sorry. I don't know where that came from."

"It's okay. You're right, anyway."

She picked herself up and with rusty sea legs indicated to the far-off shadow. "Whatever history is hiding from us, that thing never got to do what it was supposed to do. Something or someone got in the way. Obviously she got out and somehow managed to skirt round the blockade. There is no record of any battle, so I think it's safe to assume the whole time she never once engaged the enemy."

"Hillary, Wilmington had to stay an open port. Why expend so much sweat and blood building what we now know was a state-of-the-art fighting ship, only to have it sneak off in the night and slip past the enemy? What's the purpose?"

"I don't know, Frank. I'm just trying to understand. To fill in the blanks. But I think it's fair to guess after the war the people watered her story down to just a fairytale because she let them down and they were angry. She abandoned them and the people were ashamed."

Her face looked suddenly haggard. Frank could see the lines even in the night, gravity pulling age into her complexion. "And this guy in Maryland told you all this?"

She nodded with her eyes. "He may be full of shit still, but he is credible." She watched the other side of the river approaching halfway away.

"What?" he said.

"It's nothing."

"Bullshit. What's going on in that head of yours?"

"He knows."

"Knows what?"

"That she's been pulled up. They know everyone who's been involved in this. You, Charley, Qeb. And me too, because I had to go and open my big fat gob. They know David's been swinging his weight around down here greasing palms and opening doors, doors that Washington never wanted opened. But it was at the end, something he said. Or more it was the way he said it. Something in his voice—it actually frightened me, if you can believe that."

"What was it?"

She landed her toughest look on him. "He said we need to be careful."

"Careful? Are you sure that's what he said?"

"He said there are people—when they hear we have this ship—people could get hurt."

"Hurt. Hurt how? What people?"

Her expression shifted from tough to fear: a fear he had only once seen in her a long time ago. "You and me type of people. Maybe even killed."

"Killed? Killed for what? Why is this asshole frightening you like this?"

"He can access information most of us can't." Duress filled her face. "He wouldn't say how he knew of course, but for whatever reasons that thing was sunk, it was never supposed to be found again, at least not for a very long time. He said Washington was behind the developers pushing that woman to sell; that it was never about development; that it was about buying the land and shutting down the rumors.

"Then David beat them at their game, without even knowing it. And now there she is out in the open for everyone to see. I'm afraid, Frank. I'm scared to death we may have opened up a mess we never should have opened."

Frank shook his head. "I don't see it. The government is letting Admiral Dewey's flagship—the very last ship of its kind—rot at her moorings up in Philadelphia. Nobody's doing a damned thing about it and yet they care more about a beat up old wreck from 150 years ago? I mean—"

Whoop, whoop, whoop!

Hillary flashed round.

Frank craned his neck from behind her.

The darkness off their stern cracked open with flashing blue lights.

From up forward, Bob exclaimed, "Oh Shit!"

"What is it, Bob?" Frank said.

"Something I completely forgot."

"Damned stupid curfew! I forgot all about it. No one's supposed to be out here till after the thing tomorrow."

Whoop, whoop, whoop!

The flashing blue lights were gaining fast. A voice in the darkness stormed across the water, "You there in the boat, throttle down and heave to."

"Bob, we can't stop now. We're halfway there. Just keep going."

"Are you crazy? I can't do that."

"They can follow us over. I'll explain to them when we get there."

"Frank! It's the police, for chrissakes."

Bob throttled down. The high-speed tilt of the Regulator 32's deck sagged to just level as her twin Evinrude outboards settled into a throaty purr.

Frank jabbed the air, pointing to *K-Four*, "Bob! Qeb and Charley could be in danger." He cupped his hand over Bob's hand on the throttle and forced the lever forward. A flood of rich fuel kicked the engines back to life.

The voice in the blue light barked again. "Aboard the boat, heave to."

Hillary pointed to something emerging from the night. "There they are."

It was one of those inflatable boats, blue with a rigid hull beneath two round air thingies. White letters emblazoned on the thingies boldly boasted Wilmington Police Department.

A blinding light popped on, spilled across the ripples in the water, and bitch-slapped each of them hard in the face.

Frank raised his arm to block the glare. He struggled with Bob, forcing the throttle all the way.

Bob clamped his other hand round Frank's piano player wrist. "Frank, don't be a fool."

Whoop, whoop, whoop, whoop!

"Frank! You'll get us all arrested."

Frank's grip melted.

Bob throttled back and the Regulator settled again to a stop in the middle of the river.

The police boat crabbed up alongside. Its two outboard engines tumbled to a cautious idle. A big-boned guy with chevrons on his sleeves and scrutiny in his eyes swayed on practiced sea legs in a cramped excuse for a deck just behind a phone booth pilot house centered in the boat. Its roof was cluttered with technical gizmos and gadgets mounted to it.

From inside, a second cop—a kid at the wheel, anxious and excited—gawped at them all from an open sliding window. The big cop with chevrons flicked a signal the kid's way. The kid reached up and threw a switch. The spotlight's glare pulled in on itself and fizzled out.

Chevrons leaned over and gripped Bob's boat by her gunwale. He wrestled the two craft closer together till they kissed side-by-side. His wary searching eyes, gleaming white orbs in near pitch-black skin, pinged on Bob at the wheel. "Sir, keep away from the controls."

Bob showed the man his empty palms. "You got it, officer."

"This boat yours?"

"Yes officer."

"There's a curfew. You should know that. No boat traffic on the river till after the ceremonies tomorrow." Chevrons scrutinized a tall lanky guy with a beard standing just next to the guy at the helm. He looked guilty as sin of something. There was a hatch just behind the guy, just forward of the helm. It looked like it went into some kind of space.

"What's behind there?"

"The head. A microwave. And some storage bins. Nothing much else, really."

"Is there anyone down there?"

"No sir."

"What about up forward?"

"Just some empty seats," Bob said. "You can come aboard and take a look, if you want."

Chevron's nod was barely perceptible. His attentions wheeled rearward on the boat to a tall woman gripping her balance from a chubby chrome fishing rod rack bolted to a large square box in the boat's center. Further aft, a second petite and rather pretty foreign looking woman on a pontoon seat shoehorned into the boat's back was sending him to Hades with her eyes.

"Where's everybody going in such a hurry?"

The woman in the seat blurted out, "There!" She indicated to the island, to the lights by the big ship that came in that day. "My son is on that *thing* with my husband. I am worried about them."

"Worried, ma'am? Why, if you don't mind my asking?"

Hillary butted in. "We think they're in danger."

Chevrons' ears flinched. There was a strange edge in the tall woman's voice.

"What kind of danger?" he asked the smaller woman. But she wasn't talking.

Chevrons reconsidered the darkness and the barren river surrounding them. He called to his partner in the pilothouse. "Keep your eyes open, you hear? You see anything else moving around out there—I don't care what it is—don't you waste time looking. You tell me."

"Yes Sergeant."

Frank wormed aft around Hillary to Olufemi seated near the engines. "Femi got a letter. She's my brother's wife. Femi, show him the letter."

Olufemi pulled something from her coat pocket.

From the cramped deck of his police skiff, Chevrons reached over and accepted the letter from her. With both hands he fished for light, tilting the paper first to the city, couldn't make out the words, and tried tilting it to the glare from the island.

"It's from the Brunswick County Coroner," Frank started.

"I see that, sir."

"Sorry." Then Frank saw. The police boat—they were drifting apart. And the cops weren't noticing.

"Says here they want to bury someone named Tim-Lee Polk."

Chevrons tottered a bit on his feet and immediately caught the gap growing between them. He snatched again at the Regulator's gunwale. With his other hand he extended the letter back across to Frank who returned it to Olufemi.

"What's that letter got to do with you all being out here breaking a curfew?"

"Tim-Lee Polk was my nephew Qeb's best friend." Frank indicated to Olufemi, cramped up in her seat all in on herself with worry. Her expression to Chevrons was clear: *Go away!*

"Qeb is Femi's son. He's over there on the island with his father. He was killed—Tim-Lee, I mean—in a diving accident."

"And now they're asking the family to come take his body."

"Exactly. And that's the problem."

"Why?"

"Because they already buried him, that's why. Or they were supposed to have. Eight weeks ago. I think it was eight."

"You lost me. And who do you mean by 'they'?"

"Tim-Lee Polk's family. His sister showed up at my house asking Qeb for help. He's my nephew—"

"Yes, sir, you already said that."

"But you see, she told Qeb she already buried him. That was last July. I think."

"You're not sure?"

Frank searched his panicking memory. "Yeah, it was July. I'm sure now."

Chevrons doffed his ball cap and rubbed the confusion from his close-shaven scalp. "What kind of name is Qeb anyway?"

Olufemi's anger slipped down from her eyes to the tip of her tongue. "It is Egyptian!" She jutted a proud chin his way. "We are from Egypt."

"I see. Muslims then?"

"We are Christians! Not Muslim."

"Do you have ID, ma'am?"

"Oh, for God's sake, she's my sister-in-law!" Frank reported, with obvious insult. "She's a legal resident, papers and all. She's got all her shots too."

"There's no need for that kind of talk, sir." Chevrons passed scrutiny over each of them through a long silence, reached a decision, donned his cap back on his head, and said to Bob at the helm, "Sir, I think you and your friends best come about and follow us back to the docks."

The small woman in the seat hugged herself and wailed.

"Now see what you've done," Frank yelled, "She's worried sick and all you can do is upset her."

"Sir, calm down."

Frank took a step toward him. "But you're not even listening."

Chevrons' hand crept to his side and unsnapped the strap over the pistol in his holster. "Sir, why don't you take a seat by her?"

"I don't need to take a seat!"

Chevrons extracted his sidearm halfway. "Sir, I need you to sit down now. Robert!"

The kid cop's head popped out through the pilothouse window. "Yes Sergeant?"

"Radio in. We have trouble in the river."

Hillary blurted out, "Oh bollocks! What trouble?"

Chevrons' eyes flashed at her.

"We're scientists, you idiot: archaeologists, not terrorists. Look at us. Do we look like we are out to blow something up?"

"No one said anything about blowing things up, ma'am. Not till you did just now." Chevrons hardened his hold on Bob's boat for balance with one hand and tightened his grip on his sidearm with the other. "Please step out from behind that thing where I can see you, ma'am."

"Oh, this is great. Okay, there. I'm out in the open. As you can see, I have no bombs."

"I'd be careful with your words. Your name is, ma'am?"

"Stop calling me ma'am! My name is Hillary Bascombe. *Doctor* Hillary Bascombe."

Chevrons frowned. Her accent too was foreign; two foreign women on the same boat. Men with guilt in their faces, with two foreign women, good looking, out on the water in the middle of the night, breaking a security curfew, in an expensive fast boat, making for the island long after closing hours.

Hillary backpedaled in a vain attempt to recover. "Officer, that ship they brought in today—it's not what people think it is."

Chevrons' sidearm slowly slipped back home down into its holster. His gaze slipped across the quiet water over to the island and the thing the big ship had on its back. "So that's not a boat I'm looking at?"

She groaned, exasperated. "Of course it is! But there is something aboard her, something not good: something that some people might kill people for."

Deep furrows blossomed over Chevrons' sudden alarm. "Kill. Kill whom, ma'am?"

"Will you stop it with the ma'am thing? Anybody who's aboard her when they show up looking for it, that's who."

"Looking for what?"

Hillary shook aggravated fists at him. "We don't know. We *can't* know till we get over there, which we would be if you weren't here right now."

Frank clopped aft and faced off with Chevrons at the gunwale. "For all we know they're there right now."

"Sir, step back."

"But you're the cops. Can't you see? You can just forget the curfew and take us over there."

Chevrons squinted back into the harsh halogen lights bathing the docks on the island. "There's no one over there but those ships and that truck on the pier."

"What truck?" Frank lunged forward next to Bob for a better look. "That wasn't there earlier. Something isn't right. You need to take us over there."

Chevrons worked his way round Bob's stern and stepped onto the boat's transom. That way he could see the truck more clearly. It was a box truck rental parked next to the gangplank of the bigger ship. "Doesn't seem to be anyone around. Maybe your people left already."

Frank stomped his foot on the deck. "Goddammit, what is wrong with you?"

"Sir! Do not take the Lord's name in vain. I will not have that!"

Frank expelled a subjugated sigh. He suddenly felt like they were all backed into a corner with a precocious delinquent. "Don't you think we should at least go over and look?"

"What I think sir is it's time I saw some ID." Chevrons turned to Olufemi and then to Hillary. "You two ladies especially."

"Bugger!"

"Excuse me, ma'am?"

"Someone could be getting hurt right now and you want to play the bureaucrat?"

Chevrons' expression darkened. He spotted a place on Bob's deck and set one foot inside the boat.

"Enough of this!" Hillary exclaimed. She shot forward to the wheel by Bob.

Chevrons wavered with the boat's sudden rocking. He struggled for balance straddling the bulwarks, one foot on the transom and one foot on the deck. "Lady! You stay put."

Hillary elbowed Bob in the ribs. "Out of the way, Bob."

Chevrons' hand leaped at one of the outboards. His long and strong fingers gripped the rounded cover over the engine nestled inside it. His other hand fumbled for his sidearm. "Stop right there. Get away from those controls."

Hillary prodded the throttles, revving the engines to life.

Chevrons felt the power vibrating through the cover beneath his hand.

From the police skiff Officer Robert hollered, "Sergeant! We got back-up coming."

Chevrons' single-handed grip on the engine was slipping. And his left foot was sliding backwards on the slippery transom. He threw his right hand behind him and palmed the gunwale to break his fall, and released the safety on his gun with the other.

He raised the gun at Hillary with the end of his barrel swaying right, then left, then right across her back. "Stop now! You're under arrest, all of you." He hoped none of them knew that a safe cop never carried with a round already loaded in the chamber of his side piece.

Hillary shot him a look from over her shoulder that made his scalp cringe.

"I think we've had just about enough of you!" she hollered back at him. She shoved the throttles forward, kicking the engines wide awake. The boat's bow rose skyward and the stern transom dipped low. Water washed ankle deep round Chevrons shoes.

Hillary peeked behind her appreciating his predicament and rammed the throttles all the way.

With his pistol in hand and grasping thin air for balance, Chevrons toppled backwards heels-over-head into the river with a howling splash.

28-TRUE COLORS

Work lights dangled from every convenience, their garish white bulbs sharing no heat in *Recluse*'s cramped gun deck, known by the sailors who had once manned her as her gun battery. The battery's ten gun ports—a couple were part way open, but most were frozen shut with wetted age—hindered any reprieve from the air trapped inside, close and heavy with the stink of boiled sea foliage.

Four cannon and the shattered remains of two others occupied the battery. "These are way ahead of their time," Charley said, admiring them. "They're breechloaders. They load from the back. I didn't think they were around till 1900-something."

A veil of accumulated silt, dry and gritty to Charley's touch, clung to the cannon barrels, to their carriages, and deep into the pores of the battery's deck and bulkheads, as well as the ceiling—so low that he could reach up and lay his palm flat against it.

Charley absorbed the waterlogged coolness beyond the ceiling's surface, hearkening to the voices of the dead trapped in their memories. A ghostly chill reached out and embraced him, and pestered the aches in his sleep-deprived joints, but no one was talking. He hugged himself for warmth, shivering in a feeble breeze seeping through the battery's sally port.

Outside the port and across the pier, *Recluse*'s septuagenarian companion, the *North Carolina*, groaned in a restless slumber, pained by her aging joints.

"It was in the manuscript," Qeb said about the breechloaders. "Peter Howe mentions them. Special British cannon." He worked at a spot in the deck with his shoe sole. One hundred and forty years of sand and muck had been flushed from the battery by Kittering's men once she was settled aboard *K-Four*'s back.

There were two gun ports on each side of the battery, port and starboard. At two of the ports, there were still guns. But the cannon from the two other ports had somehow been broken apart and their shattered carriages lay in splintered pieces across the deck.

Charley indicated to a fat bronze crescent screwed into the deck beneath the back carriage wheels of one of the two cannon still intact by the side gun ports. The crescent was about a foot wide and must have weighed a ton. "I've seen this set-up before. This bronze rail here—it's a kind of track for the carriage wheels to roll over. The smooth hard surface makes it easy to swing the gun's weight one way or the other."

The rail beneath the long-idle, cast metal carriage wheels looked never used: smooth and unlabored. He pointed to the front end of the gun carriage. There was a trunnion bolted to it, inserted down into a beefed-up hole in the deck.

"That trunnion there is a fixed point around where the gun can swing." He tapped one of the carriage wheels with his shoe tip. "They would swing the back of the gun here along the crescent so they could angle the front through the port there to shoot."

He swung his gaze and indicated to the tail end of the gun carriage all the way up forward. There was another bronze metal insert in the deck, but this one was at the back of the gun, not at the front.

"That one looks like it works the other way around. See how the trunnion is at the back, and the rail is under the front wheels of the carriage instead?" He mulled over the three gun ports up front: one center, one at a slight angle to port, and another to starboard.

"It looks like they could fire through any one of those three ports with just that one gun. First through the center hatch over the bow in the attack, presenting as small a target as possible to the enemy." He swung his arm to the port just to starboard, but not all the way over to the side of the battery. "Then as they rounded their target—the wheels at the front of the gun would roll along the curved rail to fire through that port there on the right, keeping up their fire as they pulled alongside the enemy for a full-on broadside with these other guns."

He pointed past Qeb to the aft end of the battery. There was a second crescent and insert just like the one up forward, and another three gun ports. "Same thing back there, so that's six cannon fired from ten gun ports."

When *Recluse* had broken the surface and the last of her filthy contents had been washed away, the crew had sponged down her insides in a heavy bath of oils a young David Kittering had concocted years ago. The patent for it had marked the beginning of his wealthy climb.

Slathering the deck, the bulkheads, and the ceiling, with all their nooks and crannies was a brutally labor-intensive trick that would dull the ravenous attack of fresh air hungering after the freshly exposed and defenseless wood and metal brought to the surface. The smell of it was retched, but it worked like a charm, and held fine till better protections could be applied.

Momentarily, they shared questioning glances. Was that a police boat siren they just heard? They listened quietly into the silence. Then the siren repeated.

Charley shrugged. "A crazy night out there."

"Probably some drunk breaking the water curfew," Qeb suggested.

Charley appreciated the outline of a square hatch in the far front of the gun deck: a way down into the hull. "Tomorrow, after the specialists get here and remove those powder kegs from down below, we'll go down there and take a closer look around."

He walked along the center of the battery, spying four large squares in the deck, bulky wood framing with lattice work in their centers. "These must be ventilation gratings for air movement between the decks."

He stopped at the top of a ladder in the back half of the battery, just before the aft gun trunnion. It led down to where earlier Kittering's men had discovered some strange engines with French in their castings.

He eyeballed the length of the gun deck to forward. There were three other ladders: one leading down into a dark space below and two others leading up. One lead up to and out onto the spar deck. The other one, farthest forward near the hatch in the deck, went up to the pilot house for steering the ship.

Echoing footsteps on the aluminum gangplank outside drew their attentions to the sally port in the sloping broadside of the battery, and though the port's hatch too was plated—and had been a beast to open—Charley could not help but wonder at the ironic weakness it presented in *Recluse*'s otherwise formidable armored design. Still, the sally port was so small you had to scrunch up and crouch through it not to knock your noggin against its thick casing.

It was their only way in, and their only way out.

"Are we expecting company?" Charley said.

"I can't think who. You think it has something to do with that police siren we heard?"

"I don't know."

Qeb spied the sally port, gripped by the darkness outside. "It can't be the guards back already with their suppers. What should we do, Dad?"

"Just hang tight till we see."

A cautious head face down and hidden by a knitted hood edged into the sally port.

"Who are you?" Qeb challenged.

The hood rose, exposing their impromptu visitor, and for just the thinnest sliver of a second Charley thought he read startled alarm in the new face.

A besotted smile blazed across Qeb's features. "Gemma!"

He strode to her, slipped on the deck, nearly fell, pulled a groin muscle, recovered himself, ignored the pain, stole three more strides and banged his knee—"Ow!"—and grasped her outstretched hand.

"I'm so happy you made it," he proclaimed, helping her with one hand while kneading his throbbing knee with the other. "(Dude, that hurts!) But, Gemma, it's so late. I figured you weren't coming till tomorrow."

"I wanted to surprise you," she said, stepping down into the battery.

Qeb caressed her in a way that alarmed his father. The kid was falling for her fast, and deep. "I wish you could have come along to see when we brought *Recluse* up."

"I'm sorry, Qeb. But mother—she, you know?"

Qeb bowed his head. "I know. She hurts. Still..."

Gemma collapsed the distance between them with a tender kiss and chuckled. "What ever are you doing here in this dank cold? Why aren't you over there celebrating with everyone else? I have to say," she said, somehow fortifying her Tennessee hills drawl, "I sure am glad I didn't go looking for you over there first. The traffic is dire. I would never have made it back over to here."

She scanned their surrounds. "No guards. You're not worried about souvenir hunters?"

"Mr. Kittering hired some guards. You just missed them. Dad sent them across the river into town to get themselves something to eat. Since we're here anyway, he gave them an hour."

She wide-eyed Charley. "Well, they're going to need that hour alone just to get back. I suppose the crew of this big ship can watch over her."

Qeb shook his head. "David let them all go into town. But we have the Watch in the engine room, and one or two guys up on the bridge."

Gemma measured the insides of *Recluse*'s battery. "It's big in here." The way she came seemed like the only way in. She counted the gun ports. All of them, save one, were closed. No other way for anyone outside to see in. The gaudy strings of work lights killed any shadows in the claustrophobic space. Nowhere to hide. It was like inside someone's tomb.

She hugged herself and scrunched up her nose. "It stinks in here. How ever can you stand it? And aren't you even hungry?"

"Who can think of food when we're standing in a ship everyone said didn't exist?"

She stroked his face and suggested, "Let me take you and your father to dinner?"

"Sounds good; I'm starving. We just need to wait till the guards get back."

"Can't you ask the guys on the ship to watch till they get back?"

"They have their own jobs to do," Charley interrupted.

She shot him a dismissive glance. The edge of her lips warped. Just barely, but he caught it.

She rested her arms on Qeb's shoulders and round his neck and pulled him closer. The touch of her breasts, even through their clothes, sparked an instant response in him. "What about that big thing next door? There must be someone watching that monster."

Qeb blushed. He knew from her glimmer that she was enjoying him hardening against her. After their first time, it seemed he would swell up from so much as a simple twinkle in her eye. "I—I don't know. Maybe no one worries about anyone sneaking up there and stealing something."

He swooned in the spicy snap of her perfume. If she were a pool, he would strip naked and nose dive right into her. He couldn't resist cupping her waist in his palms through her open, zip front hoody; the very same black thing she had worn on her visit to the cove, with pipe leg corduroys, black too. And lace-up boots with the socks puffing from their tops. Beneath her hoody she wore a clingy turtleneck, midnight blue this time. It was a dangerous look, a steamy kind of dangerous that excited him in a way he wanted to last forever.

"I could just eat you up right now."

The heat of her body against his palms loosed butterflies in his belly and fired the nerves from the nape of his neck down to the rounds of his heels. A clutch of freckles beneath her eyes scurried across her nose from cheek to cheek.

"Isn't there any way I can drag you away from here?"

She stroked his forehead with the back of her fingers, titillating the nerve endings over his brow. No other girl had ever touched him like that. "You're not playing fair."

"You two go," Charley interrupted. "I'll hang around till the guards get back."

But Gemma insisted, "We are *not* leaving you behind in this horrible place."

"Okay, you win," Qeb said. "Both of us will go get some dinner with you."

She beamed, triumphant.

"Right after the guards get back."

Her smile collapsed. The black centers of her green eyes shrank to tiny dots. She backed away from him, tossing aside his grip on her. "So I don't even rate you taking me to dinner?"

"Gemma, what's the big deal? Can't you wait with us for just a bit? I'll show you around."

Her visage iced over. "I'm so sorry, Qeb. I really did try."

"Why are you mad at me all of a sudden? Try what?"

Gemma's gaze darted to her right, onto Charley. He wasn't looking. It was time. She put more distance between her and Qeb, turned to the sally port, and let go a shrill whistle that forced Qeb to shrivel.

Almost instantly, four box-built goons donning black watch caps ducked through the port. None of them could have been over five-five, but each one of them bore broad shoulders and a lot of beef beneath black knitted sweaters and loose fitting black trousers over swarthy skin.

The last one stepped down into the battery and stopped in his tracks. He peered at Qeb and Charley from beady chocolate eyes over a complexion ravaged by acne pits and two huge scars. He shared a speechless nod with Gemma who then turned back to Qeb.

"Why did you have to be so stubborn?" Her Hillbilly burr had suddenly evaporated. She flashed a look to Goon One, the ugly one.

Charley traced her gaze to a snub black pistol in Goon One's hand. At the sight of the mean silencer dangling from its end, he muttered, "Crap."

"Gemma, what's going on?" Qeb said.

She sighed thinly. "I so hoped that things would not have to go this way. Dinner with me in town, that's all you had to do. A nice diversion while my men did their job."

"Did their job? What job? Who are these guys, and why's that one got a gun?"

"Qeb, don't!" Charley said when his son closed on her.

Goon One raised his barrel to just inches from Qeb's right eye.

"And why do you sound different all of a sudden?"

"Back away from them, Qeb," Charley said.

"Listen to your father," she said.

Qeb searched her eyes for answers. They were suddenly cold and distant in a way he was seeing for the first time. "Whatever this is, I'm glad your brother, Tim-Lee, isn't here to see it."

"He wasn't my brother."

The deck beneath Qeb rocked him off-kilter. He fished behind him with his feet, searching for a foothold, stumbling over his confusion. "What do you mean, not your brother?"

She set a consoling caress upon his cheek. "You should sit down. You look like you're going to be sick."

He swatted her hand away. "All this time—everything—us—it's all been an act?"

"Your accent's changed too," Charley said. "So who are you?"

"Who I am isn't important. And for your safety, you shouldn't know."

Qeb said, "What do mean, for our safety?"

Charley added, "What do you want? Why are you here?"

"My employer has property aboard this ship and I'm here to retrieve it."

"Property? Who today would have property on a 140-year-old wreck that till just yesterday nobody even knew existed?"

She smiled maternally. "Patience. Now please go stand next to your father."

"No! Not till you explain—"

Goon One's silencer kissed Qeb's temple. Qeb surrendered with raised hands. "Fine, I'm going." He shuffled backward with his wounded knee and pulled groin through a fog to his father's side. "Why are you doing this? You at least owe me that."

"Maybe I do. But first I need you to sit down." She indicated to the centerline of the ship. "There. Both of you." Two other goons waited with line in their hands by the ladder going up to the open spar deck. "My men will tie you there."

When she followed behind Charley and Qeb over to the ladder, Charley chanced a grab at her. Goon One's pistol was on him in an instant.

"Don't be a hero Charley Morgan," she said. "If he kills you, do you think we could leave your son as a witness?"

Charley's expression chilled. "You're very good at this, aren't you?"

"I'm effective, if that's what you mean."

Qeb's trashed love for Gemma now lay all crumpled and wadded-up on the deck beneath her feet. "Good at lying is what he means!" he snapped.

He and Charley slid down against the ladder. The damp chill in its fibers leached through the fabric of their shirt backs, with the deck's hard cold squashing their butt cheeks.

She circled round them as goons two and three tied them up. Charley noted the bandage covering Goon Two's right ear. Blood was clotting its weave. It looked painful.

A weak point.

When they finished, Goon Two took up post at the sally port. Goon One, with the gun, loitered behind Gemma. Goons three and four wormed down through the small hatch in the deck up forward where the powder kegs were.

Charley warned them, "I'd be real careful what you touch down there."

"They know what they're doing."

"There's powder down there. Old powder. There's no telling how unstable it is. One wrong move and they could blow this thing and you with us to Hell in a flash."

"There's no powder down there, Mr. Morgan."

"Oh really?"

"Yes really." Her expression was self-satisfied.

"I guess that's why the kegs are marked POWDER then."

She dismissed him and said to Qeb, "You wanted an explanation. I guess you deserve one, so here it is. I don't live in Tennessee and I don't have a brother named Tim-Lee. I don't have any brothers or sisters and I never knew my parents. They died when I was little. Whoever they were, I guess they had money, because I don't know where the money came from, but I grew up in a very exclusive boarding school in Texas overlooking the Rio Grande."

"So you're a rich orphan who lies and steals!"

"I only lied to you because I had to, to do my job. I didn't like it, Qeb. Please believe me."

"How can I believe you when you're doing this?"

Charley steered her back on subject. "You were saying?"

"I was saying that, living in Texas on the border with Mexico, it's not hard picking up the language. I'm fluent actually."

"Great. You're bilingual. Put it on your resume. What's it got to do with this?"

"My employer wants their property back. My employer is the Mexican government. I work for the Secretariat of Finance." She caught calculation in Charley's ire. "Please don't try checking. You'll only look foolish."

"An American working for the Mexican government. That's new. And I don't know if you noticed, but you don't look any more Mexican than I do."

She indulged herself a flippant curtsy. "Thus my appearance makes me perfect for the job."

"Great. You don't need a tan or a hair color. So tell us, why is the Mexican government interested in a crumbling old shipwreck from a North Carolina swamp?"

She scorned her surroundings. "We don't care about this old thing. It's what's hidden inside her we care about."

Qeb measured his thoughts and suddenly burned with realization. "It was you, wasn't it? You killed him. You killed Tim-Lee." His accusation was fierce.

Her shock dilated behind fluttering lashes. "No! That wasn't my plan. That was an accident."

Qeb's face swelled with disbelief. "Then...you *were* there."

Shit! She had stepped right into his trap. "You're rushing to conclusions." Her hands flexed and fisted, searching for a comeback. "That wasn't us. We had nothing to do with that."

"Everything between us has been a lie. Why should I believe you?"

Gemma searched the sloping bulkheads as if a ready answer might be branded into the thick planks of wood steeling the armor plates on the battery's outsides. "Please believe me, Qeb. It was all just a horrible unfortunate accident."

"But you were *there*. You could have at least—"

An abrupt racket reached up from below decks. One of the goons hollered something up to Gemma, incomprehensible to Qeb or Charley. Gemma offered the ceiling her best victory smile. She answered the man with a single foreign word and kept her gaze tacked to the ceiling, rummaging her memory.

"Tim-Lee left us an easy trail to follow. We traced his movements for months. We checked his apartment; hacked into his laptop. He was so reckless, leaving it out on the table like that, just like the way you found it. Remember?"

Yeah. He remembered. "But he was just a student, no danger to anyone."

She pulled her gaze from the ceiling down onto him. "Of course he wasn't."

"Then why did you kill him?"

She gripped her hand into a fist before her face and seethed at him. "We didn't kill him, dammit!" She expelled her pain with a heavy breath. "Why won't you listen?"

"Then who did?"

She reconsidered him with veteran eyes. "You might not like what you hear."

"So I should just go on believing you did it?"

"That's not what I want between us: you thinking I'm a murderer."

Her face softened a bit.

"My employers were interested where his efforts were taking him. After a point, he seemed to lose momentum. I reported that it looked like he was giving up, and we were ordered to pack up. But then something changed. Maybe when he fell across the manuscript? He was suddenly moving about with more direction, more purpose, and we realized quickly that he had uncovered some clue or clues, and that he was really going to find it.

"I will admit I thought this assignment was crazy. I mean, tracing after some kid chasing a fantasy shipwreck? Really? I mean you and me—we both know no one believed it."

"Except your government."

"They're my employer, not my government."

"And these guys with you—would they say the same thing?"

"Never mind that."

She didn't smoke, but she looked to Qeb like she needed a cigarette, bad.

"When it happened—when your friend was killed—we were only watching him from a distance, except for my one diver in the water." She indicated to Goon Two standing guard at the sally port. "When your friend came up to the surface, he was clutching something. My diver could tell from the look on his face he had found something big."

"So you all saw Tim-Lee alive?"

She nodded yes. "When Tim-Lee saw my diver in the water, he must have seen our boat too and panicked, because he tried swimming across the open estuary, heading for the other side. You saw how choked with reeds it is there. We would never find him if he made it into there.

"So my diver chased him down. Not to hurt him. That was the last thing we wanted, any of us. All we wanted was proof: something to say we were right, that we were on track. The last thing we needed was something bad happening and attracting local attention. If he only let us see what he found we would have learned what we needed, and that would have ended it.

"We followed after them to pick them up—my diver and Tim-Lee. We never saw them out there. I promise you, Qeb. We never even heard them coming. Not till it was too late."

"Saw who? Who didn't you see?"

"That water is all black. I guess it made them difficult to see in their dark wetsuits, because that's when the other boat ran over them."

"Ran over them? Who, Gemma? Who ran over them?"

She shook her head at the planks beneath her boots. "Those two boys. Those two stupid boys." Her gaze, slightly pink, met his befuddled eyes. "It was them, Qeb. They killed Tim-Lee Polk, not us. They ran him over and they killed him." She pointed to Goon Two's bandaged wound. "And they nearly took off his ear."

"What about the boys; what did you do?"

"They saw us coming and sped off."

"And you didn't go after them?"

Her face flushed with offense. "You think we're that cold that we would just leave your friend or my diver behind? What kind of person do you think I am?" She indicated to Goon Two again. "My man was hurt too, Qeb."

Qeb edged into understanding. "And that's why you wanted to visit the families. What were you thinking, going there?"

"I had to plant fear where it needed to be. Once they saw me, I knew their little tongues would wag. No one would ever go back to that cove, at least not those murderous little brats. They would be too scared, and their parents would be happier for it. And you and me, Qeb"—She wheeled her gaze over the battery's insides—"we would have all the privacy we needed together to find this ship. And didn't we?"

The second boy—the one whose mom gave them the grey bricks—he had behaved so strangely when she finally came up to the door. Now Qeb knew why: the kid had recognized Gemma as the woman in the other boat with the big men.

A chilly emptiness swept through him.

"So, they lied to the police about what happened, and you said nothing. And then you kept it from me that it was them the whole time. You came to me pretending to be the mourning sister, begrudged by the police of answers to your brother's death, who had the wrong story from the beginning. And all this time, you knew who killed him."

"What would you have me do? I could not report it to the police the way it happened. Exposing my team was out of the question."

Dread suddenly gripped Qeb. "Oh my God. That means—" He leered at her with derision. "You never really buried him. Tim-Lee is still down there, lying in the County morgue. Isn't he?"

She shook her head. "By now the County has probably buried him."

"But his family, Gemma! What about his family? What about them? They don't even know he's dead, do they? Christ! They don't even know."

"I'm sure the school has informed them—"

"The school doesn't know, either! They wouldn't know, because you're the only one who came down here asking questions. The police would figure—you being family—that they had no more obligations to tell them. And Professor Laird—he would just figure Tim-Lee's off again on his crazy quest. He'd just worry about expelling him later, after the dig."

"Summer's over, Qeb. The dig's probably done and his family knows by now."

"You don't know that."

"You need to calm down."

"Kiss my ass!"

There was another racket below decks. Charley squirmed in his bindings. "Let's just hope you're right about those kegs. What are they doing down there?"

"I already told you, retrieving my employer's property."

Charley shot her an odd look.

"What you did in Egypt—I admire you for that, discovering the impossible. That was lucky beyond imagination." She swept her foot in a coquettish arc over the dust on the deck. "And now it seems you've done it again, only this time you proved a myth was real." She turned to Qeb and added, "Your father has put another feather in Mr. Kittering's hat. Your Uncle Frank will get his career back, and now you can rub this victory in Professor Laird's arrogant face."

"Sounds nice," Charley said. "So what's the catch?"

She glanced furtively and smirked. "The catch is you don't get the real prize."

Qeb shuffled from one numb buttock to the other. "What prize?"

Gemma knelt down before him, her eyes tracing the curve at the end of his brow. "Very soon now, you're going to see."

She pressed her palms against her knees to help herself up. She hollered something in Spanish to the two goons in the hold. One of them replied back. She seemed satisfied with that and said, "We have a little bit of time. Maybe it's time for a story."

Her burnished black tresses traced her neck and rounded her shoulders like a brook over a stony fall, their soft shine protesting the harsh glare of *Recluse*'s disagreeable work lights. Her lips, confessing subterfuge with every syllable they spilled, enticed him with their savory stirrings. Why not forget *Recluse*, toss school, and accept Tim-Lee's death for what it was: a horrible accident? Accidents happened all the time, didn't they?

You can escape with her away from all this.

Just the two of them. Together.

You're a fool!

"Do you remember, Qeb, what you told me about those three gunships?"

"What? Yeah, I guess so."

"Oh come on. No need to be so sullen. What were their names?"

"Fine. The *Fredericksburg*, the *Virginia* II, and the *Richmond*."

"There was a battle, wasn't there."

"Trent's Reach."

"What happened at the battle? Please, don't look at me like that. Your father might like this."

Qeb explained to his father, "They were all sunk, scuttled by their own crews."

Charley raised a curious brow.

"And what did Stephen Laird tell you?"

"He thinks the confederates put their treasury on those ships. He believes—"

"Never mind him. What do you believe?"

Qeb shifted in his bindings. "They had no hope of fighting past the Union fleet; no chance of escaping to the open sea."

"And so?"

She was right and he knew it. He knew it because he felt the same way. "Laird's wrong. His dig on the James is a waste of time."

"Tell us, why is that?"

He answered her from down his nose, "Because there is no gold."

"No gold?" A sudden polish shined her gaze on him. "But Qeb, there is."

His brow collapsed under the weight of confusion. "What?"

"I said there is gold."

She fondled his flummoxed features with benevolent eyes, sitting there on his butt on the cold hard deck. Striking, stung, cute, indignant, intense and seething. And sensitive: he was her wounded lover; her wounded *virgin* lover. Yes, he'd had girlfriends, but he had never—not before her.

Dammit! This was the crappy side of her work: seamy, thoughtless and cruel. Maybe.

There's no room in your life for someone else. There never will be.

The job always came first.

"What do you mean, there's gold?"

"Stephen never mentioned his ancestor, Percival?"

Qeb squished his eyes closed, searching. Stephen. She spoke his name like she knew him.

"I guess not. Let's see." She put a finger to her lip. "Percival Laird was born in Liverpool, England, to an immensely wealthy family that had built its financial empire in founding and shipbuilding. When the South seceded, Percival emigrated here to secure exclusive contracts for his family, supplying the South with materiel, all the while—and unbeknownst to his family, I might add—casting himself a politically influential career in the future Confederate States of America."

"The way you said Professor Laird's name just then—do you two know each other?"

"Of course not! Now shush; I'm going somewhere with this. Percival was close to Treasury secretary Trenholm. By the end of the war he was Trenholm's closest confidant. When the government was collapsing, all of Trenholm's trusted friends were fleeing Richmond, abandoning him to the approaching Union army. But despite the cannon balls shattering the city, despite the fires and the panic in the streets, Percival remained at Trenholm's side."

Her syllables flowed with an unusual eloquence. It was a strange adjustment for him: the hills girl he thought he knew was long gone now. "How do you know all this?"

"It's what I do, silly." She leaned into a stolen peek outside. Satisfied with the absence of any movement in the night, she continued. "But still, we lose Percival's whereabouts after the winter of 1865. He's not in Richmond anymore. We know Secretary Trenholm gave him an assignment outside the capital, but not where it took him. He does reappear in Richmond after the war, but only shortly. It seems his hopes for recapturing his wealth and influence were dashed by bad press, castigating him for complicity in the South's collapse."

"Complicit how?"

"My job in this has been to connect the dots. The dots tell me Percival had a secret, one that he took to his grave when he died in 1887."

"I'm guessing from that look you're giving me that you know the secret?"

Her swollen glimmer told him she hoped he would ask. "His secret was the whereabouts of a missing shipment: a shipment Secretary Trenholm entrusted him to smuggle from the country. A shipment of confederate treasury gold."

Qeb hung speechless, mustering her facts. "How do you figure that when you just said nobody knew where he went or what he was up to? And if that's true, why is Professor Laird so sure the gold's lying down there in the mud with the *Fredericksburg*?"

"Because that's what Percival wanted everyone to believe. It's what he wrote in his memoirs."

"Memoirs—there are memoirs?"

"There are always memoirs, Qeb. You of all people should know that. Professor Laird's disadvantage is he believes them. I know better."

"Wait. You read them?"

"Percival lied, to his descendants and to History."

Qeb leaned into his bindings, the pressure of the ropes cinching his chest and biceps. "So, if you read them, where are they now?"

She replied with a single finger over strict lips.

He sank back against the ladder behind him. "So much for anything between us!"

"Percival's assignment was a ploy to fool the Union into thinking the entire confederate treasury was lost to the river bottom at Trent's Reach. But after the war, even then so soon after, salvage workers found nothing. The wrecks were forgotten and the gold was written off as a hoax. And that's how everything played right into Percival's hands."

Qeb squirmed against the hurt of his bindings, powerless to help how hot she still looked, sneaky as she was and wondered, was that what was making him all the more horny for her?

"What does all this have to do with you and the Mexican government, and tonight?"

"Tonight? You can thank Stephen Laird for tonight." She laughed a little too arrogantly. "If that big mouth hadn't so blatantly publicized the possibility of gold on the *Fredericksburg*, all this going on up here would never have caught my employer's attention. We would not be here. And we would certainly never have crossed paths with your friend, Tim-Lee. That would have been a shame. So if you think about it, Tim-Lee's death could be blamed on him."

Qeb couldn't pull his mind together. Professor Laird responsible for Tim-Lee's death? That made no sense.

In a funk, he watched her reconsidering the chilly insides of the gun battery surrounding them. Cannon covered in petrified silt standing watch at their silent port like obedient guard dogs. Bolts blackened with age and as big around as a $20 Double-Eagle gold piece marked the centers of the hexagonal armor plates outside, girded to their heavy wood understructure by large square nuts seated hard against washers the size of coffee coasters.

The girl he knew as Gemma ran discerning fingers over a parade of vertical seams flagging the bulkhead's inward sloping rise from the gun deck to the ceiling. Beneath her touch, the scuff of the wood planks and the dips in the seams was marred only where window-sized gun hatches interrupted their regimented flow.

"Ouch!" she exclaimed, snapping her hand away. Beneath a swelling dollop of crimson on her fingertip poked a small sliver. Sucking the wound, she rolled her eyes. There was maybe just a hint of beauty after all to the ship's ugliness, to the deadliness of her purpose.

"Professor Laird says this ship is a child's fairy tale." She plucked the sliver from her skin and flicked it to the deck. "He's wrong, and your friend, Tim-Lee, is right."

Qeb glowered at his shoes. "*Was* right, you mean. And he led you right to it."

"Don't forget with you by my side."

"Excuse me, but is there a point to any of this?" Charley growled, with his butt all numb from the hard deck.

"Uh...yes. Yes, there is. Two points, Mr. Morgan. Point one is Percival Laird's lost gold. Point two is it's neatly stowed beneath that tight posterior of yours."

Charley glowered at the deck around him. "Bullshit!" But something in her expression said otherwise. "You're joking, right?"

"Twenty-five thousand Mexican escudos is no joke."

Charley envisioned the number. Twenty-five thousand. "Mexican *what?*"

"Escudos. Pieces of Eight. Sent by Emperor Maximilian to fund his newest ally, the Confederate States of America," she elaborated. "And if I did my homework correctly, there are another seventy-five gold ingots all tucked away nicely down there with them."

Heavy grunting drifted up through the hatch from down below. Something toppled over, followed by garbled syllables. Charley didn't need to speak the language to know a cuss when he heard one. He tapped his noggin against the ladder behind him and groaned, "The powder kegs!"

"That's right. The powder kegs. All fifty-nine of them." Behind her, goons three and four muscled one of them up through the tiny hatchway. The thick sound of it striking the deck bespoke the mass of its contents.

Its outsides had an unsteady patina of damp chocolate brown, with faded black hand-scripted writing on it. Four wood bands tightly wound around it held the thing together. Their rough and knotty grain gave them a ropey appearance. At one of the ends there was a plug all the way to one side, just near the top rim of the keg.

After the keg, a faceless voice spoke. A hand reached up and waggled something, and slapped it down beside the keg. It sounded heavy.

"There. You see? I was right," she boasted.

Qeb traced the cuts in the deck at his heels across the planks over to the thing, a small grey brick. He was muted for a long thoughtful moment. Then it registered.

The three bricks in the kid's ditty bag! That one looks just like them.

What had he done with the bag? He dared not look up at her, talking now to Charley. She would guess his thoughts instantly. "Let's play a game," he heard her say. "If one escudo is 0.7614 Troy ounces of gold, multiplied by 25,000 that's just over—"

"—19,000 ounces of gold," he piped up.

She wheeled her eyes off Charley to him. "You're still with us." She pulled something from her pocket and twiddled it between her fingers. "In 1865 gold was $18.93 American per ounce, making our 25,000 coins worth about $360,200 then, or in today's dollars at $445 an ounce, that's...?"

"Somewhere near eight and a half million dollars."

"Qeb, you are *so* sharp."

Goon Three's head popped up through the hatchway. He called her over and handed her something. She took it and stood there studying it while he was telling her something, flashing his eyes at Qeb and Charley between sentences. She nodded once and he disappeared back down the hole.

"Isn't it beautiful?" she said, returning to them. The escudo coin in her fingers flashed in the light. She compared it to the other one from her pocket and cooed. "Oh, look! They match." She practically pirouetted as she knelt to show him.

Qeb yanked his pain from her to his father. "I don't understand what's happening."

"It seems our kegs down there aren't powder after all."

Qeb grimaced past the nausea percolating in his belly. "We never checked the kegs. It's my fault."

"Nonsense. You know we couldn't risk moving them till they were cleared first."

"But she told me. I just didn't pay attention."

"What do you mean? Told you what?"

Qeb recounted for his father the time he and she went to Tim-Lee's apartment. "She showed me that same coin. She said Tim-Lee sent it to her, that he said there might be more." He gave her a pained once-over. "Tim-Lee didn't send you that coin. You took it from him, didn't you—that day he was killed?"

She resigned her discovery with a heavy sigh. "It was in his hand the day of the accident. My diver got it from him before..." She set the coin from her pocket down on the deck beside him. "You keep it."

The eagle on the face of it shone proud. Qeb stared at it sneering back at him. The last thing Tim-Lee had touched.

"If you hadn't been there, he wouldn't have panicked and swum out in the water where those boys ran him over." He raised red and wetted eyes to hers. "And after—why did you have to involve me when you already knew where the wreck was? You didn't need me."

Gemma shot Charley a look. Her confidence faltered under the pressure of his sage expression. "She had no way to get to the gold," Charley indicted. "She needed you because you knew someone with the resources to finish the job. Isn't that true?"

She shrugged and admitted to Qeb, "He got me. You know? People might think you're really smart, Qeb Morgan, but your self-assured arrogance is your weakness. I knew if I showed you that coin, it would nudge your ego and get the better of you. You would go to your father for help."

"How could you be sure the gold would be here?" Charley said.

"We couldn't. But if it wasn't, no one would be the worse off for it, would they?"

"Qeb's dead friend might disagree with you there."

Another keg rose up through the hatch and thumped onto the deck amongst an accumulating horde of other kegs. It toppled over onto its side and tinkled a stream of gold coins out from a mouse hole in its lid. She counted slowly and snapped her attention to Goon One with the gun and blurted something in Spanish. Instantly, he darted outside. Goon Two stayed put guarding the entrance. Outside an engine revved up.

Gemma reached down and tucked the coin on the deck into Qeb's shirt pocket. Behind her the final drumroll of kegs thunking onto the deck picked up cadence.

Outside, brakes squeaked to a halt. A door slammed, a roll door rose and banged to a halt. The gangplank boomed under bounding footsteps. Goon One stormed back inside and slapped Goon Two on the shoulder. They tromped past Qeb and Charley to the floor hatch and began huffing and puffing the 25-pound kegs off the ship.

Gemma glanced at the time on a flip-phone she pulled from her hoodie pocket. "It won't be much longer now."

Qeb searched her from behind. "So, that day near the cove..."

She turned to him, knowing.

"Was that just part of the job?"

A soft smile swept across her. The wood near the cove: they'd made love there, naked and tense love in the grass with the excitement of being caught by the wary old crone with the shotgun.

"You played me along like a fool."

She came over and knelt beside him. "You're no fool. You're a brilliant young man. And you'll go far...if you dump that streak of pride."

Charley, sitting next to Qeb, scoffed, "You're a real pro, lady."

She ignored him and pressed her lips to Qeb's ear. A crimson blush swept over him.

All done, goons three and four struggled up out of the hatch in the deck and bore hands helping goons one and two offload their bootie.

"If the gold really belongs to Mexico," Charley said, "why not claim it through diplomatic channels?"

She laughed from deep inside. "Along with the ingots, those kegs are worth almost ten million dollars. Do you really believe that with the relationship between our countries—with the sentiments of your people toward Mexico—that we would enjoy any chance of getting it back? Americans hate us. To them we're all drunks, drug pushers, and whores. Any Washington politician even thinking of handing over so much money to my people could kiss his career good-bye."

Goon One whispered something to her from the sally port. She nodded and said, "We're all finished here."

"We've seen your faces. We know who you are. You're just gonna leave us here?"

Her expression hardened. "Killing people, Mr. Morgan? We don't do that."

Still kneeling before Qeb, she said, "Not a word about the gold to anyone. Not even to Professor Laird, no matter how good that vengeance might feel." She waxed maternal, empathizing with his hurt. "You're very sweet, Qeb."

He shuddered under the touch of her hand on his cheek.

"This will pass. You'll get over it. Soon as the right girl finds you, you'll forget all about me."

"I don't even know who you are."

"I'm sorry. But it's best that way."

She caught Charley studying her. "You're a lot like another woman I know," he said to her.

"If it's a particularly uncompromising English archaeologist I'm thinking of, I'll accept that as a compliment."

He snorted a singular laugh. Outside, heavy feet were double-timing over the gangway.

"In a bit, your guards will return and find you unhurt."

Goon Four stuffed himself through the sally port and murmured something. Her brows arched and her eyes blazed.

Charley caught the words *barcos* and *policia*.

She shared some sharp syllables with Goon Four and waved him out. Her head snapped right and her eyes latched onto Charley.

"Sounds like someone's coming," he said.

"As I said, we don't kill people. But the people watching our backs can be inclined to do so. So please don't do anything that might make you or Qeb another statistic."

Instantly for Qeb, it all hit home as her stride wisped over the old wood deck. She was leaving!

Each step she took was taking her farther away from him. His heart was freaking out, snare drumming its beat against his insides. His lungs pleaded for any shred of the last air she had breathed. He forced his head round, searching for bits of her his memory could snag before she vanished forever.

At the sally port, she threw one leg over the frame and stalled.

She wasn't looking his way. Can't she at least look his way?

With her grip on the sally port she seemed to reach a decision and took that second step across. Flattened, he watched the last of her slip through and away. The gangplank outside beneath her feline steps whispered her departure. His ears curled, straining to hear her voice on the pier just one last time. It mattered not that he didn't speak her tongue.

The roll door dropped with a crash. A smaller door slammed.

The idling engine revved to life. A shifter clocked into gear.

Wheels rolled. Gravel crunched.

And Qeb collapsed into a heaving jumbled mess.

30-THE DOUBLE WHAMMY

David Kittering collared his neck in the warmth of his jacket against the morning chill that was sweeping none too gently across *K-Four*'s wide open well deck. This kind of pre-winter weather seemed to hit him harder with each new year, firing up the arthritis in his sexagenarian bones so bad that he had to arch his whole body back just to look up high enough to check on his men working twenty feet above him.

Energetic Kittering Enterprises technicians were buzzing all around *Recluse* like bees at a picnic, on special scaffolding circling her at her waterline where her sweeping hull met her armored freeboard: the thin side of her that once separated her open deck from the waves. Here and there the technicians pecked and probed. Sampling. Testing. Studying.

David had published a loud announcement that on the weekends the public were more than welcome to visit *K-Four* and thrill at the historic ship, wonder at her rakish armor, and peer though her open gun port—still just one for now—into her yet to be opened gun deck, where inside, one of Mr. Armstrong's breechloaders, righted and scrubbed, sat bathing in warm show light just for their viewing pleasure.

There was no charge. It was totally free. After all, *Recluse* was their history. The only hint of money changing hands was a humble sign at the base of the gangway affirming: DONATIONS THANKFULLY ACCEPTED.

Nobody came.

"My God, look at them. How long has it been like this?" Frank loitered beside David at *Recluse*'s bow on the fringe of her shadow, soaking up whatever heat the pre-mid-morning sun could afford to share.

"Since the welcome ceremonies last week," David said.

Across the narrow strip of water separating *Recluse* from the USS *North Carolina*, early-bird visitors to the grand battleship were lining the rails tracing her main deck. Here and there, beady eyes on hesitant faces copped guarded glances from the safety of distance. Rumors were shared behind cupped hands, punctuated by accusatory fingers jabbed in the direction of the once just-a-legend ironclad.

"I don't think they like us here," Frank decided.

"I suppose they feel foolish," David said. "They never believed in her, and now here she is shoved in their faces big as day."

"How can they not be curious, not even a little?"

"Maybe it's for the best. We have a lot of work ahead of us."

Frank escaped his disappointment by clocking his attention around and up to David's platoon of technicians laboring away the post-breakfast hours wiping down *Recluse*'s armor, renewing the coat of Kittering's mystery oil solution for fighting corrosion.

There was a sudden commotion in *Recluse*'s bowels that made him jump.

David patted Frank's shoulder. "It's just the engineers. They're removing the engines. They're coming up your way to Morehead City. I imagine you'll like that."

The little hairs lining the edges of Frank's beard crackled. David was watching him. David wanted a reaction. He deflected with, "So they didn't leave on their trip yet?"

David squinted into the sleepy morning sun. It was just a couple inches over *Recluse*'s back now. The chill would be gone soon and his arthritis would quit hissy fitting. "No. Not yet." He slipped a satisfied smile. "They're not leaving with Qeb in the state he's in."

Frank studied his nephew busying himself with something on *Recluse*'s hull. The boy was holding something back from him, unwilling to share it.

"Have you thought any about my offer?"

Something kicked down low in Frank's bowels. "I need more time think about it."

David crossed his arms from the chill. Winter had always been his favorite time of year when he was young and had all that brown fat. "That's the good stuff. It keeps us warm when we're younger," his doctor said to him when his joints first started to protest the weather he loved so much. "It's also the stuff we lose first, making the cold less tolerable as we age."

Thanks, Doc. I really need to hear that.

It sucked sometimes, getting old.

The sound of truck doors closing turned David's attention to the small lot tracing the new pier where his people parked, completely away from the parking used by the tourists. It was Charley and Femi, coming to visit. Try to get something out of Qeb before the kid imploded in on himself.

David mentioned, "Charley is in, you know?" instantly pleased by the befuddled expression gripping Frank's face.

"And Femi went for that?"

"It means he'll be home and she'll have him to herself again."

Frank jammed both hands into his trousers pockets. "I'm not as spontaneous as my brother."

"That's why I need you, to balance Charley's impulsiveness."

"I appreciate that. I still need to think it over."

David indicated to Qeb, standing well out of earshot. "Qeb's coming too."

"What?"

"I've hired him on. He's coming to work for Kittering Explorations, in Morehead City."

Frank focused tighter onto his nephew under the shadow of the ship. Qeb was immersing himself with the ship's hull where the engine's underwater exhaust came out. It was the kind of rote piddling around a man does when he's hiding from his own thoughts. "Don't do that, David. He's practically graduated. You can have him when he's done."

"He doesn't need a doctorate, Frank. The kid's brilliant."

"That's not enough, and you should know better."

David faced off with Frank and rapped his finger on the side of his head. "It's what's in here that matters. Take a look at him, Frank. He's a mess. Right now more than anything he needs a diversion: a break from the fucking books; a chance to use his mind." He turned away from Frank, and his tone grew harsh. "This thing is taking off, with you or without you. I'm going to need your answer soon."

The premature crow's feet invading the edges of Frank's eyes darkened. His thoughts were a shambles. His autumn graduate students were already arriving for their last semester with him, digging into their pre-semester work—what little work he had for them. His lab was down to bare bones now. Even the pH bath with Charley's plate was gone now, safe and sound with David's people before the UNC lab jerks could seize it.

"I can't leave my students, even if the school doesn't care about them."

David crammed his tongue in the purse behind his lower lip, smothering the snitty retort he was aching to spout out. His nasal exhalations sounded like some beast pacing in a cage. His attention retreated back up to his technicians with the oily rags. They were all heading inside the battery. There was plenty of work to do inside, delaying actions fending off Mother Nature's hunger for *Recluse*'s iron and steel and her waterlogged wood hull and interior, preserving her lickety-split to prevent her total collapse.

It would be a hand-wringing sixty days before Kittering Explorations' new facilities just getting started up in Morehead City would be ready to receive her and get her out of the elements so she could be properly refurbished. As soon as *K-Four* pulled away with *Recluse* on her back, the shovels would hit the dirt here on Eagle Island. The concrete pier where they were now, that the Wilmington citizens had funded, was just the beginning. It would finish with a fully covered, climate controlled interior including a dry well in which *Recluse* would sit such that her deck was level with the carpeted floor that would circle her well with interpretive displays. The best artists from the area would string fine silken banners over the well end to end, gently fluttering in a softly fanned breeze giving the impression of water all around her.

David drew in a deep nasal breath of delicious autumn air, feeding his suddenly elated spirit. It was only now hitting him just how much this could all prove to be his professional life's best accomplishment. He was personally matching construction funds, one dollar for every quarter the public could share. It would hog out an enormous hole from his retirement nest egg. But he'd seen the concepts for the museum. It would heat the coldest of hearts. Damn! It felt so good. He hoped he would be around to see it finished. But his last checkup had delivered a bombshell.

Stupid doctors. What the hell do they know anyway?

And that kid, Tim-Lee Polk. He would make sure the whole world knew what the kid had done for these people, even if he still didn't know himself who Polk really was. That sister of his, the one Qeb was all head over heels about—certainly she would like it.

That's when it popped into mind. "Wait a minute. Where's that girlfriend of his?"

Frank's brow arched instantly. "Gemma? You know, now that you bring her up, he hasn't mentioned her at all. Not since—it's like she just vanished."

"Has he said anything at all about that night you found him and Charley?"

"Not a word. He won't talk to me." Frank rolled a worried eye over his nephew. His posture was stooped now, as if the weight of the world was on him.

David rocked on his feet. "Who would tie them up like that?"

"Shit, David. I'm still stuck at the why."

"What about Charley? What does he say?"

Frank flipped a fast eye over *Recluse* looming over them. "Just that this is Qeb's discovery and it's up to Qeb when to do any talking."

"That's just like him. The man irritates the hell out of me. I don't know why I like him so much."

"Hey, I'm his brother. It's worse for me."

A movement in the corner of Frank's eye coaxed his attention to a man half-stepping down the pier, heading their way. Every few steps he would stop in his tracks as if changing his mind. "It looks like we might have our first visitor. He doesn't look like he really wants to be here. He's a big guy. Look at that hair. Do I see a ponytail? I wonder who that is."

David pulled a hanky from his windbreaker and wiped his new glasses, a recent necessity for his fading vision. He set them back on and stiffened just slightly. "That, my friend, is Dr. Stephen Laird."

Frank felt a sudden pinch in his colon. *Laird.* He nodded up to the armor plates, imagining the little stamp on each one of them. "*That* Laird?"

"*That* Laird." David called to Qeb. Qeb shot him back a pained expression that pleaded for solitude. David indicated in the direction of the pier. "Looks like you have a visitor."

Qeb followed David's finger. The sight of his former professor just coming up now to the bottom of their gangplank made his blood curdle. He was the last person he wanted to see.

Stephen Laird set one foot on the all-aluminum gangplank and shot Qeb a look, waiting.

Qeb wrenched his melancholy feet from the deck and trudged with contrary steps over to the top end of the gangplank.

Laird accepted Qeb's cue and proceeded up the sloping plank, hugging something inside his coat close to his side, his strapping frame echoing deliberate footsteps till he scaled the plank to the top.

Two short feet separated the two of them. Haunted didn't do justice defining the expression on the Laird's face. Qeb could practically count the beats in the vein over his former professor's eye. The big man's attention had drifted to something beyond Qeb's shoulder, and his free hand had snatched the rail beside him. Qeb could swear it was shaking.

"Professor, are you okay?"

"What? Oh. Yes. May I come aboard?"

Qeb inched back clearing the way for him.

Laird stepped down onto *K-Four*'s deck with his fascination locked onto *Recluse*. "She looks practically ready for sea, even now. One might say almost hungry for it."

Qeb coerced himself into polite conversation. "There's damage to the hull on the other side, a big bulge like something kicked her hard from the inside. The techs found a cannon ball wedged in the hull. A solid shot used for busting through things, they said. There's a smash through the gun deck. And two cannon are all in pieces, so they think the two are connected somehow."

"Cannon, you say?"

"Six of them, all breach loaders."

"*Breach* loaders?" An appreciative glow washed over Laird as if he were recollecting lost time with a forgotten relation. "Fancy that, would you."

"Professor?"

"Mm?"

"How are things going? I mean, with the *Fredericksburg*?"

Laird's expression toppled noticeably. His barrel chest heaved a heavy sigh. "You didn't hear then? They shut me down."

"No, I didn't hear. But then how would I?"

Laird nodded at Qeb's implied slant. Maybe he deserved that.

"The politicians finally won. Of course, when don't they? We were evicted. I should have seen it coming, I suppose. The powers that be in Richmond said if we left without argument there would be no fines for mussing up their precious river James. Can you believe that? You've seen that river. It's a malodorous swill." Still, he donned a rascally smile. "I made a scene anyway. I'm almost disappointed you weren't there to see it."

That was different. Professor Laird being whimsical. Qeb wasn't sure he liked Laird whimsical.

"So, what are you doing now?"

Laird savored a long breath. "Keeping busy, reaching out to old ties, rekindling forgotten friendships. And calling due some old favors."

He fiddled with the buttons on his overcoat, opening it up. "Still, there has been some tying up of a few loose ends from the dig. What's the American saying: The job's not over till the paperwork's done?" He smirked a bit, like he got pleasure from recalling that saying.

Laird tested the deck with his shoe. "Of course, I have been thinking. It may be time."

"Time?"

He offered Qeb a vaguely gutted look. "Retirement. I'll be coming into some very good money soon, at least enough for two lifetimes. Maybe I'll just putter about in some nice quiet place where no one ever goes or has ever heard of. I've always fancied a place on the coast. Corsica perhaps. But look at me. What a tosser I am whinging on about myself. I can certainly see right here you've been keeping busy. Fancy showing me around, what you've been up to?"

Qeb glanced over to his uncle and Mr. Kittering. They were watching them, closely.

"I guess so. We can start here." He circled the hull with Laird, showing him the intricacies of *Recluse*'s underbelly. When he dropped her name for the first time, Stephen Laird halted behind him in his footsteps.

"How did you learn her name?"

"Hints from a man who helped build her." Qeb explained the story behind Peter Howe's manuscript. "I would show it to you, but David insisted on putting it in safe storage."

Stephen stole a glance at David Kittering standing with another fellow beyond the bow of the recovered wreck. They were watching him with Qeb. And there was a third man, somewhat rougher round the edges, with a petite sort of woman under his arm watching from the safety of a ship's door to the big superstructure dominating the massive bow.

"I would love to see it," he said of the manuscript. "Maybe another time."

"Uncle Frank says I should publish it. The things in it about this old ship—he says people would love the story." When he said, "I'll have to be sure Tim-Lee's name is on the cover," a ruffled look crossed Stephen Laird's face.

Stephen craned his neck to overhead where the technicians wiping down the armor had disappeared. "Shall we go up there?"

The scaffolding circling the ironclad's main deck, at what would have been the water level if she were floating, gave Qeb and Stephen an up front and personal view of the steel plated deck and the sloping gun battery. The two-piece gun port hatches that split down their middles and swung to the sides to fire had all been opened to ventilate the musty interior. Inside, big electric fans powered by heavy power cables were force feeding fresh air through fat flexible tubes snaking down into *Recluse*'s bowels.

Stephen peered inside one of the open hatches and recoiled. "Whew! She's got a stink about her."

"Mr. Kittering says he knows a few tricks of the trade to get rid of that. I don't know what that means, but the man—he makes things work."

Stephen glanced down over the scaffolding at Kittering down on the deck. "Yes, he is quite the man. Is something wrong?"

Qeb squished up his face. "There's something I should show you, but it might creep you out." He indicated to a spot on one of the armor plates. "It's over here."

With both hands tucked in the warmth of his overcoat, Stephen leaned closer for a peek. When he saw what he saw, his jaw muscles flexed. As he leaned closer, Qeb noticed that just inside his open coat dangled a thin leather courier bag strapped over his shoulder.

Stephen straightened up and jutted his chin at the mark. "I'm sorry to disappoint you if I'm not surprised. In a way that's partly why I'm here. You see, I brought you something."

A playful morning breeze slapped at the ends of his overcoat. This October seemed much more glacial than previous ones. Where were the balmy winters global warming had been promising? He cleared the snot from his nose into a hanky. He was getting a cold.

"This chill in the air—let's go back down and get out of this cold."

When Qeb suggested a table and coffee in *K-Four*'s galley, he declined.

"I'm not here for very long."

They descended back down to the well deck and took cover from the breezes beneath *Recluse*'s stern, with her long tall rudder and paisley screws looming behind them.

Stephen rifled into his courier bag, fumbling with it for a minute, cussed under his breath and pulled something flat from it. "This is for you: something to add if you publish that book."

He extended to Qeb a slender journal with weathered black fabric binding down its backbone and a tannish, water-stained cover. A tiny brass colored doohickey on the cover poked up through a slot in a cloth tab stitched to the back cover that arched round to the front to seal it shut.

Qeb accepted it with bewildered fingers. "I don't understand."

Stephen leaned closer, almost towering over him. "You will when you read it."

Qeb teased the cloth tab off the brass thingamajig and lifted the cover open. Its tired binding expelled a sober crackling. Inside, creamy pages stained brown at their edges and peppered with foxing carried hand-scripted text all through it, calm and orderly at the start, but a little mad towards the middle.

"What is this?"

"A diary, I suppose. A journal, if that suits you. Here." Stephen extricated a photo from betwixt the back pages. "It was written by him. Go ahead. Don't worry."

The man in the photo was from a faraway time. He was staring past Qeb as if he were watching someone off in the distance. His hair was wild and quickly greying. His posture was stiff and unsatisfied. The collar of his plain shirt beneath a tight fitting suit jacket had a stranglehold on his neck. His clothes and the chair in which he sat were staid and simple. He was not a rich man, but not starving either.

Beside him on either side hovered two buxom women sporting ascetic expressions and thick forearms. Their uniforms were a blend of white frock over lighter colored dresses—blue maybe—that draped down to just below their knees. Whitish stockings over thick ankles reached down to clunky shoes that looked like they could do serious damage to a man's shin.

The photo was aged to a piss yellow. Qeb couldn't help the urge to bring it to his nose. It smelled like old water.

"He's my second-great-granduncle," Stephen revealed when Qeb asked him with his eyes. "The third of four sons of John Laird of Laird & Sons Shipbuilding. There were three other sons: John, Henry, and William. Henry was my great-great-grandfather. That photo was taken in 1873."

"And these women?"

"They're not family."

"Who are they?"

"They were his attendants." Stephen replied to Qeb's queer expression with a slightly discomfited sucking through his teeth. "You see, he was somewhat of an embarrassment to the family. His father, Sir John Laird was compelled to have him committed."

"You mean to an asylum, for crazy people? What did he do?"

Stephen indicated to the journal. "It's all in there. But in short, he was over here in America during the war with Mr. Lincoln. But, not working for Lincoln."

It took Qeb a moment to register. "You mean for the other side, like a spy?"

Laird smiled sadly. "If only it were so grand. No. He had aspirations of making a name for himself in the new Confederate States after it won the war." Laird ran an investigative palm over *Recluse*'s old wood hull. "Rather misguided, as it turned out."

Qeb tacked over the madman in the photo. Insanity ruled his eyes. "So, what happened?"

"When things didn't turn out the way he had hoped—when the South surrendered—he was forced out of Richmond with the rest of the leadership. He went to Washington to make a new place for himself, lobbying to rebuild the dismantled southern railroads. And of course, to recover his place in influential society he had enjoyed during the war."

Stephen brushed some moist flotsam from his hands. "And that is when he got into trouble. You see, it's all in there—well, not all of it. But he went off on a wild tangent, soliciting financial support from his wealthy acquaintances."

"For the railroads?"

"No, not at all. Nothing like that." Stephen's gaze returned to *Recluse.* "It was to recover a shipwreck."

"A shipwreck?"

"In the circles in which he lived, to solicit persons you lobby professionally for money to fund personal endeavors steps out of line with decorum, and the law. It shatters trust and your ability to do your work. And it could all blow up in his face."

"Did it?"

"Oh yes. He was sacked from his post and shunned by Society. And very quickly, by 1870 in fact, he was practically penniless. To save the family name from scandal, Sir John Laird was compelled to pay for his return to England, where they slotted him into a modest post within the company."

"So things turned out for him then."

Laird laughed. "If only. No. Apparently a lost war and societal shame taught him nothing, and soon he was back at his old tricks pressing for funds for an expedition to the American coast. He never says where in that journal exactly. Just that it was a ship with a fortune. The family refused, of course. So he solicited close family friends. Some of them were titled. When that didn't work, he lobbied the banks. It was a scandal of immense proportions that threatened to destroy the family completely. And that was that. There was no alternative. They put him away for good."

The ship with a fortune crystalizing in Qeb's mind was without question. Laird's ancestor surely must have meant the cargo aboard the sunken *Hermione*. She had wrecked in the surf near the beach. The man in the photo wanted to recover the controversial alloy plates the family had forged for Mr. Lincoln's enemies. The alloy would be a precious commodity to England's defense.

Still, the Crown would never let the family sell to anyone outside the country. It seemed like a stretch to say the plates would make Laird & Sons any kind of fortune. When Qeb suggested such, Laird was distinctly abashed.

"Armor plates? Who's talking armor plates? We're talking about gold, Qeb: Mexican gold. Coins and ingots. Worth thousands."

Mexican gold. The very words slugged Qeb hard. "Why are you telling me all this?"

Laird's expression shifted to one of almost celestial wisdom.

"Qeb, let me put it all into context for you. It was my family who built the Confederate raider *Alabama*, and it was my family who were scandalized by the British admiralty for constructing two seagoing ironclads for the South. Together they could have devastated the Union fleet, so they were seized before they could be sent across the pond and possibly drag Britain into a heated war with Mr. Lincoln. Not that we learned from our mistakes. There is also if you will"—He offered a palm up to *Recluse*—"forging special steel armor for ironclad gunboats."

The man in the photo looking up at Qeb had changed. In just the tiniest way he could swear the ends of his tight lips had edged into a slight smirk.

"What was his name?"

"Mm?"

"His name. You never said his name."

"It was Percival. Percival Laird." Stephen stroked the edge of one of the big screws. "I think he meant your ship, Qeb. I think Percival meant *Recluse*."

Qeb kneaded Percival's image between his thumb and finger till a tiny tear cracked the photo's edge, and he suffered the sudden double-barreled burdens of Stephen Laird's hand upon his shoulder and realization in his heart.

"You knew."

Laird's hand left his shoulder. The force of his presence blocking the sun gripped Qeb's courage. "The whole time, you knew. You just pretended to be mad at Tim-Lee, but Tim-Lee was doing exactly what you wanted him to do: to find *Recluse*. Because you knew Tim-Lee was right." He flagged Percival's photo back at him. "You knew because of him."

Stephen Laird diverted his eyes to the sky.

"Maybe this Percival guy never revealed all the details, but you read his diary and you believed him. You knew somehow he was telling the truth, and somewhere there was a fortune buried."

"You tell me, Qeb. You always seem to know it all. Why would I waste my time and money up on the James with the *Fredericksburg*?"

"Because it was easier pretending you didn't know exactly where to look while you let Tim-Lee find her for you." He shoved the photo back at Laird. "Take your stinking photo." He extended the journal too. "And this."

Stephen refused them. "They have no meaning to me anymore."

"Well I don't want them."

"I thought you wanted to tell her story. With that and with Peter Howe's manuscript you have everything you need to do it."

Qeb pulled away from him. "How did you know his name? I never told you—" Astonishment swept over him. "You already knew."

Stephen sucked chilly air through exasperated teeth, enraging an old filling. This wasn't going down as smoothly as he hoped. He fished again into the shoulder bag hanging inside his coat. Qeb didn't notice that when his hand came out a small object fluttered down onto the deck from inside his coat.

"Look, you found the ship. Take Percival's bloody journal. Don't be foolish, Doctor. You know you want it."

Doctor?

Now Laird was just being mean. This was, of course, why he was really here then: to rub it in. He was going down and he was taking him with him. The wry smirk on his chin said it all.

"Like I said earlier, Qeb, I had some loose ends to tie up." Stephen extended a large flat envelope to him. "Here. This is for you."

Qeb doe-eyed the white flat in Laird's hand. There was a subtle tremor to the man's grip. "So, this is it," Qeb guessed. He slipped Percival's photo into the journal and tucked it under his arm, and accepted the flat with ginger fingers.

The waxy pull-off was still on the envelope's glue strip, never sealed. The UNC logo was emblazoned in raised letters on the front corner where the return address resided. He opened the flap and peered inside. Two letters crowned with the school's letterhead peered back at him.

He swallowed the bile building in his throat. These were his judgment papers, the final stroke of the gavel decreeing his scholastic demise. Yes, he had abandoned Stephen Laird's dig; he had tossed his responsibilities; and he had accepted that. But he had done it all for a friend.

A friend who died!

But the gears of the academic machine must turn. Callous, intolerant, and unforgiving. He knew this was coming. It was just that on paper, it would make the permanence of it all that much more nauseating.

Slowly, he extricated the letters. His eyes, not wanting to see, darted left to right, absorbing the text filling the front sheet. As he read it, a lightheaded tingle crept over him. His foothold on *K-Four*'s deck faded. "But how?" he said, glued to the words on the sheet congratulating him on his pending receipt of his doctoral degree. Signed at the bottom were a series of swanky approvals.

"But...you kicked me off. You said you were going to dismiss—"

"Pshah! That was all bluff. Surely you should know me by now."

"But how? I haven't proven my skills to graduate."

Stephen indicated to *Recluse* looming over them. "With that, I sincerely disagree. And why the maudlin expression? One should think you would be elated."

"Tim-Lee's the one who deserves the credit for finding her, not me. And he got nothing."

Stephen traded the letters around for Qeb to read the other one. The same letterhead, the same rank-and-file text, the same swanky signatures. Only this one was conferring upon Tim-Lee his master's degree.

There was a metallic rattle in the air.

"You did this for him?" But by now Stephen Laird was heading down the gangway. "Professor Laird. Wait."

Laird turned on his heel at the bottom of the gangplank. "Oh. And another thing, Doctor Morgan. Percival lost his own small fortune on that same ship. I should think you might want to find that."

Qeb stared at the journal with shifting curiosity. "Stay. I want to talk. What fortune? Where?"

As he back-stepped down the pier, Laird cupped his hand to his mouth. "I can't stay. I have a hot date with a new love in Acapulco.

Just look around. It's got to be in there somewhere. I'm only sorry that letter came too late for your friend. But his family will appreciate it."

Stephen Laird halted in his steps. Donning a devilish grin he said, "Maybe you can give it to that sister of his."

The olive drab creases in Stephen Laird's coat joggled with the man's departing stride, tugging Qeb's imagination after them.

Sister? Sister. Tim-Lee's sister...

Laird was standing at the far end of the pier. No wave, no send off. Just a long silent stare.

Qeb suffered a slight pinch to his heart. "Professor Laird!"

That's when he saw it.

Where Laird had been standing, he must have dropped it and hadn't noticed. Soaking in a wafer thin sheen of water on the deck lay a small white square. A circle of red print on it was quickly washing to pink. He coaxed it up with careful fingers and read the streaking stamp of a passport photo service. In Liverpool. Merseyside. In England.

With his guard down, he rolled the thing over and gasped.

The face in the photo on the other side—her eyes—he knew them. And they knew him.

They reached deep down into him packing a chill all through him. Dismayed nerves let the big envelope slip from his grasp. The fragile journal tucked beneath his arm dropped to the deck with an unheard slap. Numbness stole his balance. The face on the square blurred to a glob. With an unseeing hand, he searched for the reassuring support of *Recluse*'s hull against his quavering palm.

He craned fuzzy eyes down the pier to its farthest end, but Laird was gone. His brain farted and his gaze oozed into the scrubby twisted pines on the far side of Eagle Island. The pines, starving for decent soil, bowed and waved with spindly arms, coaxing the numbness from him and taking the chill with it, but leaving the image behind, tucked between his fingers.

Her hair was blond this time.

Why did Laird have this?

And her eyes were a different color. They were hazel now.

Or was it then, when the photo was taken? How does Laird even know her?

But it *was* her.

A soft touch caressed his arm. Without looking, he knew that touch. The aching in his heart melted away. He turned and offered the best smile he could manage for his mother.

"I didn't know you were here."

"Your father and me—we are both here. For you my son," Olufemi said.

Qeb searched *K-Four*'s forward superstructure, past David and Uncle Frank, standing a decent distance away, out of earshot.

"He's in the mess," she said. "We have been talking."

They were talking. That scared him. He guessed his fear was obvious, because she stroked his cheek and said: "We will be fine. There are changes coming. Some you will not like, but you will be the man I raised and respect them."

"What does that mean?"

"It means your father is staying home here. It means you will be seeing him more now."

"And you?"

She knew what he meant. She settled a not too nice gaze on David Kittering. "There has been too much separation. That is stopping. I have insisted." She turned to him. "But you are in pain. I see it running all through you like sickness."

He handed his mother the photo. As she looked at it, he wondered at her strength and beauty. She had her green card now and had been drumming conversation about US citizenship. She had sold his childhood home in Qena, had packed everything up that she didn't give away, and she had followed him to North Carolina to be closer while he was in school.

There was a new side to her now he had never seen before. She was studying art and taking classes with a woman on the coast, and had come alive. Her work was beautiful. The artist inside her—it was like cracking a clam and finding the biggest pearl ever.

She handed the limp photo back to him. It was obvious what he was thinking. "It is someone else, Qeb. Someone who just looks like her."

He knew better. She was just being his mother. It was her alright, because of those freckles. Those damned adorable sexy fucking freckles. The freckles would always give her away.

Laird said 'Mexican gold.' You heard him.

He realized aloud: "Acapulco..."

"Acapulco?"

"Professor Laird said he was going to Acapulco." Qeb massaged his forehead searching for his senses. "I—where is that?"

"Acapulco?" It was Charley from the mess. "Somewhere in Mexico, I think."

Mexico. Mexican gold.

Qeb worked the photo through his fingers, snatching half-seconds between his conspiracy theories to admire the two of them. His parents, still together.

The goons who took the gold, Laird going to Mexico, and the wetted photo of his lover wearing different eyes and different hair. It all slammed home with the subtlety of a hit-and-run. Tim-Lee's death wasn't any accident: they killed him. They killed him for the gold. And somehow Laird was in on it the whole time.

It was worse than a lie. It was a lie on top of a lie. Chrissakes! It was fucking murder.

And you trusted them.

He was such a sap. Laird had played him like a tarpon on a reel.

They should mount you to a plaque on his wall.

Qeb's gut was stomping the inside of his asshole wanting out, right now. This was all too much. His legs went all wobbly and he slipped down onto his butt and crumpled up to a seat on the deck, pulling his knees to his chest to hide, and to smother the welling pain inside him.

As acid fluxed into the belly of his throat, he re-read the address of the English photo shop and flipped back to her face.

When she had this taken for her passport, what name had she used then?

He was sure of one thing. It wasn't Emeline Polk.

And it sure as hell wasn't Gemma!

Austin Haynes is a veteran navy petty officer with 25 years SCUBA and hardhat diving experience. His childhood heroes included *Sea Hunt* star, Lloyd Bridges, and famed ocean explorer Jacques-Yves Cousteau. He has dived cliffs, caves, wrecks, and reefs in seven seas including the Mediterranean and Red seas. During his navy career, he performed hull maintenance and screw changes on nuclear submarines and large ships; and provided air recompression chamber services to medical patients and the local dive community.

He is a passionate student of Civil War maritime history, and Civil War reenactor. A former resident of the Old North State, he currently calls South Florida home with his wife, Patty, drumming up more ocean archaeology adventures for the growing Morgan family.